D1126732

EMMA

EMMA

F. W. KENYON

THOMAS Y. CROWELL COMPANY
New York

TO
VERNON H. H. SCURRAH, M.A.

Who bludgeoned me into writing this story

Who said, "You may keep your Josephines and Napoleons, give me Emma Hamilton and Lord Nelson!"

Who added, "Now there's a woman for you!"

And whose stentorian laughter still rings in my ears

1

Captain John Willet-Payne, temporarily without a ship and employed meanwhile at the Admiralty, gave the clerk an amused look.

"Private and confidential business, you say? And the young woman refuses to give her name? I can think of no young woman in London who could possibly have that sort of business with me. My conscience is perfectly clear—at the moment."

"The young woman is most pressing, sir."

"I notice you say 'woman,' not 'lady.'"

The clerk grinned. "Well, sir—"

"Is she . . . pretty?"

"More than that, sir. Beautiful, but rather common."

Willet-Payne laughed heartily. "A happy combination. You may as well bring her in."

He took up his pen, noticed that he had forgotten to put the date at the top of the letter he was writing, and wrote in: *May 6th, 1781*. A moment later the clerk ushered the young woman into the room. She made her entrance quickly and eagerly, and at the first glimpse of her Willet-Payne dropped his pen and rose abruptly to his feet.

He flattered himself that, at thirty, he was a man of wide experience, even a connoisseur of women, but never before had he seen one so arrestingly beautiful as this. Her auburn hair, loose about her shoulders, was a sheer delight; her parted lips enough to drive a man crazy with desire; her eyes, large and candid, two separate pools of mute appeal. He felt an inclination to stand back, as if before some exquisite painting, and admire her, feature by feature. Rather common? Why that? Simply because her faded yellow gown was cheap and shabby, her straw hat battered and her gloves worn?

"It's real good of you to see me, sir."

Willet-Payne shuddered slightly. Her voice, for all its fullness and warmth, was the one flaw. He failed to place her provincial accent, but obviously she was not a Londoner.

"Sit down," he invited, "and tell me your name."

She took the chair he pointed to, and arranged her gown with all the grace of a duchess.

"It's Hart, sir. Emma Hart." Her earlier eagerness was giving place to

1

an attitude of slight anxiety. "*Mrs.* Emma Hart, to be truthful, sir."

He frowned. "Somewhat young to be a married woman, Mrs. Hart."

She looked down demurely. "Not married any more, sir, but widowed." The faintest sigh escaped her lips; all the sorrow of the world was in the droop of her shoulders. "It's a hard life, sir, if you let things get you down."

"Which you never do, I feel sure." He was smiling easily now. "Tell me what brings you here, Mrs. Hart."

Eager again, she leaned quickly forward. "It's my cousin, sir."

"Your cousin?"

"He was took by the press gang this morning, sir. Too young to go to sea, he is." She was having difficulty with her aitches now. "It's cruel 'ard to think of him being forced like that."

Quick tears had come to her eyes, enhancing their limpid beauty. At first he had thought them gray in color; now—as, deeply moved, he gazed into them—they seemed to change to a dark violet. Her lips trembled into speech.

"I'm sure you could help get him off, sir."

Willet-Payne pursed his lips. "What made you come to me, Mrs. Hart?"

"It was Jane Powell, sir. I used to be in service with her. You was kind to 'er once an' she hasn't forgot it."

"It would be more correct," he said, laughing delightedly, "to say that *she*, in the not unusual fashion of her class, was kind to *me*—until I grew tired of her kindness and found somebody else."

Emma slumped in the chair and was instantly a picture of resignation.

"Sooner or later gentlemen always get tired of girls like Jane an' me."

"Quite the little philosopher, I see!"

"If you mean I try to make the best of things, you're right there."

Her eyes were holding his in mild inquiry. She neither liked nor disliked the look of him, and having taken note of the underlying hardness of his gray eyes, she thought she knew him for what he was, a gentleman who would demand just one price for anything he might do for her.

"You must love your cousin very much," he commented.

"Oh, I do, sir, I do!" She was all eagerness again.

Willet-Payne, still on his feet, moved round her until he could see her face in profile. He thought how boyish she looked, a pert attractive

2

guttersnipe, and fortunately clean. He took an impulsive step towards her, and as he did so the door opened. "Damnation!" he hissed, and turned to face his apologetic but curious clerk.

"Well, what is it?"

"Begging your pardon, sir, but there's a Captain Nelson asking to see Lord Sandwich."

Furious, Willet-Payne said, "You knew Captain Nelson was expected, you knew his lordship would be waiting. Take the captain up, confound you!"

The clerk fled, but not without a backward glance at Emma. Willet-Payne, still ruffled, gave her his attention again.

"You want me to break the law, Mrs. Hart. Rather a lot to ask of a man in my position."

"Is it, sir?"

The very innocence of her tone made him suspect that she was laughing at him. He cleared his throat.

"Tell me your cousin's name."

"It's Connor, sir. Charlie Connor. He's fourteen, no more."

He went to his desk and made a great show of writing down the name.

"I know you can help me, sir," Emma prompted.

"Yes." His eyes searched her face and body. "I think I can. I shall know for certain tomorrow."

"I'm to come here again tomorrow—is that what you mean?"

Willet-Payne smiled briefly. "I have rooms near the Adelphi. Number 10 Argyll Place. I suggest that you meet me there at four in the afternoon."

Emma nodded gravely and repeated the address under her breath.

"I'll be there on time, sir. An' thank you kindly," she added warmly.

Tongue-tied, he watched her as she rose and went unhurriedly from the room. Her movements were utterly graceful. The cheapness of her clothes, the commonness of her voice, her obvious illiteracy meant nothing. Completely carried away, he thought, she walks in beauty! And then he laughed at the extravagance of such a phrase. She was young and healthy and willing. Willing? He pondered over this.

I wonder!

Emma knocked a second time at the door of Number 10 Argyll Place. She shivered and drew more closely about her shoulders the thin black cloak her mother had lent her. The afternoon was cold

3

and bleak with low dark clouds hurrying across the sky. She thought how pleasant it would be to be rich—to have clothes both warm and fashionable, own a carriage, eat the best and richest food, have servants to wait on you. She had no idea how she would get these things, but a feeling, deep and calm, told her that get them one day she would.

The door was opened at last, not by Captain Willet-Payne but by a tall stranger who stood there looking down at her and laughing gaily.

"Emma, without the slightest doubt!"

She looked up at him coolly. "I never clapped eyes on you in my life."

"Lancashire," he said, slapping his thick thighs soundly.

"I beg your pardon, sir?"

"I was referring to your atrocious accent."

"Then you was wrong," she scoffed. "Cheshire, that's where I come from."

"A near enough guess," he laughed. "Come in out of the cold."

He led her through the dark hall into a drawing room, heavily and drably, if expensively furnished, with pictures of race horses on the walls and wine decanters on the massive sideboard. A bachelor's room, Emma thought knowingly. She gave the stranger an inquiring look, her attitude that of a timid country girl, tremulous, a little afraid.

"Willet-Payne is still at the Admiralty. Here, sit by the fire and warm your hands."

"You was sitting there yourself," she said demurely.

"I prefer to stand now, my dear, to stand and admire you, just as I did one day last year at that rogue's, Dr. Graham's, in the Adelphi. I have a good memory for faces, you see, and . . . figures."

Emma laughed easily. "You saw a sight more of my figure then than you do now, sir." She sat down and extended her outstretched palms to the warm glow of the fire. "It's true I used to pose at Dr. Graham's Temple of Health, but my mother, she said it wasn't no way for a decent honest girl to earn a living, posing like that with nothing on but a veil. And of course, sir,"—she looked up at him candidly —"it wasn't, truly it wasn't."

"So you left that den of iniquity, eh?"

Emma sighed. "An' went into service."

He turned up his eyes. "What a shameful comedown, a delightful creature like you forced to work as a servant."

4

Emma repressed a giggle and looked at this stranger quizzically. He was taller than Willet-Payne, and handsome, in a raffish sort of way. She liked the careless way he wore his fashionable, expensive clothes, and admired his crisp dark hair, drawn loosely back and lightly powdered. Quite an air about him, there was. Dashing, that was the word she wanted, dashing and really sporting. She could picture him riding to hounds and drinking himself under the table afterward. She grew conscious of his wide-set eyes. They seemed to smile but were hard and calculating, just as the laughter that bubbled up in him all the time wasn't what she would call *real* laughter.

"Why such a startled look?" he demanded. "You must be used to masculine admiration by now, and being stared at in the streets."

"Men are very rude at times, I do admit."

"Ah-ha!" He slapped his thighs in delight. "Saucy as well as beautiful. So beautiful," he went on glibly, "I can scarce believe my eyes. Small wonder Willet-Payne chattered about you like a madman. I do believe I shall take you to Romney one of these days and let him paint you. Gad, but your face would make his fortune."

"My, sir, how you do run on!"

He turned to the sideboard. "A glass of wine, my dear? Port, perhaps, or Madeira?"

"Well now, when I can get it, I'm partial to a drop of port."

Sitting by the fire, sipping the wine, warmed by both, she grew conscious of a richer, wider world, a world of leisure, gracious living, admiring men.

"Emma . . . yes, I like the sound of it," he was saying.

"Oh, so do I, sir," she said eagerly. "That's why I took it up."

"So, you—er—took it up."

"Yes. You see, I was christened Amy an' never could abide the name. First I tried Emy, then Emly, then Em-i-ly—oh, an' lots more, but Emma was the one I liked best."

He came and stood over her, legs thrust strongly apart, wineglass in hand.

"Tell me about yourself," he invited.

Emma took another sip of wine, then screwed up her face thoughtfully, almost painfully, like a child making a tremendous effort over her schoolbooks. And in the singsong passionless voice of a child she began to tell him about her birthplace, the little village of Nesse, where her father was a blacksmith.

"But he died, Dad did, when I was only a few years old, an' I can't

5

remember him. Later on Ma an' me went to live with Granny at Hawarden in Flintshire." She screwed up her face more than ever. "But I think Ma married again just before that; an', being unlucky, soon lost her second, too. I can't remember Mr. Cadogan either."

Still in the childlike voice, without emotion, without real expression, she described how her mother had taken in washing at Hawarden to make ends meet, and how later, the ends not meeting, she herself became a nursemaid at the age of eleven.

"Then I came with another family to London, an' after that I was a lady's maid an' a shopgirl an' a kitchenmaid. After which I was at Dr. Graham's Temple of Health, till Ma come to London and made a real to-do about it."

"How old are you, Emma?"

"Seventeen, sir, but much older than that in the ways of the world. A real wicked world, Ma calls it."

"I expect it is, otherwise how dull it would be! What happened to your husband? Did he die, or leave you, or is he just an invention?"

Emma clapped her hands. "Much too clever, you are, sir. You see, when I went to Dr. Graham's I thought it would be more respectable if I was a married woman."

"And then, for some reason, you killed him off, this mythical husband."

"Yes, sir. To tell the truth, I thought Captain Willet-Payne would be more likely to 'elp me if he thought I was a widow."

He laughed loud and long at that. "But why the name Hart?"

"It took my fancy, sir, that's all. Sounded sort of posh."

"I can see, my dear, that you want to improve yourself."

"Course I do, an' I will, one of these days. But I'll still be me, underneath, won't I, sir?" She rose from the chair. "It's my cousin Charlie I'm worried about now. Will the captain be long?"

"I should think not, he being so anxious to see you again. I noticed a fire in the bedroom, too, and would you believe it, a warming pan in the bed. Let me warn you, my dear, payment before action, that is what Willet-Payne will demand, after which he might well forget all about your unfortunate cousin."

"Oh, no, he wouldn't be *that* cruel!" Emma cried.

"I know my friend a great deal better than you do. In any case, his influence is not as great as you might think it. Whereas mine— Well, a word in the right quarter, a wave of the hand, and your cousin will be restored to you."

6

Emma looked at him shrewdly. "And *you* wouldn't demand payment before action, would you!"

"Certainly not," he said, in mock indignation. "A rake I may be, but I am also a gentleman."

"A country squire, I'd say," Emma ventured.

"Ah, you think I look the part?" He sounded pleased. "My place is Up Park at South Harting in Sussex." He paused and chuckled faintly. "By the merest chance Up Park is in need of a congenial housekeeper, and do you know, I think I have found one."

"Have you, sir?"

"Let us make a bargain. If Mrs. Emma Hart will take the position, I for my part will promise to secure Charlie Connor's release."

Tempted, Emma considered this gravely. "Just a housekeeper, sir?"

The faint chuckle came again. "I did mention the word congenial."

Emma puzzled over this. "Meaning easy-going, sir?"

"An excellent description, my dear!"

He asked her to give him her address. She hesitated for a few moments. She and her mother were temporarily lodged with one of her mother's married sisters who lived in a quiet, humble little alley off Oxford Street. She hesitated one moment longer; surely there was more to be gained from this grand country squire than from Captain Willet-Payne! And yet, could she really trust him?

"Well?" he demanded, impatient now.

She gave him the address, upon which he told her that his own private traveling carriage would call for her at eleven o'clock the next morning.

"My carriage will take you to Nerot's Hotel in King Street," he went on. "That is where I stay when in town, and there you will find me waiting for you with your cousin. I shall join you immediately and take you back with me to South Harting."

An exciting idea had occurred to Emma. She looked up at him innocently. "As housekeeper I'll be allowed to employ my own staff, won't I?"

"Of course," he said, humoring her.

"Thank you kindly, sir."

He was at the window now, looking out. She, too, had heard the carriage pulling up outside.

"Willet-Payne," he chuckled, "but rather too late. Come along, Emma, out the back way."

He hustled her quickly from the room, along the narrow passage and into the lane at the back of the house.

"There's one thing you haven't told me," Emma said, "an' that's your name."

"No more I have! It's Fetherstonhaugh. Sir Henry Fetherstonhaugh."

"My, a blinking Sir! An' what a mouthful, too!" She kissed him impulsively on the cheek. "Tell you what, being congenial, as it were, I'll make it Fether for short."

"Housekeeper!" Mrs. Cadogan snorted. "An' at *your* age! As if it isn't plain as the nose on your face what he meant by that!"

Emma and her mother were in Sir Henry Fetherstonhaugh's carriage, rolling majestically in the direction of King Street. Not really listening to her mother, Emma smiled happily. What a stir the grand carriage had made outside her aunt's, what with the liveried coachman and the handsome, well-groomed horses! This, she told herself complacently, was just the beginning.

"A fine how-do-you-do, I *must* say!" Mrs. Cadogan complained.

She was a motherly little woman, older in appearance than her forty years and inclined to stoutness. She wore a voluminous black shawl, mended in many places, and a drab, well-worn gown, but these things went unnoticed when one looked at her face. She had the rosy cheeks of the countrywoman, well-scrubbed and shiny; but mostly it was her eyes that held one's attention, mobile, expressive eyes. They jeered now, with a vengeance.

"Besides, it wouldn't be decent, posing for them painters!"

"Hush, Ma," Emma said soothingly, "we'll soon be there."

Mrs. Cadogan rearranged her shawl with capable, work-worn hands and refused to be hushed. "This Captain Willet-Payne an' this Sir Henry Something-or-other—fine gentlemen, no doubt, but a couple of rogues where a girl like you's concerned. The less you 'ave to do with them the better."

She was crying now; and Emma, touched by the tears and ready to cry in sympathy, tried to laugh her out of it.

"You haven't always been better than you should be, Ma, an' well you know it."

A watery smile came to Mrs. Cadogan's face. "That's a cruel thing to say, Emma. You ought to be ashamed of yourself."

"Well, I'm not, so there! Dry your eyes, Ma, and look on the bright side. If I don't go on with this, what's to become of Charlie? I know 'ow to look after myself."

Mrs. Cadogan looked slightly mollified. "You'll have to be as clever as a cageful of monkeys."

There was silence during the rest of the short trip to Nerot's, with Mrs. Cadogan sitting in the depths of her corner seat in what Emma always called "one of Ma's huffs." When the carriage drew up at the imposing hotel Emma squared her shoulders in the second-hand traveling coat she had bought with the last of her money. Worn as it was, it was well-cut and fitted her perfectly.

"There they are! You keep out of sight, Ma, an' wait."

But before she could get out Sir Henry came strolling toward the carriage, followed by a bewildered and still frightened Charlie Connor.

"Well, my dear," Sir Henry said, "I kept my word, you see."

"An' I'm ready to keep mine," Emma told him cheerfully.

He stopped short at the sight of Mrs. Cadogan.

"Ma," Emma said quickly, "say good morning to Sir Henry Fetherstonhaugh."

Sir Henry looked nonplussed. "Your—*mother?*"

Emma looked urgently at her young cousin. "Run for your life, Charlie. Go on, don't gape at me!" And as he took to his heels: "Tell your aunt I'll write to her!" She gave Sir Henry her most impish smile. "I'm sure Up Park can do with a good cook, an' Ma, she's one of the best. Good plain cooking, or fancy dishes, whichever suits you. And her Lancashire hotpot—just you wait till you taste it, Fether!"

"This," he said angrily, "was never part of the bargain."

"You said I could employ my own staff," Emma cooed. "Still, if you'd rather I didn't come, after all . . ."

Sir Henry laughed harshly.

"Move over, Ma," Emma said, "an' make room for the master."

Mrs. Cadogan moved over, and Sir Henry, after the slightest hesitation, got in without a word. Emma leaned out of the window and addressed the coachman in the grandest manner imaginable.

"Come, my man, whip up the horses!"

All through the journey Sir Henry had been silent to the point of sulkiness, but now, having shown Emma over the spacious mansion, his features were beginning to relax. He was proud of the house, its sweeping parkland and the view it commanded of Portsmouth and the

Isle of Wight, and Emma's wide-eyed admiration pleased him. She was standing with him now in the room he had told her was to be hers, and her eyes, alive with excitement, were darting hither and thither, resting fleetingly on the great fourposter, the tapestried hangings, the rich thick carpet.

"It's a grand room, just for a housekeeper," she laughed.

Sir Henry took her by the shoulders and turned her till she was facing him squarely.

"You know quite well what was meant by housekeeper."

"That's true enough," she admitted soberly.

"Then why in heaven's name bring your mother?"

She laughed lightly. "To tell the truth, we was in a proper fix. No work, neither of us, and only staying with my aunt on sufferance, as it were. Seemed to me as good a way as any of finding a comfy home."

He laughed admiringly. "A clever wench, as well as a beautiful one. It endears you to me all the more."

She thought he was about to start fondling and kissing her, and she was ready to submit with a suitable grace—a bargain, after all, was a bargain—but instead he released her abruptly and, turning to a large wardrobe, flung open the mirrored door.

"Obviously you need clothes. I think most of these will fit you. If not, make the necessary alterations yourself."

Emma stared in amazement at the array of gowns and cloaks, the numerous elaborate hats, the piles of shoes and fancy slippers. With a little cry of sheer delight she half-climbed into the wardrobe and snatched up a velvet gown, dark yellow and cut daringly low. Caring for nothing but the childlike happiness of the moment, she tore off her own shabby gown and squirmed into the clinging velvet. Posing before Sir Henry, she struck an attitude of abandoned gaiety.

"Who did all this stuff belong to?" she asked.

"Who do you think, my dear?"

Emma chuckled richly. "The housekeeper before me, I s'pose."

"Who else?" he said merrily. "She left hurriedly, poor soul, with nothing but the things she stood up in." His tone now gave Emma a little stab of apprehension. "The gown, I seem to remember, was green, and a little too tight."

The stab of apprehension came again, but she chose to ignore it. She knew how to take care of herself, she was sure of that.

She said, "Where's Ma going to sleep?"

"Where else but in the servants' quarters? Your mother is here on probation, just as you are, though in a very different capacity, my sweet little Emma. I think I am making myself clear."

"Oh," Emma tossed her head, "Ma's easygoing too, spite of the things she says."

"Splendid."

"You said on *probation* . . ." Emma struggled with the unfamiliar word. "Meaning—if I don't suit I'll be sent packing?"

"Meaning precisely that. However, I shall know tonight whether or not you . . . suit." He lounged to the door and removed the key from the large brass lock. "There is a bar, too, but I trust I shall not have to remove that also."

"A bargain's a bargain," Emma said candidly.

He opened the door and left her, and for the next hour she became completely engrossed in the clothes placed so unexpectedly at her disposal. She tried everything on, posing in varying attitudes before the mirror as she did so. A few alterations were necessary, but her mother, cleverer with her needle than she was, would soon take care of that.

"Seems to me I'm in clover," she told her reflection gravely. "An' all because I wanted to do Charlie a good turn."

Presently she heard the sound of a carriage in the drive, and a few moments later raised voices floated up to her from the hall. One was Sir Henry's; the other she recognized as Captain Willet-Payne's. Ructions! she thought. Well, she had half-expected something like this. Giggling, she picked up her skirts and ran lightly down to the hall to watch the fun.

Willet-Payne saw her first. She was smiling demurely.

"Ha!" he barked. His face was flushed and angry. "Obviously," he spluttered, "you knew the trick Harry was going to play on me. I can only assume you were a willing party to the whole dastardly business!"

Emma began to suspect the truth. "So Fether hadn't any influence at the Admiralty at all."

"Not a scrap," Sir Henry admitted, "except through John here."

Spluttering still, Willet-Payne told her exactly what had happened.

"According to Harry, you grew tired of waiting at Argyll Place yesterday, but agreed to meet me there this morning, providing your wretched cousin was released. Meanwhile Harry was to meet your cousin, who by then would be set free on my order, and bring him to Argyll Place too. And all the time he was scheming to cut me out and bring you here!"

11

"Which I did!" Sir Henry laughed.

"Of all the damnable, lowdown, skunkish—!"

"Oh, come, man," Sir Henry interrupted sharply, "where is your sense of humor?"

"Pah!" Willet-Payne exploded.

"It was a mean thing to do," Emma said. "Still, I can't help laughing just a little bit myself."

Willet-Payne turned his back on her, but not before she had caught his eyes searching her with a new interest. She nodded her head wisely; it was, of course, the velvet gown, revealing as it did the warm ivory contours of her breasts.

"The laugh is partly on me, too," Sir Henry said, as he explained how he had been tricked into bringing Mrs. Cadogan as well. "So you see, John, I am saddled with the two of them."

Willet-Payne permitted himself the slightest of chuckles. "Serves you damn-well right, Harry!"

Sir Henry agreed. "Are we friends again? Will you stay the night?"

"We-ell—"

"Oh, come, it would take you till well after midnight to get back to London."

Willet-Payne's eyes narrowed. He smiled faintly, a secret inward little smile, Emma thought it. He looked quickly from her to Sir Henry.

"I don't relish the thought of the journey at this time of night. I'll stay, Harry, providing you open that special port you were saving."

"Why not?" Sir Henry agreed. "This, after all, is a celebration. For three to begin with, later"—he glanced lazily at Emma—"for two."

Willet-Payne laughed harshly. "You miserable dog, Harry!"

Emma lay in bed, naked as she usually slept, but in any case she had been unable to find a nightgown in the otherwise extensive wardrobe of her predecessor. It was well after midnight, and try as she might she was finding it hard to keep awake. It had been such a long exciting day, an unbelievable day, really—a day she felt she might have dreamt, not really experienced. The men were still downstairs, sitting long over their port, singing a little, arguing, then singing again. More than likely Sir Henry would come up too fuddled with wine to pester her much.

Sleepily she thought of her mother, indignant still but willing to admit that it did look as if they had fallen on their feet, if only for a short time. "It won't last, you mark my words." Emma didn't see why it shouldn't last, if she was clever enough, on which cheering thought she fell into a light sleep from which she woke, hours later it seemed, with the smell of a snuffed-out candle in her nostrils.

She could hear heavy breathing; and, raising up on her elbows, she saw a dark shadow against the window. She shrugged philosophically and waited. The shadow moved. "You're late, Fether," she said, but a mere grunt was the only reply she received. The smell of wine was strong but it hadn't befuddled him all that much, judging by the way he took her in his arms, roughly and impatiently. Soon she was asleep again, only to be roused a second time. She lay still for a moment, listening to the heavy knocking at the door.

"Emma! Emma, wake up!"

It was her mother.

Reluctantly Emma sat up in bed. "What's the matter, Ma?"

"It's Sir Henry," Mrs. Cadogan replied. "Better come an' 'elp me with him. He's 'ad a nasty fall—drunk as a lord, he must 'ave been—an' fair cracked his skull."

The man at Emma's side moved and began to laugh.

"I always did have a stronger head for wine than Harry," he chortled.

"Captain Willet-Payne!" Emma gasped.

Willet-Payne yawned. "I drank him under the table in no time. He must have got to his feet after a while and tried to come upstairs."

"Tit for tat!" Emma cried, and laughed till the tears rolled down her cheeks.

The village doctor had come and gone. Sir Henry, a great bandage around his head, sat slumped in a chair. His eyes, as they swiveled from Emma to Willet-Payne, flashed angrily. He was sober enough now and groaned dramatically every time he moved his head. Willet-Payne, partly dressed, lounged against a table, an unkind smile on his flushed face.

Emma, wearing a thin wrap, her thick auburn hair tousled, sat on the edge of a chair. She hardly knew what attitude to adopt and was waiting cautiously. She wondered how much Sir Henry suspected and was half-prepared, should the truth come out, for instant dismissal.

"It goes without saying," Sir Henry snapped at his friend, "that you set out deliberately to get me drunk."

"Ah, but a most worthy vintage," Willet-Payne drawled, his eyes sweeping Emma from head to foot.

13

"To get me drunk with just one purpose in mind," Sir Henry added harshly.

His eyes, too, swept Emma from head to foot. She shrugged resignedly. If he sent her packing, he sent her packing. Something else would turn up.

"You deny it, of course!" Sir Henry challenged.

"Why should I?" Willet-Payne laughed. "It's too rich a joke to keep to myself."

Sir Henry glared at Emma. "Without a doubt you were a willing party."

She shook her head vehemently. "I thought he was you. I was asleep when he come up."

"All's fair in love and war," Willet-Payne murmured.

"Of all the skunkish tricks—!"

"Oh come, man, where's your sense of humor?"

"Pah!" Sir Henry shouted.

Since there seemed little chance of making him laugh, Emma rose to her feet and stood facing him. Then she posed before him, just as if she were at Dr. Graham's Temple of Health, placing a hand on her hip. "Seems to me it's finished before it's begun. Am I to go now, or wait till morning?"

Sir Henry looked at her thoughtfully. Then he glanced at Willet-Payne.

"Do you want her yourself, or was it just to pay me out?"

"It was just to pay you out, but I'll tell you what, we can always toss a coin."

"Done!" Sir Henry cried. He was looking less angry; there was the faintest twinkle in his eyes. "But let Emma do the tossing."

"I don't know that I want to," Emma snapped, her quick temper getting the better of her. "I won't have a couple of drunken sots gambling over me like this! That I won't!"

"Delightful," Willet-Payne commented, and placed a guinea in her hand. "Now toss, Emma."

"Tails," Sir Henry said promptly.

"Heads," Willet-Payne added unnecessarily.

Emma tossed the guinea. She stood there watching it glitter in the candlelight, following its course as it bounced from the carpet and rolled on the polished wood of the floor. Her mind was working quickly. Honest with herself, she admitted that she cared little for either Willet-Payne or Sir Henry, but of the two she preferred Sir

14

Henry. And why? Because the master of Up Park was obviously a man of considerable wealth. She allowed the guinea to settle, then ran and picked it up.

"Well?" both men demanded.

It was heads.

"Tails," she pronounced, without the slightest hesitation.

Sir Henry smiled his satisfaction; Willet-Payne, she thought, gave her the queerest of looks, and turning the coin in her hand she realized why. There was a head of his Majesty King George the Third on either side.

Sir Henry's smile of satisfaction broadened and soon he was laughing heartily.

"How right you are," he told Willet-Payne, "a rich enough joke indeed."

He half-rose in his chair, his eyes now on Emma alone, his intention quite clear to her, but before she could mask her faint dismay with a show of eager willingness he groaned, clapped his hand to his head and fell back into his chair.

"Poor old Harry," Willet-Payne laughed. He turned sharply on Emma. "My guinea, if you please!"

She held his eyes steadily. "I'd rather keep it, thank you. Who knows, it might come in handy some day."

2 Emma tripped at the top of the stairs, thus giving her drunken pursuer a slight advantage. Scrambling to her feet, she flew down the corridor, all too conscious of the heavy stumbling feet close on her heels. The man was Ainsworth, one of Sir Henry's shooting and drinking companions. She had never liked him, loathing his bloated face, his piglike eyes, his gross ridiculous figure.

Somehow she reached the door of her room and fumbled frantically at the handle. At last the door flew open, but Ainsworth was upon her, his arms grasping her clumsily from behind, the heat of his breath on her neck.

"Got you, my beauty!" he shouted, and swung her round.

It was useless to call for help. All night Sir Henry, a cynical smile on his lips, had watched first one, then another of his drunken companions pestering her. Sickened now by Ainsworth's foul breath, she squirmed and kicked, but unavailingly. Disgust welled up in her as she felt the slobbering mouth searching for hers. In another moment she might faint.

"Release her, you crazy sot!"

The voice came sharply, like the thrust of a rapier, taking both Emma and Ainsworth by complete surprise. Over the bulk of Ainsworth's shoulder she caught a glimpse of the man, tall he looked, slim and austerely dressed. She recalled having vaguely noticed him during the evening, but had no recollection of his name. Ainsworth recovered from his surprise, jeered under his breath, and renewed his amorous attack. A moment later he was sprawling, whimpering slightly, on the floor at her feet. Leaning against the wall for support, Emma looked gratefully at the young man.

"Oh, thank you, sir!" She thought he must be a great deal stronger than he looked. "Thank you ever so much."

He inclined his head, then quickly averted it. A faint color tinged his cheeks. She realized that with her gown ripped beyond repair she was now naked to the waist. Still with his head averted, he addressed her in short, precisely uttered sentences.

"I doubt if you know my name. It is Greville. Charles Greville. I

16

arrived late. You scarcely noticed me. Nor did the others, since I neither drink nor gamble to excess. I should advise you to lock your door. If I can be of assistance to you at any time, please call on me."

He looked at her for one swift, penetrating moment, added a brusque good night and strode lightly down the corridor, leaving Ainsworth groaning and cursing on the floor.

Emma went quickly into her room and barred the door.

"Well, that's a queer one, that is," she said aloud.

A feeling of loneliness overcame her, and quick tears came to her eyes. "I must be in one of my moods," she admonished herself. "Life's 'ow you find it an' it's up to you to make the best of it." Nevertheless, she was near to regretting having come to Up Park, to say nothing of having dragged her mother with her. She had worried a lot about Ma lately. It hurt to see her unhappy and reproachful, shunned by the other servants and merely tolerated by Sir Henry.

She began to think really hard about Sir Henry. He was neither kind nor actually cruel to her. He spent money on her when he had a mind to, but never gave her money to spend herself. He allowed her the freedom of the house and on occasion, once she had mastered the horse he gave her, took her riding with him over the downs. She knew he was not in love with her, though just what being "in love" meant she didn't rightly know. He took her when he wanted her, just as he took a glass of wine, quickly and violently. And often, afterward, he seemed to dislike her, speaking to her roughly, as to an inferior. "I'd leave him tomorrow," she told herself frankly, "'cept that I like soft living."

She began to wonder what he would do when he learned what had happened. Perhaps he was beginning to suspect already, for she often caught him looking at her carefully, the same way her mother did, though Ma's look held anxiety, his just cold appraisal. She counted on her fingers. Another two months and it might begin to show.

"My, I am getting sorry for myself," she scoffed and, turning on her side, composed herself for sleep.

Her last conscious thought was of the queer young man, Charles Greville. Silly, when you came to think of it, because, grateful as she was to him, he wasn't her sort at all.

Emma sat in the shadows, watching the men at their cards. There were only four of them tonight—Sir Henry; Charles Greville; Willet-

Payne, who came but rarely; and a George Romney, who had apparently come with Greville last night but had gone early to bed. Ainsworth and the rowdier ones had departed that morning, leaving Up Park unnaturally quiet, so much so that Sir Henry was uneasy and not in the best of moods. To make things worse, he was losing at cards and, in consequence, drinking too much.

She gave her attention to Charles Greville. She placed his age at about thirty, though his manners made him much older. A refined lean face, he had, with slightly prominent cheekbones, large eyes, and a rather long thin nose. She knew more about him now, having learned from Sir Henry that he was the Honorable Charles Francis Greville. Just think of it, his father was the Earl of Warwick! No wonder he was so very distinguished looking!

"Well, gentlemen, whether you like it or not, I myself have had enough."

It was Greville who spoke, coldly, precisely, politely.

"Since when was it good manners to rise from the table winning?" Sir Henry sneered.

Greville gave him a mild look. "You may have your revenge tomorrow night, Harry."

"And me, too," Romney laughed. "Greville and Willet-Payne are the only winners."

"Trouble with you, George," Sir Henry said nastily, "you haven't been able to keep your eyes off my pretty Emma."

That was true enough, Emma thought. Mr. Romney had watched her all evening, not the way Sir Henry's friends usually watched her, though, but quietly, calmly, almost studiously. She remembered then that he was the painter Sir Henry had mentioned at their first meeting. He was summing her up, she decided, trying to make up his mind whether or not he wanted to paint her. She felt drawn to him, liking his gentle smile and his friendly observant eyes. He was older than the others, old enough to be her father, she thought.

He rose from the card table. "I *have* been a bit rude, and I *do* apologize."

"A lovely creature, just as I told you," Sir Henry said.

"More than lovely," Romney corrected. He came to Emma's side and addressed her directly. "I'm sorry I stared at you like that. Be a good girl and forgive me."

"Why," she cried, noticing for the first time that he spoke with a slight provincial accent, "you come from Lancashire, don't you?"

18

Romney made a face. "And you don't come far from there. Would it be Cheshire?"

"Cheshire it is, Mr. Romney!"

Sir Henry was on his feet now, lurching a little, more the worse for wine than Emma had first thought.

"Well, there you are, George," he said harshly. "You have one thing in common, you and Emma—humble birth."

Romney smiled. "And I'm sure we are neither of us ashamed of it."

"Not for a single minute!" Emma agreed.

"Talent such as Romney's," Greville put in, his voice more precise than ever, "like beauty such as Mrs. Hart's, raises one above the limitations of birth and station."

"Why, thank you, Greville," Romney said, his voice solemn, his eyes alight with amusement. He turned to Emma again. "It goes without saying I'd like to paint you."

Emma clapped her hands. "Sir Henry said as 'ow you might."

Sir Henry mimicked her scathingly, "Sir Henry said as 'ow you might. What delightful language. How easy to see, gentlemen, that my little treasure has her feet firmly fixed in the gutter. Come, Emma, stand closer. Better still, get up on the table. Lift the candles, Greville. I want our brilliant artist to have a really good view."

Emma hesitated; Romney and Greville exchanged a look of embarrassment.

"No, wait!" Sir Henry chuckled. "Stay where you are, in the shadows, but slip out of your clothes. Romney, to my knowledge, is uninterested in nudes; I want to change his attitude."

There was a moment of silence; Romney and Greville were more embarrassed than ever.

"This," said Greville, fastidiously, "is in rather bad taste."

"Bad taste?" Sir Henry was growing quarrelsome. "What the devil do you mean?"

"Greville is right," Romney said placatingly. "I can appreciate Mrs. Hart's beauty without—well—hurting her feelings."

"Feelings!" Sir Henry roared. "My dear good Romney, they don't have feelings, Emma's class of people."

Emma turned from him quickly. She wanted to laugh, she wanted to cry. She even wanted to fly at Sir Henry and scratch like a cat. Eager to escape, she moved toward the door.

"Emma!" Sir Henry shouted.

She ignored him and began to run.

"Damn you, wait!" he cried and stumbled after her.

Romney caught him by the arm. "What a host you are, Harry. Our glasses are empty."

"Are they, by God!" Sir Henry roared. "Never let it be said that a guest of mine stands with an empty glass."

Emma paused at the foot of the stairs. Somebody was following her, but the footsteps were not Sir Henry's. She turned and there was Greville, a severe look on his face, his usually smooth brow creased in a frown.

He said: "I want to say how sorry I am."

She tossed her head. "Kind of you, I'm sure!"

He was looking at her pensively. "You are the most beautiful girl I ever saw or am ever likely to see. That there should be tears in your eyes is therefore a sin."

Tears there were and she knew it, and was angry with herself.

"Tears, me foot! We don't 'ave feelings, my class."

"That, of course, is nonsense." He was speaking with the utmost sincerity. "Nor does it follow that a person in your position, a person who has had few or no advantages, should be unworthy or incapable of better things."

"Just let me go," Emma begged. "That's all I want."

Greville bowed stiffly. "Of course, Mrs. Hart. But please remember that I want to be your friend, that if you need help at any time you can always turn to me."

"That's real kind of you, Greville," she cried impulsively.

He smiled faintly. "Greville . . . Yes, I rather like to be addressed like that by you. Good night, Emma."

She went slowly up the stairs, her heart strangely warmed. Greville didn't look it, didn't quite sound it, but she was sure he was the kindest, most considerate man in the world.

When she reached her room she found her mother waiting for her.

"Ma! There'll be 'ell to pay if Sir Henry catches you here at this time of night."

Mrs. Cadogan gave her an angry look. "Much I'd care if 'e did. I want to talk to you, Emma. I want to talk to you real serious."

Here it comes, Emma thought, and waited.

"Well," Mrs. Cadogan demanded, "whose is it?"

"I don't know what you're talking about, Ma."

"Is it Captain Willet-Payne's or Sir Henry's?"

Emma gave up all pretense. "If it comes to that, Ma, I don't know that I can rightly say."

Mrs. Cadogan burst into tears. "You're a bad wicked girl, that's what you are!"

Emma supposed she might be, natural enough as it was for a girl in her position to have a baby, and natural enough half the time not to know who the father was; but her mother's tears, hurting her, made her fly into a sudden rage.

"So that's all the thanks I get for saving Cousin Charlie! And what would 'ave 'appened to us if we 'adn't come here? Tell me that, Ma!"

Mrs. Cadogan dried her eyes on the kitchen apron she wore. "Oh, well, I suppose you was just unlucky. You always did 'ave a kind heart, I'll say that much for you. What worries me now is Sir Henry won't like it. More than likely he'll turn us out when he knows."

"Perhaps he will, perhaps he won't."

"Good Lord alive, girl, you don't seem to care!"

There was a knock at the door.

"Sir Henry!" Mrs. Cadogan gasped, and ran to hide behind the curtains.

Emma shook her head. "Don't be silly, Ma, *he* never knocks."

She opened the door and there stood Greville, just a little hesitant, the frown on his forehead again. He held a piece of paper in his hand.

"I have given the matter some thought," he said, "and have decided to return to London early tomorrow with Romney. Fetherstonhaugh is not *quite* the sort of person I care to associate with. To be frank, Mrs. Hart, except for the fact that he met my uncle in Naples during the Grand Tour I would never have known him." He handed Emma the piece of paper. "This is my address."

Emma took the paper and painstakingly read the address.

"You *can* read?" he said.

"After a fashion," she replied.

"You can also write, I hope?"

"After a fashion," she repeated.

"Ah, splendid!" He sounded relieved. "You see, if anything should happen here to hurt you, I want you to write to me at that address. Will you promise to do that, Emma?"

"Oh, Greville, how good and kind you are!" she cried, and kissed him on the cheek.

He stood back from her quickly, startled and, she thought, ridiculously confused.

21

"You promise?" he said.

"I promise," she said solemnly.

He bowed, turned abruptly, and went quickly down the corridor. Emma folded the piece of paper and tucked it between her breasts. Her heart was light; she felt like dancing and singing.

"Well, there you are, Ma," she said, turning in triumph to Mrs. Cadogan, "now you know what's going to happen to us if Sir Henry turns us out."

"I go to London tomorrow. If you are still here when I come back at the end of a week, so much the worse for you."

Then, after issuing this ultimatum, Sir Henry fell into a chair and slumped drunkenly forward across the table. Satisfied that he would remain like that for some time, Emma took up a candle and went quickly to the library. There she found pen, paper, and ink, and sat down to write to Charles Greville. Actually she had never written a letter before in her life. Lips compressed, eyes narrowed in an effort at concentration, she applied herself to her task with considerable misgiving.

Laboriously she wrote the first line.

Sir H. as told me to go.

She pondered this for several moments and grew desperate. If only her mother could help her! But Mrs. Cadogan, who always signed her name with a cross, knew even less about letter writing than she did. She tried again and was pleased to find that, after half an hour, she had written several lines. Leaning forward until her nose was nearly level with the pen, she pressed on with her task, doing her best to put into words what had happened, but making no mention of the cause of the quarrel. He would, she hoped, invite her to join him in London. Her condition would then be more than obvious, but whether he liked it or not it would be too late—oh surely it would!—for him to change his mind. Finally, with a great sigh of relief, she wrote the last line.

Oh Greville, wot am I to dow?

So moved was she by what she had written that the tears were streaming down her cheeks. Greville would help her, she knew he would! And then, why, then she would love him devotedly for the rest of her life.

"Emma! Emma, where are you?"

It was Mrs. Cadogan, running along the corridor, and by the sound of her voice, quite agitated. A moment later she was in the room, panting with the unaccustomed exertion.

"Emma, it's that Mr. Greville!"

Emma sprang up. "But it can't be, not already!" She had been able to send her letter only that morning after Sir Henry, true to his word, had departed for London, saying as he left, "Remember, I never want to see you again."

"It's 'im all right," Mrs. Cadogan gasped.

"I'll go down, Ma," Emma said.

She found Greville in the hall, looking uneasy but at the same time most determined.

He said quickly: "I met Sir Henry on the road. I returned from Kendal last night. I am now on my way to Portsmouth. He told me— Well, he—" His voice trailed off in confusion.

"That he was finished with me?"

"Er—yes."

"An' he said why?"

"Yes, Emma."

She gave him the saddest of looks. "Not that it isn't plain to see, if you look at me really 'ard."

Greville averted his eyes.

A moment later he said: "Please don't cry, Emma."

She had no intention of crying, but judiciously she simulated a tearful attitude. Folding her hands across her breast, she let her shoulders droop and became a picture of utter dejection.

"Oh, my dear child!" Greville exclaimed, deeply moved.

She sobbed just once. "It isn't that I'm complaining, Greville. I 'ave nobody to blame but myself."

"You have Sir Henry and Willet-Payne to blame," he said angrily.

"I was weak an' easily led," she sighed.

"You never said a truer word, girl!" It was Mrs. Cadogan, who had joined them unnoticed. "Question is, what are we goin' to do!"

"Yes indeed," Greville agreed. His manner was a little hesitant. He kept glancing at Emma, and quickly away from her again. "Er—I take it that Sir Henry has made no provision for you whatsoever."

"Not so much as a brass farthing!" Mrs. Cadogan snapped.

"Shameful, shameful!" Greville cried, but still his manner was hesitant. "I—er—I naturally want to help you all I can."

Emma thought suddenly that she knew what the matter was. If he took her to London, the sight of her, in her present condition, would embarrass him. It would even appear that he was shouldering the blame, was indeed responsible. She was sorry for him in his indecision and thought, "Poor Greville!"

He was looking at Mrs. Cadogan now. "What had you thought of doing?"

"If I 'ad my way," Mrs. Cadogan replied, "I'd take her back to the country, to me mother's at Hawarden, but we ain't got the money to get us there."

Emma saw Greville's face clear. "I have a little money with me. Enough for that, I'm sure." He took out his purse, opened it and peered closely into it. He counted the contents not once but twice, came to a decision and gave several coins to Mrs. Cadogan. "There, I think you had better take charge of the money. The very best thing you could do, go to Hawarden, though *afterward* . . ." The indecision was on him again.

"Afterward . . . ?" Emma prompted.

Greville frowned. "Er—you must write to me."

Emma half-turned from him. "I do understand that a girl in my condition isn't a pretty sight. Good-by, Greville, and thank you ever so much."

He frowned again. "No," he said, carefully weighing the matter, "I fail to agree. In a way, you are more beautiful now than ever before. The sadness, the resignation, and behind them both the hope and the courage." Pleased with his summing up, he almost smiled, and he added triumphantly, "If Romney could see you now he would want to paint you and he—by heaven, yes!—he would call it Genesis."

And with that he turned and fled.

3 Greville sat at his desk in the little study of his small, well-ordered house in Edgware Row, Paddington Green, and frowned at the two unopened letters lying before him. He glanced fastidiously around the room. He had recently moved from a larger house in the new Portman Square and still found these rooms too cramped. However, beggars could not be choosers, and it was consoling to think that the air of Paddington Green was healthier, even if the district itself was not so fashionable.

He looked at the letters again, carefully examining the handwriting of each. One came from his uncle, Sir William Hamilton, British ambassador to the Court of the Two Sicilies, the other from Emma Hart. He thought with distaste of the other letters Emma had written. What a paradox that a creature so beautiful could be so ignorant, so abysmally illiterate. Yet the letters, he reflected, beneath the ill-spelled phrases, were full of warmth and gratitude, and suggested a latent intelligence which, if carefully cultivated, might one day match the girl's physical beauty.

He opened his uncle's letter first. Uncle and nephew were the greatest of friends, the friendship taking precedence over the ties of blood. From the very first they had made a point of ignoring the relationship and calling each other "Greville" and "Hamilton." Of all the things they had in common, an appreciation of beauty was the most pronounced. Sir William was a great collector of paintings and marbles and bronzes, and mostly their letters to each other consisted of comments and criticisms which revealed the deepest similarity of tastes. It was as a connoisseur of the beautiful that Greville had written to Sir William in Naples about Emma, describing her appearance in minute detail.

"If I did not know you for what you are, my dear Greville," Sir William now wrote in reply, "I would say without hesitation that infatuation had got the better of sound common sense; and that you had described, not an *objet d'art*, as you call her, but a creature of flesh and blood with whom, unable to help yourself, you had fallen in love."

Greville smiled thinly. The phrasing had something of an unkind ring about it.

"I do agree with you," Sir William further wrote, "that it is nothing less than a mortal sin that a creature so beautiful should remain so ignorant."

Greville nodded wisely to himself.

"It is a shameful waste, my dear Greville, and I advise you strongly, most strongly indeed, to follow your suggested plan of offering her your protection, your protection in the purest sense of the word"—Was Hamilton laughing at him?—"and attempting that most difficult of things, the making of a silk purse out of a sow's ear. If what you say of her nature, her natural brightness and cheerfulness, is true, she would, I feel sure, make a very apt pupil."

Greville dropped the letter. Yes, yes, but there were difficulties, grave difficulties. Confound it all, he was a comparatively poor man! His sole income of five hundred pounds a year was barely enough for his own modest needs. And yet this opportunity of creating a perfect piece of art was damnably tempting.

He opened Emma's letter, and so distressed was he by the poor phrasing and the bad spelling that at first he entirely missed the significance of her main piece of news. She was "distrackted" since she had not "hard" from him for some time, and once again she knew not what to "dow." "Greville, wot shall I dow?" And then he read again her reference to the child, a reference which, confused as it was, suggested one thing only.

"Great heavens—stillborn!" he exclaimed.

What a different complexion it put on this matter that had troubled him so sorely! He reached for a sheet of notepaper, then hesitated as he thought of Mrs. Cadogan. For warm-hearted Emma would insist upon bringing her mother. Still, why not? He rose and strode excitedly about the room. Servants were an expense he could well do without. By all accounts Mrs. Cadogan was an excellent cook—a plain one, of course, but plain food was healthy food, and cheap. Without doubt she would be glad to work for her keep. A cook-housekeeper, that would be an excellent arrangement. And a chaperon too. Why, the very thing! A cook-housekeeper-chaperon!

He returned to the desk, took up the pen with decision and began eagerly to write. The future, he concluded, would be nothing if not interesting.

Emma and her mother had arrived at Edgware Row and Greville,

26

greeting them courteously and paying off the hackney coach, had ushered them indoors.

"You must be tired after the long journey," he said.

"A bit shook up," Mrs. Cadogan admitted.

"Me, I enjoyed every minute of it," Emma cried.

He smiled tolerantly. "Such delightful high spirits."

Mrs. Cadogan, he thought, looked more like a countrywoman than ever. Her cheeks were rosy and shining, her eyes beaming with good will. He had, he felt sure, made a good bargain. He gave his serious attention to Emma. Her distressing experience, so fortunate in its outcome, had matured her figure. The girlishness had gone; she was the complete woman, her body rounded and comely. He hoped fervently that she would remain just like this and not go to fat, as so many of them did.

"Come," he said briskly, "let me show you to your room."

Carrying the ladies' small and shabby portmanteau, he led the way up the narrow stairs to a neat but sparsely furnished bedroom. He opened the window and drew their attention to the view of the common.

"One might almost assume that we are in the depths of the country," he said. "I trust you will both be comfortable here."

"We will an' all," Mrs. Cadogan told him contentedly.

But Emma was looking at him in faint bewilderment. She had expected a room to herself, not one to be shared with her mother, but perhaps—yes, that would be it!—perhaps he intended her to go to his on such occasions as were considered necessary.

With a little cough, Greville suggested that he should show them the rest of the house. There were two other bedrooms, one his own, the other reserved for guests, and above a tiny attic used for storing boxes and trunks. On the ground floor he allowed them to peep into the dining room and drawing room, then led them purposefully to the kitchen, off which was a tiny pantry.

"And now, Mrs. Cadogan," he said, "I feel sure we would all enjoy a brew of tea."

While Mrs. Cadogan busied herself in the kitchen he took Emma back to the drawing room, invited her to sit down and drew her attention to Correggio's "Venus" hanging on the wall. He remarked regretfully that it belonged to his uncle, the ambassador. "I live in fear that he might write at short notice and ask me to send it out to

27

him." Emma looked at it politely, expressed her appreciation with a little cooing noise and then gazed, one by one, and solemnly, at the Dutch pictures, the Roman vases and the Greek urns he pointed out to her. Finally, as if returning with an effort to mundane things, he asked her if she had fully comprehended his letter.

"A bit 'ard to understand, some of it, but I think so, Greville."

"My object," he said punctiliously, "is to superintend your education. You will, I feel sure, be a very apt pupil. First and foremost I must correct your speech; not only iron out the provincial accent, but teach you how to speak and write real English. To speak and write English in its purity is the duty of all who use it. You understand that, Emma?"

"Oh, yes, Greville!"

"Splendid!" He rubbed his hands together. "Splendid! I also think that later your voice should be trained."

"Make a singer of me, too? That's rich!"

"But not impossible, Emma. To be able to sing a little in a pleasing voice is in a lady a necessary refinement."

"Make a lady of me, too! That's even richer!"

Greville frowned. "You would like to be a lady, surely?"

Emma's eyes twinkled. "I am what I am, an' always will be, here." She touched her heart. "But I may as well 'ave all the airs and graces, too."

"Most wise of you," he told her tartly. "And now, to turn to more mundane things, mundane but necessary . . . I want you to understand that my income of five hundred pounds a year does not make of me a rich man."

"It seems like a fortune, Greville."

"Nevertheless, it is sometimes insufficient for my needs. Happily, my uncle in Naples assists me from time to time with gifts, and I have—er—expectations, but for the time being economy will be strictly necessary. You will keep books, Emma, and once I have shown you how to do it, write down every single item of expenditure. Thus we will be able to watch ourselves and keep a tight rein on extravagance. Ah, Mrs. Cadogan!"

Mrs. Cadogan had entered with the silver tea tray.

"Tea, for instance," he went on smoothly, "is extremely expensive and must be used sparingly. However, if we set our minds to it I see nothing against our existing here at Edgware Row in at least modest comfort. Have you any questions, Emma?"

28

Emma almost said, Are you as stingy as you sound? But her heart was so full of gratitude that she hesitated to hurt his feelings and quickly shook her head.

"Of course, there's Mr. Romney," she said. "Are you going to let 'im paint me?"

Greville considered this. "Later, but not just yet. At Romney's studio you will meet many members of fashionable society. It would place you at a disadvantage to do so without first having acquired a little polish."

"It would show you up, and that's a fact," Emma said candidly.

"Yes," Greville agreed, not unkindly, "it would show me up."

"Mr. Romney knows me for what I am."

"True, but Romney is my good friend and will betray neither your secret nor mine." Greville's features relaxed somewhat. "But enough! It would be a pity if I sounded too much like a schoolmaster. Shall we drink our tea now?"

Mrs. Cadogan had finished in the kitchen and gone up to bed, leaving Emma and Greville in the drawing room looking, Emma thought, like an old married couple. Greville sat, not quite at ease, in his chair, reading steadily and now and again making comments on the book; while Emma busied herself for the first time in her life with a tapestry. She wanted to laugh, and, at the same time, because she felt lonely in this strange new house, she also wanted to cry.

Occasionally Greville's eyes rested on her broodingly, and each time this happened she thought, It's coming; but he quickly resumed his reading, moving from his chair only to refill his glass with port. This made Emma's mouth water, but she concluded ruefully that the drinking of port was not ladylike.

Presently he yawned and closed his book with a snap.

"If I am tired, you must be doubly so after your long and tedious journey."

He rose. Emma did likewise and stood docilely before him, waiting. Now, oh surely now! For a long moment he looked at her steadily. She returned his look with all the appeal she could summon to her face.

"What is it, Emma?" he asked, as if she had spoken and he had not quite heard.

"Oh, Greville, I'm not *that* tired. You're so good and kind, I wish I knew 'ow to thank you properly."

He came closer, a little smile on his lips. She waited expectantly.

29

"We may as well start as we mean to go on," he said, his precise tones freezing her heart. "Your aitches, for instance. 'How', Emma, please! Not—er—''ow'."

"Oh, Greville!" she said, a little sob in her throat.

"It is not my intention to be harsh," he said gently. Turning, he picked up a candle. "Come, let me light you to your room. After tonight it will be your task to snuff the candles and lock the doors. Come, Emma!"

She followed him up the stairs, feeling woebegone and desolate and more puzzled than ever. It wasn't natural, she kept telling herself, it just wasn't natural. At her door she looked at him desperately. With his face glowing in the light of the candle, his body in the shadows, he had a ghoulish look.

"Why don't you go straight to bed," she suggested, "and let me bring you a nightcap?"

He shook his head. "Thank you, no. I have had my fill for tonight. I am, you know, an abstemious man." He inclined his head. "Good night, Emma. Sleep well."

"Good *night!*" she said, and flounced into her room.

She found her mother sitting up in bed.

"Well," said Mrs. Cadogan dryly, "this *is* a surprise."

"Is it!" Emma snapped.

Mrs. Cadogan looked at her curiously. "Did you quarrel, Emma? Did you tell 'im the truth about the baby an' then quarrel?"

"I didn't tell him, Ma. You said yourself 'e wouldn't want a baby here."

Emma still wondered what to do for the best. Without actually telling an untruth, she had deliberately suggested in her letter that the baby had been stillborn. Having done that, how could she tell him now that she had a daughter a few weeks old in the care of her grandmother at Hawarden and suckled by a friend there with a baby of her own and more milk than she knew what to do with?

"I won't tell 'im just yet, Ma. Maybe never at all."

Thinking of Greville again, she began to undress, tearing off her clothes angrily. If he didn't want her, well, she didn't want him! She snuffed out the candle and smiled sadly in the darkness. Come on, Emma, be honest with yourself! Whether it was just out of gratitude or not, she was sure she was in love with him and she knew she wanted him. *In love with him?* Was what she felt *really* love? How hard it was to understand this queer feeling! She sought for words to express it.

It was all mixed up with the little-boy look she associated with him. Sort of wanting to protect him, which was silly when *he* was protecting *her*. Maybe that was what real love was, she thought solemnly.

Restless, more wide-awake than ever, she listened to her mother's even breathing, then she stole softly on bare feet from the room. At Greville's door she paused for a moment. She could hear him moving about. She waited till all was silence; thought, Brazen, aren't you!; and turned the handle. The door was locked.

She went slowly back to her own bed and got in at her mother's side. She felt as if Greville had struck her, even called her a dirty name. Yet why had he taken her up like this? Not just for the sake of educating her, surely! She remembered a phrase in his letter. *My protection in the purest sense of the word* . . . And the other bit about her mother being a chaperon. A chaperon in the purest sense of the word, too, it seemed!

Then she thought of what he had said about her going to Romney's studio, the need of a bit of polish before meeting fashionable people. And how Romney would keep her secret and his . . . All these things came together suddenly and gave her what seemed to be the only possible explanation. Greville was planning to make her his wife!

"And 'im the earl of Warwick's son!" So excited was she that she began to shake her mother. "Ma, wake up! Ma, do you know what? I'm going to be the countess of Warwick one of these days!"

31

4. Romney said apologetically, "Just a minute or two more, that's all I need, Emma."

"Well, I *am* a bit cramped," Emma said.

Cramped or not, she was still quite carried away, exalted, almost, by the pose she had fallen into, so naturally and so easily. And yet, when you came to think of it, how laughable it was that she, Emma Hart, should be down on her knees in the guise of a nun at prayer! Sacrilege, some people would call it.

"What a genius you have for posing," said Romney. "How do you do it, my dear?"

"Well, I sort of picture myself the way you want me, and . . . there it is. And I really feel it, too. I do, Romney, honest I do!"

"In other words, a born actress."

"Oh, I wouldn't say that. I can pose, but I'm sure I can't act." She laughed softly at a passing thought, but quickly composed her features again, her eyes raised in beatific contemplation of the infinite. "Not that the life I'm leading these days doesn't make it easy for me to feel like a nun."

Romney smiled. "Indeed."

"He's a queer one, that Greville, an' no mistake. You should ask him to come and pose for you as a monk."

"Perhaps I will," Romney laughed. "Head a bit higher, please. Yes, that's right."

Emma had been with Greville for nearly six months now, and he was pronouncing himself moderately pleased with the progress she had made. Her English, he said, had improved amazingly, while her accent was only noticeable in moments of excitement.

On the whole, immersed in her lessons, she was content with life and not too unhappy, in spite of Greville's indifference. These regular visits to Romney's studio in Cavendish Square did much to break the monotony, and her attachment to the painter had grown deeper with every visit. The love that existed between them, as Romney said, was pure, untouched by physical demands. She was more than just a model, he had told her many times; she was the greatest inspiration an artist could ever find. "My divine lady," he often said.

Her own attitude to Romney was more that of a daughter than anything else. She found it so easy to talk to him, perhaps because they had indeed humbleness of birth in common, he being the son of a cabinetmaker.

"Well, that will do for today," Romney said.

Emma relaxed, rose slowly to her feet, and went to change into her own clothes, quickly becoming herself again as she threw aside the nun's robe. Later, the habit being well-established now, she went to make tea. Thus occupied, she thought of all the happy weeks she had been coming to Cavendish Square. Greville hadn't been too willing to begin with, but Romney had talked him into it. She had come the first time, weeks before Greville was willing to pronounce her ready, because Sir William Hamilton, writing from Naples, had asked for a portrait of his nephew's "protégée."

"But remember," Greville had cautioned, "when you meet people at the studio, concentrate on listening intelligently while saying as little as possible." This she had done with satisfying success, meanwhile studying carefully the grand people she met, listening to their refined accents, taking full note of their easy, almost casual manners. She knew that a change was taking place in her; she could feel it happening. But underneath, she told herself, she was still "me" and always would be. All the same, it was a bit of a joke to know she was fooling so many people, especially the men.

When she returned to the studio with the tea Romney was busy with another unfinished portrait.

"You work too hard," she admonished.

He smiled and came to take the cup she offered him. "Work is life to me, Emma. *This* work. And not only does it give me pleasure, it earns me more money than I would ever have believed possible." But he was growing depressed now, as he sometimes did. "Still I don't think ambition and happiness often go hand in hand. Don't ever grow too ambitious, Emma."

She knew he was thinking about his wife, who had refused to come to London with him. He had told her once before about his marriage and the two children. There had been no quarrel, just a gradual growing apart of two people who had nothing left in common.

He went back to the portrait he had been working on. "How disillusioning romantic love can be! Be careful, Emma, fall in love by all means, but never blindly and crazily."

"Oh, I'm levelheaded enough," Emma said, "'cept—I mean except about Greville." She heaved a deep sigh. "I don't know what to make of him; truly, Romney, I don't."

33

"But he's kind to you, isn't he?"

"Yes, he's kind enough." She shrugged. Things were as they were and there was nothing she could do about it. She laughed dryly. "He keeps me a bit short of money. I have to watch every penny. Still, I expect things will be different when he's the earl of Warwick."

Romney looked up sharply from the canvas. "What nonsense has he been telling you?"

"Oh, he never talks about his family, but when his father dies—"

"My dear Emma," Romney interrupted gently, "his father is already dead. The present earl is Greville's elder brother, married, with a son to follow him. The chance of Greville ever becoming earl of Warwick is remote."

"Oh—damn!" Emma cried. She was exasperated and disappointed, yet underneath amused enough to laugh at herself. "It was Sir Henry who told me. I must have mistaken him. Or else he lied, just for the fun of tricking me. Oh well, it doesn't matter."

Romney came to her and patted her hand. "What I like so much about you, Emma, is your cheerfulness. I often think that cheerfulness is the greatest of all the virtues, perhaps the only one that really matters."

Emma gave him an impish smile. "Looking at it that way, I'm the most virtuous woman in the world."

Romney smiled, but seriously he said, "I think you must have had hopes of becoming the countess of Warwick."

"That's right," she chuckled.

"Has Greville ever given you the impression that he wants to marry you?"

Emma frowned over this. "No—I mean, he hasn't *said* anything. But look at the way he treats me. Real respect it is. And educating me to take my place in fashionable society."

"Come and look at this portrait," Romney said quietly.

Emma went with him to the easel. She saw a young woman, not beautiful, not even pretty, but obviously haughty and well-bred. A born lady, without a doubt.

"The Honorable Henrietta Midleton," Romney told her, "one of Lord Midleton's daughters. An heiress, in short. Worth thirty thousand pounds to any man who marries her, I believe."

"Well, I hope she's paying you a handsome fee."

"A hundred guineas, no less." Romney turned and faced her squarely. "What I have to say will test your cheerfulness to the utmost. The Honorable Henrietta is Greville's fiancée."

Emma had never felt more flabbergasted in her life. "That's a lie, Romney!" she said angrily.

"No, Emma, it's the truth."

"An heiress. Thirty thousand pounds! He wants her for her money!"

"Can you blame him? A younger son with no expectations."

"He told me he *had* expectations! He did, Romney!"

"He must have been referring to his uncle, Sir William Hamilton, whose only child died some years ago. But Sir William still has a wife and is, in any case, hale and hearty and by no means an old man."

Emma's anger was subsiding, but she was more puzzled about Greville than ever.

"Why did he take me up, Romney? That's what I can't understand. The way things are, I'm not to be his wife, nor his mistress either."

Romney gave a sly laugh. "Which, of course, is not remotely amusing."

"No!" Emma snapped, and stamped her foot.

"No?"

"No, Romney, no, no, *no!*" Her voice, shrill on the last 'no', broke suddenly. "N-not in the least amusing," she said weakly, and then, in spite of herself, she started to laugh. Presently, breathless with it all, she sank into a chair. "But what does it mean, Romney, Greville's silly attitude?"

Romney chose his words very carefully. "Greville has an artist's feeling for beauty without an artist's ability to express that feeling. So he took you up, I think, because he saw an opportunity, one single opportunity, for presenting to the world a thing of complete beauty."

"A thing—that's me!"

"Yes, my dear." Laughter was bubbling up in him.

"But I'm flesh and blood, too, Romney!"

"And you love him dearly."

"No, I hate him! I hate him!" Emma's eyes narrowed. "When does this Miss Midleton come for her next sitting?"

"Tomorrow at three. Why?"

Emma rose. "Thank you!"

"Emma, my dear—"

She smiled sweetly. "Good afternoon to you, dear Romney." She kissed him swiftly on the cheek. "Fiancée indeed!" she exploded.

Back at Edgware Row Emma found Greville deeply engrossed in the housekeeping accounts. He looked at her vaguely as she entered his study and motioned her to sit down. She was quite calm now. The anger had gone, leaving in its place a simmering resentment, and resentment, up to now, had been foreign to her nature. She thought, it's real mean of me, but I just can't help myself. The Honorable Henrietta Midleton indeed!

"Emma," said Greville, looking up sharply, "I find it impossible to account for the sum of one shilling and one halfpenny. But quite apart from that we seem, of late, to have verged on the side of rank extravagance."

Emma grinned. By "we" he naturally meant "you."

"Take the butcher's account. A steady increase over the last few weeks until now—dear me, Emma!—out of all proportion."

She tossed her head. "You like the best cuts and they're always dearer at this time of year."

"Butter is still the same price, yet more has been spent on butter this month than last."

Emma felt a little stab of alarm. She could only hope that, capable as he was of going to the tradespeople and asking the prices, his sense of dignity would prevent it. Having decided now never to tell him about the baby, it was necessary to send money to her grandmother at Hawarden, and the only way she had of getting money was to cheat with the housekeeping.

She said quickly, "I do love butter, Greville."

"That," he said dryly, "is obvious, since you are inclined these days to plumpness."

"Romney thinks it becomes me."

"He, I grant you, should know. But take care, my dear Emma, that plumpness does not become fatness. Now the matter of hackney coaches. You seem to have taken an unconscionable number of late."

She smiled. "Unconscionable" was a word he admired and used whenever he could find a place for it.

"It's too far to walk to Romney's," she said.

"Eight times in the month," he protested.

"No, Greville, nine."

"Ah, then that accounts for the shilling!" he cried. "But what of the halfpenny? Please don't think me cheeseparing in this instance. It is only that I like to be exact."

Emma screwed up her face. "Wait a minute. Yes, I gave a ha'penny to a beggar and don't remember putting it down."

Greville beamed. "Splendid. Everything is accounted for." His beam faded. "But the general expenditure, my dear, must be kept down, really it must."

Emma laughed shortly. "Just as well you don't intend getting married. You could never afford a wife."

He smiled thinly. "A wife, Emma, is not in every case an—er—encumbrance."

She knew quite well what he meant by *that!* Anger flared up in her again. What a sly rat he was, for all his grand manners.

He took up his pen and began to write. "To a beggar, one half-penny," he said, as he wrote. "Oh yes, and the additional hackney coach . . ."

"Put down two," Emma said, suppressing a giggle. "I'm taking another tomorrow to the same place."

Romney, rather flustered, made the introduction with the best grace he could summon up.

"Mrs. Emma Hart—the Honorable Henrietta Midleton."

Emma inclined her head gracefully and murmured that she was most happy to make Miss Midleton's acquaintance. Her attitude was that of a perfect lady, poised, just a little casual, even a little haughty and suitably languid.

"Miss Midleton," Romney said, "was admiring my unfinished nun."

"Yes indeed," Miss Midleton said warmly.

Emma looked at her quickly. The warmth of the voice had been entirely unexpected. It gave her a little stab of conscience. Aristocratic and haughty though Miss Midleton looked, she was obviously a young woman of vast inexperience, untouched by life as it really was.

"Please do not think me rude, Mrs. Hart," she ran on, her voice twittering nervously, "if I say that the original is even more to my taste than the painting." Instantly she grew confused and laughed, rather like a horse neighing. "But what am I saying, my dear Mr. Romney!"

Romney smiled good-naturedly. "I'm far from satisfied with the work yet, Miss Midleton."

"But I did not mean— Oh dear, how very clumsy of me! The work is excellent, Mr. Romney, though I am not an authority as Charles is. I should like Charles to see it, except that it might make him want to see the original, too, and *that* would never do." Again came the neighing laugh. "No, never! Ne-he-heee!"

"Charles?" Emma said politely.

37

Romney cleared his throat.

"My fiancé, Mrs. Hart."

"Quite a coincidence," Emma simpered. "I, too, know a Charles. Not my fiancé, of course, but a very dear friend nonetheless."

Romney cleared his throat again. "A not uncommon name, Charles."

Emma looked at him innocently. "My Charles is an authority, too, where art is concerned." Better, she thought, to get it over and done with quickly before she relented. "I was so fortunate to meet him. Life can be so hard for a poor widow in straitened circumstances." She sighed elaborately. "Even so, I hesitated for some time before I decided to accept his protection."

"Emma, my *dear*—" Romney tried to interrupt.

"Dear me, what have I said?" Emma asked, wide-eyed. "Am I embarrassing Miss Midleton?" She looked at the Honorable Henrietta, whose cheeks were faintly pink. "But of course not! Miss Midleton, like myself, is a woman of the world."

Miss Midleton giggled nervously. "Dear me, dear me, what would dear Papa say!"

"Indeed," Emma went on, avoiding Romney's eyes now, "I feel that we have much in common, Miss Midleton, and could become good friends. Do forgive me for presuming on so short an acquaintance, but would you care to take tea with me some day soon?"

"I should be delighted," Miss Midleton stammered.

Emma inclined her head. "I have a little house in Edgware Row, Paddington Green. It belongs to Charles, of course, but I like to call it mine. Some day next week, Miss Midleton?"

"Edgware Row?" Miss Midleton's voice rose on a shrill, unladylike note.

"Yes, the number is fifteen. You would like Charles, I feel quite sure of that."

"Fifteen!" Miss Midleton gasped. "Is he—Charles— Oh, please tell me who he really is!"

"Gladly, Miss Midleton. My friend is the Honorable Charles Francis Greville. Is it possible that you are already acquainted with him?"

But Miss Midleton, clutching her throat, was falling into a quiet, ladylike faint from which, while Emma retired to the hall, George Romney hastened to revive her. Later, when he had assisted her to her carriage, extravagant in his apologies, he took his divine lady by the ear and led her back to the studio.

"So it's true," he said, smiling faintly.

"What's true, Romney?"

"That in every woman, however generous, however warmhearted, one can find, if one searches hard enough, the bitch."

Emma woke with a start. She raised herself on one elbow and listened. Somebody was rapping sharply at the bedroom door.

"Emma! Emma, I want to talk to you. Get up at once!"

She smiled in the darkness. Three days she had waited for this, the big scene she had pictured in her mind, and now it had come. She could tell that by the angry tone of Greville's voice.

"Emma!"

"Coming, Greville," she replied softly.

She got quietly from the bed, careful not to disturb her mother, and slipped into a black silk wrap. After Greville had left Edgware Row that evening she and her mother had gone early to bed. She had hoped that he was going to visit Miss Midleton; now she felt sure that he had indeed done so. She opened the door and closed it quietly behind her.

"Goodness, Greville, what's the matter?"

He scowled at her. "Come downstairs, Emma!"

The candle he was holding shook in his hand. He led her down to his study in grim silence. She glanced at him obliquely. No longer the quietly composed, eminently restrained Greville she had previously known, he was seething with anger. Stamping mad, she decided, and began to feel a little frightened. Was it possible that she had gone too far?

In the study he strode about, flinging up his arms dramatically, his anger increasing at every step he took. Emma could hardly believe her eyes. It looked as if he was human after all, really human. Her mind was working rapidly. A half-smile flitted across her face. If she could keep him like this, angry and human . . . ! It was, after all, a heaven-sent opportunity, roused from her bed, warm and rosy with sleep, wearing nothing but the black silk wrap, a recent present from Sir William Hamilton in Naples . . .

"Greville—"

"Vixen!" he spat at her.

He looked and sounded so ridiculous that she had trouble keeping back the laughter that rose in her throat.

"You planned the whole thing! Obviously you did!"

39

"Greville, what *are* you talking about?"

"After seeing Henrietta I went straight to Romney. Oh, he pretended the innocence that you are pretending now, but in the end I forced him—*forced* him, I say!—to tell me everything that had happened."

"Poor Greville," Emma said, her voice a gentle sigh, "did Miss Midleton jilt you?"

"She never wants to see me again. I, for that matter, never want to see *you* again. But first—!"

"Oh, but Greville," she protested, "an accidental meeting like that!"

"The meeting was *not* accidental!"

"If Romney said that he wronged me deeply."

Greville came close to her, placed his hands heavily on her shoulders and shook her violently.

"You asked about Henrietta's next appointment," he thundered as he shook her. "You went to Cavendish Square at that time yourself. Good heavens, Emma, do you take me for a fool!"

The wrap nearly came away in his hands, which at this stage was more than Emma wanted. He straightened it absently and stood back from her.

"Tomorrow I shall send you home to your grandmother."

"And Ma, too?"

"How many times have I told you not to say 'Ma'? Yes, and your mother, too."

"You'll miss her cooking, Greville."

"Go back to bed, Emma!"

"Servants cost money and you've had her free all this time."

"I told you to go back to bed!"

"But won't you listen to me first?" Her voice broke of its own accord. "Oh, Greville, Greville!"

"Excuses, excuses! Why should I listen to excuses!"

She looked at him pleadingly. "You might have known that I would meet her at Romney's in the end."

"I knew nothing of her visits, Emma, nothing! Lord Midleton commissioned the portrait unknown to me. I have seen very little of Romney lately, you know that. Great heavens, had I realized that Henrietta was going there I would have kept you well away from Cavendish Square. For the last time, Emma, go back to bed."

She wondered what to do next. She asked herself what possible attitude in her very considerable repertoire of attitudes could be employed to soften his anger. In a flash of inspiration she remembered

Romney's painting of the nun at prayer. Instantly she fell to her knees in a similar pose, but instead of gazing beatifically into space she leveled her eyes, round and solemn and childlike, on Greville's face, and instead of clasping her hands across her breast she extended them, flutteringly, toward him in supplication. The supplicant, she thought, not the nun at prayer. Good gracious no, not half-naked like this, her bare rounded knees peeping through the black silk wrap, and her breasts partly exposed.

"Oh, Greville, I was ever so wicked, I know I was."

"Please don't say 'ever so'!" he snarled.

She swallowed contritely. "But 'ow could I 'elp it if I—"

"*How! Help!*" he shouted, beside himself. "Get up, Emma. Go to bed at once." She was sure that she could recognize a faint alarm in his voice. "Do as I say, Emma. At once!"

She crawled toward him, not like a fawning animal, but with all the grace she could put into her movements. The wrap trailed behind her, clinging only to her shoulders. She was, she felt sure, a most entrancing and appealing sight.

"Greville!" she sobbed, and flung her arms round his knees.

"This," he pronounced, "is more than I bargained for."

"Please say you forgive me," she begged. "Please! I only did it because I love you. I love you so dearly, Greville, yet you care nothing for me, nothing at all!"

"My dear Emma," he said, a desperate note creeping into his voice, "in my own way I love you just as dearly. Be a sensible girl and go back to bed. Perhaps, in the morning, when I have slept on it, when my anger has cooled, we shall discuss this unhappy matter again, sanely and—er—quietly."

"Greville, dear kind good Greville!"

She looked up at him, her beautiful eyes swimming in tears. She clung to his knees all the harder.

"Do get up," he said thickly.

"I can't, Greville. I feel that weak. All the life has gone out of me. Oh, Greville, Greville . . . !"

He reached down jerkily and raised her to her feet. She flung her arms around his neck and kept them there, lightly forcing his head down. She had intended to simulate grief, to weep dramatically, but now, gratifying her infinitely, the tears were flowing of their own accord. She knew that if he turned from her now her heart would be broken forever.

"Emma," he wailed, "this is madness."

She pressed herself softly and fully against him. "I'm so cold, Greville."

"Madness!" he repeated, and put his arms round her.

After he had kissed her, clumsily but with an eagerness that was completely satisfying, he lifted her in his arms. "I'm too heavy for him," she thought comically, but he held her there, carried her from the room and went on up the stairs, staggering alarmingly as he reached the top. Panting, he reached his own door, kicked it open and carried her in.

"Madness," he kept saying, "madness!"

Emma awoke to find Greville staring down at her. The pale early sun was streaming through the window, the curtains of which had not been drawn the night before. She stretched luxuriously and smiled up at him.

Once again he said "Madness," but in a different tone, calmly and sadly.

"Madness like that is nice," she chuckled. "Don't you think so, Greville?"

"Nice enough," he said curtly.

"But Greville, surely—"

"Yes, yes," he said testily, "I enjoyed it. But don't you see, the true artist creates. He creates but never possesses. I feel I have betrayed myself, made a mockery of my artistic integrity. Everything is spoiled now, everything."

"Do you know what I think, Greville? I think you must have wanted to betray yourself lots of times while I've been here."

"Yes, yes, but I was always strong enough to resist."

"What nonsense you talk! Everything is perfect now, not spoiled. Don't you see that in possessing you created, too! You created a woman who loves you more than ever now. Can't you see it, can't you *feel* it, dear, dear Greville?"

He scowled at her. "You have the look of a well-fed cat. I can even imagine you with nice long whiskers."

She reached up her arms and drew him down to her.

"Madness!" he said again, but in the tone he had used the night before.

And Emma, eyes closed, lips parted, smiled contentedly.

5   "I wonder how many times you have sat for me now," Romney said.

Emma laughed merrily. "Better ask Greville. It's down in the accounts. Every time I've come here in a hackney coach, I mean." She reflected for a moment. "He did say last month that I would soon reach the two hundred and fiftieth sitting. Just think of it, Romney! Two hundred and fifty hackney coaches at a shilling a time. What a fortune!"

"For Greville, yes," Romney agreed solemnly. "Of course, it flatters him that I should find you such a great inspiration. If it weren't for that he might never have brought himself to spend the money."

Romney was putting the finishing touches to his latest "Emma." This time he was painting her as a bacchante. She had posed as a saint and a sibyl, as Joan of Arc and Cassandra, as Nature and Sensibility. And in these, as in all the other countless poses, he had declared fervently that she was perfection itself.

Emma, reclining on the couch, her long hair streaming about her shoulders and down her back, was thinking lazily of the three years she had lived at Edgware Row with Greville. She thought in particular of that night he had discovered the trick she had played on Henrietta Midleton. How kind fate had been, making him rouse her from her bed like that! The madness, as he called it, had continued for a time, then faded to a regular habit; and life had gone smoothly forward.

She had never been so happy before. Her "real" establishment had brought her the one thing that was lacking. Of course, Greville at times had proved a difficult man to live with, and until the news had come from Italy, he had often reproached her for depriving him of a wealthy wife. But after the news came, news of his aunt's death in Naples, he had seemed almost pleased by what she had done. "With Hamilton a widower," he had told her happily, "I am now his sole heir."

Nevertheless, Sir William Hamilton might well live for many years yet; it was still necessary to watch expenditure, and this Emma did painstakingly, striving to make the best possible bargain with every single tradesman. "Commendable, most commendable," Greville said; and, after the first year, instead of buying clothes for her himself,

43

he allowed her what he called the handsome sum of twenty pounds a year for pocket money.

She laughed to herself now as she wondered what he would say if he knew that in spite of her ability to keep expenditure down she still cheated over recorded prices. He would hardly say "Commendable, most commendable!"

"There are them as would say you was a bad mother," Mrs. Cadogan had once reproved her.

"Is that what you think yourself, Ma?"

Mrs. Cadogan had considered this. "Yes, Emma, an' no. She's well cared for, you see to that. You left 'er when she wasn't no more than two weeks old, an' you've seen 'er just twice since then. Way I look at it, take a kitten from a cat at birth an' it soon forgets."

"But a cat doesn't think and feel, Ma!"

"No more it does. What do *you* think and feel, Emma?"

"I sometimes think a lot but I never seem to feel much. Not even when I see her. I just pretend, that's all. Maybe if there was a father to take an interest it would be different."

Well, she had made her choice three years ago—poverty at Hawarden, or security at Edgware Row—there was no use fretting about it now.

Romney looked up from his work and asked her, in French, if she was tired of the pose. She replied, in French, that she was a bit, but not too much. Her education, to Greville's delight, had progressed rapidly. Her English, when she gave her mind to it, was perfect. She could write a legible hand, even a good, intelligent letter. She could read poetry quite prettily and her voice, now partly trained, was sweet and clear. The only thing that annoyed the precise and exacting Greville was her inability to spell correctly. With English spelling eluding her he had thought it foolish to embark on a new language, but was ready now to admit that the time spent over French lessons was not being wasted.

Romney sometimes asked her if she was ever bored, living so quiet a life. She considered this now. She *did* live a quiet life and she *did* at times feel just a little bored. She had expected Greville to take her about in society, but this he had never done. There were two things against it, he said. A gentleman never took his mistress about with him; and, quite apart from that, his poverty made it necessary for him to live in retirement from the fashionable world.

Yes, it *was* a quiet and sometimes dull life. The only people she

44

ever met were those who frequented Romney's studio, gentlemen of leisure, mostly; some had offered her their protection and one, newly rich, elderly, and not quite a gentleman, had offered her marriage. Each offer she had declined prettily. She preferred Greville, queer one that he was. "I must love him very deeply indeed," she told herself solemnly.

"Emma, my dear—"

Romney's voice startled her.

"Oh, did I move? Do forgive me."

He threw down his palette. "Enough for today, Emma. I was going to offer you a penny for your thoughts. Such a faraway expression it was. Not the bacchante expression at all."

"I was thinking—" She hesitated. "Oh, Romney, if I were to die now, this very moment, I would die happy."

"One of the tragedies of life," Romney said somberly, "is that one cannot die at such a moment."

He sounded so doleful that tears of sympathy sprang to her eyes. Seeing this, he was contrite and apologetic, and urged her to remain the sweet unspoiled Emma he had always known; but his black mood continued all through their habitual tea drinking, and nothing she could say would bring even the faintest of smiles to his face.

"I have an awful feeling," he confessed, "that life will change for you soon and I shall never see you again."

"But what nonsense!" she cried.

At Edgware Row she found her mother in no better spirits. And Ma was usually so cheerful and contented.

"Maybe it's just me constipation," Mrs. Cadogan said dolefully, "but where is it all goin' to end? That's what I want to know."

"A nice big brew of senna pods will buck you up," Emma said cheerfully.

"You know what I mean, Emma. You and Mr. Greville, that's what I mean. Lasted longer than I expected, it 'as. That restless he is these days. Hadn't you noticed?"

Emma laughed heartily. "He did the accounts this morning. There was sixpence I couldn't remember having spent. He'll get over it."

But Greville's mood that night was no better than Romney's or her mother's. Emma sat at his feet while he sipped his port, and with her head against his knee she told him how sorry she was about the missing sixpence. He said gloomily that it scarcely mattered. She couldn't understand all these moods. It had been such a lovely day, bright sunshine and a clear atmosphere, the sort of day you felt as if you were walking on air.

"What you need is a change," she suggested. "You ought to go and see your relatives in Scotland."

"Impossible!" he snapped.

"Meaning the expense, Greville?"

"Meaning the expense!" He pushed her roughly aside and got up to stride about the room. "This genteel poverty, how I detest it!" He went to refill his glass, gazed at the almost empty decanter, and said, "Pah!"

Emma tried to smile. "Do you know what I think? I think you must be constipated, like Ma."

He looked at her balefully. "Scarcely a ladylike remark. And please, I have mentioned this before, say 'Mother', not 'Ma'."

A sudden flare-up of temper got the better of her. "To 'ell with being ladylike!"

"Pray remember your aitches, Emma."

"Hell, then! Hell, hell, hell!" The temper disappeared as quickly as it had come. "Oh, Greville, are you feeling sorry you took me up?"

"A little, perhaps. How do I know?"

"Greville!"

"Forgive me," he said gruffly. "If I am ever sorry it is because of the way my plan went awry."

She knew what he meant by that. "But you enjoyed it, didn't you?"

He turned his back on her. "There are more important things than the pleasures of the flesh. Yet, confound you, Emma, I enjoyed it—for a time."

She shook her head sadly. And still she loved him, she loved him with all her heart.

"What would have happened if your plan hadn't gone awry?" she asked curiously.

He swung around and looked at her broodingly. "I would now have the pleasure of regarding you as one regards a perfect work of art."

"And what would have happened to me, Greville?"

He looked immeasurably puzzled. "Bless my soul, I never thought of that."

"I'm a woman, Greville," she said quietly. "I'm flesh and blood, not a marble statue to be sent to your uncle in Naples."

He gazed at her with the oddest expression in his eyes.

"No," he said slowly. "I quite see that, not a marble statue to be sent to Naples." In a moment he was striding about the room again. "But life must have purpose, Emma. To go on in the same way, day after day, month after month, year after year— One can scarcely call that living. Stagnation, that is what it is, stagnation."

"But if you're *happy*, Greville—"

"Happiness is a delusion. One may as well be dead as continue without purpose, without ambition. I—" He broke off with an angry gesture. "Good night, Emma. Remember to put out all the candles and lock and bolt the doors."

She watched him leave the room and thought what a fool he was, making himself miserable when it was the easiest thing in the world to be happy. All you have to do is give yourself the chance, she thought.

She put out all the candles, locked and bolted the doors, and went up to bed. She paused to try Greville's door when she came to it. For the first time since that night three years ago, he had locked it.

She shrugged philosophically. Oh, well, it was another day tomorrow. Let him be miserable all night; he couldn't go on like that forever.

"He'll get over it," she said.

"He wants you," Mrs. Cadogan said, and made a face.

"Where is he, Ma? Still in the study?"

Mrs. Cadogan nodded. "Ructions, by the look of things. Stamping mad, I'd say."

Only a few minutes ago Greville, tired and travel-stained, had returned from Pembrokeshire where, at his uncle's request, he had been making a tour of inspection of Sir William's estates. He had expected to be away only two weeks but had been gone the better part of a month. That something had happened to anger him, something in some way concerning her, had been obvious the moment he reached Edgware Row. She had rushed out eagerly to greet him; he had pushed her curtly aside and marched in grim silence to his study.

"Better hurry," Mrs. Cadogan said.

Emma found Greville sitting at his little desk. He still wore the heavy traveling coat. His face, particularly about the nose and mouth, had a pinched look. The letters that had accumulated during his absence still lay untouched on the desk.

"Emma," he thundered, "I want you to tell me the truth about that child at Hawarden."

47

Unprepared for such a question, she gave a great start of surprise. "Why, Greville, what child?" she stammered.

"The child in your grandmother's care. The child called 'little Emma.'"

"I don't know what you're talking about!"

"I want the truth, Emma; I *saw* the child."

"You—you've been to Hawarden?"

He nodded. "I met an old friend in South Wales. I went north with him. We visited several country houses. Finding myself near Hawarden—we were at Chester, if I remember rightly—I decided to call on your grandmother. Now, Emma, the truth, if you please!"

"What did Granny tell you?" Emma asked, playing for time.

"A number of things. For instance, that your name was never Hart. That you were never married, still less widowed. Not, of course, that this matters, except that it proves you a ready liar. Finally the old lady told me how good you were to the child, how you sent money regularly."

Emma thought, It's the money, as much as anything.

Greville said, "Your child was *not* stillborn—is that right?"

She nodded, decided on her line of attack, and grinned at him impishly.

"But Greville, why are you so solemn and grim? You don't know how silly you look."

"Silly?" he ejaculated.

"Yes, silly. Silly, silly, silly!"

He cleared his throat. "Your grandmother suggested that you kept the birth a secret because you were afraid I might take no further interest in you. Is that right?"

"Yes, Greville, it is. You wouldn't have, would you?"

"My dear foolish Emma," he said, almost pityingly, "I was interested in you when you were—hum!—in a certain condition, and I helped you. I think—yes, I *think* I would have continued to help you."

"But you wouldn't have let me bring the child to London, would you?"

"No. No, no, indeed I wouldn't."

"There you are then! I did the right thing."

His anger was passing. "I admit that you did. At least, you did exactly what I would have asked you to do if I had been told in the first place."

"Oh, but don't you see, Greville, I couldn't be sure of that! I was afraid you wouldn't want to see me ever again."

"Be that as it may, Emma"—his voice rose on an indignant note—"there is still the question of—"

Knowing that he was going to speak of the money she had sent to Hawarden, she interrupted quickly: "Is little Emma well? What did you think of her?"

"She was in excellent health, and I thought her a beautiful child. And quite advanced for her age, I would say. But Emma—"

"Oh, Greville, aren't you just a little sorry for me?"

"*Sorry* for you?"

"Having to keep it to myself like that. Think of the way I suffered! The anguish of having a child and never being with her! There were times when I could hardly bear it!"

Greville laughed shortly. "Oh, hold your tongue! I refuse to be put off a moment longer. You sent your grandmother money. How did you manage to do it?"

Emma shrugged, and told him the truth. He raised his hands as if struck a mortal blow.

"It just shows you what a good manager I am, Greville!"

"What a good deceiver, you mean!"

Emma gave him a shrewd look. "Would you have let my baby starve?"

"Emma!" he protested, in a shocked voice.

"What *would* you have done, then?"

He gave this question a moment's thought. "I expect I would have made a separate provision for your child." He frowned. "Yes, undoubtedly I would."

Emma laughed tinklingly. "There! Left to myself I saved you money. You made provision without *knowing* you were doing it."

"That scarcely seems logical to me," he said heavily. "To reason like that suggests a twisted mentality. By heaven it does! I very much fear, Emma, that at heart you are a woman of absolutely no principles."

Emma chuckled. "Isn't every woman, at heart?"

He ignored her and began to open his letters.

"What happens now, Greville?" she asked bravely.

"Eh?" He was absorbed in a letter.

"Are you going to make separate provision, or do you want me to go on just the same, saving you money?"

"One moment!" His eyes were sparkling now as he read the letter. "I just want to know where I stand, Greville—"

"Emma!" He jumped up from the desk, waved the letter in the air. "This is from Hamilton! He's coming on a visit! Ah, what a time we shall have, the three of us!"

"The *three* of us?"

"Hamilton speaks of especially looking forward to meeting my protégée. As I say, what a time we shall have, the three of us!"

"But can you afford it?" Emma asked innocently.

A sly, attractive smile crossed his face. "Hamilton has plenty of money."

6 Everything was in readiness for Sir William Hamilton's arrival. Emma, taking a last-minute glance at the room which she and her mother had prepared for him, agreed with what Mrs. Cadogan had already asserted: all was as neat as a new pin. The sound of a carriage outside drew her quickly to the window. A moment later she saw Greville rush out and heard his voice raised excitedly in welcome. She continued to peep through the curtains but was careful not to disturb them. Now Greville was helping his uncle down from the carriage, or at all events trying to!

"My dear good Greville," Sir William's pleasantly accented voice floated up to her, "I may be fifty but I am by no means decrepit. I pride myself on my fitness, now more than ever before."

Emma remembered that Greville wanted her to be in the drawing room to greet his uncle, wanted her to look composed and calm and lovely. She hurried downstairs and took up her position near the small carved cedar table where presently she would serve tea. She was wearing a gown of dusky pink velvet, high-waisted and cut low, but not *too* low, and in her abundant auburn hair was a wide blue ribbon. She looked much as she had looked when Romney had painted her as Nature, her eyes and lips ready to smile, to laugh outright if necessary, yet the whole effect one of modesty and innocence and carefree youth.

She had only a few moments to wait. Greville was soon at the door, standing deferentially aside while his uncle came briskly into the room. Emma quickly noted the powdered wig, the lace ruffles, the bright-blue breeches, the pale-yellow hose, and thought how gay he looked in contrast with his somberly clad nephew.

Sir William came to a sudden halt and turned to Greville, now at his side. Emma could see that it was a tense moment for Greville: he was anxious, expectant, unable even to make a formal introduction. Sir William looked at her again. She held her pose, her eyes meeting his, not boldly (Greville had warned against boldness), not timidly (he had warned also against timidity), but with a gentle frankness.

"Delightful!" Sir William cried. "The reality is far more entrancing than Romney, with all his skill, was able to make her."

Greville smiled his relief.

Sir William took Emma's hands in his, kissed each chastely, then stood back from her, to appreciate her beauty to the full, he said.

Emma, still neither bold nor timid, continued to return his scrutiny. She thought the family resemblance between uncle and nephew quite strong, though Sir William had finer features, deeper-set eyes, and a more sensitive mouth. She had heard him admitting to fifty; she knew he was fifty-four, and that, for all his trim soldierly appearance and vigorous movements, seemed very old to her.

Her mind dwelt on all that Greville had told her about him. His father had been Lord Archibald Hamilton; his grandfather the third Duke of Hamilton. More important still, Sir William was the foster brother of the king, having been brought up in the same nursery as his majesty. He had been a soldier in his youth, an officer in the foot-guards, and had served in Holland under the Duke of Cumberland. Later he had become a member of Parliament, then he had gone to Naples as envoy extraordinary and had succeeded in bringing about the neutrality of the Kingdom of the Two Sicilies in the American War of Independence. His title—he was a Knight of the Bath—had come after that, and he had finally returned to Naples as British ambassador. As for his private means, marriage with an heiress had brought him estates worth five thousand pounds a year.

"Well, Hamilton," Greville was saying tentatively, "are you . . . satisfied?"

"*More* than satisfied," Sir William replied. "I never saw such beauty, such natural grace." He moved about in front of Emma, then walked right round her. Greville did the same, still just a trifle anxious. "She is better than nature," Sir William added.

"It was my intention," Greville admitted gravely, "that in time she should put nature herself to shame."

"You succeeded, my dear Greville!"

"You really think so, my dear Hamilton?"

"Assuredly, assuredly!"

Emma, wanting to snort derisively, continued to smile and pose. They were discussing her as if she were a piece of statuary or a painting, not a flesh and blood woman. It was insulting. And yet, on the other hand, the evident admiration was sweetly flattering.

"Nevertheless," Greville said fastidiously, "she was more attractive a year ago. She is inclined to fatness now."

"No, no, my dear Greville," Sir William protested. "Plumpness,

plumpness merely. Plumpness, I always think, is a sign of good nature and a happy disposition."

Emma looked at Sir William with greater interest, but his eyes still held little more than a steady impartial appraisal. To him—damn him!—she was still just a work of art.

"*Chacun à son goût,* my dear Hamilton," Greville remarked weightily. "Which means . . . my dear Emma?"

"Each to his own taste," Emma replied obediently.

"Ah," said Sir William, "the French lessons you spoke of are in progress."

"Yes, and an apt pupil she is, a very quick learner."

"And the rest of her education?"

"Apart from the fact that she is a very poor speller—"

"Pooh!" Sir William interrupted, "so am I. So, for that matter, are you!"

"My *dear* Hamilton—!" Greville scowled. "*Apart* from the fact that she is a very poor speller, she has come on exceedingly well, as you will discover for yourself when you talk to her at length. Any subject you care to discuss, even your pet subject, volcanic phenomena. And by the way, how many ascents have you now made of Mount Vesuvius?"

"Twenty-two in a matter of four years," Sir William replied promptly, and then he began to tell Greville about his latest collection of volcanic earths.

Unnoticed now, Emma slipped out of the room to her mother in the kitchen.

"Ma," she said, with a grin, "he's just as queer as Greville, and that's the truth."

Greville came briskly and importantly into the drawing room where Emma was waiting for him. She thought what a striking couple they were going to make at the theater, he so aristocratic and handsome and polished, she so poised and calmly beautiful in the new black silk gown Sir William had insisted on buying for her. "A little expression of gratitude for your excellent hospitality," he had said gaily.

Greville was looking at the clock. "One more minute and the hackney coach I ordered will be late," he said fretfully.

"Time enough to start worrying when the minute's gone," Emma laughed. "Have a glass of wine, Greville, and give me one, too."

Greville hesitated, then poured out two glasses of port.

"But this," he warned, "must not become a habit."

"Of course not," Emma said gravely.

The time was slipping quickly away and soon Sir William would be returning to Naples. Emma knew she would miss him quite a lot, not so much for his own sake, but because of the mellowing effect he had on Greville.

"Did you enjoy your trip to Scotland?" Emma asked Greville.

"Immensely."

He and Sir William were recently returned from what Sir William had gaily called a royal progress through England and up to Scotland, staying en route at numerous country houses and having, Sir William said, the time of their lives.

"I hope it won't be too dull for you when your uncle goes back," she said.

"It will be just as dull for you," he replied broodingly. "With Hamilton no longer here to spend money on us, we will be obliged to face the restrictions of near-poverty once more. In short, it will be necessary to review our financial position. And speaking of *that*, you have not yet told me anything about your visit to the child at Hawarden."

During the absence of uncle and nephew, Emma and her mother had gone on a short trip to Hawarden. So far as the child was concerned, it had not been a success. She had found little Emma, young as she was, a composed and independent individual.

"She didn't remember me," Emma told Greville.

"One could scarcely expect her to," he said.

"She was a bit suspicious of me at first. She thought I might be an aunt, and sometimes she called me 'Auntie.' "

"Did you correct her?"

"Well, no, I didn't. Oh, Greville, I thought it might be better for her not to know who I really am."

"True, unless you propose to go back and live at Hawarden."

"Greville!"

He changed the subject quickly. "I thought Hamilton looked tired when he left this morning. He really does set himself too hard a pace."

"Oh, well, he'll have a quiet enough time, spending the day with the king."

"Yes." Greville's eyes twinkled for a moment. "His majesty is quite a different proposition from those royal rakes, his sons."

"Is the Prince of Wales as wild as people say?"

Greville was looking at the clock again. "The hackney coach is now late." He put down his glass. "I might tell you, Emma, I am still of two minds about taking you to the theater."

"Oh, but you promised, Greville!"

"In a weak moment, yes."

Emma pouted. "You wouldn't be so cruel as to break your word."

"What a child you are," he said, smiling indulgently.

Sir William had invited them to the theater many times, but she had never yet been alone with Greville. Always when she had begged him to take her he had spoken with a long face about the expense, but she sometimes wondered if he felt that to be seen alone with her in public would in some way compromise him. Greatly daring, she had accused him of this in his uncle's presence, and with a sickly smile he had muttered something about the certainty of people embarrassing him by turning to stare at her. "She is almost *too* beautiful," he had added, and Sir William, laughing merrily, had declared that it was an embarrassment he himself would gladly welcome.

"Ah," Greville said, "at last!"

Emma had heard the hackney coach too, and went to get her cloak.

The curtain came slowly down on the end of the first act, and Emma began to clap heartily. Greville gave her a sideways glance of disapproval.

"Really, Emma! Too much enthusiasm attracts attention."

Emma made a face. Greville himself was clapping with gentlemanly restraint.

Their seats were in the second row of the dress circle. Emma had hoped for a box—Sir William always had a box—but Greville had said no, a box would be uneconomic. Uneconomic was a word he seemed to like the sound of and often used now. Emma began to look enviously at the people in the boxes.

"Goodness gracious!" she exclaimed.

"What is it, Emma? Do please keep your voice down."

A little chuckle escaped her. "He's up to mischief, and no mistake."

"I beg your pardon?"

"Spending the day with the king! A good story *that* was!"

Greville had seen Sir William now, in one of the boxes, and the lady with him.

"Just look how pleased she is with herself," Emma whispered. "Do you know her, Greville?"

Greville shook his head violently. "She is a complete stranger to me!" He had grown quite pale. "By heaven, when a man of Hamilton's age practices deceit because of a woman—!" Greville was on his feet now. "Remain here," he ordered, and he made his way toward Sir William's box.

This, Emma thought, was going to be fun, and she watched eagerly as Greville entered the box. Sir William looked vastly taken aback, but recovered himself quickly and made an introduction. Greville bowed stiffly; the lady graciously inclined her head. She was fashionably dressed, not young by any means, but pleasant looking and still handsome. Greville chatted politely for a few moments—what an effort it was for him, too!—then withdrew from the box. "Now for ructions!" Emma thought, as he rejoined her.

"A widow," he muttered.

"Goodness, how did you find out?"

"Not by asking, certainly. I hope I know my manners." He was shaking with anger. "She is a Mrs. St. Simon. Apparently he met her at Lord Queensberry's. Pah! Hamilton and a *widow!* I dislike this, Emma, by heaven I do!"

"Shush, Greville, people are beginning to stare."

He cast a hasty glance about him and blushed.

"A second marriage must be prevented at all costs," he said in a heavy whisper. "You understand, *at all costs!*"

So disturbed was he that he wanted to leave the theater at once, but Emma persuaded him against it. Sir William had caught her eye now and was nodding and waving pleasantly. For them to disappear suddenly, she pointed out, might seem suspicious.

"Very well," Greville agreed. "Let us by all means be circumspect."

When Sir William returned to Edgware Row, he looked, Emma thought, like a naughty but quite defiant schoolboy. Jauntily he helped himself to port and began to discuss the play. Greville listened to his comments impatiently, and in silence.

"A widow!" he burst forth at last.

"A widow, yes!" Sir William smirked.

"She, too, spent the day with his majesty, I presume."

"All things are possible," Sir William said complacently.

"Hamilton, what an old fool you are!"

"Greville, I beg you to mind your own business!"

"My *dear* Hamilton—!"

"Mrs. St. Simon is a most charming lady."

"Her reputation is anything but that!"

56

"'Pon my soul, Greville—!"

"A widow she may be, but she is also an adventuress."

"Oh, come, Greville! Come, come, *come!*"

"An adventuress of the cleverest order. I know of three men she has ruined already."

"Ruined?" Sir William began to look uneasy.

"By blackmail," Greville said coldly. "They were, I admit, of much less importance than you." He shrugged. "Her aim in your case is much more likely to be marriage. Undoubtedly she already sees herself as ambassadress at Naples."

"God bless my soul!" Sir William ejaculated.

"Naturally she covets the high position you hold."

"But even so . . ." Sir William said weakly.

"I doubt," Greville concluded scathingly, "if his majesty the king, for all the love he bears you, would approve of such a marriage. Providing of course you were actually contemplating marriage."

Sir William mopped his brow. "Nothing was further from my mind. A little dalliance—" He smiled feebly. "Just that, no more."

Greville smiled his relief. "When do you meet her again?"

"I—hum—am to take tea with her tomorrow afternoon."

"Send her a brief note of excuse."

Sir William squared his shoulders. "I am, my dear Greville, a gentleman. I must keep the appointment."

"Then make it the last one."

"I will, indeed I will!"

Badly shaken by the lies Greville had told him, he went reluctantly to take tea with Mrs. St. Simon. When he returned he was even more upset. Emma would never have thought it possible for so fine a gentleman—and a diplomat, at that!—to show such agitation. She quickly gave him a glass of wine while Greville hovered anxiously by. Sir William drained the glass at a single gulp.

"Greville, I'm sunk!"

"My dear Hamilton!"

"To dwell on the conversation that took place between me and Mrs. St. Simon this afternoon would be futile, but during it one thing became most clear. Dear me yes, *most* clear! The wretched woman has every intention of turning our friendship, slight as it is, into—heaven help me!—into marriage."

Greville was just as agitated now. "Have you committed yourself in any way?"

57

"I trust not, I hope not!"

"There is nothing in writing?"

"Nothing, nothing, thank heaven!" Sir William dropped heavily into a chair. "You must help me, Greville, you must help me!"

"And indeed I will, gladly."

"You have a plan?"

"Yes, my dear Hamilton, I believe I have!"

Later Greville discussed his plan privately with Emma. Sir William, worn out and anxious, had gone to his room to rest, first having assured Greville that, deep in his heart, he had never had the faintest thought of a second marriage. He had loved his late wife too sincerely. No one could ever take her place, no one!

"This Mrs. St. Simon," Emma said, looking with amused eyes at Greville, "you really were telling lies about her?"

"Obviously," Greville replied impatiently.

"She hasn't ruined anybody in her life?"

"I should think it most unlikely."

"And to think that you once called *me* unprincipled! Unscrupulous, that's what you are!"

"And I propose to be more unscrupulous still. She is, I imagine, a dear sweet creature, though not averse to making a second marriage with a man as wealthy and important as Hamilton. Now listen, Emma, listen carefully." He paused for a moment and frowned. "I imagine you remember the ease with which you prevented me from marrying Henrietta Midleton."

Emma chuckled. "That I do."

"I see no reason for amusement, Emma!"

"I'm sorry," she apologized.

"But for you I might now be married to one of the most eligible young women in London!"

"Oh dear, and I thought you had forgiven me for that long ago."

"I may have forgiven you, but the memory still rankles. Pay attention, please, and try not to interrupt. I propose to give a little musical evening here next week and invite Mrs. St. Simon. You, for your part . . ."

He broke off, smiled thinly and then, his manner more precise than ever, began carefully to outline his little plan.

Emma had just concluded her second song of the evening. She had sung to Greville's pianoforte accompaniment, the pianoforte being a recent present from Sir William who himself played the viola. After a moment's silence polite applause resounded in the small drawing room, polite, that is, on the part of everybody except Sir William. He, following out Greville's strict instructions, once more clapped his hands wildly and cried, "Bravo, bravo!"

It was essential, Greville had stressed, that he should give the impression that he was deeply, even idiotically, infatuated both with Emma's singing and with her beauty. Well, he was certainly doing it, she thought, even to the point of ogling her. She glanced at Mrs. St. Simon who, puzzled at first, was now staring at Sir William with a shocked expression on her face.

It was only a small gathering. More than a dozen people, Greville had said, would overcrowd the little room. Romney was there—his expression as he too glanced at Sir William was one of amused surprise —as well as two or three of his artist friends known slightly to Emma. In addition there was Gavin Hamilton, a cousin of Sir William. Emma had met him several times and liked him, he was such a tease. He was Sir William's age but looked younger. Most of his time he spent in Italy, where he dealt in antiques and painted a little.

The applause died away. Greville rose from the pianoforte, took Emma by the arm and led her purposefully in Mrs. St. Simon's direction. "Remember," he hissed in her ear, "success or failure, it all depends on you." He made a few graceful remarks to the widow, then withdrew, leaving Emma facing a somewhat truculent lady.

"A quite pretty voice," Mrs. St. Simon almost barked.

"How kind you are," Emma simpered.

There was a pause, dragged out so long that it seemed as if no further conversation would be possible. Mrs. St. Simon, however, recollected her manners.

"Sir William tells me you are studying singing."

"Yes indeed!" This was an ideal opportunity; Emma took it without hesitation. "And soon I shall be going abroad to further my studies."

Mrs. St. Simon shot her a questioning look. "Abroad, in such a case, means Italy."

"But where else, Mrs. St. Simon!"

"You have Rome in mind, no doubt."

"Oh, no, Mrs. St. Simon, Naples. Sir William is so impressed with my voice that he intends to give me the advantage of the best singing masters in Naples."

Mrs. St. Simon smiled stiffly. "How kind of him."

"Oh, yes! So kind, so thoughtful, so very generous. We shall be going out with him when he returns."

"*We?*" Mrs. St. Simon's smile was less stiff. "Ah, yes, Mr. Greville will be taking you."

Emma shook her head. "Greville has no intention of visiting Naples. I meant my mother and I." She laughed tinklingly. "Dear Sir William, bless his innocent heart, feels it would be more proper if my mother were to act as chaperon. Of course, for a man in his position . . . But goodness, it will deceive nobody."

"I should imagine not!" Mrs. St. Simon was beginning to cluck, Emma thought, like an elderly hen. "Your mother's presence certainly deceives nobody about your relationship with Mr. Greville."

Emma smiled her sweetest smile. Greville, she saw, was hovering nearby, well within earshot.

"No, it doesn't, does it!" she agreed. Then she glanced swiftly at Greville. His face said clearly, enough. "Please excuse me, Mrs. St. Simon. I know Sir William is anxious for me to sing again."

She slipped back to the pianoforte where Greville joined her.

"Well?" she asked.

"Watch," he said.

Mrs. St. Simon, still like an elderly hen, was making her fluttering way to Sir William's side. Her face was pink; she appeared to be breathless with exasperation. Greville lounged after her, engaging Gavin Hamilton in conversation as he went. He halted within earshot of his uncle and the indignant widow, and while pretending to listen to Gavin's latest story about the Prince of Wales, strained his ears.

"So you find the dear Emma charming," Sir William was saying.

Mrs. St. Simon had passed no such remark but she said dryly: "Very."

"So natural, so innocent," Sir William enthused.

"Innocent!" Mrs. St. Simon jeered.

"At heart," he went on eagerly, "a child with a child's good nature."

Mrs. St. Simon was growing pinker. "If she is all you say, I wonder your nephew can bear to part with her."

"Ah, so Emma has been telling you about the coming trip to Naples."

"She has, Sir William!" Mrs. St. Simon barked. "And I must say that to endanger your personal reputation like that seems foolish."

Sir William wagged his head. "The good Mrs. Cadogan will be there to silence malicious gossip."

"You—you *simpleton!*" Mrs. St. Simon gasped.

Sir William remained silent, smiling feebly. For a moment he caught Greville's eye and looked as if he would like to wink. Things were undoubtedly going well.

"May I ask you a question, Sir William?" Mrs. St. Simon said.

"Assuredly, assuredly."

"If you were to marry again,"—she dropped her eyes modestly—"would you still insist on giving this scheming young woman"—up came her eyes in anything but a modest expression—"your protection?"

"Indeed I would," Sir William said stoutly. Greville's eyes were on him, boring into him. He recollected himself. "Indeed I would," he repeated, "even though, up to now, I have not contemplated a second marriage. No wife in her right mind could possibly object to my—hum—interest in so talented a girl as Emma."

"You must be insane, quite insane!" Mrs. St. Simon gasped, and turned on her heels, which brought her face to face with Greville. "I find," she said haughtily, "that I have an insufferable headache, and since Mrs. Hart is about to sing again . . ." She left the sentence unfinished, inclined her head coldly, and walked from the room.

Sir William and Greville shook each other gravely by the hand.

"My dear Greville, how can I ever thank you!"

"My dear Hamilton, if you must thank anyone, thank Emma."

"Nevertheless, the idea was yours. You were inspired, absolutely inspired. If there is anything I can do for you, *anything*, pray let me know."

Greville smiled, a smile which, seen by Emma from the other side of the room, made her wonder just what he was planning now. It was his mean smile, the smile that boded ill for someone.

"Come to my study, Hamilton," Greville said. "Yes, there *is* something you can do for me. It would be impossible to discuss it here . . ."

Emma watched uncle and nephew leave the drawing room.

"He's up to mischief," she told herself. "That's plain as the nose on your face."

"Well, have you started packing yet?" Greville asked.

Startled by his voice, Emma turned quickly from the pianoforte where she had been practicing dutifully. There was a fixed smile on his face, a smile that revealed no real friendliness.

"Packing?" she echoed, and then remembered that Sir William was

61

anxious for the three of them to spend a few days at some watering place. "Where are we going, Greville? Has Sir William decided yet?"

Greville's smile remained fixed. "I meant in preparation for your journey to Italy."

Emma laughed uncertainly. "Oh, that story I told Mrs. St. Simon last night."

"Which she believed, my dear, so convincing was your acting. I almost believed it myself, and so did Hamilton. In fact, it gave him a happy idea."

"Oh . . ." said Emma, her heart sinking.

"He wants to repay you for the help you gave him," Greville went on smoothly. "He thinks that a trip to Naples might be an excellent way of doing it."

Emma turned back to the pianoforte and began to pick out notes with one finger. She thought she knew now what mischief Greville had been planning last night, but she had to be sure.

Over her shoulder she said, "You'll be coming, too, of course."

Greville laughed shortly. "It would be quite impossible for me to leave England at present, Emma."

Emma went on picking out notes with one finger. "What would you do while I was away—find another heiress and try to marry her?"

Greville gave a little start. This was nearer the truth than Emma knew. As he had pointed out to his uncle last night, his financial position was intolerable; the sooner he made a satisfactory marriage the better.

"I'm sure it was you who suggested Naples, not your uncle," Emma accused.

"On the contrary, Emma. He has had it in mind for some time. He admires your voice and is most keen for you to have it fully trained."

"Foreign parts wouldn't appeal to me," Emma said. "I'd be lost outside England."

Greville made an impatient gesture. "Travel is broadening to the mind, Emma. It will give you polish. It is the one experience you still need."

Emma raised both hands and banged them down on the keys, making a jangling, discordant noise.

"I won't go, an' that's flat!" she raged.

"Temper, temper!" Greville reproved.

She swung round on him. "Oh, take that silly grin off your face!" She pointed a derisive finger. "Cheshire cat, Cheshire cat!"

Greville made an effort to keep his own temper. "This is a splendid offer, Emma. To reject it without a moment's consideration is not only foolish but ungrateful."

"Words, words, words! How you love them!"

Greville stepped quickly toward her. She thought he was going to strike her. All her temper disappeared; her shoulders drooped, her eyes filled with tears. Greville took her by the shoulders and shook her again and again. She submitted without protest, and when he stood back, panting, she fell naturally into an attitude of utter sadness. The sight of her, she felt sure, was enough to melt the stoniest of hearts.

"You're tired of me," she moaned. "You want to get rid of me. Oh, Greville, and I love you so much, so very much." A little sob caught in her throat. "I don't know why I do, Greville, but I do, I do! Please don't send me off to foreign parts!"

She could see that Greville was moved, but not sufficiently so for his resolution to be undermined.

"Any other girl would jump at the opportunity," he said impatiently. "I find it hard to understand you, really I do!"

It occurred to her then that her attitude *was* extraordinary. She even found it hard to understand herself. Life in Naples, under the protection of the British ambassador, would be a very grand affair indeed. Oh, but how terrible it was, how truly terrible, to be so much in love with Greville.

"I only intend you to go for a few months," Greville said brusquely. "I have business to attend to in England, business connected with Hamilton's property. He has been kind enough to make me his sole representative here. Shall we say six months at the outside? I shall then join you and bring you home."

He sounded sincere, but Emma was unwilling to believe him.

"You give me your word, Greville?"

"If you think it necessary."

"What about Ma?"

"She shall go with you. As you told Mrs. St. Simon, it would be more proper."

"But Ma in Naples! Ma at the British Embassy!"

Greville shrugged. "She could be kept in the background. And in any case she would never learn Italian, and her English, or what *passes*

63

for English, would not be understood by Hamilton's Neapolitan friends —any, I mean, that she might inadvertently meet."

Anger flared up in Emma again. "What a nasty snob you are! Ma—well, she's just Ma, she's good and kind and I won't 'ave anybody belittling her."

"Your aitches, Emma, your aitches!"

"That finishes it!" Emma stormed. "Wild 'orses won't drag me to Naples now!"

"Emma!" Greville said sternly.

She flung herself, sobbing, into his arms. "Oh, Greville, I'm sorry, truly I am, but I just can't bring myself to leave you. An' I won't, damn you, I won't!"

Defeated, Greville allowed his arms to hang loosely about her, and bitterly he thought of the confidence of his argument last night when his uncle had insisted that the girl loved him too much to be separated from him. "But Hamilton," he'd said, "the excitement of the new life, the demoralizing effect of the climate, the importance of your position in Naples—those and many other things can be relied upon to change her outlook in next to no time." All that confidence, and now this lamentable failure . . .

"Greville!"

He thrust Emma away from him and turned to face an excited and alarmed Sir William who, flinging himself wildly into the room, was waving a letter in his hand.

"What is it, Hamilton?"

"A note from Mrs. St. Simon. Delivered just now by hand. A note, God bless my soul, of apology!"

"Apology?" Greville frowned.

"Take it, Greville. Read it, man, read it!"

Greville took the note and read it aloud.

> *Dear Sir William,*
>
> *Please forgive me for my inexcusable rudeness last night. I realize now that if I did not misjudge you I should be more tolerant. In my heart I still regard you as a very dear friend. Please call on me at the earliest possible moment and tell me that you forgive me. Ever your admiring*
>
> *Amelia St. Simon*

Emma began to laugh. "Well, you are in the soup now, Sir William."

"Pah!" Greville cried. "What are you going to do, Hamilton?"

"Ignore the letter, ignore it! And—bless my soul, yes—leave for Naples without delay. Be a good fellow, Greville, and start packing for me. I have a hundred things to do, his majesty to see, the foreign secretary . . . !"

And he rushed from the room as wildly as he had entered it.

Emma looked at Greville. She laughed impishly. "Forgotten me, he has, an' that's a fact."

Greville turned on his heels and left her without a word.

7 During the month that followed Sir William's hasty return to Naples, Greville was sulky and bad-tempered, and often so cruelly sarcastic that Emma welcomed his decision to spend a few weeks with friends in the country.

Nevertheless, his absence left her desolate. Unhappy with him, she was unhappier without him. She hoped she would never see him again; she knew she would die if she didn't. It was a curse to love like that, she told herself tragically.

He had left her no address—all he had said on departing was "Watch the accounts most carefully"—but from Gavin Hamilton, who called from time to time at Edgware Row ("itching to make love to me, he is!") she discovered his whereabouts and wrote him a long sad letter, telling him that when he returned she would do anything she could—anything!—to make amends.

There was no reply. She wrote again, an even wilder and more incoherent letter. Again there was no reply. Finally she wrote a third time, her excuse being to forward two letters which had arrived from Italy, obviously from Sir William, who had also written to her.

This letter was short but full of Sir William's thanks for the pleasure which "just knowing her" had given him. He said how sorry he was that she had not been able to accompany him to Naples. "But I see no reason, my dear Emma, why you should not join me in the near future." He painted a glowing picture of life at his house, the Palazzo Sessa, and told her that an apartment was waiting for her and her mother. "The moment I hear that you are coming out I shall have the rooms redecorated in the most comfortable English style." He remained her true friend and everlasting admirer.

Her true friend . . . ? Was that all he wanted to be? She smiled wanly at the thought and recalled how in bidding her good-by he had kissed her fully on the lips. Not a fatherly kiss, as you might have expected, but a kiss, brief as it was, with a touch of fire in it. A kiss which suggested that he no longer regarded her as merely a work of art to be admired coldly and never touched. He was, of course, more experienced than Greville, but old, so very old. Even if she were not in love with Greville, she could never think of a man thirty-four years older than herself *that* way. No, never!

66

She remembered her earlier dream of a richer, wider world, a world of leisure, gracious living, admiring men. What, then, of Naples? What, then, of life at the fine Palazzo Sessa, a fairy palace, if all Sir William had said was to be taken seriously? Life there, surrounded by Sir William's fancy foreign friends, would surely go farther than any of her wildest dreams. Any girl in her right mind would snatch at the chance of being the mistress of an ambassador. Something was sadly wrong with her. Why, she wasn't even tempted!

Greville came home in better spirits than she had expected. Sir William's letters, of course! she decided, but when she refused to talk about Naples his good humor, such as it was, evaporated, and he took her roundly to task for the illiteracy of the letters she had written him.

"It irritates me beyond endurance," he said, "to find you incapable of spelling such a simple word as woman." He brought out one of her letters. "Look at this. W-H-O-M-A-M. Preposterous! And here again, two l's in valuable. And again! T-E-A-D-O-U-S for tedious. What a mockery it makes of all my efforts!"

"I shall never write to you again," she said sadly.

"So much the better!" he shouted. "Since you refuse to discuss Hamilton's kind and generous invitation we may as well go through the household accounts."

Emma chuckled maliciously. "I haven't put a single thing down since you went away."

He all but tore his hair. "How much money have you left?"

"Not a penny, so there!"

For the next week he was icily polite to her, speaking only when he found it absolutely necessary to do so. Finally she took her troubles to Romney; and Romney, saying how desolate he would be without her, advised her to go to Naples. She asked him scathingly if Greville had been getting at him. Smiling comically, he admitted that Greville had indeed asked him to speak to her persuasively about Naples.

"But I do think," he added, "that the change of scene would do you good."

Greville had been getting at her mother in the same way, too.

"As for me," Mrs. Cadogan said, "I wouldn't mind the trip. In for a penny, in for a pound, that's me, Emma."

And then, quite suddenly, after another letter from Sir William, Greville's iciness melted.

"Emma," he asked gently, "how much do you really love me?"

"With all my heart. You know that, Greville."

"Which means you would do anything for me, yes?"

"Anything but go to Naples!"

"But Emma, surely you would go there on my behalf, especially to be of service to me?" He was smiling engagingly.

She felt that Greville, in such a mood, was not a man to be trusted. "I don't know what you mean."

"Let me put it this way. It is only by borrowing against my expectations that I am able to maintain you and your mother and the child at Hawarden. Either you go to Naples and help me, or it will become uneconomic for me to continue my protection."

"What do you mean by *help* you?"

Greville laughed shortly. "Hamilton is showing an interest in another confounded widow."

"I don't think you're telling the truth," Emma said suspiciously. He gave her a haughty stare. "I am not in the habit of telling lies!"

"Very well, I'll go if *you'll* take me."

He sighed elaborately. "I wish I could take you, Emma. Believe me, I love Italy and would welcome a few months of the carefree life there."

"Then—"

He shook his head. "Hamilton's affairs are troublesome and need my constant attention. I give you my word that later, say in three or four months, I will come out and fetch you."

Emma began to feel cornered and sought desperately for something with which to strengthen her argument against Naples. She thought of the child at Hawarden.

"It's cruel to expect me to desert little Emma."

Greville made an impatient gesture. "You deserted her three years ago."

"Oh, Greville, what a dreadful thing to say!"

"How many times have you seen her since then? For that matter, how many times have you *wanted* to see her?"

Angry with herself because she found it impossible to weep a little, she tossed her head airily. "That's neither here nor there. It's her keep, that's what troubles me. Would you expect me to ask your uncle for money to send to my grandmother?"

He looked at her in alarm. "Certainly not!" His eyes narrowed. "Did you ever tell Hamilton about the child?"

"No, I didn't."

"So much the better. I prefer Hamilton not to know."

"Why ever not, Greville?"

He hesitated. "It might lessen his good opinion of you."

"You mean," Emma said shrewdly, "he might not want me then."

"I mean nothing of the kind," Greville said hastily. "He regards you as a thing of beauty and purity. To disillusion him would be—hum—cruel. I myself will make full provision for your child during your—hum—absence in Italy. There, will that satisfy you?"

Emma felt utterly defeated. "You do give me your word that you'll come and fetch me?"

"I have already given it."

"Your solemn word, Greville?"

"My solemn word, Emma."

"Well, in that case . . ."

He embraced her swiftly. "Thank you, Emma. What a good sweet child you are."

She released herself. "Is Ma to go, too?"

"Of course."

"But Greville, I'm frightened. Just think of it, two defenseless women traveling all that way alone!"

"Defenseless? I doubt it," he laughed. "However, Gavin Hamilton is going out soon. You and your mother shall travel with him. Come now," he ran on recklessly, "you will need some new clothes for the journey. It will be cold, so you will need something warm. I can spare twenty pounds." He pulled himself up. "At least, I can spare fifteen."

Emma found herself laughing hysterically. "Loosening the purse strings, are you! Well, *that's* something!" She controlled herself and said slowly and solemnly, "Greville, if this is a trick to get rid of me I —I'll never forgive you. I mean it, Greville, I mean it!"

She stood on the deck of the channel packet, looking back with tears in her eyes at the now distant coast of England. She wore a heavy cloak to keep out the February cold and her large straw hat, more suitable for summer in Italy than winter in England, was tied to her head with a silk scarf. She had never felt so miserable in her life. Leaving home like this was as bad as losing an arm or a leg; it hurt just as much, she was sure of that.

Gavin Hamilton, muffled up to the ears, was standing at her side, talking about the crossing, which he thought would be a smooth one. She ignored him, just as she had ignored her mother who, even before the ship put out, had sought shelter below deck.

She thought of the leave-taking with Romney and could still see his doleful face, and hear his words, his tragic assertion that he knew he would never see her again. Calling her, as he had so often done, his divine lady, his heaven-sent inspiration, he had declared that he would never paint again, which, of course, was nonsense.

She could still see Greville's face, too, and his smile of complete satisfaction. She loved him and hated him and despised him; she was sure now that it was all a trick. He would never come to Italy for her, never!

Gavin was still talking, describing enthusiastically the cities they were to visit and pass through on the journey which lay ahead of them.

"I hope you realize, my dear," he said flirtatiously, "how fortunate you are, with me to look after you."

"Yes," Emma said obediently.

"Then smile!" he begged. "Beautiful as you are in any mood, I prefer a smile to this somber look of tragedy. Life is just beginning for you, not ending."

"Please leave me alone, Gavin."

He put his arm round her. "He isn't worth all this misery, Emma."

"I know he isn't," she agreed, trying to be reasonable. "But please, I don't want to talk about him."

"Then let us talk about the navy," Gavin said, and drew her attention to a warship in the near distance. "The *Boreas*, Emma. She carries twenty-eight guns, and do you know, I met her captain in London a few weeks ago."

"Did you . . ." Emma said listlessly.

"Nelson, that was the name. A queer, grumpy little chap, I thought, but very capable, they say. Yes, Nelson—at least I think so."

"I don't care what his name is!" Emma burst out. "Oh, do please leave me alone, Gavin!"

Gavin shrugged, excused himself and left her. She was immediately sorry about the outburst and resolved to apologize later. Nelson, she thought, inconsequently, a naval officer. And that reminded her of the long-forgotten Willet-Payne. But for meeting Willet-Payne she would never have met Sir Henry Fetherstonhaugh, nor Greville himself. Nor Sir William Hamilton. If she hadn't met Captain Willet-Payne she wouldn't be going to Naples now. And all because she had tried to do Cousin Charlie a good turn!

"Nelson," she thought again. She couldn't get the name out of her mind.

"Oh, damn him, whoever he is! Damn him, damn him, damn him!"

And that made her feel just a little better.

They were on the road again.

Gavin, who had many friends in the French capital, had wanted to stay longer in Paris, but Emma had persuaded him against it. The sooner they reached Naples the sooner she would get a letter from Greville. He had promised faithfully to write within a few days of their leaving London, which meant that his first letter, conveyed by the faster mail coach, would be waiting for her at the Embassy on arrival.

"Well, Mrs. Cadogan," Gavin said, "what did you think of Paris?"

"A sight better than I expected," Mrs. Cadogan replied.

"No more wicked than London, eh?"

"Lord save us, no, Mr. Hamilton. Though mind you, there wasn't no way of telling what them foreigners was jabbering about."

Emma scowled and said sourly, "Me, I'd rather have London any day."

And then she wriggled back in her seat, wrapped the traveling blankets more closely about her, and made up her mind to remain enveloped in gloomy thoughts. They were traveling by private carriage, not by public coach, an expense upon which Sir William had insisted. Mrs. Cadogan, swathed in shawls and blankets, sat at Emma's side, her lively eyes darting from window to window, taking in and enjoying everything. Gavin sat opposite, trying his best to catch Emma's eye; and when at last she found it impossible not to look at him, he pursed his lips and narrowed his eyes until his face wore a perfect imitation of Greville's mean look. Unable to prevent herself, Emma laughed just once, shortly and sharply.

"Better, much better," Gavin said.

She tossed her head. "Can't say I'm really amused."

"Good Lord alive, girl," Mrs. Cadogan expostulated, "you sound as cheerful as if you was going to a funeral. What Mr. Hamilton thinks about this nonsense I can't imagine."

"The child will come round, Mrs. Cadogan," Gavin said, "if only we give her time."

Emma looked at him steadily for a moment, then dropped her eyes. She knew very well what he meant by "come round." Oh, yes, she was growing fond of him, as fond as she ever could grow of a man so much older than herself; but loving Greville as she did, how could she permit even the smallest flirtation? Faithful till death, that was what she was, she thought wonderingly. It was a tremendous thing,

71

this real love; but why, oh why, did it have to make her so wretched? She sighed and came to the doleful conclusion that there must be a more serious side to her nature than she would ever have thought possible.

Hating the journey as Emma did, she soon grew impatient with the constant changing of horses and lost count of the towns and villages where they stopped for the night. Even Mrs. Cadogan was less cheerful by the time they reached Geneva. "Fair shook up, I am," she said, and readily agreed with Gavin that they should spend a few days there "to pull themselves together" before continuing the journey.

On their last day at Geneva Gavin took her to what he called the best vantage point for a view of the lake. It was dusk, with a magic quality in the air and a bewildering beauty on the lake as the fading light turned the icy blue of the water to a deep warm red, then a rich full purple. Tears came to her eyes as she stood at his side. Never in her life had she felt such utter loneliness.

Gavin sighed elaborately. "Beauty can be so cold and unsympathetic. And I refer to *your* beauty, not the lake's."

"I can't help the way I'm made," Emma apologized. "I really am sorry, Gavin."

"Pooh!" He laughed lightly.

She studied him candidly. "Thank goodness I haven't broken your heart."

"Greville!" Gavin laughed. "I could wring his confounded neck."

"And so could I," Emma said thoughtfully. "It's horrible, feeling like this."

By the time they reached Rome and the end of their journey was in sight, Emma had thoughts for nothing but the letter which would be waiting for her at Naples. More than likely it would be full of the things Greville had never been able to say to her, he being so reserved. He would tell her—she knew he would, she hoped he would!—that he was missing her so much that he proposed to join her in a matter of weeks, not months. She would love Naples then! With the three of them together again it would be just like London.

Before Emma's party left Rome Gavin came to her with a letter he had received from Naples.

"Not from Sir William," he said, "but from his niece, Mrs. Mary Dickenson who, incidentally, is my second cousin."

Emma remembered having heard of this Mrs. Dickenson. She was spending a long holiday in Naples and often acted as hostess when

72

Sir William gave one of his grand official dinner parties at the Embassy.

"I hope Sir William is in good health," she said politely.

"He most certainly is!" Gavin chuckled. "He might have been afraid of Mrs. St. Simon, but according to Mary he is finding Lady Clarges a little too charming."

"Would Lady Clarges be the widow Greville spoke of?" Emma asked.

"I imagine so."

Emma felt happier now about Greville. He had been telling the truth about a widow in Naples after all, not just trying to trick her.

"Lady Clarges is an old friend of Sir William," Gavin went on. "She is staying with Mary Dickenson but hopes, I feel sure, to move to the Embassy very soon. I do hope," he mocked, "that you are not going to fail Greville and let her."

"I won't fail him," Emma said resolutely.

"Mary, let me warn you, thinks that such a marriage would be most suitable, so you will have her to contend with as well. Very severe, very proper, is Mary Dickenson."

"Meaning she won't approve of me, Gavin."

"Not for one moment."

"Well, you needn't sound so pleased about it!"

Gavin grew quickly serious. "I never liked Mary very much myself. It will give me the greatest pleasure in the world to take sides with you against her."

They reached the outskirts of Naples in the early evening of a cloudless sunny day. It was nearly the end of April. Gavin had ordered the coachman to stop the carriage; and now, tugging at her arm, he was crying, "Look, my dear, look!"

They were at the top of a steep hill with the city lying beneath them, a city bathed in the bright haze of the late sun. Excitedly Gavin pointed out the many churches with their rose-tinted domes and towers, the Italian palaces set in their colorful gardens, the bewildering network of narrow winding streets crammed with tall cardboard-like houses—"And the bay itself," he shouted, "the serenity of the water, a deeper blue even than the sky—oh, surely its beauty touches you, Emma! This is not just another city, my dear; this is heaven itself."

She shrugged. "How you do run on, Gavin. Shall we go?"

With dusk crowding about them, they began the descent into the surging life of the city, passing under low archways and through narrow streets that opened out into wide squares and market places crammed with people, some singing, some strumming guitars, all gaily dressed and carefree.

Darkness had fallen by the time they reached the British Embassy; but the house itself, with all the shutters thrown open, was a blaze of light and the strains of music drifted out to the street.

"Ah, a party!" Gavin cried, and jumped down from the carriage. With elaborate ceremony he helped down Mrs. Cadogan, then Emma herself. Once on the ground, Emma stumbled and Gavin caught her in his arms. A mischievous look crossed his face.

"My dear, how unfortunate, a sprained ankle!"

"There's nothing the matter with my ankle," she said.

"I insist that there is!"

Then he lifted her in his arms and carried her purposefully into the house. In the wide hall obsequious servants appeared as if from nowhere and grouped themselves about Gavin. Emma kept saying "Let me down!" and "What will Sir William say!" but Gavin ignored her while the servants, some of whom greeted him by name, clapped their hands and laughed in delight.

A moment later the double doors of a reception room were thrown open and Gavin strode in, revealing to Emma's startled eyes a dazzling array of ladies and gentlemen. The music stopped, there was a sudden hush—"You could 'ave 'eard a pin drop," Mrs. Cadogan said later— and all eyes were centered on Gavin and the travel-stained girl in his arms.

"Gavin! Emma!"

Emma saw Sir William then. He came hurrying toward them, a magnificent, commanding figure in full court uniform. He looked so startled that, in spite of her depressed spirits, Emma wanted to laugh out loud.

"Emma, my *dear!*" he gasped. "Is anything the matter?"

"A sprained ankle," Gavin said.

"God bless my soul!"

"And cramp, too, William. That, no doubt, was why she fell from the carriage."

Sir William glanced hastily over his shoulder at his guests, still silent, still staring.

"Put her in a chair, for pity's sake!" he begged.

A servant brought a chair. Gavin gently lowered Emma into it. Sir

William, somewhat flustered, murmured that their arrival was a complete surprise. He had not expected them for at least two more days. He made a quick signal, two servants approached, and he said, "Carry Mrs. Hart to her room."

"Come, come, William," Gavin cried, "surely an introduction is called for."

"Introduction?" Sir William was still flustered.

"Better an introduction now," Gavin chuckled, "than an explanation later, eh?"

Again Sir William looked over his shoulder. He cleared his throat twice, but Gavin, placing his hand on the back of Emma's chair, spoke first.

"Ladies and gentlemen, permit me please, on my cousin's behalf, to present his beautiful protégée. Mrs. Emma Hart, ladies and gentlemen, newly arrived from England."

"Ahem!" said Sir William.

Sheepish, Emma thought, real sheepish he looked, but his head was high and defiance was gathering in his eyes. The silence continued for one moment more, then a quick murmur of voices filled the room. The gentlemen began to gather round her chair while the ladies, drawing together, remained politely aloof. Emma, listening to the Italian voices, thought peevishly, Why can't these foreigners speak English! But she knew from the smiling faces and ogling eyes that every little spate of words was a compliment.

"Oh, Sir William," she cried, "what a way to burst in on you!"

Sir William bowed gallantly, took her hand in his and kissed it. One man cried "Bravo!" while another said in broken English, "This then is the so beautiful portrait come to life."

Sir William spoke to the servants again. A moment later Emma was lifted in the chair, another servant led the way and Gavin and her mother brought up the rear. Glancing back as she was carried from the room, Emma saw that the ladies were chattering like magpies while Sir William, surrounded by his male guests, was answering as best he could a volley of eager questions.

Upstairs, on the first floor, Emma found that a little suite of four rooms had been reserved for her. There was a bedroom for herself, another for her mother, a drawing room, and a little anteroom. All were furnished, as Sir William had promised, in the English style. She was impressed and almost ready to be content, if not really happy. Then she thought of her startling entry in Gavin's arms.

75

"Gavin, I don't think Sir William was too pleased."

"We took him by surprise, I admit."

"But Gavin, why did you do it?"

"I beg your pardon, my dear?"

"You know what I mean! And I knew you were up to mischief as soon as the carriage stopped. I could see it in your eyes."

He laughed and chucked her under the chin. "I wanted to help you, Emma. Or rather, I wanted to help you help the wretched stuffy Greville. As soon as I heard the music I knew Lady Clarges would be here."

"And is she?"

"She is. And Mary Dickenson too. You should have seen their faces! Horror—stark undiluted horror!"

More servants were in the room, bustling about with trays of food, decanters, and wineglasses; but before the hungry travelers could touch the refreshments Sir William entered, signaled to the servants to withdraw, and looked sternly at Gavin.

"That was a little indiscreet, surely, Gavin!"

Gavin looked hurt. "What else could I do, William? A lady in dire distress. You would have done it yourself."

Sir William began to laugh and slapped him on the back. "You have forced my hand. I meant Emma's arrival to be—hum—discreet. My intention had been to bring her only gradually to public notice." He turned quickly to Emma, who was still sitting in the chair in which she had been carried up. "My dear sweet Emma, taken by surprise like that, I greeted you most briefly. Please believe me when I say how happy I am to have you here in Naples." He turned next to Mrs. Cadogan. "And you also, my dear Mrs. Cadogan. I trust you will both be happy and comfortable during your stay, and a long stay I will do my utmost to make it."

"Please can I have Greville's letter?" Emma said.

"Letter?" he echoed.

Emma's heart sank. "There isn't any letter?"

"Why, no, my dear. Er—not yet."

"Oh . . ." Her voice sounded hollow in her own ears.

Sir William said hurriedly: "You must give him time, Emma. If he wrote only a week after you left the letter might not yet be here."

"If he wrote . . ."

Sir William patted her hand, murmured something about the sweet impatience of young love and said that he must return to his guests. He was pleased, she knew it instinctively, that Greville had not yet written. Perhaps he even knew that Greville had no intention of writing. There was some sort of understanding between uncle and nephew, she was sure of that.

He paused at the door to say, "Ought we to get a doctor to look at that ankle?"

Emma shook her head. "Ma's real good with sprains."

"Well," said Mrs. Cadogan, the moment he had gone, "fallen on our feet this time. An Eye-talian palace to live in, by the looks of things. It don't seem possible. My, how we do come up in the world!"

Emma smiled wanly. "But Greville hasn't written . . ."

Emma stood at the corner window of her own lofty drawing room at the Palazzo Sessa and gazed unseeingly across the bay. After only a few days in Naples Sir William had brought Emma and her mother to this villa at Caserta where, it seemed, he spent most of his time. Not caring much for the official Embassy in the city itself he had leased this *palazzo* from the Sessa family and was gradually and enthusiastically stocking it with his ever-growing collection of art treasures. "And now," he had said, when Emma had first set foot several weeks ago in the *palazzo*, "a treasure more beautiful than any piece of marble, than any picture, is here to grace the rooms and give them life." Flattering, this was, but it made her just a bit uncomfortable.

The view from the corner window was entrancing. She looked at it now, looked at it with real concentration, gazing slowly along the wide sweep of coastline from Sorrento to Cape Minerva, and finally settled her eyes on the island of Capri, a jewel in the deep clear blue of sky and sea. She remained unmoved. Her heart was dead, and the fault was Greville's.

She turned her back on the view, went to the writing table, spread a sheet of notepaper before her and took up a pen. She stared angrily at the white blankness of the paper. Since her countless pleading unhappy letters had brought not a single reply, perhaps a little boastful mention of Sir William's kindness and generosity would stir the heartless Greville. She began by telling him that she was learning Italian rapidly and that the singing master was delighted with her voice. Would that please Greville? She doubted it, since her earlier account of the disappearance of Lady Clarges from Neapolitan society had brought forth no reply.

She smiled faintly as she thought of Lady Clarges. Before the lady

77

had recovered from the shock of Emma's startling arrival, Gavin had been at pains to assure her that the beautiful young protégée had long been Sir William's secret mistress, and had been brought to Naples to continue in that capacity. That had been enough for the delicate sensibilities of Lady Clarges, but not enough for Sir William's niece, Mary Dickenson. Mary had sworn, Gavin said, that she would lose no time in removing Emma from Sir William's life.

This threat disturbed Emma in no way. She even hoped that Mary Dickenson would succeed, for removal from Sir William's protection would mean only one thing, a speedy return to London. She had met the niece just three times since her arrival, each meeting being accidental and brief. For, up to now, Sir William had kept Emma in the background, never permitting her a place at table when he gave an official dinner party, a fact which had given weight to the gossip that she was indeed a secret mistress. She wondered if he was ashamed of her, and whether or not he regretted having brought her to Naples; but that could hardly be possible when he was so kind and generous and thoughtful, not only to herself but to her mother, too.

She went on with the letter, describing in detail the gowns Sir William had bought for her. She said how she liked the simplicity of the muslins, so suitable for the hot weather, and how "really enchanted" she was by the hand-painted white satin which had cost twenty-five guineas. She grew conscious that she was smiling as she wrote and thought wonderingly, "Goodness, it's the truth I'm telling, I am enchanted by the white satin, even if I didn't know it till now."

"Well, well, how splendid to find you so happy this morning!"

She turned quickly, and there was Sir William beaming down on her.

"I knocked," he said playfully, "but apparently you were too engrossed in your letter to hear me."

He strolled to the window, where he stood for a few moments admiring the view. When he turned to face her again his manner was grave.

"My dear, I have a letter for you. The handwriting is Greville's."

He took the letter from his pocket; Emma jumped up from the writing table and pounced on it. He held it away from her quickly.

"Wait, Emma." The gravity of his manner deepened. "I want to warn you that I suspect the nature of the contents. I have heard from Greville myself, you see."

He held out the letter. Emma hesitated.

"He isn't coming to fetch me?"

"No, Emma."

"And he doesn't want me to go back?"

"Well—no, my dear."

She held out her hand. "I'll read 'is letter myself."

But Sir William held it from her again. "Greville, for obvious reasons, finds it necessary to make a satisfactory marriage." He smiled faintly. "Financially necessary, financially satisfactory. That was his main reason for wanting you to come to Naples."

Tonelessly Emma said: "Is 'e married already, Sir William?"

Sir William shook his head. "But he has hopes again of Miss Midleton." He laughed merrily. "Especially since, no longer supporting a mistress, he is a reformed character."

Sir William's tone was dry and this, along with the twinkle in his eyes, made Emma want to chuckle, but she set herself sternly against it.

"Let me 'ave the letter, please."

He gave it to her, saying quietly and sincerely, "Keep in mind always, Emma, that I love you dearly and want to protect you against too much unhappiness. I am ready, believe me, to do anything I can to make you forget my ungrateful nephew."

But Emma was scarcely listening and with the letter ripped open was hurriedly devouring the contents; hurriedly at first, then not so hurriedly, then finally, with the precise words and phrases a blur before her eyes, not reading it at all.

"My dear sweet child . . ." Sir William began.

She turned from him quickly, from his outstretched arms offering her comfort, and ran to the window. One short sentence of this cruel letter of dismissal remained clear in her mind. *It is your duty to oblige Hamilton.* Sorrow and anger battled with each other. Oblige Hamilton! She knew what that "oblige" meant! Her eyes were dry now, and anger got the upper hand. She began to hate Greville, to hate him more than she would ever have thought possible. If Greville were within reach she would murder him and kill herself. Kill yourself? a little clear voice seemed to say in her mind, don't be such a fool, girl! You have the world at your feet. To the devil with the Honorable Charles Francis Greville!

Sir William was at her side now. He placed an arm lightly about her shoulders.

"The most enchanting view in the world," he said.

"Oh, yes, yes, Sir William!" she cried. "So much beauty," she went on softly, "and it doesn't hurt now, like—well, like beauty used to. First it hurt, then it didn't mean anything at all, but now—Oh, yes, the most enchanting view in the world!"

Sir William smiled. "I think—Do you know what I think, Emma? I think you have grown up quite suddenly."

"I might have, and that's a fact."

"Do you still want to go back to England?"

She frowned over this. "I don't rightly know, an' that's the truth."

"Go back if you really want to. I should only grow to despise myself if I kept you here against your will. But if you go I will see that you are adequately provided for."

She kissed him impulsively. "You're so kind! I don't want to go back; I want to stay here."

"You make me the happiest man in the world," Sir William said humbly. "Shall I write and tell Greville your decision, or would you rather tell him yourself?"

"I'll tell him myself," she decided, and felt herself growing hard and bitter.

The moment Sir William had gone she went back to the writing table, tore up the unfinished letter, and found a new sheet of note-paper. She had grown up now, Sir William was certainly right about that, grown up in a matter of seconds. She felt contempt for Greville, yes, but also a growing longing to pay him out, to make him suffer at least a little.

She remembered Sir William's humility; she recalled again that phrase of Greville's, "oblige Hamilton." No, by heavens, she would make Sir William marry her. Yes, marry her! She took up the pen and wrote exactly that to Greville. "I will make Sir William marry me." How Greville would laugh. He would laugh, then put the empty threat from his mind. Ludicrous, he would say, utterly ludicrous.

Ludicrous it was and she admitted it.

"But I'll do it," she told herself fiercely, "I'll do it!"

8 Sir William had said, "A select dinner party, ten guests at the most."

Emma thought of this now as she dressed carefully with her mother in bustling attendance. This was to be her introduction to Sir William's more important friends in Naples, her presentation, as it were. She smiled. For the hostess was to be Mary Dickenson. And even though Mrs. Dickenson hated Emma, Sir William still expected her to present his protégée to his Neapolitan friends.

"My, there'll be ructions," Emma chuckled.

Mrs. Cadogan removed the last of the curl papers. "There now, 'ave a good look at yourself."

Emma rose from the dressing table and posed in front of the long gilt-framed mirror. She looked at herself critically from head to foot, from the mass of auburn ringlets to the toes of the pink silk shoes. For this first important social appearance she was wearing Sir William's most expensive present, the white satin gown. She nodded approvingly and, rearranging the folds of the gown, decided that it gave her almost a virginal look.

"Right pleased with yourself, I must say," her mother sniffed.

"And why not, Ma?" Emma laughed. "It wasn't much fun being miserable. I don't rightly know how I managed to put up with it all that time." She struck a new pose. "Will I do, Ma?"

"You look real grand, girl, but aren't you putting on a bit of weight?"

Emma nodded. "It's the Italian food. But Sir William doesn't mind about it. He likes a woman to be plump. Ma, are you happy here?"

"Happy enough, Emma."

"Are you sure, Ma?"

Mrs. Cadogan considered this for a moment. "There ain't much to do an' the jabbering foreigners are a sore trial at times, but"—a slow smile crossed her face—"living the life of a lady suits me grand. To begin with I was worried like, wondering 'ow it would all end, but now I live from day to day an' try to be—What's that fine word you sometimes use, Emma?"

"Philosophical?"

"That's right. All the same, 'ow *will* it all end?"

Emma chuckled. "Just you wait and see, Ma."

Mrs. Cadogan frowned. "Don't you think it would sound sort of better, living in an Eye-talian palace an' all, if you started calling me Mother?"

"Goodness," Emma mocked, "and you never much of a one for airs and graces."

Mrs. Cadogan grew serious. "Oh, I like 'Ma' best myself. It's Sir William and his fine friends I'm thinking of. An' another thing, Emma,"—she was becoming pink and flustered now—"I've been thinking it wouldn't do no harm to try a few improvements myself. Not wanting to show you up, that is. I'm wondering if you'd be good enough to take me in 'and, Emma."

"If you want me to—Mother."

"Writing, to begin with. I still can't do much more than sign my name with a cross. After that a bit of reading, and then maybe I could tackle the language."

"Speak Italian, *you*, Ma?"

"Yes, Emma. To tell the truth, it fair riles me to hear 'em jabbering an' not understand a single word."

Emma smiled. "All right, Ma, I'll take you in hand."

"Thank you very much," Mrs. Cadogan said gravely.

There was a knock at the door, and Sir William came briskly into the room. Emma thought he looked just a little worried; but when she greeted him with "Well, Sir William, will I do?" he beamed on her and said he had never seen her look more delightful.

"Only one thing is lacking," he said, and she saw that he was taking a string of pearls from his pocket. "There!" he cried, when he had adjusted them around her throat. "Look at yourself in the mirror." The soft luster of the pearls against the whiteness of her throat left her speechless. "They belonged to Lady Hamilton," he told her. "I want you to keep them, Emma." Before she could thank him he went from the room, muttering that Mary Dickenson had arrived and must be given a few last-minute instructions. His tone made it clear enough to Emma why he had looked worried.

"Pearls!" Mrs. Cadogan chuckled. "Next it'll be diamonds."

"That's more than likely, Ma."

"Yes, but is it *honest*, Emma?" Mrs. Cadogan went on seriously. "Taking his presents and giving him nothing, I mean."

Emma smiled. "Coming on nicely, Ma. That's two aitches you didn't drop."

"Don't put me off, girl!"

"Sorry!" Emma laughed. "Giving him nothing, you say? Aren't I giving him the pleasure of my company? And aren't I the most beautiful thing in the house, as he keeps telling me? Better than any of his pictures and statues, that's what he says."

"That's as may be, but 'ow long do you think he's going to be satisfied with just that? He's not as old as you try to make out. Leastways, he's not *too* old."

Emma was fingering the pearls. "They belonged to Lady Hamilton . . . The *first* Lady Hamilton," she added softly.

Mrs. Cadogan gave a little shriek. "Good Lord alive, girl, you don't mean *you'll* be the second!"

"Don't I, Ma?"

"He'd never do it, not a fine gentleman like Sir William. Not unless he was tricked into it."

"I'll have to be clever, I do admit," Emma said, "if I want"—she roared with laughter—"if I want to become Greville's aunt."

Mrs. Cadogan laughed, too, but she said soberly, "You'll never do it, girl."

Emma curtsied to herself in the mirror. "I've a notion it all depends on what happens tonight with this Mary Dickenson."

It had been arranged that a servant would call her as soon as the guests began to arrive; but, remembering Sir William's worried manner, Emma decided to go down at once. She was halfway down the wide staircase when Mary Dickenson's voice arrested her. It was high, as only the very best of well-bred voices could be high, and strained and querulous.

"Surely you realize, Uncle," she was saying, "that you are behaving a little unwisely."

"My behaviour is my own concern, Mary," Sir William replied heatedly. "Kindly mind your own business, my dear."

Emma peered down cautiously into the hall. Sir William looked agitated but willful, Mrs. Dickenson indignant and grimly determined. She was about Greville's age but appeared older and, for all her refinement and breeding, frumpish.

"In this instance," she went on insistently, "I *am* minding my own business. I must tell you frankly, Uncle, that as hostess here at the Palazzo Sessa I find it impossible to present to your guests a young woman of Mrs. Hart's reputation."

"A high-handed attitude, 'pon my soul it is!" Sir William spluttered.

"Uncle, Mrs. Hart must not be present tonight."

"Emma, I assure you, certainly will be present!"

"Very well, then, I shall consider it my duty to ignore her. Your guests, I feel sure, will understand my attitude and sympathize with it."

"I know them too well to expect them to sympathize with rudeness."

"Rudeness? *Really*, Uncle!"

"For you to make a scene would be intolerable!"

"I trust," Mrs. Dickenson said haughtily, "that I know how to cut a person without making a scene. Take my advice. Keep the young woman upstairs. People are gossiping enough as it is."

Sir William laughed recklessly. "I thrive on gossip."

"But *Uncle*, think of your position. Think of the damage you might do yourself at court if you accept this—this *creature* publicly."

"Good heavens, Mary," he protested weakly, "you speak as if she were my mistress."

"How am I to know otherwise? In any case, in the eyes of the world she is certainly your—*mistress!*"

Sir William tried to laugh nonchalantly. "Then the damage is done already. But not at court. Dear me no! You know as well as I that King Ferdinand is not as strict as all that."

"I was thinking of our own court," Mrs. Dickenson said coldly, "not the easygoing Neapolitan Court."

"Pooh!" said Sir William, shaken nonetheless, "our own court is far enough away."

Emma sensed that he was fighting a losing battle. She crept quickly back to the top of the stairway; then, humming a cheerful little air, a Neapolitan song she had recently learned, she tripped lightly down, a picture of youth and gaiety and innocence.

"How do you do, Mrs. Dickenson," she said politely.

Mary Dickenson averted her head. Sir William cleared his throat, looked pleadingly at his niece, then swiftly, a little foolishly, at Emma. She thought that the sight of her was giving him confidence.

"Mary," he said sharply, "Emma spoke to you."

Mary Dickenson remained silent, her gaze directed on Emma but her eyes looking coldly through her.

"Mary . . ." Sir William pleaded.

"For the last time, Uncle, will you or will you not be guided by me?"

84

Sir William looked at Emma again. She fell instantly into an attitude of the utmost dismay and distress, but meanwhile she watched him coolly as he struggled to make up his mind. She saw by his face that he was gaining additional confidence and at the same time growing angry.

"By heaven," he said softly, "I shall neither exclude Emma from the dinner party nor permit you to cut her before my guests."

"That is tantamount," Mary Dickenson said haughtily, "to asking me to leave the house."

Emma bowed her head. She clasped her hands lightly in front of her and allowed her shoulders to droop. Before she cast down her eyes she saw Sir William flinch at the sight of her utter dejection.

"Come, Mary, be sensible!" he said sternly.

"I am being sensible, Uncle!"

"I refuse to be coerced!" he thundered, and rang for a servant. "Mrs. Dickenson's carriage!" he ordered tersely when the servant came.

Emma raised her eyes cautiously. Mary Dickenson was standing there irresolute. A slow deep flush was spreading from her neck to her cheeks. A few moments later, after an intolerable silence, the servant announced that Mrs. Dickenson's carriage was waiting. With a gesture Sir William invited his niece to precede him from the hall. She did so with a dignity so ridiculous that Emma wanted to laugh. When Sir William returned his eyes were still burning with anger.

"You were quarreling about me," Emma said sadly.

"I fear we were, Emma."

"That was a pity." She looked at him beseechingly. "Is there anything I can do about it, Sir William?"

"There is indeed, child!" He was growing quite excited. "From now on, as long as you live under my roof, you shall be hostess here. Mary forced my hand, but 'pon my soul I am more than pleased about it!"

Sir William's face was stern as he paced up and down his study, glancing from time to time at Emma but remaining silent. "Gracious," she thought, "what have I done!" They were spending a few days at the Embassy in the city and here, last night, she had received his guests a second time. The dinner party, she felt sure, was just as successful as the one a month ago when she had taken Mary Dickenson's place. True, she had flirted with a preposterous Italian count, but as far as she could remember Sir William had noticed nothing. Had her singing been at fault? Hardly that, when he had accompanied her so happily on his viola and the guests had applauded unstintingly. Perhaps her spur-of-the-moment posing had upset him; she had wondered afterward if it had been in the best of taste.

"Sir William," she faltered, "why did you send for me?"

He glared at her and strode to his desk.

"Do tell me what I've done to displease you," she pleaded. "Is it because of the way I posed last night? After all, when the count asked about Romney . . ."

Sir William shook his head. "It was natural enough to demonstrate the ease with which you used to pose for Romney. It delighted my friends. Your Joan of Arc was especially effective. I think you could cultivate the posing for future dinner parties."

"Do you really?" She looked at him anxiously. "But *something* is wrong. Is it Mother?"

He sat down at the desk. "Your mother is an excellent creature. I have no complaints, and I admire the determined effort she is making to learn Italian."

"I know!" Emma pouted prettily. "I've been spending too much money."

"You have spent a lot, but not too much. That is what money is for, to be spent." He picked up a letter. "The trouble, Emma, is that you have been making threats."

"Threats? *Me?*"

"You have threatened poor Greville with disinheritance."

"Goodness, *have* I?"

"At all events *partial* disinheritance." He rose, a picture of towering indignation. "You wrote to him and told him that you would pay him out by making me marry you."

Emma's hand went hastily to her mouth. "Lord save us!" she gasped, sounding exactly like her mother, "so that's the trouble."

Sir William bore down on her. Really frightened now, she thought what a fool she had been to write to Greville like that. Sir William stood over her. Out shot his hands, and grasping her shoulders he began to shake her, none too gently.

"Oh, Sir William—!" she gasped, and then she saw the twinkle in his eyes.

He released her. "There, you little baggage, I'm not the actor I thought I was."

Emma giggled in relief. "What did Greville say?"

"He said he thought it might amuse me to know your intentions. He said it was, of course, preposterous."

"Which it is," Emma said candidly. "It was just that I was angry with him."

Sir William took her quickly and easily in his arms and kissed her. She closed her eyes and found herself kissing him back, kissing him until they were both breathless. Not even with Fetherstonhaugh had she experienced such intensity. And Greville, compared with his uncle, had been a babe in arms, his passion, if passion you could call it, a fluttering thing, like a dying bird.

Sir William released her. "What led you to think, you little goose, that I should need any making?"

"Oh, but you couldn't do it, Sir William, you just couldn't." She saw the eager look on his face. "C-could you?"

"I am surely free to please myself in such a matter," he said, a trifle pompously. "Subject, of course, to his majesty's approval."

"The king of England, you mean?"

"Yes. It would be necessary for a man in my position to gain his majesty's consent before marrying."

Emma saw then the impossibility of it all.

"It will take time, my dear," he went on jauntily, "need cautious handling. But make you my wife I shall. I give you my solemn word."

This giving of his solemn word somehow irritated her. Greville had given *his* solemn word that he would join her in Naples. Not that Sir William wasn't a gentleman of a different kidney, and King George and he were foster brothers, there was that to remember. All the same . . .

"Me being what I am?" she said, lowering her eyes.

Sir William smiled happily. " 'Pon my soul, Emma, what are you but the most beautiful young woman in the world?"

"All the same, there are things you don't know about me."

He looked grave for a moment. "I know that Greville found you at Up Park." He laughed dryly. "I also know the sort of man Fetherstonhaugh is, but you were very young, inexperienced and easily tempted." He patted her shoulder indulgently. "The past has nothing to do with the future."

"There's something else you don't know. You don't know about the child."

"What child, Emma?"

She told him the whole story, even mentioning the possibility that

Captain Willet-Payne might be the child's father. He listened gravely without interrupting. She thought, Well, I've finished myself now.

"So you see, Sir William," she said, "you can't marry me now, not a fine gentleman like you."

Sir William smiled. "These facts would be disturbing to his majesty. They shall, of course, be kept from him." He frowned. "I wonder why Greville never told me about your child."

"He thought you might not want to keep me here if you knew."

"Yet you tell me yourself, my dear."

"I had to be honest with you."

"Even at the risk of my sending you away?"

Emma nodded miserably. "Yes."

"Dear Emma," he said gently, "your courage endears you to me more than ever, perhaps because at heart I am a very simple person and value honesty. You were unfortunate. Why should I turn against you because of that? Just think for a moment of the good your misfortune has brought about. Not only has it led to my own personal happiness, but through Romney—who met you at Up Park, remember! —it has given beauty to the world."

Tears flooded Emma's eyes. "How good and kind you are, dear, dear Hamilton!"

"Hamilton . . . yes, you must call me that, now!"

He took her in his arms again, and she rested there, her head on his chest, listening to the quick excited beating of his heart.

"Dear sweet Emma," he murmured. "Small wonder that Romney called you his divine lady." He kissed her hair lightly. "Your incomparable beauty makes it a sacrilege to touch you." But he kissed her again, on the lips this time, and again and again, with mounting intensity. "Emma," he whispered, "it will take so long to gain the king's permission, so long, and I have waited a countless age already. Need I wait . . . longer?"

She pushed him away. She was truly grateful for all he had done for her. Grateful . . . She tried to be honest with herself. It was gratitude she felt, not love. Affection yes, a deep and lasting affection, but not love.

"Emma . . ." he urged.

She buried her head in his breast again. Was it to be yes, or no? Then she reached up her arms and locked them about his neck.

"Tonight, Emma?"

"Lord save us, Hamilton," she chuckled, "what's wrong with now?"

9 Gavin Hamilton, lounging in a chair, chatting with Emma as she sat at her writing table, remarked that time was rapidly slipping away. Emma looked up from the letter she was writing to Greville in faraway London. A little frown puckered her forehead.

"Yes," she agreed, "much too rapidly."

"William," he commented, "is looking older."

"Am *I* looking older?" she demanded.

Gavin chuckled. "Considerably."

"I thought that dressed like this I looked younger than ever," Emma said huffily.

She had spent the early part of the morning superintending the work now going forward in the newly constructed English garden of the *palazzo* and was still dressed in the colorful costume of a young peasant girl, a form of dress Sir William thought suitable for gardening. She herself considered the tight scarlet bodice and the flowing multicolored petticoat especially becoming. True, the scarlet clashed with auburn hair, gave it a deadened look, but she had drawn her hair tightly back and covered it with a bright blue kerchief.

"Are you leaving for Rome this afternoon," she asked pointedly, "or going with us to Naples?"

Gavin grinned. "You have little hope of getting rid of me as quickly as that. I shall spend a few days with you at the Embassy. Oh, come, Emma, this isn't like you, being cross with an old friend. I merely meant that you were showing a certain maturity. How old are you? Twenty-four, twenty-five? Whatever it is, you are more beautiful than ever. Maturity suits you. I can see character in your face now. That empty expression of youth has completely disappeared."

"Thank you very much," Emma said, pleased with him now.

He laughed shortly. "Character, did I say? I also suspect a growing hardness, a bitterness. Could it be the bitterness of unfulfilled ambition?"

"I hate you today, Gavin!" she snapped. "Please be quiet and let me finish my letter."

She bent over the letter again, but instead of taking up the pen she fell to brooding. Gavin might just as well have come right out in the

89

open and said: "You'll never be the second Lady Hamilton now."

She sometimes wondered if Sir William had tricked her, if he had ever really intended marriage. He had, of course, written to the king, but while doing so he must have guessed what the reply would be. His majesty, expressing surprise that his dear Hamilton should be contemplating a second marriage, had asked pointedly for details of the fortunate lady. Awkward, most awkward, Sir William had considered this. To tell the exact truth would be foolish; to invent for Emma a background she did not possess would be equally foolish. Wiser, he had said, to wait until his next visit to London. "So much easier," he had said, "to bring my foster brother around to my own way of thinking when I can *talk* to him."

That was three years ago; and here they were still in Naples, and the subject was never discussed these days. There were times, however, when Emma neither thought of it nor cared very much. She was virtual mistress of the Embassy and the Palazzo Sessa; she was admired wherever she went; artists came from all over Europe to paint her—Sir William now had a veritable gallery of Emmas—and people vied with each other to gain invitations to the select Embassy dinner parties. She was, in fact, an unofficial leader of Neapolitan society. Unofficial . . . that was a word she hated. How much happier to be Lady Hamilton and received at the Court of the King of the Two Sicilies.

As for her more intimate relations with Sir William, he made few physical demands on her now; after the first flush of his second youth he had grown almost apathetic. Yet in all things he was her willing slave and worshipped her openly, so openly that the more critical of his friends sneered at him behind his back, sneered at him but at the same time envied him the possession of his divine lady. And money! She had never had so much to spend in her whole life. As she had been delighted to tell Greville in a recent letter, she was able, without turning a hair, to lose many times the yearly allowance he had made her at a single sitting at the card table.

"Frowning like that," Gavin remarked, "will make you old before your time."

She ignored him and tried again to concentrate on her letter to Greville. Poor Greville, she thought condescendingly, he was still a bachelor, still unsuccessful in his search for a rich wife. She bore him no resentment now. She even wrote to him regularly. Her letters were friendly and full of gossip, and in them it pleased her to boast of her success in Naples and the generosity of his uncle. But she had never mentioned Sir William's three-year-old promise to marry her. *That* was to have been a big and shattering surprise. And besides, she had known instinctively that Greville would do everything possible to prevent such a marriage.

She took up the pen now and continued the letter. She told Greville that she was sending him some more money, through Mr. Coutt's bank in London, for the child at Hawarden. (She had not told Greville that his uncle knew about the child.) This written, she instructed Greville to send her more gloves from London. She chuckled to herself as she wrote, "You will charge them, as usual, to Hamilton's account."

At this point a servant entered unobtrusively, addressed her as "Excellenza," a form of address that always delighted her, and presented her with a large, important-looking letter. She saw in surprise that the letter was sealed with the seal of his majesty the king of the Two Sicilies. She had seen it often on letters received by Sir William but had never received a letter so sealed herself. She tore it open quickly, read the brief contents and clapped her hands. So excited was she that she leaped up and did a little dance around the room.

"What now?" Gavin asked curiously.

Placing a finger to her lips and returning purposefully to her writing table, she seized a pen and with swift strokes completed her letter.

"Tomorrow night, dear kind Greville," she wrote, "I go at the especial invitation of his majesty, King Ferdinand, to a royal ball."

The new little maid, a black-eyed, swarthy-skinned peasant girl whom Emma had found during a recent trip to Sicily, said what a pity it was that the *excellenza* should find it necessary to hide so handsome a petticoat, trimmed as it was with crepe and spangles.

"Ah, but we know it is there," Emma said gaily, and stood very still while the girl arranged the purple satin gown to their mutual satisfaction.

A moment later Sir William came into the room looking, Emma thought, just a little agitated. She dismissed the maid.

"The ball has been abandoned," he announced.

"Oh, *no*, Hamilton!" she cried.

Sir William sat down and told her that there was disturbing news from Paris. The rabble had risen, he said, and stormed that political prison, the Bastille.

"But Paris is so far away," Emma pouted. "Why abandon a ball because of what has happened there?"

"My dear Emma, a gesture was necessary. The queen of France, remember, is a sister of Maria Carolina."

"As if that matters when I was to have been the most attractive woman at the ball," Emma complained.

"It was inconsiderate, I do admit, for the French to start a revolution." Sir William rose, handsome as ever, immaculate and distinguished in his court uniform. He bowed and kissed Emma's hand. "You will still be the most attractive woman at the palace. We are to go there, in any case, to an informal gathering."

Happy again, Emma curtsied deeply.

"Have I got it right?" she asked. "I've been practicing all day."

"No aristocrat could do it more gracefully," Sir William said gallantly.

In the carriage later he could talk of nothing but the trouble in France. It had been brewing for a long time, he said, and he predicted that it was the beginning of a new and terrible era, perhaps for the world at large as well as France itself.

Before they reached the palace he said, with a puzzled look on his face, "The news from France reached King Ferdinand the night before last, even though I was only made acquainted with it this evening. In short, it arrived before your personal invitation was sent out. The invitation was even sent *after* the decision to cancel the ball was made. It seems most odd. I suspect an intrigue. I shall make some discreet inquiries tonight."

But Emma's mind was entirely taken up with her coming presentation. An informal gathering, she thought. Well, that would make things easier. Perhaps she would be able to write to Greville again tomorrow to tell him that she had been asked to sing, or even perform her attitudes, always so well-received at the Embassy dinner parties. Yes, the attitudes, which had grown out of her earlier posing for Sir William's friends, might make a very good impression on King Ferdinand.

"I think I should warn you," Sir William was saying, "that this will not be a *real* presentation. There will be—hum—nothing official about it."

"What do you mean by that, Hamilton?" she asked in surprise.

"You may not even meet their majesties, and if you do it will be unofficially, in one of the anterooms. What I am trying to tell you, Emma, is that you are not about to be presented at court."

Surprise at his words left her speechless.

"It is a question of etiquette," he said, growing flustered. "Believe me, I would be the last person to hurt your feelings. Had it been possible you would have been presented three years ago, 'pon my soul you would!"

"But the invitation—"

"Yes, yes, Emma, quite, quite. But as I said, odd, distinctly odd. Ah, here we are!"

The drive had come to an end.

Though Emma had seen the royal palace of Caserta many times and had once, during their majesties' absence, been taken on a tour of inspection, she entered it now as if for the first time. Quite awed, but not willing to admit it, she stepped down from the carriage and stood for a moment in one of the vestibules of the immense portico; then, graceful as ever, a placid countenance masking the doubts with which Sir William's words had filled her, she mounted the great state staircase. In one of the main reception rooms, with its gilded walls, its tapestries and frescoes, nervousness all but got the better of her. She felt dwarfed by the vastness of the room and intimidated by the grandness of the ladies and gentlemen who thronged it.

"Courage, sweetheart," Sir William whispered.

"Thank you," she whispered back, and stared boldly about her.

She recognized many of the ladies and gentlemen, and under the encouraging smiles of the ladies and the admiring glances of the gentlemen her nervousness began to disappear. Soon she and Sir William were surrounded by a growing group of people, all resplendent in full court dress. Sir William made easy, gracious introductions here and there. His tone of voice suggested subtly that it was an honor to be introduced to Emma Hart, the blacksmith's daughter. Not, of course, that he mentioned this almost forgotten fact; she was, "My protégée, a young countrywoman of mine." Never before had Emma felt so warm a feeling around her heart, nor so much affection for Sir William.

On his arm Emma moved slowly about the reception room. Beneath the apparent gaiety she sensed a tenseness and continually caught such whispered words as "Paris" and "the Bastille" and "Revolution." They were joined in the end by Acton, the prime minister, the man described by Neapolitan gossips as Queen Maria Carolina's favorite. Emma had met him a number of times at the Embassy and had never been able to make up her mind whether or not she liked him. He whispered for a moment with Sir William, then led them from the

93

crowded reception room to one of the smaller anterooms; and there, for the first time, Emma came face to face with King Ferdinand and Queen Maria Carolina.

Sir William made the presentation with unhurried dignity and Emma's curtsy, he told her afterward, was perfection itself. King Ferdinand received her graciously, his dark eyes at the same time swiftly searching her face and figure. Ordinary lewdness she could tolerate, but lewdness combined with inanity made her want to laugh. She thought how ridiculous he was, the too-fat figure smothered in black velvet and gold lace, the hair over-powdered, the face now wreathed in a slow and silly smile. She could well believe that what gossip said was true: the queen, not the king, ruled the kingdom of the Two Sicilies.

"It is to be hoped that you speak French," Maria Carolina said, in that language. "Italian I can scarcely endure."

Emma replied in French that she had a reasonable knowledge of the French language. Her majesty murmured condescendingly that Madame Hart's accent was passable. She then made a gesture which appeared to be a signal to the king, for his majesty immediately took Sir William by the arm, muttered something about a new portrait by Madame Le Brun, and led the ambassador from the room. They were followed by Acton, leaving Emma alone with the queen.

"Come," her majesty commanded, "we shall converse, the one with the other."

Maria Carolina, undoubtedly a regal figure, was nevertheless a disappointment to Emma. Surely all queens should be beautiful! The Hapsburg lip fascinated her and seemed to detract from the fineness of the slim hands and slender neck. Yet when you really looked at the dignified carriage of the woman you forgot all else except, perhaps, the eyes—lively, searching, shrewd.

"You do not like that man, my king," she stated.

"Your Majesty—" Emma faltered.

"It was written in your face. You think him a fool."

"We-ell . . ."

"Without a doubt he is. But understand, please, care must be taken. He has in his life two interests. Two interests only. The hunting of such creatures as wolves and boars, and—women, the second being in itself an extension of the first. You are sure you fully comprehend the French language?"

94

"Yes," Emma replied promptly. "His majesty hunts wolves and boars and—women."

Maria Carolina looked at her coldly and continued: "One would think that thus engaged, by day and by night, he would trouble me not at all. But no! No! Twelve children I have already and there will be more. I was married at an early age, as was my poor sister, the queen of France. At an early age, you understand! I have the look of a woman of forty, forty-five. I am thirty-five. Did I say twelve children? I think thirteen, fourteen possibly. Some of course have died."

She paused. Talking nonsense, Emma decided, and at the same time summing her up.

The royal eyes narrowed. "Is it true that you are in secret, as gossip has it, the wife of Hamilton?"

Emma shook her head. "Not even in secret, Your Majesty."

"Ah, then you are, as some say, of lowly birth, otherwise he would not be so great a fool. Or you possess a husband, yes?"

"No, Your Majesty."

"So! Of lowly birth merely. But you have beauty, which I envy. What an idiot, that Hamilton. To lose you would be so easy." Smiling distantly she made a gesture of dismissal. "That is all. You may withdraw. I shall send for you again, when we will talk at greater length. It was I, please understand, who commanded your presence, not the king."

Surprised by this revelation, Emma mentioned it to Sir William during the drive back to the Embassy.

He smiled. "The queen is most concerned—and rightly so—on her sister's behalf. She believes, as I do, that revolution will sweep through France like a raging fire—unless some outside power can be persuaded to intervene."

"Meaning England?"

"Precisely, my dear. Maria Carolina therefore plans to make a friend of you in order to gain more influence with me, England's representative here in Naples. She plans it on the assumption that I am and always will be your willing slave."

Emma remained silent for a moment, stunned and awed by the picture she saw of herself playing an important role in international affairs. It was something she had never for one moment contemplated.

"But why," she asked, frowning, "did she send me an invitation to a ball she knew would not take place?"

"To flatter you, to pave the way for meeting you in private. When she sends for you again it will be another private meeting."

Emma laughed bitterly. "I'm not fit for public recognition, you make *that* clear enough."

He cleared his throat and tried to change the subject. "What she fails to understand, this intriguing queen, is that the most I can do is make recommendations to my government. I myself have no power to involve England in a war with France. Nor would I wish to bring about such a thing if I had that power."

"But your recommendations *could* influence any particular situation, couldn't they?" Emma said shrewdly.

"Undoubtedly, but my first consideration is the welfare of my own country."

"And *I* could influence *you*, Hamilton."

"No one more so," he said gallantly.

Emma smiled to herself. It was easy to see how a clever woman could make herself the power behind any man, king, ambassador, or otherwise. Her anger and indignation were fading.

"What else did the queen say?" Sir William asked.

Emma gave him a faithful account of the conversation, omitting nothing, not even her majesty's reference to the gossip about a secret marriage.

Sir William chuckled. "I, too, have heard the gossip."

It was an opportunity to remind him that nothing further had been done about his promise to marry her, but Emma chose to ignore it.

"The queen didn't seem all *that* friendly," she said.

"She will improve on acquaintance," he assured her. "I know her well. The coldness and condescension hide a warm heart, and she has promised to send for you again. Cultivate her. You have nothing to lose by it."

Emma laughed. "I'll do my best, and of course I won't tell her how impossible it would be to move you when you don't choose to be moved."

He wagged a playful finger. "You can move me in all things but state affairs, and well you know it, you little baggage."

"State affairs and—and one other thing!" she burst out.

He grasped her meaning at once and his face grew grave.

"You know the attitude of my foster brother, King George," he said hastily.

Emma gave him a long sad look and remained silent.

"Yes, yes," he said, even more hastily, "I gave my word and I am, I do assure you, a man of my word. Now I am only waiting till we go to England, so that I may speak to my foster brother personally."

"I don't believe we will ever go to England," she said sadly. "You are much too happy here. Set in your ways, you are, what with climbing Vesuvius and collecting marbles and bronzes, and writing little lectures about volcanic earths. Why, Vesuvius would have to blow up completely to move you!"

"We might go sooner than you think," he said lamely. "Yes, indeed. Patience, Emma, patience!"

But another year passed and still the promised return to England seemed as far off as ever; yet it was, without doubt, the happiest year Emma had so far spent in Naples. Queen Maria Carolina's friendship, guarded and cool and unofficial as it was, gave a certain importance to Emma's position and brought her new friends. Life was full of parties and receptions, balls and grand dinners. More and more artists came to paint her, sculptors to model her. It was all so flattering, so much more intoxicating than the strongest wine.

And meanwhile, in spite of the gay, lighthearted tempo of life in Naples, Emma surprised herself by taking a deeper and deeper interest in European affairs. This she did under the instruction of Maria Carolina who, though Sir William pooh-poohed the idea, considered herself a stateswoman of considerable ability. Her condescension melted slowly, imperceptibly, while Emma grew to admire her and tried to model herself on such a clever woman. Sir William watched all this tolerantly and raised only one objection.

"My dear," he said, "you are in danger of becoming onesided in your outlook, a mere echo of Maria Carolina. Study European affairs by all means, but do so independently, objectively. Otherwise—dear me yes!—I might find an enemy in my own camp."

"Instruct me yourself, then," Emma challenged.

This he eventually did, and many were the hours they spent together reading and discussing history.

"Quite the scholar I am," she said, laughing at herself.

Such was the state of affairs when, with the revolution in France gathering greater momentum, graver news reached Naples. Maria Carolina summoned Emma and Sir William to the royal residence in Naples, the Palazzo Reale, and told them about the unsuccessful flight of the king and queen of France.

"This," she cried tragically, "is the beginning of the end."

Sir William, showing a courteous sympathy, agreed that the situation in Paris was most serious.

"There can be no second flight," Maria Carolina went on. "The rabble will see to that. How, I wonder, will the king of England receive this dreadful news?"

"He will be shocked and dismayed, Your Majesty."

"And your Mr. Pitt who, I understand"—she was sneering now—"is the real master of England, how will he receive it?"

"He, too, will be shocked and dismayed," Sir William replied smoothly.

"Yet he will cling with stubbornness to his policy of peace!"

Sir William smiled. "There is such a thing as public opinion, and that, in England, is the real master."

The queen shrugged angrily. "Pooh, madness!" And she added, "How, then, will this real master of England receive the news?"

"In the same way, Your Majesty. For some months now public opinion in England has revealed a growing anger with France. In the long run public opinion will force the issue. It always does, in England."

"How smug you sound, Sir William! And 'in the long run'! In the long run it might be too late! In the long run my sister may have met her death!"

"Oh, come," Sir William laughed easily, "exile perhaps, but not death."

"It has happened before," Maria Carolina raged. "Even in England. Think of your Charles the First. He went to the block. Was that an issue forced by English public opinion?"

Sir William smiled benignly. "Ah, my dear Madam, who knows?"

Emma, looking at him admiringly, thought his attitude a fine example of diplomacy. Smooth words, polite smiles, no betrayal of personal feelings. Except, of course, that he had addressed Maria Carolina as Madam instead of Your Majesty, but politely, so very politely. Smug, of course, as the queen had said, like so many Englishmen, but how could he help it, poor dear, having been born that way?

Presently Maria Carolina dismissed him imperiously but kept Emma at her side, scowling at first, then growing somber, then finally saying sadly,

"You can do nothing with him, nothing?"

Emma had no wish in this instance to do anything with him, but she affected a similar sadness and slowly shook her head.

"If I were Lady Hamilton it might be different."

"And that is an impossibility."

"Yes," Emma agreed. "Perhaps I made a grave mistake in the beginning."

"Ah, yes, these men!" Maria Carolina cried. "Yes, I understand the mistake you made."

Emma's eyes filled with tears. "But he does love me."

The queen laughed dryly. "As the ridiculous English have it, he worships the ground you walk on. The ground, mark you. What an imbecility!"

"It's just that he won't stir himself to go to England to ask the king's permission," Emma said.

"What good would that do?" Maria Carolina asked, impatient now. "So stuffy, that king, and mad, too, they tell me. Did he not throw away the colonies in America? He would never consent."

Emma's tears were flowing now. "But King George being Hamilton's foster brother . . . I mean, Your Majesty—"

"Foster brother?" Maria Carolina said sharply. "I knew nothing of that!" Her eyes narrowed; her impatience vanished. "That is different!" She was almost purring. "Our dear Hamilton in that case will have influence in London greater than any ordinary ambassador. Therefore we must, as you say, put our heads together." The words were tumbling out now. "The good Hamilton loves you and he is growing old. Without you he would be lost. It is a habit, yes, yes, yes! but to the old, habit is vital. Therefore, my dear Emma—ah-ha!— therefore you will give him one big fright."

"Fright?" Emma asked, noting that for the first time the queen had addressed her by her Christian name.

"Acton I think is the very man—yes, Acton! A pretended *affaire*, a hint that you are tired of waiting and are about to leave him for another man."

Greatly daring, Emma said: "But would you like that, Your Majesty? Even a pretended *affaire*?"

Maria Carolina frowned. "It is true that you have a dangerous beauty and Acton might grow serious. Very well, we must think of someone else." She clapped her hands. "But yes, the handsome Caracciolo, younger than Acton, younger than Sir William. With Caracciolo the fright would be greater."

99

"Caracciolo . . ." Emma mused.

She knew him well. He was a member of a noble family, a minor prince, who, beginning his career in the navy, was now minister of marine. She had always found him amusing and enjoyed his undisguised admiration, his charming, voluble flattery. She felt sure that an open response on her part would shake Sir William, who had many times laughingly remarked that he would need to keep an eye on Caracciolo.

"Yes, Francisco Caracciolo it shall be," Maria Carolina went on enthusiastically. "Acton shall make the arrangements, discuss the matter with him, give a ball at which the first blow shall be struck!"

"And you think this will help to make me Lady Hamilton."

"I can think of nothing else."

"As Lady Hamilton, would I be officially received at court?"

"Assuredly. No longer the hole-and-corner friendship, but open to the world."

"How wonderful!" she cried, with clasped hands and shining eyes. In reality Emma thought the plan ridiculous, but she had learned her lesson in diplomacy.

"Such delightful simplicity," Maria Carolina purred. "And now to plan this little campaign. Ah, but what fun it will be, my sweet Emma, what fun!"

And fun it was, though there were times when Sir William's alarm and distress made Emma feel conscience-stricken.

The ball, which was to have been the first blow, was delayed. A more gradual approach would be better, the queen decided, and so, following her eager instructions, Emma began by treating Sir William with unaccustomed coolness. She refused to accompany him when he suggested a drive. She made a habit of going to bed early, and she started to evade rather than reject his physical approaches, infrequent as they were. Puzzled by all this, he asked if she was feeling ill. She replied that she was in perfect health, thank you! The hurt, bewildered look that came to his eyes upset her, but she hardened her heart.

That was the first step. The second was taken when Maria Carolina sent for Sir William, ostensibly to discuss the situation in Paris. Later she gave Emma a word-by-word account of the conversation.

"Sir William," she had begun, "I wish to discuss a matter more personal than the revolution in France. More personal to you, I mean."

"Indeed, Your Majesty?"

"You will without doubt think me presumptuous, but for your own good I am prepared to take that risk."

Sir William remained silent, politely waiting for her to continue, but she was quick to see the passing flicker of apprehension in his eyes.

"It is of the lovely Emma that I wish to speak," Maria Carolina went on, and again came the flicker of apprehension. "There is—forgive my making such a remark—a considerable difference in your ages. Perhaps thirty-five, forty years, yes?"

Sir William cleared his throat. "Not *forty*, Your Majesty."

"She is, of course, devoted to you; but have you never thought that such devotion might at times become a strain, might indeed be preserved out of that most thankless of all feelings, gratitude?" She gave him a moment to consider this, then continued: "It is always difficult for an elderly man—I shall not call you an old man—it is always difficult, I say, for an elderly man to retain the love of a young and beautiful woman."

"Emma," Sir William stammered, "is loyal . . ."

"Nevertheless," the queen went on relentlessly, "a younger man might some day cause her to forget her loyalty."

"Never!" he cried, and tried, unsuccessfully, to laugh.

Maria Carolina looked grave. "Let us consider the position as it is at present. You brought Emma to Naples. You set her up at the Embassy and the Palazzo Sessa. You let her be known as your protégée. You gave her a position in Neapolitan society. You continued her education until now it has reached a point resembling perfection. Nature has made her beautiful; *you* have made her accomplished. In short, my dear Hamilton, you have set her in the place of your late wife and withheld one thing only, her right to be known to the world as the second Lady Hamilton."

"There have been certain—ah—difficulties." He was growing vastly uncomfortable.

"I believe you when you say that; but can the dear Emma be blamed if, after all this time, *she* believes the difficulties are of your own making?" He started to speak, but the queen pressed quickly on. "Marriage is the only thing that will make her wholly yours. The only thing that will bind her to you for the rest of your life. Unless, of course, it is not now too late."

"Too late?" he cried.

The queen shrugged. "When hope is deferred bitterness can creep

101

in. A woman's heart can stand so much, and then—what is that delightful word Emma uses? Ah yes, and then—*ructions!*"

Sir William mopped his brow. "Has Emma been confiding in Your Majesty?"

"No, no, but I am a woman of perception."

"Perhaps you have heard gossip?"

"Gossip?"

"You mentioned a younger man . . ."

"I know of none, but I see that something she has done or said, or not done or not said, has filled you with suspicion."

"Yes!" he gasped, "dear heaven, yes!"

Later, after this conversation had been discussed in full by the queen and Emma, they decided that perhaps the next step might not be necessary. They waited for several days, but though Sir William was ill at ease, more distressed than ever, and though he seemed at times on the point of speaking, he made no move.

"And so, the third step!" Maria Carolina announced.

Acton, ready at all times to bow to her wishes, duly gave the ball she had planned, and since she herself was to be present it was regarded by all Naples as a social event of the utmost importance. Emma, not very happy about the part she was playing, remained coolly elusive where Sir William was concerned and deserted him entirely for Prince Caracciolo, who declared with his usual gallantry that he looked forward to many repetitions.

Shortly after midnight the queen called Sir William to her side and kept him there. He was miserable and dejected, and paid scant attention as she discussed once again the situation in France, outlining her suggestions for a pact of mutual aid between her country and his.

"It is my firm belief," she said, "that revolutionary France will soon become a menace to the peace of Europe and a threat to the freedom of Naples."

Sir William nodded absently, his eyes on the dancers.

"I will speak frankly, my dear Hamilton. In the event of war we would be utterly lost without the protection of British warships."

He glanced at her vaguely, then back at the dancers, his eyes searching for Emma and Caracciolo.

"In return," Maria Carolina urged, "we would gladly offer you the use of our available troops." Then, without changing her tone of voice, she added, "If you are looking for Emma—"

He gave her his instant attention. "Emma?"

"She left the ballroom some little time ago with Caracciolo."

"Oh . . ." he said miserably.

"It is possibly no more than a mild flirtation . . ."

He looked at her squarely. "This has been going on for some time."

"I suspect that it has. You propose to let it continue, yes?"

The dejected look passed quickly from his face. He straightened his shoulders.

"By heaven, no!" he said angrily.

Without excusing himself he went hurriedly in search of Emma. He found her on the terrace, the prince at her side.

"The hour is late," he thundered, and offered her his arm.

Emma, just a little frightened at his anger, left Caracciolo without protest.

Sir William led her in silence to their carriage, and in silence they drove back to the Palazzo Sessa. His anger was still so obvious that she wondered if she had gone too far. As he helped her down from the carriage he said curtly, "I want to talk to you."

She followed him to the library, running a little to keep up with his long strides.

And then, in the library, his anger fell from him and he sank wearily into a chair. His face was gray; his eyes were full of pain.

"Are you ill?" she asked quickly.

"Ill? Yes, in a way I think I am." He swept up his arms in a grand gesture. "Lovesickness and jealousy, that is the nature of the disease."

"Emma, you must make an end of this flirtation with Caracciolo. You understand?"

She fell on her knees at his feet, looked up at him, and laughed impishly.

"You sound like a husband."

"I do? And yet I have not that right." He rose and strode across the room, turned and came back to stand over her. "Caracciolo has much to offer you. True, he is married and could never make you a princess, but he possesses great wealth. He could set you up in splendor. Have I delayed too long, Emma, have I?"

Emma jumped impulsively to her feet and ran quickly into his arms. She knew that Maria Carolina would have advised against this capitulation, but her heart told her it was the only thing to do.

"Oh, Hamilton," she sobbed, and clung to him.

He raised her face to his and kissed her gently, almost reverently.

"You came close to breaking my heart," he said.

"As you have done to breaking mine," she sobbed.

He held her away from him. "Well, which is it to be, Caracciolo's mistress, or an old man's wife?"

"Oh, Hamilton, need you ask!"

"Begin your packing tomorrow," he said briskly. "We leave for London at the end of the week."

10 And now they were actually in London again, Emma, Sir William and Mrs. Cadogan, after a leisurely journey overland to France and a calm June crossing of the English Channel. Emma, seated in the carriage with Sir William at her side, her mother opposite, was finding it hard to hide her excitement. Since the great decision had been made Sir William had been kinder, more loving and more attentive than ever, often declaring that when she was out of his sight, if only for a single moment, he was plunged into the depths of despair. "A bit in his dotage," Mrs. Cadogan was apt to comment, much to Emma's annoyance.

"Well," Sir William was asking them both, "does it please you to be in London again?"

"Oh, yes, Hamilton!" Emma cried.

Mrs. Cadogan shrugged. "I don't care where I am, just so long as we're not separated, Emma and me."

"Separated, Emma and you?" Sir William exclaimed. "I see no reason why you ever should be."

His future mother-in-law shot him a quick look. "Not even when you're fair and properly married, the two of you?"

Sir William looked askance at her "fair and properly," but his eyes soon twinkled and he assured her warmly that the coming marriage would not make the slightest difference.

"When we return to Naples I intend you to be in charge of both the Embassy and the Palazzo Sessa."

"Good Lord alive!" she exclaimed. "Well, I promise you this, Sir William, I'll keep them in order, them thieving Eye-talian servants."

"And save me much money, eh?"

"I will an' all!" she laughed.

The carriage stopped. They were in Piccadilly, outside the house that Greville had rented for them; and there, opening the door, was Greville himself.

Emma said quickly to Sir William, "You haven't told him we're going to be married? You swear you haven't?"

Sir William smiled indulgently. "I swear I haven't. You shall have your wish and tell him yourself; but treat him gently, my dear, treat him gently."

Greville came forward to help the travelers down from the carriage. Cordial as his manner was, it was clear to Emma that he, like herself, was a little uncertain, a little on guard.

First he greeted his uncle. "Hamilton, my dear fellow!" Then Mrs. Cadogan. "Ah, the excellent Mrs. Cadogan, blooming as ever!" And finally, his eyes running over her swiftly, "Emma, how splendid to see you again."

In the house, while Mrs. Cadogan was giving orders to the servants about the luggage, Emma was able to study him carefully, as carefully as he was able to study her. By the look of things, she thought, it was daggers drawn already.

"It seems," Sir William was saying, "as if you are in residence here, my dear fellow."

Greville shook his head. "No, no, Hamilton. It was quite by chance that I was here to welcome you. Your letter from Paris gave no exact date. I engaged the servants a week ago—a skeleton staff only, mind you—and merely called to see that all was in order."

"Splendid, splendid! Emma will undoubtedly find it necessary to engage many more. She has learned, you see, how to do things on a grand scale! And now, my dear Greville, let us have a good look at you."

"Do you see any change in him, Emma?" Sir William asked.

Emma looked at Greville quite coolly now. She asked herself what she felt, now that she had seen him again, what indeed she had expected to feel. She had loved him so deeply; he had meant everything to her. She had wondered, wondered anxiously, if the sight of him would restore that old compelling love, yet looking at him now she knew that such a thing could never happen. She was relieved, yet disappointed, too. The tragedy of growing up, making progress, finding new values. He was just a man she would have passed in the street without a second glance.

"Older, of course," she said at last, "and—yes—more mature." Then, remembering how he and Sir William had inspected her during her first meeting with Sir William at Edgware Row, she walked right around him, head quizzically on one side. "Stouter, too, don't you think, Hamilton?"

Greville's face darkened.

Emma stood back from him. "Considerably stouter."

"No one could say that you yourself had grown thin," he said tartly. "The climate of Naples must have agreed with you more than I expected. So relaxing, and so demoralizing, too." He turned quickly to his uncle. "I heard a rumor that you had been recalled by the government. Surely, after your years of valuable service in Naples, that is not correct?"

"Dear me, no!" Sir William laughed.

"Then this is just a holiday visit? Your letters have given me no real details, you know."

Sir William tried to hide a smile. "In a way, yes, a holiday visit."

"There will doubtless be consultations with Mr. Pitt," Greville tried again.

"Doubtless, doubtless."

Greville looked swiftly at Emma's impassive face, then he addressed Sir William again.

"How stupid of me! You were summoned to London because of the general situation in Europe."

Sir William shrugged. "My dear fellow, I am not regarded as sufficiently important for that."

Emma caught his eye, signaling "Leave me with Greville," and, understanding the signal, he signaled back "No gloating." Upon which Sir William excused himself and, calling Mrs. Cadogan, went on a tour of inspection of the house.

There was a stiff little silence.

"Well, Greville?" Emma said at last.

"I trust you had a pleasant journey," he said politely.

She nodded happily. "A week in Florence, and almost two weeks in Venice. Then Milan for a few days and a day or two here and there on the way to Paris."

"How nonchalant you sound!" he jeered. "Quite a little jaunt. Hamilton must be in good form, in spite of his age."

"There's no need to speak of him as if he was a decrepit old man!" Emma said angrily.

"He will be sixty-one this year."

Another stiff little silence fell between them.

Emma wondered how best to bring up the subject with which she was bursting.

"You are still a bachelor," she said.

"Yes."

She smiled sweetly. "So sending me away didn't help."

"No."

"Are you still trying to find a rich wife?"

"Without success," he said shortly.

She thought she saw the opening she was looking for. "Poor Greville, are you badly in debt?"

"In debt, but not badly."

"Still, it must be unpleasant, always trying to make ends meet," she said. Then she added condescendingly, "If matters become desperate I might be able to give you a little assistance, later on. Please don't hesitate to call on me, Greville."

He looked at her angrily. "Are you trying to insult me?"

"Why, *Greville*, dear—"

"And where, pray, would you get the money?"

Emma smiled sweetly. "From the man I'm going to marry. From my future husband. From—"

"By heaven!" he cried. "I thought there was something odd about this visit. You—!" He broke off and laughed nastily. "Hamilton would never be such a fool."

"No?"

"My God, this is preposterous! Preposterous!"

"Oh, Greville," she said softly, her heart full of love for Sir William, "when two people have lived together so long, found so many things in common, been so happy together—they could never separate, never."

"Separate?" He seized on the word. "So that was it! You slowly enslaved him, then you gave him his choice, separation or marriage. You—! And to think that I sent you out to Naples, fool that I was!"

Emma touched him quickly on the arm, quite sorry for him now, ready almost to apologize, eager to offer him her friendship. He dashed her arm away.

"The marriage has not yet taken place, Emma. I tell you now, I tell you solemnly, I shall prevent it if I can."

He turned on his heels and went swiftly from the room.

Emma heard him a moment later in the hall shouting, "Hamilton! Hamilton, where are you?"

She went after him quickly, fear gripping her heart. She saw now that Greville should not have been told until the marriage was an accomplished fact.

She reached the hall just as Sir William came down the stairs.

"What, not going already, Greville?" he said breezily.

Greville took a deep breath and began what Sir William afterward described as a veritable tirade. He reminded his uncle of Emma's past;

he spoke heatedly of Fetherstonhaugh and Willet-Payne; he sneered at the difference between Sir William's age and Emma's. He accused Emma of trapping an old man into marriage, not because she loved him, but because of the position the marriage would give her. Gone was the precise and dignified Charles Francis Greville; in his place stood an alarmed and hysterical man. Finally, taking no notice of the blackness of his uncle's face, he cried:

"Why, after all this time, must you insist on marrying your mistress? It—damn it all, Hamilton, it is not the sort of thing a gentleman does!"

"Enough, Greville, enough!" Sir William thundered.

"But the insanity of it, Hamilton! You bear an old and honorable name, and you want to give it to *that* creature!" He pointed a quivering finger at Emma. "Beautiful, yes; charming, yes! I admit it, I admit it! More beautiful than ever, but at heart a slut!"

Sir William took a threatening step forward, but his anger had weakened him. His face was pale now and his hands were shaking. Emma's heart went out to him; he looked so old and pitiful.

"You ought to be ashamed of yourself!" she told Greville violently.

"I took you out of the gutter," he raged. "What a fool I was!"

"Leave us, Greville, for pity's sake leave us," Sir William begged. "I love you dearly, you know that, as dearly as I love Emma, whom you gave to me. Leave us now, and when you are calmer, come back and let us be good friends again."

A cunning look crossed Greville's face. "Perhaps when I tell you that Emma has a child at Hawarden—"

Sir William stopped him. "I know about the child."

Greville made a helpless gesture. All the fight seemed to have gone out of him.

"You are still determined to marry her?"

"I most certainly am!"

Emma, watching Greville, saw another cunning look cross his face. It was there for only a moment, then quickly disappeared.

"You came to England for that purpose, Hamilton?"

"Yes."

"But—why? Surely you could have married just as easily in Naples?"

"It was sentiment," Emma said quickly. She was afraid of Greville now, yet not sure why. "We wanted to be married in our own country. That was all."

Greville smiled faintly. "Asking first the blessing of his majesty the king, no doubt."

"He and I are very old friends," Sir William said confidently.

"Of course," Greville acknowledged.

He bowed ironically to Emma, told his uncle that he would gladly call again soon and went quickly from the house.

"He's up to mischief!" Emma cried.

Sir William pooh-poohed the idea. "He can do nothing and he knows it. Quite obviously he still loves you, though he himself would be the last to admit it."

"He never loved me!" Emma said hotly. "He only tried to create in me a part of himself, and that was what he loved. He loved himself, Hamilton. And he is determined still to be your sole heir."

"He can do nothing," Sir William repeated. "I shall wait on his majesty tomorrow. We shall be married within a week."

But two weeks passed before Sir William was able to see the king. His majesty was at Windsor, suffering a slight indisposition, and unable to receive anyone. "Indisposition" was the official report, whereas rumor had it that the king, known to be mentally unstable, was languishing in a strait jacket.

Meanwhile the Piccadilly house was thrown open to Sir William's many friends; and Emma, the poised and charming hostess, was an instant success. The toast of London society, Sir William declared, pleased and flattered by it all. Emma was pleased and flattered, too; but she knew that he was exaggerating. Time enough to talk of being the toast of London society when Sir William's friends began to invite her to their own grand houses. She was not Lady Hamilton yet. Sir William, giving his dinner parties, was inclined to put the cart before the horse.

During the second week she went to visit her grandmother and little Emma at Hawarden. Mrs. Cadogan accompanied her, and to their dismay they found the old lady in failing health. Emma immediately engaged a young widow of the village to look after both her and the child, but she knew that a more permanent arrangement would have to be made before she returned to Naples. The girl herself, now nearly ten and tall for her age, showed little interest in Emma. She had even forgotten that she had once mistaken her for an aunt.

"Much use it is getting sentimental over it," Mrs. Cadogan said practically when Emma burst into tears. "You made your choice years ago. Tell the child the truth now and you'll unsettle her. Nice thing that would be, with you going back to Italy an' maybe never seeing her again. Leave things as they are. Better to do nothing than make things worse."

"I could take her to Naples, Ma."

"Could you? Sir William wouldn't like that."

"No," Emma said sadly, "he wouldn't."

Back in London, Emma met George Romney again. She had gone eagerly to the Cavendish Square studio the morning after her arrival from the Continent, only to find that the artist was away. His greeting now was warm enough, but she had a feeling that it was an automatic, surface kind of warmth. His general appearance shocked her; he was untidy now in his dress and looked so much older.

"You deserted me," he told her somberly.

"And you said you would never paint again," she tried to tease him. "But of course you did."

The faintest hint of a smile crossed his face. "Heaven help me, I did."

"Making yourself more famous than ever, Romney."

"Fame! Pah! I hate the word. The trouble is, I achieved my ambition too soon. All that was left afterward was repetition."

Grieved on his account, she wondered what to say to him.

"You used to call me your inspiration," she said. "If inspiration left you when I went to Naples, well, here I am again, ready to sit for you whenever you want me."

Romney shrugged. "So very kind of you."

Tears came to her eyes. "Oh, Romney, you break my heart."

"You want me to paint you in that pose, then? Emma, the broken-hearted?"

With the tears still in her eyes she flew into a little fit of temper. She berated him soundly. She told him that he, the most talented artist of the day, ought to be ashamed of himself. He hung his head. He said contritely that he was sorry, and he begged her to forgive him.

"Be a good girl," he said. "Go and make tea, just for the two of us, like you used to in the old days."

This Emma did, and as she sipped the tea with him she chatted gaily, gossiping about life in Naples, finally telling him of Greville's attitude to her coming marriage with Sir William.

"The second Lady Hamilton!" Romney exclaimed. He sprang up, almost his old self again. "I know how I shall paint you, just as you are

111

today, in your white organdy gown, your auburn ringlets down your back, a look of quiet triumph in your eyes. And I shall call it 'The Ambassadress.' "

Emma clapped her hands. " 'The Ambassadress'! Yes, that's what I shall be when I go back to Naples! The Ambassadress!"

He sank back into his chair and scowled. "You had never looked at it like that before?"

"Well, to be honest, Romney, maybe I had."

"Perhaps I ought to paint you with a *cunning* look of triumph in your eyes, not a quiet one. A look betraying your real reason for marrying Sir William Hamilton."

"Now you want to make me hate you!" she flared up.

Romney held her eyes for a moment. "You are marrying the old man for love? Just that? Love?"

"But I do love him. I love him dearly!"

"And if he were poor, ill-educated, a blacksmith, say, like your father was?"

She turned away from him.

"How cruel you are to me, Romney," she cried, the quick tears in her eyes again. "If Sir William had been poor I would never have met him. And please remember, I went to Naples unwillingly. Would you rather I had died there of a broken heart?"

Romney looked at her broodingly. "Is it really mended, that heart of yours? Or do you still love that stupid Greville? Would you, for example, give up all that Sir William has to offer you if Greville promised you marriage today and love everlasting at Edgware Row?"

Emma gave a full-throated laugh. "Lord save us, Romney, never!"

But in her heart she thought sadly, It's too late for that, now . . .

The house in Edgware Row looked smaller.

Staring at it from the hackney coach, Emma thought, No, I never lived here, never! She hesitated, wondering whether to get out and knock, or tell the coachman to drive her back to Piccadilly. She was restless, a bit on edge; and, not knowing what to do with herself while Sir William went to see the king, she had thought suddenly of Edgware Row and Paddington Green with its little church and tall elm trees. She realized now that she had been irresistibly drawn to Edgware Row ever since her return to England.

"Please wait," she told the coachman, and got down.

Greville, whom she had not seen since the day of her arrival, seemed vastly taken aback when he answered her knock. "Emma," he exclaimed, and much to her amazement a look of alarm crossed his face. "If you have come to make a scene—!" he protested.

"A scene? Oh, Greville, it was just for old times' sake."

"Really?" He smiled thinly and seemed somewhat relieved. "So that is your present attitude. Emma the sentimentalist."

She held her quick temper in check. "Aren't you going to ask me in?"

He shrugged and stood back for her, then followed her into the drawing room. Like the house, it too looked smaller, more confined; yet somehow, after glancing around at the familiar furnishings, she began to feel at home. She quickly noticed new works of art and recognized one or two pieces sent to Greville by Sir William.

"As you see, my collection increases," he said airily. "Of course, I need a larger establishment."

"Which, of course, you can't afford," Emma said gently.

"No," he scowled.

"May I go through the house?" she asked.

"If you wish."

He followed her in silence as she made her tour of inspection. How silly of her to have thought that she had never lived here! It seemed now that she had never lived anywhere else. A lump came to her throat as she stood in Greville's study, pretending to admire his latest mezzotint. So easy it was to picture him sitting at the desk, going through the household accounts and at the same time reading her a severe little lecture.

Naples seemed so very far away. The life she had led there, the exciting, pleasing success of it all, was a misty dream, something that had never happened.

She said softly, "Does the ghost of the girl I used to be ever walk in this house, Greville?"

"What a fanciful suggestion!" But he was looking uneasy. He made as if to take her in his arms, then quickly restrained himself and said stiffly, "I do admit that I have missed you at times."

This reluctant admission made her smile.

"Did you ever replace me?"

"No."

He was trying his best not to look at her, trying and failing.

"Have I improved, Greville?"

He nodded briefly. "You are, if possible, more graceful, and your face, if not your figure, is more beautiful. You are, of course, too plump. Twenty years from now you will be not only fat but gross. I can see that clearly. *Gross*, Emma!" He sounded quite angry. "But your face, I predict, will remain beautiful."

"I hate you," Emma said lightly.

"For the rest, your speech is better, the grammar passable, but the accent is still noticeable. I have listened carefully and up to now you have not dropped a single aitch." He bowed ironically. "My congratulations."

"Maybe you could love me now if you never did before."

"Love!" he scoffed.

"Greville," she said softly, "kiss me."

Much to her surprise he took her in his arms. She kissed him back and clung to him, trying to recapture the love, the desperate love, she had felt for him. Trying and failing, and feeling the quick tears of vexation spring to her eyes.

She pushed him away, holding him at arms' length and looking at him critically. He was discontented and unhappy. She could tell that by the strained look on his thin handsome features. She could see weakness there, too, and indecision.

"Please forgive me," he said stiffly, "for the scene I made with Hamilton. It was undignified. I was not myself. I regretted it bitterly afterward."

"It doesn't matter. No real damage was done."

"No," he said curtly, "the real damage was done later."

"What do you mean by that?"

"You will learn in due course." He turned away from her. "I thought you already knew. That was why I asked if you had come to make a scene." He came closer again and took her by the arm. A moment later he was leading her from the room. "Let me escort you to your carriage." He paused for a moment with her at the door. "You must try to forgive me, Emma, but I had to do it."

"Had to do *what?*" Emma all but screamed.

He refused to say more, helped her into the hackney coach and turned on his heels.

"Greville!" she shouted.

He looked back over his shoulder.

"I doubt," he said, smiling, "if I shall ever have the pleasure of calling you 'Aunt,' now."

All the way back to Piccadilly she brooded over his words. He had done something, but . . . what? He had interfered in some way, but . . . how?

Sir William was waiting for her, and she could see by his face that things had not gone well. He refused to meet her eyes, and so nervous was he that only by keeping her temper and questioning him patiently was she able to get at the truth. Yes, the king had been pleased to see him; yes, his majesty was in good health again; y-yes, the question of the marriage had been discussed.

"He refused his consent," Emma said, "but you're afraid to tell me."

"Well, now, his majesty realizes that he cannot *prevent* me from marrying you."

"But he did refuse his consent?"

Sir William laughed shakily. "Poor George is somewhat browbeaten by the queen. And to complicate matters there are these illnesses. Rumor was right about the strait jacket. And do you know, the poor fellow was in such a state that he talked for sixteen hours during the last bout, sixteen hours of nonsense and never a stop."

Sir William was, of course, doing his best to evade the issue.

"But surely it wasn't necessary to consult the queen!"

"Her majesty herself was present, my dear."

"Then it would have been better to wait."

"Indeed yes, but I had no choice. Her majesty wasted no time in bringing up the subject."

"She—?"

"Bless my soul, Emma, she knows almost everything there is to be known about you, and from her point of view, strong moral character that she is, you are—hum—beyond the pale."

"Greville!" Emma shrieked.

"Yes, yes, I fear so. Her majesty did admit that Greville had waited on her. Naturally I—hum—tried to reason with her. I said I had forgiven you long ago. I pointed out that you were young, innocent, unprotected. I—"

"Forgiven me!" Emma cried. "And have you forgiven yourself for taking me, seducing me? Have you, Hamilton, have you?"

"You—Gracious heaven, child, you had been seduced—hum—several times before I—" The look in her eyes made him flinch. "Before you made me the happiest man in the world," he amended hurriedly.

"Tell me just what the queen said," Emma demanded.

Sir William sighed. "Her majesty was in a towering rage. By that, of course, I mean that she was very very angry, not that she shouted and screamed. She said—dear me, she said, 'Marry the trollop if you must, if you are fool enough, but if you do, remember that we shall find it necessary to replace you at Naples.' The righteous indignation of these strongly moral women, bless my soul, it has to be seen to be believed."

Mopping his brow, he collapsed into a chair. With difficulty Emma controlled her anger and disappointment and got him a glass of wine.

"And another glass for yourself," he said. "We must drink a toast."

Emma laughed hysterically. "A—*toast?*"

"To our forthcoming marriage, Emma. To the happiness of the future. My mind was made up before I left their majesties' presence. To retire from public life will hurt me not at all. I shall buy a little place in the country—somewhere near Bath, perhaps, and we shall live there happily for the rest of our lives."

Emma, suddenly practical, said, "Did you tell the queen that?"

"No, no, but in a day or so I shall offer my resignation."

Emma went to the sideboard and slowly poured the second glass of wine. Naples was strong in her mind. She had only to close her eyes and she was back there, she the friend of Queen Maria Carolina, she the woman who had dreamed of playing an important part in European affairs . . .

Marry Sir William and live quietly in the country? What utter nonsense! She would be the ambassadress or nothing!

"Hamilton," she said quietly, "these are critical times and you are needed in Naples. *You*, not some new man who knows nothing of conditions there."

"Bless my soul," he cried, half-rising in his chair, "I cannot let you make the sacrifice."

"No, Hamilton, we'll go back together, the ambassador and the ambassadress. You just wait and see."

"But how in the name of heaven are we to bring that about?" Sir William asked.

Emma laughed sadly. "I wish I knew, Hamilton."

11 It had come at last, the first of the invitations she had hoped for but had not dared to expect. She stood at Sir William's side, eyes sparkling, lips slightly open, her face, Sir William said, more lovely than ever. The Duke of Queensberry's ball! She could scarcely believe it. And at the especial, the most pressing, invitation of his grace.

"Just pinch me, Hamilton," she whispered. "I'm sure I'm dreaming."

Sir William smiled amiably. "Most gratifying, I do admit."

The duke had just danced with her; his compliments had been extravagant and he had vowed that soon he must get Romney or Reynolds or one of the others to paint her, "Just as you are tonight, my dear." Thinking of this, she glanced at herself in one of the mirrors. There was no doubt about it, white satin suited her better than anything else. Sir William always said so, and Sir William had excellent taste. He had chosen this gown himself, liking the gold embroidery and the pale blue sash.

Other gentlemen were flocking about her now in the crowded ballroom, coming in twos and threes, inviting her to dance and on the point, she was ready to swear, of quarreling amongst themselves about her.

"No, no," she said, for the second time, "Sir William has engaged me for the next dance."

"In point of fact," Sir William declared chirpily, "I have, in another sense, engaged her for the rest of my life."

Emma thought he was making rather an exhibition of himself; but he was sweet and good, and more eager than ever to tender his resignation. They had argued about it only that afternoon; she was still determined that by means yet to be discovered they should return to Naples as man and wife.

Now she was waiting for Greville to come back from Scotland, where he had gone to escape Sir William's anger. There was just a chance that if he went to the queen and withdrew his spiteful story royal consent would be given. "He will never do it," Sir William had said, but Emma felt differently. Greville had gone too far, had brought himself close to complete disinheritance. She would promise him that a will would be made in which Sir William would divide his estate equally between the two of them, providing he, Greville, gave her majesty proof (documents could be forged) of Emma's high-born ancestors.

She was refusing a third gentleman when Sir William, surprisingly humble, interrupted her with the protestation that he preferred, after all, to watch the next dance. "His royal highness the Prince of Wales," he whispered in her ear, and stepped back a pace.

"But incognito, incognito, Sir William," the prince said.

Emma looked at him quickly, battling with a sudden fit of shyness, yet deciding that shyness was the right attitude, shyness and just a hint of dawning maidenly admiration. Oh yes, and awe, too, most certainly awe!

Sir William, twittering irritatingly, began to make a presentation, but the prince, whose eyes had never left Emma's face, ignored him.

"So this is Romney's divine lady," he murmured.

"And more delightful in the flesh than Romney ever made her on canvas," Sir William gushed.

"No artist, except perhaps the Almighty, if He ever thought of painting, has skill enough to capture her as she really is," the Prince of Wales said heartily, and so loudly that a little hush fell amongst those who surrounded them. Smoothly he added: "I shall take Sir William at his word—age, in any case, has no right to such youthful beauty—and claim the divine lady for myself."

He offered his arm, and after the slightest hesitation Emma took it. The fabulous Prince of Wales, she thought, but what a boor. Though his voice had a pleasant ring, he was too hearty, too loud, too confident. In spite of his impeccable manners and the dazzling extravagance of his dress, she could see him only as a country bumpkin, a young man spoiled by his high position and the fawning adulation of stupid women. She would remain aloof, she told herself, tempt him with the unattainable. And yes, she would appear to him as Romney had seen her when painting her as a nun. Later, dancing with him, conscious that all eyes were centered on them, she wondered why she had made any decision at all about him. It must have been instinctive, she thought excitedly. Because, through him, she might have a chance of gaining the queen's consent! A chance, yes, but how to use it? That was the question.

Later still, bored with him, but maintaining her saintly pose, she recalled all she knew about him, his many love affairs, his mountainous debts, his excessive gambling, his shameful debauchery and, most important of all as far as she was concerned, the anxiety and grief his conduct had caused his royal parents. First, as a youth, there had been the actress, Perdita Robinson, followed, after countless others, by the highly respectable Mrs. Fitzherbert, with whom, according to gossip, he had made a secret but illegal marriage.

After dancing with the prince three times, Emma pleaded a headache, made her excuses to the Duke of Queensberry, who promised to give a concert for her soon at his place at Richmond, and insisted on Sir William taking her home to Piccadilly.

"No woman has *ever* treated the prince like this," he protested.

Emma smiled. "That's what I hoped. It will make him all the more eager to see me again."

"Emma, my *dear!*" Sir William cried, a look of fear crossing his face.

"You threw me at him," she teased.

"It was a matter of—hum—courtesy." He shook his head sadly. "The prince is young, of course, with so much to offer."

"Oh, Hamilton," Emma cried, and flung herself into his arms, "I detest him, really I do!"

"*Detest* him?"

"Nevertheless, I want to use him."

"*Use* him, my dear?"

"Through him I might be able to force the queen to consent to our marriage."

"Oh, come, how could you possibly do that? Her majesty will frown on you all the more if she learns that you and her disreputable son are friends."

Emma smiled. This would fit in nicely with the idea now taking shape at the back of her mind.

"Is he really married to Mrs. Fitzherbert?" she asked.

Sir William shrugged. "It has been officially denied, but many people believe that he married her several years ago. It would be an illegal marriage, of course."

Emma began to feel excited. "The Fitzherbert affair must have been opposed by the king and queen."

"Dear me, yes!"

"Is she as virtuous as people say?"

"My dear Emma, she is a good woman, not only virtuous but religious. She holds an excellent position in society and enjoys a private fortune. If young George were not a prince she would be considered most acceptable."

Emma chuckled richly. "Whereas me, with *my* reputation—!" She broke off and became deeply serious. "I think I know what to do about it."

"Emma, my dear—" Sir William begged.

"Wait and see, Hamilton, wait and see!"

She was sitting for Romney, not for the proposed ambassadress painting, but in the guise of Calypso, which the artist was working on at the wish of the Prince of Wales. His royal highness had given her not a moment's peace during the month that had passed since the Duke of Queensberry's ball. He had sent his gentlemen continually with invitations to private suppers; she had refused them all. Following this, and just when she was wondering if she had gone too far, he came to dinner at the Piccadilly house, having "commanded" Sir William, "my father's oldest friend" to issue the invitation. Emma remained aloof but gracious, so much so that on leaving his royal highness grumbled that she had hardly spoken a word to him the whole time. She replied primly that she hoped she knew her place.

And then had come Romney's urgent summons. He had been commanded by the Prince of Wales to paint her, and his royal highness had suggested Calypso. Calypso, the goddess of silence! His royal highness, it seemed, had a sense of humor.

Presently, Romney expressing himself satisfied for the day, the first sitting ended. He was more cheerful now. They took tea together, he declared that it seemed as if she had never been away, and she gladly promised to sit for other new portraits, once the Calypso was finished.

When she went to keep the next appointment the servant who showed her into the studio told her that Romney was detained with an unexpected visitor and would join her as soon as possible. As she waited she thought how like old times it was, coming regularly to Cavendish Square, but with one pleasing difference. She was not required now to keep an account of the shillings spent on hackney coaches; indeed, she came in style from Piccadilly, riding in the private carriage provided by Sir William.

The door opened, and not Romney but the Prince of Wales entered the studio.

He said brusquely, "You have tried my patience sorely. This was as good a way as any of getting you to myself."

"I bow to the inevitable," Emma said and, pointing to the unfinished canvas, added sweetly, "I thought you required nothing of me but my beauty."

His frown deepened. "Tell me what your game is."

"*Game*, Your Highness?"

He gave her a charming smile and bowed in a most princely manner.

"I know something of your background," he murmured, "your humble birth, your earlier illiteracy, your complete lack of morals, your love affairs with various men. Now, unless I am much mistaken, you are assuming a virtue you never possessed."

Emma curbed her temper, saying quietly, "I have to think of my future husband."

"What," he said haughtily, "you prefer an old man to me?"

She had not intended any reference to Sir William. In spite of herself it had slipped out, easily and naturally. Suddenly she felt weary of the whole thing and sick at the thought of going on with it. To tell the prince she disliked him would of course be indiscreet, but dislike him she did, now more than before.

She said recklessly, "I prefer security with an old man of position to the uncertainty of dalliance with a prince of your unsavory reputation."

His head shot up indignantly. She shrugged. This was the end of her scheme, and unless Greville could be forced to undo the mischief he had done she would never be the ambassadress. Back to Naples as Sir William's mistress, she thought resignedly; that, at all events, would be better than a life of obscure respectability in the country.

But his highness was smiling again. "I have never been spoken to like that before. I . . . quite like it. When can we have supper together? Tonight?"

Emma shook her head. "Not tonight, Your Highness. Not ever."

He was instantly angry again. "I asked you what your game was. You have a game, I see that clearly." His eyes narrowed. "Are you playing for higher stakes than a casual *affaire*, a mere frolic, might win you?"

She decided to confide in him fully. "That's what I intended, but it would have been dangerous. My deceit, once it was known to you, might have made you turn nasty. And I don't like men when they're nasty." Better, she thought, to put it that way than to tell him frankly that physically he revolted her. "It was a plan, you see, to force her majesty your mother to give Sir William permission to marry me."

"It—?" The prince looked puzzled. "Tell me the whole thing! Come, the whole thing!"

"Well, the idea occurred to me when I thought of Mrs. Fitzherbert, she being so good and virtuous and worthy in every way except that she's not of royal blood. I thought—well, I thought that if I tempted you but didn't give in you might be persuaded to offer me the sort of marriage you offered her."

The prince looked at Emma in admiration. "You actually believed you could wield as much power as that?"

"It seemed possible."

"And by heaven, it might have been!" he cried.

"Might have been, sir? So you *are* married to Mrs. Fitzherbert after all."

He smiled gaily. "Not even my royal parents know the answer to that."

Emma sighed regretfully. "Well, think how much more displeasing to them *I* would have been, me being, in their eyes, such a slut."

"But such a beautiful slut!" he cried, "and by heaven, sweetheart—!"

She held him away from her, saying quickly, "They would have done anything to prevent it, *anything*." She felt so sad at the thought of the lost opportunity. "Anything," she repeated.

"They would have, and they *shall*, sweetheart."

"What do you mean, sir?"

His highness took her hands in his; he patted them, he kissed them, he patted them again. She let him hold them, although she shivered at his touch.

"Gossip of my interest in you might have reached them already," he went on. "To please and help you I propose to go to them, tell them that Mrs. Fitzherbert—heaven forgive me!—means no more to me, and speak of my desire, my pressing, urgent, passionate desire to form a permanent association with you."

Emma's heart began to beat high with excitement; she could scarcely believe her ears.

"Oh, but you're teasing me!" she said.

"I shall do it at once, today." He laughed boyishly. "Oh, think of their faces!"

"I shall never be able to thank you enough," Emma told him.

"There is, of course"—his voice dropped, his eyes clouded with desire—"the matter of some small reward."

Emma's heart sank. Indecision swamped her. So much, so very much, depended on his help.

"Oh come," he said pettishly, "a woman of *your* easy virtue . . ."

Quick temper got the better of her.

"I was never promiscuous," she cried. "I've given myself to only one man at a time. The only reward I can offer you is Romney's portrait of me. Take it or leave it."

"Damn it all," he exploded, "I am paying him a hundred guineas for the Calypso!"

Emma chuckled. "And your debts, they say, are more than half a million. Will poor Romney get paid, I wonder?"

The prince laughed and released her hands.

"When the Calypso is finished I shall commission another. Romney shall paint you for me as a Magdalene." He strode to the door. "Good day to you, Emma."

"Your Highness—!"

He turned and smiled most charmingly. "I shall keep you in doubt. If I win at cards tonight I shall help you. If I lose . . ." He shrugged. "Well, we shall see."

Sir William, having been summoned hastily to Buckingham House to see the king, was back again at Piccadilly. He was so weak with excitement, or so he claimed, that he was obliged to drink two glasses of wine before he could give Emma, a most impatient Emma, an account of what had happened.

"The queen is greatly displeased," he managed to gasp at last.

"You mean about me and the Prince of Wales?" Emma demanded.

"Yes, yes, my dear. And the king, too, is most displeased. His majesty was so agitated that I feared the madness might overtake him. Quite purple in the face, he was, dear me, yes!—"

"Hamilton—"

"Why, he asked, wringing his hands, had he been cursed with such a son? He himself had never behaved like that when *he* was a young man; *he* had made a respectable marriage and settled down—"

"Hamilton, for goodness' sake, come to the point!" Emma raged.

"Temper, temper!" Sir William admonished, and sounded just like Greville.

"*Hamilton—!*"

"Very well, my dear, very well. Cruel to tease you, I do admit. His majesty looked at me sternly. 'William,' he thundered, 'how soon can you marry this young woman of yours and take her back to Italy?' He completely took my breath away, completely! 'Pon my soul he did!"

Emma burst into tears and flung herself into his arms. Her surroundings faded; she was back in Naples, back in the Palazzo Sessa. She could feel the balmy Neapolitan air, see the heavenly bay with Capri shimmering in the sunlight. Turning from all this, she was passing through the reception rooms of the *palazzo*, full to overflowing with people who bowed before her and shouted her name. She was home again, she, Lady Hamilton, the ambassadress.

"The day after tomorrow," Sir William was saying, "at Marylebone Church . . ."

But Emma was barely listening. She was thinking now of the Prince of Wales. Her heart warmed to him and her conscience smote her. So small a thing, the reward he had asked, and her gratitude being what it was . . . Yet once again the thought revolted her. She could never bring herself to do it, never! She concluded that, at bottom, she was a much nicer person than many people thought. Either that, she told herself solemnly, or she was growing hard . . .

12 Everything was exactly as she had pictured it before leaving England. The reception rooms of the Palazzo Sessa, crammed with people, made a brilliant sight. All Naples was here, eager to welcome home the ambassador and his new wife. She heard her name called on every side; congratulations and extravagant compliments were showered upon her.

And, most important of all, Queen Maria Carolina was here, a queen showing now not the slightest aloofness, calling her "Sweet Emma, my dearest friend," whispering slyly that while she, not King Ferdinand, was the real power in Naples, so would Lady Hamilton be the real power at the British Embassy.

"You and I together," she said, "will be more than a match for the French. We have a mission, *Excellenza*"—How sweet to be thus addressed by a queen!—"a sacred mission, the saving of Europe from revolution."

When it was all over, when the last carriage had rumbled away, Emma stood with her husband on the top floor of the *palazzo*, gazing in rapture at the sheer calm beauty of the Neapolitan night, soon to be lit by the moon now rising, it seemed, out of the very crater of Vesuvius.

"You have no regrets?" Sir William asked quietly. "You are truly happy?"

"As if you needed to ask such a thing!" Emma cried. "You've given me so much, honors and rank and—yes, Hamilton—self-respect. I'm the happiest woman in the world."

"Dear sweet Emma," Sir William murmured, and took her gently in his arms.

Presently Mrs. Cadogan appeared to bid them good night, a subtly changed Mrs. Cadogan, dressed in black, wearing a black apron, with a bunch of keys dangling from her waist. Now established as official housekeeper, she was ready, as she had said many times before, to save Sir William money by keeping a strict watch on the thieving Italian servants. Already they were a little afraid of her and had begun, most respectfully, to address her as *La Signora Madre*.

"Just look at that mountain!" she exclaimed.

The moon was high now, and clouded by the column of smoke, a column with a spreading, flat top, like a great gray mushroom stained by violent spurts of orange flame.

"A majestic sight," Sir William declared.

Mrs. Cadogan shuddered. "Makes me uneasy, it does. Well, good night, Sir William, and good night to you"—her eyes mocked Emma good-humoredly—"My Lady."

But Emma was looking fixedly at Vesuvius. Fancifully she saw it as a representation of France, threatening, but not quite achieving, a monstrous upheaval.

She shivered. "It makes me uneasy, too, but I'm still the happiest woman in the world.

In the months that followed, the happiness continued to an intoxicating degree, being heightened beyond all expectation by the personal importance of the new part Emma was called upon to play as ambassadress.

At the Palazzo Sessa; at the official Embassy in the city; and at the newly acquired seaside villa at Posilipo, enthusiastically renamed the Villa Emma by Sir William, she entertained not only the local nobility but all the important English visitors who passed through Naples. Resuming her correspondence with Greville (what good friends they were when separated by a great distance!) she took delight in many casual references to the lords and ladies she, the ambassadress, had sheltered beneath her "humble" roof.

Within a few weeks of their return to Naples Sir William was taken violently ill, and this illness, a distressing bout of bilious fever, left him apathetic where state affairs were concerned. All he now asked from life, he said, was to be left in peace, which meant that his activities were confined to collecting more and more volcanic specimens, ancient coins, marbles and cameos, to an occasional appearance at the San Carlo Theater and, if the mood was on him, a lazy drive to Posilipo. As for state affairs, why, he asked, should he exert himself unduly when his dear Emma was there to take the tiresome weight from his shoulders? And "Why, indeed!" Emma echoed.

This brought her into constant contact with Maria Carolina, who likewise took the tiresome weight from the shoulders of her king. Emma was present at almost every party, formal and informal, given by the queen, and going frequently to court without the need to wait for an official invitation, she often dined alone with the Neapolitan royal family. "So domesticated at times," she told Greville. "Just the king and queen, me and Sir William, when the dear man is well enough, me singing duets with the king and Sir William accompanying us on his viola."

But beneath this carefree exterior Maria Carolina was consumed with anxiety on behalf of her sister, the queen of France. Both Emma and Sir William, who had spent a week in Paris on the way out, tried to assure her that her fears were exaggerated. There was revolution in France, yes, but a revolution that had done no more than turn Louis XVI into a constitutional monarch.

"How blind you are," Maria Carolina said sadly. "I know in my heart that the revolutionary party will never rest until they have brought about my brother-in-law's complete downfall. Yet England still preaches peace. England is my one hope, but I am beginning to hate her."

"Public opinion in England," said Emma, echoing Sir William's earlier words, "will force the issue yet."

"Public opinion," the queen snapped, "has been gagged by your Mr. Pitt's peace budget. A reduction in taxation, yes, but made possible by a reduction in military forces. Pah! If only England were not an island! She would not then be quite so smug!" She took a deep, angry breath. "Will nobody realize that France is a volcano more dangerous than Vesuvius!"

As time sped by the volcano that was France continued to rumble, and soon Maria Carolina's own Austria (she never forgot that she was a daughter of Maria Theresa) was preparing to make war on the revolutionary government. This brought out an incensed Paris mob, which seized Louis XVI and made him a prisoner in the Temple.

And finally the volcano rumbled into full eruption. Louis XVI was brought to trial, condemned and executed, and revolutionary France, taking Mr. Pitt's attitude for weakness, declared war on England.

Yet the French revolutionaries held back and Marie Antoinette, though still in prison, remained unharmed. It seemed, during those first months of war, that France was face to face with disaster. Austria, Prussia, and Spain, as well as England and Saxony, were in arms against her, while within her own borders peasants revolted in Poitou and Brittany, and her most important naval base, Toulon, fell into the hands of the French royalists.

"Let England strike now, strike at Toulon, and my sister might still be saved!" Maria Carolina cried.

Emma, fussing over Sir William, made him comfortable on the painted gold and green day bed which had been placed by the window. Another attack of bilious fever had left him looking frail and much older than his sixty-three years.

"People will take me for your grandfather," he joked.

"Nonsense, Hamilton," Emma laughed, but she silently agreed with him. "Two or three days and you'll be better than ever."

"I shall never climb Vesuvius again," he said sadly.

"I should hope not, risking your life like that!"

He closed his eyes, and after a moment he asked vaguely about his nephew.

"We forgave Greville, did we not?"

"That we did, whether he deserved it or not."

Sir William opened his eyes. "And your child, the little Emma . . . What did we do about her? I seem to remember that your grandmother died."

"Yes," Emma told him, "Granny died soon after we left England. Mother's sister, Mrs. Connor, took the child. The Connors live in Manchester now."

"You send them money, I hope?"

"Of course I do, Hamilton."

"I think," he pondered, "that your child should go to a good school. I can easily spare a hundred pounds a year."

"That's very generous of you," Emma said warmly.

"Ah, it is easy to be generous when you have the money," Sir William told her. He sat up and gazed out of the window at the view he loved so much. "Dusk with mysterious fingers falls fast across the bay," he murmured, as if quoting. "Why, oh, why must man make war when beauty like this cloaks the world!"

They talked for a while about the war. Maria Carolina, wavering always between high optimism and deep depression, had received news yesterday of the royalist activities at Toulon. They were holding the naval base, the report said, with difficulty. England, Maria Carolina complained, was so *slow*. Much more delay and the opportunity would be lost forever.

"Why, look!" Sir William exclaimed, "a warship in the bay!"

Emma followed the direction of his pointing finger, seeing nothing at first, then recognizing the masts and riggings of the vessel, which seemed to hang there in the gathering dusk, fairylike and elusive.

"Is it a British ship?" she asked.

"Get me the telescope," he said.

Emma did so, and after he had peered through it for a few moments he nodded excitedly.

"Yes, British, and lying-to for the night. The captain will come ashore tomorrow. That is the usual practice."

Attended by Mrs. Cadogan, Emma was making a quick inspection of what Sir William called the Palazzo Sessa's royal suite. Despite the poor state of his health, Sir William had gone early to the port, and now he had sent a message saying that the suite was to be occupied for a few days by the captain of the *Agamemnon*, who brought excellent news and must be received like a prince.

"Everything to your satisfaction?" Mrs. Cadogan challenged.

Emma nodded. "Yes, Mother."

The "excellent news" proved to be that the royalists of Toulon had come to terms with the British admiral, Lord Hood; they were eager to form an alliance with England and had welcomed the landing of a British garrison. Sir William told Emma this while the captain of the *Agamemnon* and his young midshipman son were making themselves acquainted with the royal suite.

"I like the little captain," Sir William added. "Not a handsome man, far from it, but he inspired me with confidence. You will, I know, do all you can to make him comfortable."

"Of course, Hamilton."

"He brings a request for Neapolitan troops, otherwise it might not be possible to hold Toulon. You, with your influence with the queen, should be able to help him there."

Emma's eyes sparkled. A real part to play at last!

"He shall have as many troops as he needs," she said grandly.

She met Sir William's "little captain" before dinner was served and for the first time learned his name.

"Captain Horatio Nelson," Sir William said, in introduction, "my dear wife, Lady Hamilton."

Emma frowned over this. Sir William's manner suggested that she was being presented to the captain, not the captain to her. He was still weak, of course, from his illness, and forgetful as well as agitated.

"And Emma, my love," Sir William went on, "the Captain's son—"

"Stepson," Captain Nelson interposed.

"Ah yes, yes! Josiah—er—?"

"Nisbet," Nelson supplied.

Emma smiled graciously on the boy, trim and serious in his midshipman's uniform. His quick blush touched her heart. He could scarcely be more than fourteen, slim, shy, but with bright merry eyes.

"One of our future admirals," she said, winking at him to put him at his ease.

When they sat down to dinner in the lofty, cool, shuttered dining room, Sir William invited his guest to say grace. The captain inclined his head. "Thank you. My usual grace, then." He leaned forward with closed eyes. "God save the King and bless this food."

As the meal progressed, Emma was able to study him at leisure. She thought he looked very boyish and intense, and she hid a smile at the dandylike air with which he wore his full-dress uniform. He was short and slender, with a straight proud carriage. His sensitive mouth and his hair, tossed untidily back from his forehead, made him look even more boyish. She longed to ask his age. It didn't seem possible that he could have even a *stepson* of fourteen. Nelson? She had heard the name before. Nelson, Nelson?

"Is the *Agamemnon* your first command?" she asked.

Nelson barely glanced at her. "No, I have had others. My last was the *Boreas*."

"Ah, the *Boreas!*" She remembered her first crossing of the English Channel with Gavin Hamilton, and Gavin's enthusiasm, his talk of having met the captain of the *Boreas*. "I once saw the *Boreas* when crossing to France."

Nelson paid no further attention to her and spoke briefly, to no one in particular, of the *Agamemnon*, which he called one of the finest sixty-fours in the service. Affronted, Emma decided indignantly that he was interested in nothing but ships. He had refused wine before dinner; but now, with Sir William proposing the appropriate toasts for such an occasion—"The king!"; "The queen and the royal family!"; and "Admiral, Lord Hood!"—he filled his glass each time, drank deeply, and solemnly passed the decanter across the table. What a pompous little man! Emma thought, yet her eyes were continually drawn to his sensitive mouth. In spite of the fact that her beauty, which inspired all men, affected him not at all, she had the strange feeling that he and she had much in common.

"How splendid to have you here at such a time, Captain Nelson!" she said, determined to arrest his attention. "Your presence makes us realize so fully that the navy—*our* navy—stands firmly between us and French aggression."

Nelson glanced at her momentarily. "Yes." He turned abruptly to Sir William. "My mission is urgent. May we discuss it now?"

Sir William smiled amiably. "You must talk with my good lady. She and the Queen of Naples—or, to give her her full title, the Queen of the Two Sicilies—are thick as thieves."

Emma saw Nelson's face cloud. He was, as Sir William had said, by no means handsome, yet the smile that immediately followed the frown was charming.

"I need ten thousand men, Lady Hamilton."

"We shall discuss the matter later," Emma said, to teach him a lesson.

He looked at Sir William again. "You are perfectly serious? I am to negotiate with the Neapolitan court through your wife?"

"Perfectly serious, my dear fellow, perfectly."

When the meal came to an end Emma laughed lightly.

"Since there are no other ladies for me to withdraw with, I may as well take Mr. Nisbet on a tour of inspection." She saw the boy's quick look of pleasure at the way she had stressed *Mr.* Nisbet, and addressing him directly added, "Unless, of course, you prefer to stay and drink port with Sir William and Captain Nelson."

"I'd rather come with you, Lady Hamilton," Josiah said eagerly.

Emma smiled. She had made a conquest of the stepson, if not the stepfather.

Josiah chattered gaily and excitedly as she led him from room to room of the *palazzo*, and by the time they reached the roof he had lost nearly all of his boyish awkwardness.

With a little prompting here and there she learned that his father had died when he was a baby. This happened in the West Indies, where Captain Nelson later met his mother. Her name was Frances, but Nelson generally called her Fanny.

"She must have been brokenhearted," Emma said, "when her son as well as her husband sailed away in the *Agamemnon*."

"She put a brave face on it," Josiah boasted.

"Just as you did, I'm sure."

Josiah said yes, of course, but blushed faintly; and Emma, seeing her mistake—she had come close to reminding him that he was only a child—asked why he had chosen the navy for a career.

"Didn't you say your father was a doctor?" she added.

"Yes, but Captain Nelson is a sailor."

Admiration and hero worship, Emma thought. "I expect he seems more like your real father than—well—your *real* father."

"He's the only one I remember, Lady Hamilton."

"All the same," she smiled, "it must be a bit awkward, serving under one's own father."

Josiah laughed. "Well, it was at first, but things are all right if I remember when I'm on duty that the captain is just that, the captain." He chuckled reminiscently. "He gave us all a lecture on the quarter-deck, me and the other midshipmen. So stern he was, and he *can* be stern when he wants to. He told us how we were to obey orders without question and never form any opinions of our own about their propriety."

Emma made a face. "In other words, none of your lip, young man!"

"Yes, that's right! 'And secondly,' he said, 'secondly, you must consider every man your enemy who speaks ill of his majesty the king.' Very definite he was about that, even though the king *is* half-crazy all the time. Oh, yes, and then there was that bit about the French. He's always saying it, and he'll say it to you before he's known you twenty-four hours. 'And thirdly,' he said, 'thirdly you must hate a Frenchman as you hate the devil.'"

"I take it he doesn't like the French."

"He never did and he never will."

They rejoined Sir William and Nelson; and presently, at a word from his stepfather, Josiah bade his host and hostess good night. His eyes lingered on Emma for a moment before he left the room, and the admiration she saw in them warmed her heart in a way that made her want to cry.

Seating herself, she wondered what attitude to adopt for Captain Nelson's benefit. After all, his lack of interest in her person was an open challenge. Perhaps it would be best to fall into a pose indicative of sensibility. On the other hand a businesslike attitude, quiet, re-strained but *wise*, might penetrate his indifference; an attitude, in short, which would reveal her as the power behind the ambassador, the intimate confidential friend of the queen, herself the power behind the Neapolitan throne.

"This matter of troops—" Nelson said abruptly.

No finesse, no finesse at all! He could at least have said, "By your leave, Lady Hamilton, but the matter is extremely urgent."

"I have already suggested," Sir William said, "that Nelson and I see King Ferdinand tomorrow morning, and of course, the prime minister, while you, my dear, occupy yourself with the queen." He yawned, apologized, and added, "I anticipate no difficulty, no difficulty whatsoever."

Emma said, "Your glass is empty, Captain Nelson."

Nelson stared at it. "I have had sufficient wine, thank you." He glanced at Sir William; the old man's eyes were closed, his head was nodding. Nelson shrugged and turned to Emma; the shrug suggested that he had no option but to address her. "The assumption appears to be that the queen is the real master."

Emma nodded. "The king is an amiable and rather simple nobody. The queen is a true daughter of Maria Theresa, and in any case her marriage treaty gave her a say in Neapolitan state affairs. Still, I think you will like the king, and if you are interested in hunting he will like you." Nelson's solemn countenance made her want to joke about King Ferdinand. "His majesty used to have just two interests in life, hunting and women; now he has only one—"

"Women?" Nelson questioned mildly.

"No, Captain, hunting. The queen often said that both pursuits were one and the same thing, so naturally—"

Nelson swept this aside with a quick, irritable gesture and asked a question about the provisioning of the *Agamemnon*. It wasn't that he was shocked; Emma saw that clearly. It was merely that he was uninterested, not only in the private life of the king, but in Emma Hamilton the human being, the woman. It was a most infuriating attitude. It had never happened to her before, never!

"My poor fellows," he was saying, "have had not a morsel of fresh meat or vegetables for close on nineteen weeks."

"We'll see to that, the queen and me," she said quickly, horrified at the thought of his crew verging on starvation. "We'll do all we can to help, I promise you."

"Thank you," he said, his manner still abrupt.

She began to lose patience with him and abandoned all thought of any sort of attitude designed to impress him. In the little silence that fell between them now she studied him all over again. His uniform was rather old fashioned, as the flaps on the waistcoat indicated, and his hair was innocent of powder, yet her first impression of dandyism remained. Perhaps it was an instinct with him which he had never given himself the time to cultivate. Out of temper with him, she decided to ignore his young stepson's warning and bait him about France and the French.

133

"Queen Maria Carolina," she said, "is a clever woman. She has a real understanding of the present situation in Europe. She loves and respects England and has a lasting hatred of the French."

Nelson's head shot up. "And by heaven, Madam, I, too, hate the French. I hate their country and I hate their manners."

"And also . . . their women, Captain?"

"I met several when I lived in France for a short time. I refused to look at them."

"Ah, you were afraid you might succumb to their charm."

Nelson's face broke into a slow, attractive smile. "Those I met had the charm of the devil. I have to admit that for a time I was—tempted. I went so far as to try and learn their language—a thing of the devil, too—in order that I might converse with them; but I failed, by the grace of God, and my honor was saved. After that I told myself that, being French, they were naturally ugly."

Emma, softened a little by his smile, began to feel irritated with him again. *She* wasn't French, but he refused to look at her, really *look* at her. Did he think her ugly? Or perhaps he *had* looked at her, and was now intent on saving his honor.

"What a pity," she said, "that you will be unable to converse with the queen. She knows no English and speaks mostly in French."

"The ignorance of these cursed foreigners," he said, but he was smiling again.

"I shall be happy to act as your interpreter," Emma offered.

"Why, thank you, Lady Hamilton." But his charming smile had faded and he went on intensely, "You think I am biased in my hatred of the French; but France—and this I believe with all my heart—is and always will be a menace to the peace of Europe."

"How fierce you sound, Captain," Emma said, and glanced at Sir William. "So fierce that you have disturbed my husband's slumbers."

Sir William yawned and made his apologies. "Damned inhospitable of me. Forgive me, Nelson."

Nelson rose. "If I may be excused, I should like to go to bed early in preparation for tomorrow's activities. I also want to finish a letter to my wife."

Sir William struggled out of his chair and insisted on accompanying his guest to the royal suite. He linked one arm through Emma's, the other through Nelson's.

"I have a feeling," he said warmly, "that this is the beginning of a real friendship."

Nelson laughed pleasantly. "Get me the troops I need, Sir William, and I shall be your friend for life."

When the three of them had bade one another good night and Sir William had tottered off to his own room, Emma lingered for a few moments outside the royal suite. She was deep in thought. Just when she was disliking Nelson' most his delightful smile came to warm her heart. Delightful? Yes, but quite impersonal, too. What a damnable, irritating man he was! And narrow, too. Narrow as only an Englishman could be.

Captain Nelson spent four days in Naples.

With Emma and Sir William acting as interpreters (impossible, of course, to keep the officially appointed ambassador out of things!) he was received twice during the first day by King Ferdinand and Queen Maria Carolina. At the second meeting Nelson declared that their majesties' tremendous enthusiasm and flowery expressions of gratitude embarrassed him, but Emma was quick to note the proud lifting of his head when she told him that the people of Naples regarded him as their savior. A royal promise was made for the immediate use of six thousand troops and later, if humanly possible, the full ten thousand Nelson had requested.

"Thank you, Sir William," he said simply.

This irritated Emma afresh. *Sir William, but not me!* And to make matters worse, Nelson made a point of telling her, privately, that he considered her husband one of the finest gentlemen he had ever met. He had not even noticed—she was sure he hadn't!—that Hamilton looked old enough to be her grandfather.

Meanwhile young Josiah, making up in part for his stepfather's cool indifference, was her constant shadow. "You have undoubtedly made a conquest," Sir William teased her. "I shall have to look to my laurels." She replied tartly that the boy had better manners than his stepfather.

King Ferdinand, stirring himself, gave a banquet at the Palazzo Reale. Such was his majesty's enthusiasm that he insisted on Captain Nelson sitting on his right, a circumstance that angered Emma beyond all reason. To give a mere sea captain precedence over the king of England's minister was unthinkable! Yet, engaging Nelson in conversation later, she assured him that she and the queen, thinking it right and proper, had insisted on it. Why, she asked herself, oh, why must she find it necessary to ingratiate herself with a man she disliked?

135

"I feel," Captain Nelson told Sir William after the banquet, "that I should return the king's hospitality, but the question is, how?"

It was Emma who answered, half-hoping that if Nelson took up her suggestion he, a man unaccustomed to the graces of the fashionable world, would fail miserably as a host to royalty.

"Why not a luncheon party on board the *Agamemnon?*" she said.

Captain Nelson's quick smile made her feel remorseful.

"The *Agamemnon*, Madam, is a warship, not a gilded palace."

"You could, of course, have full use of the Palazzo Sessa," Sir William said, "but nonetheless I think Emma's suggestion an excellent one. The *Agamemnon* is your home, and more, my dear fellow, it represents the might of British seapower. I strongly urge you to do it, 'pon my soul, yes!"

"And feast their majesties on common seamen's fare?" Nelson laughed dryly.

"The entire resources of the Embassy are at your disposal," Emma said, in her grandest manner. "The best food from the kitchens, the best wine from the cellars."

"And the *Signora Madre* will give you all assistance," Sir William urged, explaining, "my esteemed mother-in-law, Nelson, and most efficient housekeeper."

"Thank you," Captain Nelson said seriously. "A luncheon party aboard the *Agamemnon* it shall be."

Preparations were begun immediately under the joint command, as Nelson called it, of himself and Mrs. Cadogan, but the party did not take place. Emma and Sir William went aboard the *Agamemnon* for an early breakfast, a simple meal with everything shipshape, but hardly had it been consumed when a message from the Neapolitan prime minister warned Nelson that a French man-of-war was cruising off Sardinia.

"Upon my honor," Nelson cried, "I must sail without delay."

King Ferdinand, who was to have been welcomed aboard with a cannonading and the hoisting of his royal standard, was informed of the need, as Nelson put it, to show the Neapolitans what a British man-of-war could do in an emergency. The *Agamemnon* was stripped of its gay bunting and the hampers hurriedly brought from the Embassy were hurriedly returned.

Good-bys were brief, though Nelson, shaking hands with Sir William, said that the gratitude he felt would remain in his heart forever. He said the same to Emma, but with less warmth, *much* less, she was sure! And the hand she extended for him to kiss he failed to see.

"Godspeed," Sir William said emotionally, "and a safe return."

"Thank you, Sir William," Nelson said quietly. "My life is in the hands of Him who knows best whether or not to preserve it. To His will do I resign myself. All I ask, whatever happens, is that I shall retain my honor and remember my duty." He turned to Emma for a moment. "A word of warning, Lady Hamilton. King Ferdinand is not as simple as you might think him. Remember that he is the brother of the King of Spain, and that Spain, in my opinion, is not to be trusted."

"I'll remember," she said haughtily, and turned to say good-by to Josiah.

The boy once again made up for his stepfather's "bad manners." Blushing and stammering, he tried to tell Emma how much he had enjoyed her hospitality; and, his eyes worshipping her, he kissed her hand with a clumsy attempt at gallantry.

"Yes, yes," Captain Nelson said, somewhat testily, "Lady Hamilton has been wonderfully kind to you. We must remember to write and tell your mother."

Emma thought that, next to Nelson, she hated Nelson's wife. She hoped she would never see him again, yet beneath this anger and indignation, this unreasoning frustration, was the strangest feeling.

Why, she thought wonderingly, I do believe I respect him more than any man I've ever met.

13

Sir William beamed on Emma.

"Without a doubt," he chuckled, "you have become the power behind the power behind the Neapolitan throne."

"It pleases you to joke," she pouted.

Sir William became instantly serious, his manner now that of a loving but disobedient child sharply reproved.

"I joke, my love, but no one recognizes the seriousness of my words more than I do."

He went on with the task of copying the letter which Emma had brought to him from Maria Carolina, a letter written by the King of Spain to the King of Naples. Emma had roused him from his bed and dragged him down to the library, for it was necessary that the letter should be returned to the Palace of Caserta with all possible speed.

The task finished, he threw down his pen.

"The suggestion that the King of Spain is flirting with France, and that the King of Naples is partly in sympathy, is interesting," he remarked. "Incidentally, it proves that Captain Nelson was right in refusing to trust Spain. How did you get this letter, my dear?"

"It was in Ferdinand's pocket. Maria told me about it during supper. It was a simple matter to make Ferdinand drunk and remove the letter, but Maria wants to replace it before he recovers."

Emma saw her husband hide a smile at her glib use of the Christian names. She scowled at him, just to let him know that a second attempt to tease her would not be welcome. He cleared his throat and said that he had received another letter that afternoon from Captain Nelson.

Emma shrugged. "Really."

Nelson, who had failed to come to close quarters with the French man-of-war off Sardinia, wrote frequently these days, mostly to Sir William, but now and again to Emma herself; and, though she had hoped that she would never see him again, his letters always left her feeling strangely elated.

"Where is Captain Nelson now?" Emma asked, and then she saw the expression on her husband's face. "Is something the matter, Hamilton?"

Sir William said gravely, "He is at Calvi, laying siege to the place, and the stout fellow has suffered what he chooses to call some *slight* injury."

Emma's heart twisted oddly in her breast. "You mean it's really serious?"

"I fear it means the loss of the sight of his right eye."

"Poor Nelson!" she cried, "I shall write to him as soon as I come back from the palace."

Sir William, referring to Nelson's letter, told her how the injury had taken place. Nelson, having planned the siege of this Corsican port, had led his men ashore and under heavy enemy fire had been struck in the face by flying sand and splinters.

"He is the bravest little man I know," Sir William said emotionally. "The heart of a giant beats in that thin frail body. Heaven be praised the injury was not greater."

Emma found herself caught up in the same spate of emotion.

"You couldn't be prouder of him than I am!" she cried warmly.

She carried the story back to Maria Carolina at the palace, enlarging on it to the point of exaggeration as the queen, bending over the still snoring Ferdinand, replaced the "borrowed" letter.

"Your hero now, this man you hate," Maria commented.

"One must recognize bravery when one sees—at least, hears of it," Emma said stiffly.

"One thing only matters," Maria said practically. "Will the British take Corsica?"

"They have already taken the port of Bastia," Emma reminded her.

"True," Maria grunted.

The queen was short-tempered these days and given to deeper depression than usual. She had been like this, Emma reflected, ever since the French, soon after Nelson's hasty departure, had executed her sister, Marie Antoinette. Nor had matters been improved by the British evacuation, three months later, of Toulon. "Thrown out by an impossible man with an impossible name!" she had cried derisively. The fact that six thousand Neapolitan troops had been thrown out too by the previously unknown Napoleon Bonaparte she completely ignored.

"They have already taken Bastia," Emma repeated. "They will take Calvi and throw the French out of Corsica. Nelson guarantees it in his letter." Nelson had done nothing of the kind, but Emma had never been afraid of exaggeration. "*Guarantees* it," she stressed.

Maria, leering somewhat, said again, "Your hero, now."

Letters from Captain Nelson continued to reach the Hamiltons at Naples, letters revealing his hopes and fears and suggesting at times that his superiors were slow to recognize his true worth. After the taking of Calvi, Emma hoped that he would put in at Naples for water and provisions, but it was at Leghorn that he spent Christmas and from there wrote about his uneasiness at the success of the French armies in Europe.

In March, 1795, eighteen months after the Naples visit, Nelson was writing again from Leghorn. He was in a happier mood now and told Sir William and Emma that he was having a miniature done by an Italian artist. But the miniature was not to be sent to Naples; it was for Fanny, his wife, "who is missing me sorely, as indeed I am missing her."

Later in the month he wrote of a "brush" with the French fleet. Corsica, he said, was still safe, but his admiral had desisted too soon, being content with a small success instead of a complete rout of the French. "Had I been in command . . ." he wrote, and added, "The boldest measures are always the safest."

Promotion came a few months later, news of it reaching Naples in a letter from Josiah. Captain Nelson was now, in addition, Colonel of the Chatham Division of Marines. "But they haven't given him a squadron yet," Josiah complained. In a later letter Nelson echoed the complaint. He had been promised a squadron, but was sick with impatience, waiting for the promise to be made good. He was tired of the Mediterranean, tired of pursuing the French and never coming properly to grips with them, and overcome with a longing for the sight of the green fields of England. Yet in the next letter, such was his rapid change of mood, he said how happy he would be to see again the glow of Vesuvius in the night sky of Naples.

Meanwhile Emma's life in Naples continued, on the surface, to be gay and carefree. She was busy organizing dinner parties, musical evenings, and balls; setting a pace with which Sir William, never in very good health these days, no longer struggled to keep up. He was becoming something of a recluse and, taking less and less interest in his official duties, was more inclined than ever to leave all things to Emma and his secretaries.

But beneath the surface gaiety of Neapolitan life anxiety grew as French success followed French success in Europe. The coalition ranged against France was badly shaken; and Spain, as further letters from the King of Spain to the King of Naples revealed, was wavering seriously, while in Naples itself there were alarming signs of unrest and underground revolutionary activities.

Nelson himself was sure that Spain was up to mischief, as he indicated in a letter telling of his promotion to the rank of commodore. "I have my squadron, it is true," he wrote, "but I seem to have little to do but send on to my admiral news of that fellow Bonaparte's successes. I suspect, and this I say in confidence, that your King Ferdinand is ready to desert us, providing Spain makes the first move."

And Spain did make the first move.

Emma was at the palace when news was brought to Maria that Ferdinand had received, in secret, a Spanish courier. Both women instantly thought, Another letter! They hoped that he would, as usual, carry it in his pocket; and Emma sent a message to the Palazzo Sessa telling Sir William that she was remaining at the palace to dine *en famille* with the king and queen.

King Ferdinand's sly smiles during dinner, his occasional little chuckles at, presumably, nothing in particular, told Emma that the news from Spain was of more than ordinary importance. Accordingly she set herself out to be her most charming, and encouraged Ferdinand, not a really difficult task, to drink quite heavily during the meal. He reached the stage of insensibility, Maria said dryly, at least ten minutes sooner than usual. A letter from Spain was indeed in his pocket. Maria extracted it and, her nimble fingers trembling, read it aloud to Emma. Nelson had been right. The King of Spain was on the point of withdrawing from the coalition and joining forces with France.

Emma made an immediate copy, and with this copy hurried back to the Palazzo Sessa. Sir William was in bed. He had suffered another attack of bilious fever and was all but helpless. With a weary shake of his head he acknowledged the seriousness of the letter's contents.

"The copy must be sent to London without delay," he said. "See to it, Emma. I lack the strength to leave my bed."

Later, when Emma had dispatched the courier to London, he said, "My dear, you have done your country a service today which, I trust, will never be forgotten."

Emma smiled happily. She would write not only to Nelson, but to Greville—in any case, she wanted Greville to send her a Dunstable hat—and tell them, oh, in quite modest language, how important a stateswoman she had now become.

Time was slipping by "stealthily," as Sir William put it, and soon Commodore Nelson was writing angrily to say that he had been ordered to assist in the evacuation of Corsica. He was depressed and disgusted, and in his next letter, breaking the news of the decision to withdraw the fleet from the Mediterranean, he spoke of the blow this was to one's honor.

Emma continued to follow his career, but memory of the man himself grew dim. He was just somebody you had formed the habit of writing to—a hero, yes, but no longer her own personal hero. Or so she felt until February, 1797, which brought news of the Battle of Cape St. Vincent and the crushing defeat of the Spanish fleet. This news was received deliriously in Naples. The coalition against France might have been broken, England might stand alone, but England was still a power to be reckoned with.

In celebration Emma filled the Palazzo Sessa with a thousand guests and talked excitedly to everyone of "our dear friend, Commodore Nelson," quite ignoring the fact that Admiral Jervis had been in command. And when news came that, in recognition of his services, Commodore Nelson had received the Order of the Bath she cried, "They'll make him an admiral, too, you just wait and see!"

But this had already happened. Promotion had come to Nelson in the ordinary course of seniority. Quite unaware of the fact, he was a rear-admiral of the Blue before going into action at Cape St. Vincent.

"I can't believe," Emma said, "that four years have passed since Nelson visited Naples."

Emma was taking tea, English fashion, with the queen at the Palace of Caserta. Tea drinking was a habit her majesty had acquired because of Emma, but she had no real love of it. They were talking, as always, about the war; and Emma, enthusiastic still, had remarked that Nelson would rise to even greater heights.

King Ferdinand joined them but he refused tea. "Did I hear you speak of Nelson?" he asked.

"You did," Emma told him, her eyes dancing. "It's an inexhaustible subject. How sorry he must be for himself," she added, taunting him, "—the King of Spain, I mean."

"There will, no doubt, be certain regrets at having joined the French," Ferdinand admitted.

Emma decided to taunt him further and at the same time issue a solemn warning.

"It is wise to mark well what happens when a nation turns against its allies. Nelson came to Naples as a friend four years ago. What a pity if he were to come a second time as an enemy."

Ferdinand sniggered and looked foolish. He remarked that her excellency's French was not as good as usual, then slunk from the room. Maria chuckled, "As your good mother would say, my dearest Emma, you are a little above yourself today."

"To tell the truth," Emma laughed, "I've been a little above myself ever since we heard of Cape St. Vincent. Still, I do apologize. I know I haven't the right to try and put a king in his place."

"Put my fat Ferdinand in his place you did indeed," Maria acknowledged. "It amused me. And when one considers that, unknown to him, he himself supplied the warning which led to the Spanish defeat, my amusement knows no bounds."

Emma held up her head most proudly. It needed only this admission to convince her that she, assisted of course by Maria, had been personally responsible for the British victory.

"Though actually," Maria added, her voice like a dash of cold water in Emma's face, "Spain's declaration of war on England was made well before the battle."

"The letter I copied helped," Emma said warmly. "Nelson himself says it gave them more time for preparation."

"Yes?" Maria teased.

"Yes!" Emma said hotly.

There was a slight commotion in the corridor, and Sir William burst into the room. His unceremonious entry and his evident agitation alarmed Emma.

"Hamilton, what is it?"

"Most dreadful and distressing news," he gasped, and thrust a letter into Emma's hands. "From Nelson, my dear."

Maria rose from her chair. "After victory, defeat!" she moaned.

Emma stared at the letter. She was quite unable to read the few lines of illegible scrawl.

"But this isn't Nelson's writing."

"It was written with his left hand," Sir William told her. "He has been injured in action again. He—my dear, the poor fellow has lost his right arm."

"Oh, Hamilton—*no!*"

"You must write him some few words of comfort, my love. He feels

143

—so ridiculous, it is—he feels that he is of no further use to his country."

A few days later a letter came from Josiah, and this gave them details of the injury, which had taken place during an attack on Santa Cruz.

"We had landed on the mole," Josiah wrote, "and he had drawn his sword. In the confusion of it all, with grapeshot and canister flying about us, I lost sight of him. I retraced my steps a short distance, and there I found him, lying unconscious. His right elbow had been shattered by grapeshot."

Tears filled Emma's eyes. The scene was there before her. She could see Nelson lying at her feet, her hero, the man she had hated because he had failed to recognize her beauty. She read on with difficulty.

"I placed him in the bottom of a boat and the movement, causing him so much pain, brought him back to consciousness. I tried to cover the elbow with my hat, but he insisted on looking at it before he fainted again. I took the handkerchief from my neck and bound the arm above the elbow until the dreadful flow of blood ceased. Lovel, the bargeman, tore up his shirt to make a sling. He revived somewhat after that, insisted on getting to his feet and helped, though in great pain, to save many of our wounded. He said, 'I have my legs and one arm left.' Oh, Lady Hamilton, I shall never forget that, never! And then, when we got him back on board, he said calmly, 'Tell the surgeon to make haste and bring his instruments; I know I must lose this arm and the sooner it is off the better.'"

Emma felt that she could read no more; the tears were flowing down her cheeks, but she forced herself to go on.

"The surgeon operated under the greatest of difficulties, with only a dim lantern for light and the ship rolling horribly. If the admiral cried out, no one heard him, and he had refused the rum which, it is said, is of help before an amputation.

"He is a greater man now with only one arm than he was with both. He claims he would rather have lost both arms than the two hundred men who fell at Santa Cruz; but they, loving him as they did, would rather have died a dozen deaths than seen him suffer like that."

Emma, still weeping, set herself to the task of writing the few words of comfort asked by Sir William; but her hand faltered, and she found it impossible to put into words the things she felt in her heart.

She knew now what the trouble had been from the first.

144

She had never really hated Nelson. Self-importance and vanity had blinded her. She gripped her pen more firmly. She wanted to write the truth, to scribble on the paper over and over again the words, "Nelson, I love you, I always have, right from the beginning." She wanted to, but the thought of his wife, whom he loved and longed to return to, stopped her. Instead she spoke of her distress and sorrow, of her wish that he could come straight to Naples and be nursed by her, and of how proud he must be of Josiah, who had saved his life.

When the letter was finished she gave way to a little fit of temper. "Oh, damn Nelson's wife, damn her!" she cried.

Emma, shading her eyes against the sun, stared out across the shimmering water of the bay. Sir William, standing at her side, shook his head.

"No," he said, "not the *Vanguard*."

Emma was unable to hide her disappointment. "But Nelson may be aboard her, whatever she is."

"The admiral's flag would be flying if he were. The most we can expect, my dear, is news of him."

It was June, 1798. Nelson, after a spell in England, had been given a new ship, the *Vanguard*, and was in the Mediterranean again, in command of twelve sail-of-the-line. He was under orders, a recent letter had told the Hamiltons, to seek out the enemy fleet and take, sink, or otherwise destroy it. Great rejoicing in Naples had greeted this news, which was all the more heartening now that the Roman Republic, so perilously close to Neapolitan territory, was occupied by French troops.

"One thing is certain," Sir William said, "if Bonaparte tries to attack Egypt, he will overreach himself. It would be an act of supreme folly with Nelson ready to cut him off from France."

Later in the morning Sir William and Emma left the Palazzo Sessa for the Embassy in Naples, and there they received the officer in command of the visiting warship. He was Captain Troubridge, often mentioned by Nelson in his letters, and his ship was the *Mutine*.

"Nelson—give us news of Nelson!" Emma cried, casting aside all formality. "Where is he? Is he in good health?"

The shadow of a frown crossed Troubridge's rugged, friendly face; and Emma, seeing it, knew that he resented her eagerness and considered the possessive way she had pronounced Nelson's name a great presumption.

"*Sir Horatio*," he replied, his stressing of the title a reproof in itself, "is in good heart." Turning from her and ignoring her pointedly, he addressed himself solely to Sir William. "I have a letter for Your Excellency from Sir Horatio. He—"

"But where *is* he?" Emma interrupted.

Without looking at her Troubridge said, "Not ten miles away, awaiting my return to the fleet." He handed Sir William the letter. "I respectfully trust that Your Excellency will be able to provide the assistance we need."

"We'll do everything Nelson asks, everything!" Emma cried.

"We ourselves can do little, save argue with King Ferdinand," Sir William said, after reading Nelson's letter. "Our friend needs provisions and, if possible, the help of Neapolitan frigates."

Emma was well aware of King Ferdinand's present attitude. His country was at peace with both England and France, and Ferdinand wanted the situation, ticklish as it was, to remain like that. Much as he might profess to hate the French, he went in constant fear of them and would rather, at this stage, offend England than France.

"I shall take you to his majesty at once," Sir William told Captain Troubridge, "but I have little hope of his cooperation."

When they returned from the Palazzo Reale, where the Neapolitan royal family was at present in residence, Sir William was shaking his head glumly and Captain Troubridge was fuming with indignation.

"I have some little influence at court, Captain," Emma said gently. "Stay here a little longer while I go and see what a mere woman can do."

"Indeed," Captain Troubridge said icily, but he agreed to delay his return to Admiral Nelson until Emma had paid a visit to Queen Maria. "Though Lord knows," he said, "I went in for some straight talking myself just now."

Maria, aware of what had happened, received Emma with sympathy, and together they went to see King Ferdinand. They found him with his prime minister, Acton.

Emma thought of all she knew about this man Acton. He had been born in Besançon, the son of a London goldsmith who had settled in France and married a French girl. As a youth he had entered the naval service of Tuscany. First the captain of a frigate, he had risen to high command until, at the invitation of Maria Carolina, he had taken on the task, twenty years ago, of reorganizing the Neapolitan navy. His love affair with the queen was notorious, and now he was not only prime minister but minister of finance as well; while in recent years he had come into an English title on the death of a cousin and was Sir John Acton, sixth baronet of that name. His sympathies were undoubtedly with England; but, like Ferdinand, he was afraid of France. Looking from him to the king, Emma came to the point at once.

"If Admiral Nelson, through lack of the aid Your Majesty can give him, is defeated by the French," she said, "your neutrality will count for nothing and French hordes will sweep into Naples."

Ferdinand protested that if he helped Admiral Nelson the French ambassador in Naples would hear of it.

"And with the French fleet cruising in the vicinity of Malta," he added, "I— No, no, it is more than I dare risk, Lady Hamilton."

"Malta?" Emma seized on this triumphantly. "So Your Majesty knows where the French fleet is!"

"It was secret information," Ferdinand faltered. "I should not have spoken."

She reflected that if she went back to Captain Troubridge with no more than this information about the French fleet she would have been of some small service to Nelson, but she wanted to do more for him.

"If Malta falls to the French," she said, "Naples or Sicily will be next."

"But with the British fleet at hand . . ." Ferdinand faltered.

"You don't want to help but expect to be protected!" Emma said cuttingly.

"We are placed in an unenviable position, you must admit that," Acton retorted.

"Nelson needs provisions," she urged, the passion in her voice surprising and pleasing her. "Keep your frigates in harbor if you must, Nelson can manage without them, but at least let him have water and provisions."

Ferdinand was wavering. "If it could be done without the French hearing of it *too* soon . . ."

Acton heaved a deep sigh. "There are times when risks must be taken. I see that clearly. Let Captain Troubridge carry letters to Admiral Nelson, letters addressed to the governors of such ports as Syracuse and Palermo."

"Bearing my signature?" Ferdinand said plaintively.

Acton kept a serious face. "Naturally, Your Majesty. The letters would otherwise be useless. Instruct the governors to give Admiral Nelson all aid in respect of provisions. Indicate that discretion is necessary, but stress *all aid*."

Then, flushed with triumph, Emma hurried back to the Embassy while the king and Acton prepared the letters.

Emma was at Posilipo with her mother, inspecting some alterations that had been made at the Villa Emma, when the message reached her from Sir William. The *Mutine* was in the Bay again, under the joint command this time of a Captain Capel and a Lieutenant Hoste, who had come ashore bringing dispatches from Admiral Nelson.

Emma hastened back to Naples, only to find that Sir William had taken Captain Capel and Lieutenant Hoste to see King Ferdinand. The whole Embassy was in an uproar, with the servants dashing excitedly hither and thither and shouting that at last there had been a great naval victory. She called for her carriage again and set out hurriedly for the Palazzo Reale.

"At last!" she told herself, echoing the servants' words.

They had seemed so long and tedious, the weeks and months that had dragged by since Captain Troubridge's visit. Following Nelson's letter of thanks—his squadron had taken on provisions at Syracuse—had come the depressing news that the island of Malta had surrendered to the French. Naturally this had cast the Neapolitan court into immediate gloom, with the queen herself saying reproachfully that the French, it seemed, were more than a match for Nelson. "After Malta, Naples or Sicily!" Ferdinand had groaned, but a few weeks later came the news that Bonaparte, ignoring both Naples and Sicily, had landed an army in Egypt.

Emma reached the Palazzo Reale just as Sir William and Nelson's envoys were leaving. Sir William, his face flushed, his eyes bright, was trembling with excitement. He introduced Captain Capel and Lieutenant Hoste; but Emma, cutting through the introductions, cried,

"Tell me everything, everything!" And, "Why hasn't Nelson come himself?" Fear gripped her heart. "Has he been injured?"

The three men looked grave.

"A head injury," Captain Capel said.

"Serious, but not fatal," Lieutenant Hoste added.

"He must come to Naples!" Emma cried. "He must take a long rest ashore and let me nurse him."

"The admiral intends to come to Naples, at all events to refit," said Hoste, staring at her hard, then blushing as she caught and held his eye. "He is badly in need of a rest, Lady Hamilton," he added lamely. "If you can make him see that you will have the thanks of the whole squadron."

"Tell me about the battle," she demanded.

Captain Capel told her that it had taken place in Aboukir Bay.

"The French were moored in a semicircle," said Hoste, eagerly taking up the story, "and very close to shore. That was a precaution taken by the French admiral, to prevent us from breaking his line, but—"

"But he hadn't counted on the Nelson touch!" Capel broke in. "Sir Horatio saw a chance of forcing a passage between the French and the shore, and took it. If only you could have been there, Lady Hamilton, to see it all!"

"If only I could!" Emma cried.

"We attacked at sunset and gave battle right through the night. The action was long and—begging your pardon—bloody. When the French flagship, *L'Orient*, caught fire and blew up, we saw by the light it gave that things were going well with us. In the end, only two French sail-of-the-line and two frigates escaped. The rest were taken or burned. In Admiral Nelson's own words, it was more than a victory, it was a conquest."

"A conquest, yes!" Emma echoed.

"Nelson is to be given a fitting welcome," Sir William said. "King Ferdinand has ordered it."

"With a French ambassador still in Naples?" Emma laughed. "How brave of him!"

She turned to Captain Capel. "Are there any personal messages from Admiral Nelson?"

"There are indeed," Sir William interposed. "He sends his warmest regards to both of us, and to you, my dear, in particular. He feels that without your aid in that little matter of provisioning this great victory might not have been possible."

Emma felt herself glowing with pride and pleasure. She ignored the "might not have been" and saw quite clearly that the battle was *her* battle; the conquest, as Nelson had so rightly called it, *her* conquest.

"And for this," she thought, "I came to Italy."

She had fulfilled a great and glorious destiny; of that she felt quite sure.

14 Emma and Sir William sat under the awning in the embassy barge, weaving their way with difficulty through the countless gaily painted pleasure craft which filled the bay. It was a glorious morning, warm enough to be unseasonable for September, with a cloudless sky and a calm translucent sea. Ever since dawn, when Admiral Nelson's ships had been sighted off Capri, the Bay of Naples had been aswarm with boats of all description, many of them, like the one now following the embassy barge, crammed with colorfully dressed, excitable musicians. Emma smiled at the gay conflict of joyous sound as "Rule Britannia" rang out on the one hand and "See the Conquering Hero" on the other.

"Little dignity but much enthusiasm," Sir William remarked.

Emma leaned forward eagerly as the barge came in full view of Nelson's flagship, the Vanguard. She had given much thought to the clothes she should wear for this momentous, festive occasion, and had finally chosen a cream muslin gown with cotton embroidery. The waist, she knew, was higher than the present fashion, but in next to no time the ladies of the court would hasten to copy it. Round her shoulders she wore a blue shawl decorated with tiny golden anchors, and in lieu of a hat she had placed across her forehead a bandeau bearing the printed words Nelson and Victory.

Alongside the Vanguard now, and recognized, they were greeted with a salute of thirteen guns. "Viva Nelson!" Emma cried, as the roar of the guns died away. Her cry was taken up by the pleasure craft and rose to an echoing shout across the bay. She herself was the first aboard the Vanguard. How she got up from the barge she was never able to remember, yet the scene of this second meeting with Nelson was one, she knew, that would remain in her mind forever. The sight of his empty sleeve smote her heart; and his frail, worn look was an agony. With a little sob, she flung herself upon him and saw with pleasure that he was just as affected as she was.

"England has much to thank you for, Lady Hamilton," he said gently, looking at her as he had never looked before.

"But more to thank you for, Nelson! Much, much more!"

She clung to his left arm and touched the empty right sleeve, and sobbed again as she glanced at the fixed and sightless eye with its enlarged pupil obscuring the blue of the iris. "Oh, Nelson, how ill they have used you!" Reaching up, she smoothed back his hair, which he wore over his forehead now, and revealed for a moment the still livid scar of the head wound. Emma knew she was making an exhibition of herself, but she cared not at all.

Sir William had come up behind her on the quarter-deck, and now he was carefully holding out his left hand to Nelson, who took it gratefully in a long firm grip. Neither man spoke. There were tears in their eyes. It was the most touching scene Emma had ever witnessed.

A great shout went up from the pleasure craft which now entirely surrounded the *Vanguard*. The gleaming state galley had come alongside, and beneath the silk awnings sat King Ferdinand, a mass, as usual, of black velvet and gold lace.

"An unexpected honor," Sir William said dryly.

"He has thrown all caution to the winds," Emma laughed. "He cares nothing now for the French ambassador."

But Nelson was frowning. "Had he given me those frigates I could have gone into Alexandria and taken Bonaparte's supplies. That would have made an end of the French in Egypt as well as in the Mediterranean, might even have led to their downfall in Europe. However . . ." He shrugged his shoulders, his face cleared and he gave a curt order. "A twenty-one gun salute," he told Emma, smiling broadly, "and only thirteen for you. The lip service one is obliged to pay to royalty!"

Emma laughed with him, but she grew serious as she said, "Never be anything but genuine with me, Nelson. Always tell me truly what is in your heart, otherwise I—" She broke off and laughed again.

"Otherwise—?" Nelson insisted.

"I might grow to hate you." She nearly added "again," but stopped in time. "Come," she cried gaily, "Lord Nelson must greet the king!"

"*Lord* Nelson?" he took her up. He was boyishly flattered and, at the same time, anxious and eager. "What news have you had that has not yet reached me?"

"None," she admitted, "but I naturally expect you to be raised to the peerage."

"I naturally expect it too," he said gravely.

The thunder of the salute in honor of King Ferdinand put a stop to all immediate conversation. When the echoes of it had died away and Ferdinand was struggling up from the state galley, Emma remembered to ask about Nelson's stepson. Josiah had not written to her since he had saved Nelson's life at Santa Cruz, but from time to time Nelson had made brief reference to him in his letters. Young as Josiah was, he had received quick promotion; he was now a captain and his ship, when Emma had last heard, was the *Dolphin*. At the mention of his stepson Nelson's face darkened.

"Was he with you at the Nile?" Emma asked.

"No," Nelson said briefly.

"Is something the matter?"

"Yes, by heaven there is! Josiah joined me later, when Lord St. Vincent sent me some frigates. His lordship was displeased with his behavior and sent him to me to see what I could do with him. He had been drinking heavily and had little or no authority over his men. Distressing, Lady Hamilton, but I am trying to be patient with him. He saved my life, and that is something I can never forget. You want to see him again, of course."

"Of course."

Nelson looked over his shoulder. "Captain Nisbet!"

While greeting Nelson, Emma had been conscious of a large young officer standing a little withdrawn on the quarter-deck. He came forward now, clumsily, and with a scowl on his face.

"But—Josiah!" she cried. "No, I would never have recognized you!"

"Five years is a long time," Josiah muttered.

He added, almost inaudibly, that he was pleased to see Lady Hamilton again, and stepped back.

"Poor boy," Emma told Nelson. "Quite put out because I hadn't remembered him. How old is he now? Eighteen?"

"Nearly nineteen. There's good stuff in him, I feel sure of that."

Josiah was forgotten during the formality of receiving King Ferdinand aboard. Panting with the exertion and surrounded by his resplendently dressed gentlemen, Ferdinand made a long and flowery speech in French and apologized for the absence of the queen, who was in bed with a touch of fever.

"Not even his majesty," Sir William said warmly, when Emma had translated Ferdinand's words for Nelson, "can say enough in praise of my bosom friend—"

"*Our* bosom friend!" Emma put in.

"True, true, my love, *our* bosom friend. Nelson's glorious victory at the Nile has never been equaled in the annals of naval history. Admiral Nelson has made himself immortal."

Nelson waved these compliments aside, yet he enjoyed them, Emma could see that. And indeed he should, she told herself. This was no time for modesty, no time at all, and she told him as much.

"Indeed yes, indeed yes!" King Ferdinand hastily agreed.

His majesty remained on board as the V*anguard* moved slowly towards the quays; and, declaring heartily that if he were not a king he would like to be a sailor, he insisted on a grand tour of inspection. "Here I am safe and happy," he cried; and Emma, who had never left Nelson's side, assured Ferdinand that on a British man-of-war *no one* need go in fear of the French. "As one does on dry land," she added.

Nelson smiled his approval and to Ferdinand said gravely, "We must waste no time in discussing the French problem. In my humble opinion, Your Majesty, the time has come for Naples, if only for its own protection, to send an army north against the invaders."

As Emma made this clear to Ferdinand in French his face began to fall.

"So beautiful a day," he complained, "so great the rejoicing, and one must talk of war. I shall abdicate my throne and join the British navy under Admiral Nelson's command."

"Admiral *Lord* Nelson's command," Emma gave it, in translation and, impulsive as ever, took Nelson's arm in hers. "I feel sure of it, Nelson, sure of it! The very least they can do for you, the very least!"

When Nelson, closely attended by Sir William, Emma, and King Ferdinand, stepped ashore, the quays were crammed with excited, gesticulating sightseers. Cry after cry of "V*iva* Nelson!" greeted him, and at a given signal, while flowers were pelted at him, fishermen released hundreds of birds from the wicker baskets they held above their heads.

"Through Nelson, liberation!" Emma cried, beside herself with excitement.

"Your Ladyship flatters me beyond all reason," Nelson protested, but he was flushing with pleasure.

She led him to an open carriage, carriage and horses alike bedecked with red, white and blue streamers, and, getting in herself, placed him on her right, Sir William on her left. She caught a glimpse of Josiah's unhappy face in the crowd and called to him gaily to follow in another carriage. He was jealous, poor boy; she could see that clearly.

"The Neapolitans have only one thought today," Emma said. "Nelson is their savior."

He smiled happily at her shameless flattery.

"Nelson is a sailor, not a soldier," he told her. "They must learn to help themselves."

Emma immediately judged it wise to fall in with his mood.

"I shall speak to the queen about an army for the north. Ferdinand will never move of his own accord. It will need Maria to *push* him. Maria and . . . me."

The thickest crowds had been left behind now; but even so, as the carriage began the steep ascent of the journey to the Palazzo Sessa, little groups of people stood on corners, waving flags and crying "Viva Nelson!"

"It should be 'Viva Emma Hamilton,'" Nelson cried, "and by heaven, as far as *I* am concerned, it is!" And over and over again he shouted, "Viva Emma Hamilton! Viva Emma Hamilton!"

"Bravo, bravo!" Sir William chimed in, nodding his head and gently clapping his hands. "'Pon my oath, my dear, it seems to me that you, too, have gained immortality."

Emma fell back in her seat. She was proud of the tears in her eyes, and so moved was she by all this adulation that it was some moments before she could speak.

"Just a small select dinner party awaits you," she told Nelson. "Nothing elaborate. We are all too worn out with excitement and emotion to cope with a large gathering. But later, later, Nelson, a grand banquet in your honor. I insist on it, I insist on it!"

"Your Ladyship is much too kind," Nelson protested weakly.

"Come, come, my dear fellow," Sir William laughed, "there is no escape. A banquet we shall indeed give. Can you make the preparations within a week, Emma?"

Emma nodded. "Though it would take a *year* to prepare the sort of banquet we ought to give him."

"A week from now, then!"

"Strangely enough, a week from now will be my birthday," Nelson said.

"Splendid! A double celebration. And a cake, Emma, a cake!"

"How many candles, Nelson?" Emma asked.

Nelson sighed. "Forty, I fear."

"Dear heaven," Sir William moaned, "the prime of life! The best age in all the years of one's life."

"No, no, Hamilton," said Emma, feeling very wise, and ignoring the fact that, at thirty-three, her best years were numbered, "the best

154

age is one's present age, however old one is, if one is truly happy."

"Nelson is truly happy today, he must be," Sir William insisted, "and so for that matter am I. But I still protest that sixty-eight is not my best age."

"Happy! We are all happy!" Emma cried. "This must be the happiest day of your life, Nelson. Or was that the day of the battle?"

"No," Nelson said quietly, "the happiest day was the day I married Lady Nelson."

Sir William beamed on him. "Well said, my dear fellow, well said."

"Lady Nelson is a very fortunate woman," Emma said softly, and tried to forget that Nelson's words had been like a blow in the face to her. "A very fortunate woman," she repeated.

"I want you to meet her some day," Nelson said. "I want you and Fanny to be the best of friends."

And that, too, was like a blow in the face.

A very tired but still excited Sir William was leading his guests out to the garden for the purpose of viewing what he called "Emma's little surprise for Nelson."

"Follow me quickly," he said, "and only look back when I give the word."

They followed him obediently, Emma close at Nelson's side, his favored officers surrounding them and, bringing up the rear, a glowering Josiah Nisbet. It was a still dark night, the air balmy and intoxicating with the scent of flowers, the darkness broken by the fitful glow of Vesuvius and, on the bay, the twinkling lights of the fishing boats.

"Now—turn!" Sir William cried. "Come, come, all of you! Turn and look back at the house!"

The little company turned. In the daylight, approaching the Palazzo Sessa, they had all seen and appreciated the red, white and blue decorations which covered the façade; now, among these decorations, flashed the words NELSON OF THE NILE and, beneath them, the single word VICTORY.

"Three thousand lamps!" Sir William announced.

Congratulations were heaped upon Emma, while Nelson told her that he was scarcely worthy of so much trouble. There was a caress in his voice that made her forget what he had said earlier about the happiest day of his life—until he added that he must remember to tell his wife when he wrote to her later.

The company began to drift back to the house; and, separated from Nelson for a moment by Sir William, Emma found her arm taken detainingly by Josiah.

"What," he jeered, "only three thousand lamps? Surely thirty thousand would have made a braver show."

Emma tried to free herself, but his hand tightened on her arm.

"Josiah, let me go!" she said angrily.

He forced her to stop and held her there until the others had passed out of earshot.

"Josiah, you've been drinking too much!"

"I always drink too much. Hasn't anybody told you?"

She looked at him with pity in her eyes. "Oh, Josiah, to think that the boy I loved should come to this! Why, you're only a boy still. It —it's shameful!"

"Yes, you did love me, didn't you!" he said eagerly. "Just as I loved you. I didn't know what it meant then, but I do now. Or perhaps I did know, young as I was. It's not just your beauty, but something else. Something in your voice, in the way you move, in your eyes when you look at a man. Do you look at all men like that, Emma Hamilton, *do* you?"

Emma twisted out of his grip and, half running, tried to catch up with the others. Josiah caught her quickly, swung her around and gathered her in a quick embrace. His lips were on hers before she could turn her face away. She struggled at first, then grew limp and unresponsive, waiting for him to come to his senses.

"Damn you!" he said, releasing her. "You said you loved me!"

She tried to control the rage she felt. "I loved you when you were a boy, just as I would have loved a son of my own."

"It would be different," Josiah sneered, "if I were a victorious admiral. You'd have my name, then, on a bandeau around your empty head."

Emma flew at him and boxed his ears, but he seemed not to notice.

"Flattering him all the time like that! And that old fool of a husband of yours egging you on. How long, I wonder, before Sir William pushes you into my stepfather's bed and says, 'Here, take her, hero of the Nile'?"

She boxed his ears again, hurting her hands but making no apparent impression on him.

"You'll be sorry in the morning," she panted.

"No, not sorry," he said, a break in his voice, "only tongue-tied. I'll

156

be tongue-tied till I drink more wine. I love my mother, remember that, *Lady* Hamilton. And I love him, too, little cock sparrow that he is. I'm warning you, keep on setting your cap at him and I'll make a *real* scene."

"Josiah—" she pleaded, all the anger gone from her.

"Oh, damn you, damn you!" he shouted and, breaking into a run, fled from her.

She went slowly back to the house. Presently she would say good night to Nelson and he would go to his room to write to his wife.

"Emma!"

She gave a little start. Sir William was coming back to look for her. Sir William—so old, so doddery, so utterly worn out with the day's excitement.

"Yes, Hamilton, I'm coming," she called.

She realized that she had very nearly said, not "Yes, Hamilton," but "Yes, Father." She laughed hysterically, then clung to him and sobbed like a child.

He patted her shoulder absently.

"Dear Emma, you are absolutely exhausted. The joy of this day has been too much for all of us."

Nelson, much recovered, but still worn and frail in appearance, sat writing a letter in the drawing room of the Palazzo Sessa's royal suite while Emma moved restlessly about and talked excitedly of her final plans for the banquet that was to take place tomorrow night. He looked up presently. She could tell from his face that he had not been listening.

"Have you spoken to the queen yet?" he asked.

"I spoke to her this morning, Nelson. She agrees with us that it is better to go out and fight the French than to sit in Naples waiting for them to make an attack."

"And the king himself . . . ?"

"Maria will appeal to his pride and vanity. If possible she will persuade him not only to raise a substantial army but to lead it himself." Emma smiled fondly. "She will draw a comparison between a brave admiral on the one hand, and a slothful king on the other."

Nelson returned her smile, just as fondly, cleared his throat, and went on with his letter. She looked at him thoughtfully for a few moments, her eyes centered absently on the Order of the Bath which was sewn to the coat of his undress uniform. His attitude puzzled her.

There was no doubt that he saw her now through new eyes, recognizing her beauty and agreeing with Sir William that no other woman in the world could rival her. He openly admired the many paintings of her that hung in the *palazzo*, especially the one in which Romney had depicted her as St. Cecilia. And last night, when she had presented her attitudes to a select company of visitors, and someone had compared her with a famous London actress, he had said angrily, "Oh, hang Mrs. Siddons!" He admired her, there was no doubt of that; he admired her almost possessively; but was that to be all? Mere admiration of a work of art?

He put down his pen.

"There!" he said.

"Another letter to Lady Nelson, of course," Emma said sweetly.

"What else!" he laughed. "I wanted to tell her how much improved in health I am, and what a debt of gratitude we owe, Fanny and I, to you and Sir William."

"We have done nothing, Nelson, nothing!"

"You have done everything, everything," he insisted. "Not only did you make my victory possible, you have given me rest and tranquillity when I most needed them."

"I thought you disliked Naples."

"I do, Lady Hamilton, I do!" His voice rose indignantly. "The more I see of life in the city the more I detest the place. The laziness, the immorality, they amaze and shock me. The court itself is decadent, full of whores and scoundrels. But for my hatred of the French I would gladly see this country overrun with them."

Emma nodded her agreement; but she was thinking, what an amazing man! Perhaps his upbringing was responsible for such an attitude. Not only was his father a clergyman, as he had told her yesterday, but his favorite brother as well. She suppressed a little chuckle. Last night she had dreamed that she and Nelson were married, Sir William and Nelson's wife having died suddenly. But just think of it! A father-in-law and a brother-in-law both parsons! And for that matter, a husband as strictly moral as Nelson himself!

"How long have you been married, Nelson?" she asked.

"Twelve years, though I have spent much of that time at sea."

"And you have no children of your own."

"No," Nelson said, frowning. "My dearest wish has been denied me. Except for that, Fanny is the best of wives. I miss her sorely. I wonder, Lady Hamilton, if you would do me the great favor of writing to her? She is naturally anxious about my health and some little word of assurance from you . . . It is not too much to ask, I hope."

It was, indeed it was, but Emma smiled. "I'll do it this very day, but circumspectly. It would never do to make Lady Nelson jealous."

"Jealous?" Nelson smiled in childlike innocence. "As if that were possible."

Irritation rose in her. It was like striking one's head against a stone wall. If he loved her at all, his love was no more than that of a grateful friend. Wanting him as she did— Yes, she now admitted to herself, I do want him!—it was enough to drive her frantic. She wanted his love, the love of the man Nelson for the woman Emma; she wanted it for the rest of her life. But he must come to her of his own accord or not at all.

"And perhaps you might mention Josiah," Nelson suggested. "Poor Fanny is as distressed as I am by his conduct. I was hoping—you were so kind to him before and he was crazy about you—I was hoping your influence now might make him ashamed of himself."

"I'll talk to him later," Emma said, knowing the impossibility of keeping such a promise, "but the young man is consumed with jealousy."

"Jealousy, Lady Hamilton?"

"Of the attention I have been giving his stepfather," Emma said lightly, but watching Nelson's face carefully.

"What nonsense!" he laughed.

He began to write another letter; but this was interrupted by Sir William, who came to say that Sir John Acton was visiting the *palazzo* and wished to consult with Admiral Nelson on the subject of France.

The moment Nelson had departed with Sir William, Emma went to the writing table and shamelessly read the letter he had written to his wife. Skimming through it quickly she found "dear Lady Hamilton" described as "one of the very best women in the world." She noted, with mixed feelings, the underlining of "very best," then read, still with mixed feelings, that she was "an honor to her sex," which was followed, disconcertingly, by "and a living proof that a reputation may be regained." So Nelson *had* heard gossip, knew something of her story, yet he seemed unmoved by it. But, A *reputation may be regained!* That was choice! She had never had a reputation to lose, except during the years she had been married to Sir William, years of—she sought for a fitting phrase—yes, years of exemplary moral rectitude! Finally

159

she read Nelson's last words to his wife. "May Almighty God bless you and give us, in due course, a happy meeting." She nearly burst into tears. To be in love with Nelson was hopeless, hopeless!

The letter he had left unfinished next held her attention. It was to his commanding officer, Admiral Lord St. Vincent, formerly Sir John Jervis. In this she found another reference to herself. "I am writing opposite Lady Hamilton," she read, "therefore you will not be surprised at the glorious jumble of this letter. Were Your Lordship in my place I doubt if you could write so well; our hearts and our hands must be all in a flutter."

"*Well!*" Emma exclaimed.

How different from the tone of the letter to his wife! And what a different complexion it put on his attitude, his innermost feelings. Or . . . did it? Knowing him as she did now she suspected that it was an unconscious attitude. There was no deliberate practice of deceit. He was a little in love with her, she thought happily, and didn't realize it.

How to make him realize it; *that* was the question!

"My love," Sir William declared, "tonight you have excelled yourself."

Nelson was quick to agree. "I never saw the like of it, Lady Hamilton. This splendid gathering is beyond my wildest dreams."

Emma smiled happily. On her right stood Nelson, dapper in his full dress uniform; on her left Sir William, benevolent and paternal, and distinguished as ever, in full court dress. She herself had chosen white again, a muslin gown embroidered with a chain stitch of gold thread. The first Lady Hamilton's pearls were around her throat and from her ears hung the tiny anchor-design earrings which a Neapolitan craftsman had fashioned for her.

The banquet proper, at which a birthday cake made by Mrs. Cadogan had been cut with suitable ceremony, was over; and now many of the sixteen hundred guests were dancing, while the rest stood about in little groups waiting for an opportunity to speak to Admiral Nelson or to receive from him a smile and a nod. And each guest wore on his breast a button and ribbon, given to him on entering the Palazzo Sessa, with the name NELSON printed on it.

"I suggest, my dear," Sir William said, "that you sing, or present your attitudes, or perhaps dance the tarantella for us."

Emma was tempted; never before had there been such a large audience, but she firmly shook her head.

"This is Nelson's night. All I want is to stand at his side."

A slight snigger followed her words. She glanced quickly from Nelson to Sir William. Neither had heard the snigger; neither had noticed Josiah Nisbet now standing just behind them. Emma gave the young man a quick look, her eyes flashing anger. He withdrew a few paces, but remained within sight, his eyes boring into her.

Anger gave place to anxiety. Josiah was drunk enough now to make a scene. His eyes had been on her all through the banquet and had grown more sullen each time Nelson had spoken to her. She remembered with a shudder the menacing way he had half risen in his chair when she had helped Nelson cut up his food. A scene must be avoided now at all costs. She came to a quick decision when the Austrian ambassador joined them and engaged Nelson in conversation.

"Hamilton," she whispered, drawing Sir William aside, "have you noticed Josiah's condition?"

Sir William nodded. "Yes indeed. Ugly, quite ugly."

"Get him to the library on some pretext or other and lock him in."

Sir William hesitated. "Really, my love, I—"

Before anything more could be said, Acton joined them, first to pay Emma punctilious compliments, then, as he drew Nelson and the Austrian ambassador into the conversation, to speak casually about the "French problem."

"Strong action is needed," Emma said impatiently, "and now is the time for it."

And Nelson eagerly echoed her words.

She touched his arm quickly and leaned against his shoulder.

"Be guided by Nelson," she said. "Nelson knows the value of attacking rather than waiting to be attacked."

She was still leaning against his shoulder, the epaulette brushing her cheek, when Josiah, for the moment forgotten, came lumbering into the little group, and pushing his way so roughly that Sir William was sent staggering backward.

"Josiah!" Emma said warningly.

He lurched toward her, his eyes black with fury. She glanced quickly at the others. It was useless to appeal to Sir William, agitated and trembling as he was. As for Acton and the Austrian ambassador, they were trying politely to ignore Josiah's rudeness. And Nelson himself—

161

poor Nelson was still weak from his injury and had only one arm. It would need physical strength to deal with Josiah now.

"I was saving you a dance," Emma said quickly. "Have you come to claim it?"

"Dance with *you*, my lady?" he sneered.

"Josiah!" Nelson warned.

Emma took him by the arm. "Come, let's dance, Josiah."

He shook himself free of her.

"Lady Hamilton," he said, raising his voice, "my stepfather is a respectable man. For my mother's sake I want him to remain like that. You understand, *Lady* Hamilton? He's a fool too, to let his head be turned by your damnable flattery. Such a fool, he can't see that he's allowing you to take my mother's place. He—"

The lad stopped short, looked about him in a dazed manner and burst into tears. It was a ghastly moment. People were crowding around now, eyes alert with interest, ears obviously strained. Fortunately, few of them understood English.

"By heaven, Josiah—!" Nelson cried, starting toward his stepson.

"No, Nelson!" Emma begged.

But Nelson had already seized Josiah by the arm.

"Oh, leave me alone!" Josiah shouted, roughly freeing himself.

And then help came from burly, indignant Captain Troubridge, who placed himself purposefully behind Josiah; though his eyes, in the moment they held Emma's, said in one piercing glance the things that Josiah himself had said. A moment later his big arms closed around Josiah and took him completely by surprise.

"Out with you, my boy," he said, and half-pushing, half-carrying Josiah, removed him from the ballroom.

"We must pretend that nothing has happened," Emma faltered.

"My dear Lady Hamilton," Acton said cheerfully, "nothing *has* happened."

The Austrian ambassador echoed his words and strolled nonchalantly away.

"Young, impressionable, imaginative, and obviously his mother's champion," Sir William remarked sagely.

Emma ignored him, linked her arm through Nelson's, and induced him to stroll about the room with her. He was pale and shaken; his hand trembled on her arm and his face held the strangest look.

"His mother's place . . ." he whispered. He was quivering all over.

"I shall talk to him later. He shall, of course, return to his ship and remain there."

"No one could ever take the place of his mother," Emma said, trying her utmost to sound sincere.

"No," Nelson agreed vaguely, and then, in an attempt at briskness, "I must talk to Acton again. There has been too much delay already." Freeing his arm from hers, he said gently, without looking at her, "Will you excuse me, Lady Hamilton?"

Emma watched him go. She wondered if Josiah had done her a service, but she feared that he had only made matters worse.

15 In the two days that followed the banquet Emma found herself running busily from the Palazzo Sessa to the royal palace of Caserta, conferring with Sir William and Nelson on the one hand, Queen Maria on the other. Nelson called her his personal ambassadress; but his manner was strained, he avoided being alone with her, and he was never able to meet her pleading eyes. It seemed clear that Josiah Nisbet, far from doing her a service, had indeed made matters worse. Finding it necessary to talk to somebody, she mentioned Josiah's scene to Sir William.

"It was unfortunate," he said, "most unfortunate. Nelson has been deeply wounded, but the wound will heal. The friendship we share with him will triumph over Josiah's crass stupidity. Ah!" he burst out, "how precious a thing is friendship."

Friendship, Emma raged within herself, *friendship!* And how blind Hamilton was! Blind and self-complacent. She wanted to say to him, "But I love Nelson, I want him, I need him!" What would Hamilton say if she did? Would he wag his head sagely and say, "Have patience, my dear, have patience?"

Then, still finding it necessary to talk to somebody, she turned to her mother.

Mrs. Cadogan said dryly, "The poor boy was fair upset, and he had a right to be."

"A *right* to be?" Emma echoed indignantly.

"Anybody with half an eye could see it. You taking his mother's place, I mean. An' deliberately, too."

"Oh no, Ma, not *deliberately!*"

"All this honor and glory, and honor and glory it certainly is, has gone to your head. Now if Admiral Nelson was just a nobody—"

"I've loved him since the first time I saw him!" Emma cried passionately. Her hand went to her mouth. "There, Ma, it's out." She threw herself into her mother's arms. "Oh, I'm so *miserable.* I don't know what to do for the best."

Not unkindly, Mrs. Cadogan said, "You're a great one at attitudes. Best thing you can do is strike a new one. What's the word I want, now? Yes, renunciation, that's it. Suit you fine, it would, an' save us all a lot of trouble."

Emma gave her mother a watery smile. "I could do it, of course."

"He's a fine gentleman," Mrs. Cadogan went on, "but he's open to flattery, like the rest. Conceited, too, and willful. Leave him alone, girl, or you'll break Sir William's heart, blind old silly that he is; and Lady Nelson's, too; and maybe your own into the bargain. There now, I hope I've said enough."

Emma kissed her mother. "If Nelson doesn't want me," she said sadly, "my heart's broken already."

On the evening of the third day following the banquet Nelson came back to the Palazzo Sessa after a visit to the *Vanguard*. Emma herself had just returned from a consultation with Queen Maria and had brought Acton with her. A decision had been reached at last; a decision due, she was sure, as much to her own pleadings as to Nelson's straight talking. Her heart glowed with pride and pleasure. Nelson might not want her as a woman, but she was still his personal ambassadress; his cause was her cause; she had worked hard in the past three days and success was now hers.

"I sometimes wonder," Acton remarked, as they waited for Nelson and Sir William to join them, "what the British government will think of Admiral Nelson's—forgive me, Lady Hamilton—of Admiral Nelson's interference in Neapolitan affairs."

"Interference?" Emma raged.

"My dear good Emma, Nelson is a sailor, an admiral, a very great and brave one; but he is not even in supreme command in the Mediterranean, still less a minister plenipotentiary to the court of the Two Sicilies."

"He is under orders," she said warmly, "to seek out the French and destroy them."

"By sea only."

"Why split hairs, Acton? The decision has been made."

Acton inclined his neatly powdered head. "Subject, dear lady, to my own acquiescence. I need more than advice from Admiral Nelson. I need help."

"And you shall have it, I promise you that," she said grandly. "Not that you haven't had help already. Nelson did destroy the French fleet at Aboukir Bay, *remember?*"

Acton bowed ironically. "We have a king and queen in Naples, we have a British ambassador, we even have a celebrated British admiral; but we also have, heaven help us," he added viciously, "Emma Hamilton, the blacksmith's daughter, mistress of the ambassador's nephew, mistress of the ambassador himself before he married her, and soon, if *she* has her way, mistress of the gallant little admiral."

"But never mistress of Prime Minister Acton!" she spat at him. "Is that why you dislike me?"

It was a silly thing to have said. Acton's conduct, though he had admired her enough during the early days in Naples, had always been irreproachable. She made a hasty apology, upon which he turned up his eyes and murmured,

"Vanity of vanities, all is vanity."

Sir William and Nelson came in at this juncture, the cool lofty room echoing with the sharp, almost irritable tapping of Nelson's heels on the parquet floor.

"Success at last!" Emma cried, her eyes challenging Acton.

Nelson merely nodded, while Sir William, smiling fondly, said, "What else was to be expected, with my clever little Emma straining every nerve? Gentlemen, I draw your attention to the one woman in the world who has brains as well as beauty."

Nelson said impatiently, "How soon can an army be sent against the French in Rome?"

"General Mack will be ready to march within ten days," Emma told him. "The king will lead, as is fitting to his royal dignity, but General Mack will *command*."

"I have little confidence," Nelson said testily, "in a general who finds it necessary to travel with five large carriages. I saw them myself. Crammed, all five of them, with personal junk."

Acton laughed easily. "How plain to see that Admiral Nelson dislikes all foreigners, the French not excepted."

"I do," Nelson said promptly, but a fleeting, impish smile crossed his face. "We have already discussed Austrian aid," he added. "Can we be sure of receiving it?"

"We have the word of the Austrian court," Emma told him, "guaranteeing us Austria's support if we act openly against France."

"Ah, but wait, my dear," Sir William interposed, suddenly and surprisingly authoritative, "the wording of the dispatch, if I remember rightly, was support if we—that is, if the Neapolitan government—act openly against the French at Malta. I have some acquaintance with the tortuousness of diplomacy," he added, apologetic now under Emma's look of annoyance, "so the 'at Malta' is perhaps worth remembering."

Nelson said: "We have the problem of Malta on our hands, too. Is there any truth, Acton, in the report that the whole of Malta, with the exception of Valetta, is ready to declare for Naples?"

Acton nodded. "With the exception of Valetta."

Nelson went on: "Is there any guarantee that General Mack *will* march in ten days?"

Acton cleared his throat. Under Nelson's sharp impatience, Emma was glad to see, his earlier opposition had fallen away.

"I should like first," he said, "to be assured of British support at, say, Leghorn."

"I am ready," Nelson replied, "to transport your troops to Leghorn, to take the place and land the troops there."

"Thank you," Acton said, humbly; and Emma's heart swelled with pride.

There was no more to be said. Acton excused himself; and, with Sir William accompanying him to his waiting carriage, Emma was able to have a few moments alone with Nelson. He was instantly embarrassed; she saw that clearly. He wandered about the reception room, looking first at one portrait, then at another, and finally came to a halt at Romney's "Bacchante."

"Nelson!" Emma said insistently.

He turned, but he refused to meet her eyes.

He said curtly, "Tomorrow I sail for Malta."

"Malta? But *why*, Nelson?"

"Whatever the people of Malta themselves are ready to declare, Malta is held by the French, who are well supplied. A blockade is—necessary."

Emma saw that it was, but she also saw that he was glad of an excuse to leave Naples. A blockade of Malta, she thought, wanting to laugh aloud, in order to escape the blockade she had placed on him.

"But tomorrow, Nelson!"

She moved closer to him; and now, for the first time since the night of Josiah's dreadful scene, he looked her full in the face. Or *did* he? Emma had the distressing feeling that his good eye looked through and beyond her, while only the blind eye, fixed and staring, dwelt on her face. It was horrible and uncanny.

He said abruptly, "Has Josiah been to see you?"

She shook her head. "No, Nelson."

"I begged him to apologize," he said.

"*Begged?*"

"No, ordered."

"It would be sweet of him if he did, but I don't expect it."

"You are much too generous," he said harshly.

She sighed. "Why apologize, when the damage has been done?"

"The damage has been done," he agreed, still speaking harshly.

Sir William came ambling back.

"I distrust the Austrians," he said, "'pon my soul, I do."

Nelson turned to him in evident relief and told him of his decision to sail for Malta.

"A wise move," Sir William agreed, "but you will not remain there? Sufficient to establish a blockade, then return to Naples, eh, my dear fellow?"

"I have lingered too long in Naples," Nelson replied. "My base, in any event, should be Syracuse."

"Well, well, you know best, my dear Nelson, but we shall miss you sorely."

"Sorely!" Emma echoed, tears springing to her eyes.

Nelson cleared his throat. "You have been too kind, much too kind. Both of you. I shall miss *you* sorely, both of you. But duty comes first, and—honor."

Emma tried once more. "You promised to transport troops to Leghorn."

"My own presence is scarcely needed for that," he said, and excused himself hurriedly.

He slept that night aboard the *Vanguard* and sailed for Malta at dawn.

After he had gone Emma thought tragically that only the sudden, convenient death of Sir William and Fanny Nelson could ever clear the way for her. This love she felt for Nelson was going to be a grand, pathetic sacrifice, a renunciation whether she liked it or not.

Emma put down her pen and reread the rapid scrawl of her letter. She had started many times to write to Nelson; but each time she had destroyed the unfinished letter, restraining, for once in her life, her natural impulsiveness. Love letters would alarm him still more, would keep him away forever.

Her excuse for writing now was that since his departure for Malta the Neapolitan court had fallen once again into indecision and apathy. She was glad of the further excuse of being able to tell him that, in recognition of his services, he had at last been raised to the peerage. He was Baron Nelson now—only a baron when *she* would have made him a duke!—with a pension of two thousand pounds a year. She was able to tell him, too, that the East India Company had granted him ten thousand pounds, and that fabulous presents had arrived at Naples from the Sultan of Turkey.

"All this for the brave Nelson," she wrote, "but not enough, not by any means enough!"

To touch him she told how one of the queen's children, the young Prince Leopold, tearful at Nelson's departure, had threatened to run away to sea, thinking thereby to meet with the admiral again.

And finally, beseechingly, she begged him to "love dear Hamilton and myself, for we love you dearly."

Impulsively she took up her pen again and added, "Sir William is the best friend, the best husband, I almost say the best *father*."

Renunciation? To the devil with it!

The *Vanguard* was sighted in the Bay of Naples twenty-one days after Emma had watched it sailing slowly out, and Nelson himself reached the Palazzo Sessa just as night was falling. Emma greeted him alone, happy in the knowledge that Sir William, suffering a touch of his old trouble, the bilious fever, had gone early to bed. Not that she wasn't sorry for her husband, but his illness did seem providential.

"Lord Nelson!" she cried. "Baron Nelson of the Nile!"

A brief smile lit Nelson's face. "A baron is the very bottom of the peerage ladder, Emma."

She noted the "Emma," used unconsciously and for the first time.

"Hamilton is furious," she said, "and so am I. He said you should have been made a viscount at the very least. *I* say you should have made a duke."

"I admit to being disappointed," Nelson said.

She took him straight to a room she had prepared for him, prepared in the hope that he would return. It was not in the royal suite, but in a part of the *palazzo* with a better, a more romantic view of the bay. And she sent word down to her chef, instructing him to cook for Admiral Lord Nelson the best meal his art could devise.

"Now," she cried, "you must see the presents from the Sultan of Turkey! Look! I have them all laid out for you."

In childlike excitement she pointed out the sable pelisse; the diamond aigrette; the purse containing two thousand sequins; and, from the sultan's mother, the elaborate box set with diamonds. She slipped into the pelisse herself, holding up the great broad sleeves.

"But, of course," she said soberly, her eyes cast down, "it was meant for Lady Nelson."

Nelson made a vague gesture. She saw then how tired and weary he looked.

"Oh, Nelson, do forgive me for running on like this!"

She made him sit down and poured a glass of wine for him.

"I have had a trying time," he said.

"But a successful one! That goes without saying."

"Yes. We took the outlying island of Gozo without firing a shot—I have the French colors to present to King Ferdinand—but the port of Valetta will prove more difficult. The French are well entrenched there. The blockade will continue, of course."

A little silence fell between them. Emma could see that he wanted desperately to keep on talking, to delay what she had now decided was "the inevitable."

"I hope you received Hamilton's dispatch about the Austrian attitude?" she said, to help him.

"Yes. Sir William was right, after all, about those two little words 'at Malta.'" He made an impatient gesture. "No Austrian assistance for Naples if any other move is made. No Austrian assistance unless the French are the first to begin hostilities."

Silence fell between them again.

Emma broke it at last with a half-fearful, whispered, "And so you came back, Nelson."

He was looking at her intently. "And so I came back."

"You were needed, you were needed badly."

He rose from the chair and turned his back on her.

"Conditions in Naples made it necessary, but I had decided to come back before I received your letter."

The words were torn from him; she was sure of that.

She waited for him to turn, but still he kept his back to her and spoke no more. It was an intolerable silence this time. Poor Nelson, she thought, what a struggle for him, what a desperate struggle! Honor and duty on the one hand, love on the other.

"Josiah came to see me," she said. "He apologized. He was ashamed of himself."

"As I am," Nelson said.

"I was hurt and insulted that night," she went on, "but Josiah did what he thought was best. Oh, in a stupid way, I admit; but underneath he was so earnest about it all that, afterward, I wanted to cry."

Nelson turned then. "What an extraordinary woman you are, Emma."

The "Emma" again!

"Josiah," he continued, "opened my eyes that night to the truth. So I went away, and now I have come back—I, God help me, who was always an honorable man, a man who placed duty before all else." He looked at her pleadingly. "Tell me, Emma, I beg of you, that you, too, place duty before all else. Tell me!"

This was not what she had expected, but she uttered the words he was waiting for.

"I do, Nelson, I swear I do."

"It was wrong of me to come to you like this," Nelson said.

"Yes," she agreed, but he had come, he had come!

"You must help me—promise, Emma, that you will!—to forget this beautiful, terrible thing that has happened to us."

"I know what you mean, Nelson," she said, "and I'll try, I swear I will!"

But when he left her, rushing away to see Acton and the king without eating the food sent up from the kitchens, the wine in his glass untouched, she was still wearing the sable pelisse, which had been meant for Lady Nelson.

During the few days that Nelson remained in Naples Emma saw him only in the presence of others. The room she had prepared for him remained unoccupied. He slept aboard his flagship, saying that the pressure of affairs made it necessary. He was constantly at the royal palace, conferring, arguing, pleading, now with King Ferdinand, now with John Acton, and Emma and Sir William were ever at his side, joining forces with him, interpreting for him.

One conference in particular stood out vividly in Emma's mind. Maria was ill again but had risen from her bed. Her condition was pitiful. All the scorn, all the former fire, had gone out of her. In a quivering voice she said that her greatest fear was that Nelson would leave the coast of Naples unguarded.

"That was never my intention," Nelson told her, with Emma interpreting. "If it had been, how could I withstand the plea of a queen I admire so much?"

"And still you quake with fear!" Maria reproached her husband.

"No, no, my love," Ferdinand protested. "I am ready at a moment's notice to lead the army."

Nelson said: "The plan was to attack the French on three fronts. A neat plan, a neat trap, but if the Austrians refuse to join us we will have to be content with two fronts." He turned to Acton. "Aid from Austria cannot be counted on?"

Acton shook his head. "Not unless the French attack first."

"By then it would be too late!" Nelson said scathingly. "How many men do you wish me to land at Leghorn for our second front?"

"Four or five thousand."

"And how many men can go north by land?"

"Thirty thousand."

"If the decision is made, why the delay? I can embark your men and sail for Leghorn at very short notice."

When this had been translated for Ferdinand's benefit, Acton exchanged a quick glance with Ferdinand, who squared his shoulders manfully.

"The lack of Austrian aid is the only thing that makes us hesitate," Acton said.

A flush of anger and despair suffused Nelson's cheeks. "Very well, then, one of two things will happen to you. You may advance and risk death by the sword, or you may remain in Naples twiddling your thumbs till the French come and depose you."

Maria threw up her arms, moaned, screamed at Ferdinand, and sobbed hysterically.

"Well?" Nelson demanded.

"There is, of course," Ferdinand temporized, "the question of financial aid from your country."

The moment Emma had translated this Nelson tried desperately to express himself in French, grew angry at his failure and said in English that there was ample public money in Naples if only the court and the nobility would cease from squandering it on themselves. He said that Naples was not worth helping unless it showed a willingness to help itself, and he added violently that he was ready to be done with the whole frustrating business and give his entire attention to the French in Egypt.

Acton's face froze, Ferdinand looked sheepish, and Maria fainted. Emma fussed over her; servants were summoned and ran excitedly about until, finally, she recovered.

"I am but a poor weak woman, desperately ill, heartbroken," she sobbed. "I shall go into a convent and leave my husband, brave man that he is, to be deposed alone."

Ferdinand looked appealingly at Acton. "The decision is made, yes?"

Acton shrugged. "The decision, I fear, is made."

Ferdinand smiled happily. "That is good! We will now review the troops!"

Nelson thought this a waste of time; but he went through with the elaborate ceremony, only to report afterward to Emma and Sir William that what he had seen had filled him with certain misgivings.

"A pretty display," he said, "but the officers seem a poor lot to me. Overdressed and handsome, damnably handsome; but nice clothes and good looks don't win battles."

When the Neapolitan troops he was to take to Leghorn had embarked, Emma and Sir William went aboard the *Vanguard* to bid him Godspeed. They stood for a few moments with him in his day cabin, Emma feeling as awkward as Nelson looked, and glad that Sir William himself was present. It was a day of dull heavy clouds and a moaning wind that made Emma shudder.

"It will be blowing a gale by nightfall," Nelson remarked.

Emma was glancing about the cabin, and her eyes had come to rest on an amazing object which had been propped up against the bulkhead immediately behind Nelson's Windsor chair.

"Nelson, that isn't a—a *coffin?*"

"Yes," Nelson laughed. "The coffin I intend to be buried in."

"But how horrible!"

"Not that I intend to be buried just yet," he said. "You see, it was made from one of my trophies, from the mainmast of the French flagship, *L'Orient.*"

"A somewhat macabre idea," Sir William remarked.

"It's horrible, horrible!" Emma cried.

"A sailor must die sometime, be buried somewhere," Nelson said curtly.

Emma and Sir William went ashore soon after that, Sir William saying, "I trust, my dear fellow, that we shall see you in Naples again in the not too distant future."

Nelson looked at Emma for a brief moment. "If God so wills it, Sir William."

Later in the day, from a window at the Palazzo Sessa, Emma watched Nelson's ships sail out of the bay and listened to the unhappy, tormented sound of the wind. She found it impossible to get thoughts of the coffin out of her mind.

"It's a bad thing," she told Sir William miserably. "We'll never see Nelson again. Never!"

173

16 Two days after Nelson's departure the army, led by King Ferdinand and commanded by General Mack, marched north; and Emma was left restlessly to wait for news. When it came, the whole of Naples went wild with joy. First it was announced that Admiral Lord Nelson had landed the Neapolitan troops at Leghorn without active opposition, then that the army under Ferdinand and Mack had marched in triumph into Rome. And almost immediately afterward, Emma heard that Nelson was returning to Naples.

"He can't keep away!" she told herself happily.

But before he arrived it became dismally clear that the joy of the Neapolitans had been premature, for rumors of defeat began to reach the capital in quick, bewildering succession. It was even said that General Mack himself had been taken prisoner.

Emma hastened to the palace, but for once she was refused access to the queen. She was told curtly that her majesty had retired to her bed with a feverish cold. Emma was skeptical and went to see Acton, but he would neither confirm nor deny the rumors.

The only information to reach the British Embassy was disconcerting.

"There have been desertions," Sir William told her, "even among the officers."

"But how can you be so sure?" she demanded.

"I have seen three officers personally known to me. They have come back to Naples in civilian clothes. And when I questioned them, all they would say was that, on the march to Rome, they went thirty-six hours without food."

"Incredible! Shameful!" Emma cried. "Yet the army entered Rome in triumph!"

"I suspect that it walked into a trap."

The many rumors were still unconfirmed when Nelson arrived. By this time Sir William, doggedly purposeful, was gathering together the art treasures he most prized and was having them packed for shipment to London.

Nelson made one comment. "If General Mack has been defeated the French will take Naples within two weeks."

He then demanded an audience with the queen. After some delay he was summoned to the Palazzo Reale. He went, accompanied as usual by his interpreters, Emma and Sir William.

Maria received them in the privacy of her boudoir. There was no doubt that she was ill. Her cheeks were tear-stained, her face ugly and bloated with much weeping.

"My heart is broken," she sobbed.

"Ask her," Nelson commanded, "to tell us all she knows."

Maria sighed and spoke briefly to Emma, who explained in English: "The French have a well-equipped army of thirteen thousand at Castellana. Ferdinand still has about twenty thousand men, but Maria says they are rabbits. The right wing of the army has been driven back."

"Has Mack been captured?"

"No, that was just a rumor."

"The truth is bad enough," Nelson grunted.

"What does Lord Nelson say?" Maria asked timidly.

"That the situation is serious," Emma replied.

"And what, my dear Emma, does he suggest?"

Emma put this question to him.

He said one word: "Evacuation."

Maria nodded sorrowfully. "There is always our island of Sicily."

As they left the palace, Emma hung back with Nelson in one of the reception rooms while Sir William, lost in thought, strode ahead.

"You look so tired and worn," Emma told Nelson. "Please do us the favor of staying ashore at the Palazzo Sessa."

He said curtly, "It is more necessary than ever that I should remain on board the *Vanguard*."

She touched his arm quickly. "Oh, Nelson, I give you my word not to—"

He looked at her briefly; his face softened.

"Dearest Emma, I trust you no more than I trust myself."

"You came back, Nelson!"

He ignored this. "I must remain on the *Vanguard*," he insisted, "and keep everything in readiness for a hasty departure. I am prepared to evacuate the royal family—please make that clear to the queen—but more important to me than the royal family are you and Sir William."

At this moment, Sir William came hurrying back to them, his face broken with alarm.

"A demonstration!" he cried. "Our carriage is surrounded."

"A demonstration against *us*?" Emma said, unbelievingly.

175

"No, no, against the royal family, I think."

They went out to the carriage. It was indeed surrounded, as was, by now, the whole palace. The mob, which seemed to have appeared from nowhere, was shouting, gesticulating, booing. At the sight of Nelson a little silence fell, and a way was cleared to the carriage. The moment Nelson was seated between Emma and Sir William the shouting and booing broke out again.

"What in heaven's name are they jabbering about?" Nelson asked testily.

Emma looked puzzled. "They want to see the king."

"The . . . king?"

"I can't understand it. Ferdinand is with the army. They know that well enough." She listened for a moment. "They say that unless he shows himself they will storm the palace."

Silence fell again.

"Gracious heaven—look!" Sir William gasped.

Emma and Nelson looked in the direction of his pointing finger.

There stood Ferdinand, on one of the balconies, bowing uncertainly, trying to smile, and bowing again. He was dressed in civilian clothes, the inevitable mass of black velvet and gold lace.

"If the king deserts his army, what can you expect of his officers!" Nelson said coldly.

The shouting and booing broke out again; and Ferdinand, as if pulled back on strings, disappeared from sight.

"Maria must have known of his presence all the time," Emma cried indignantly.

"You spoke of evacuation," Sir William told Nelson sadly, "but I doubt if the mob will allow it, now."

Emma smiled in sudden delight and all but clapped her hands.

"Hamilton! The secret passage!"

Nelson smiled, too. "Ah, so there's a secret passage."

"Yes! From the palace to the Vittoria landing stage at the Molo Figlio."

Nelson shrugged. "Indecision may continue to rule the court, but the *Vanguard*, as well as my other ships, is at the royal family's disposal. Meanwhile, in case the French sweep into the city, I shall move the *Vanguard* to a berth beyond the range of the forts. Be ready to come aboard at a moment's notice. I shall do all I can for the royal family, but my first thought is for my friends."

Emma and Mrs. Cadogan stood back in the shadows at the servants' entrance watching the trusted footmen of Queen Maria unload the coach and speaking cheerily to them as they carried the casks—it was casks this time—into the Embassy. Both women wore shawls over their heads and had cloaks wrapped tightly round their bodies, so cold and bleak was this winter's night in Naples.

"Is that the lot?" Mrs. Cadogan asked the servant in charge.

"No, no, Signora Madre, there is one more coach to come tonight."

He bowed and departed. He was dressed in plain clothes, not the usual livery, and the coach was an old, unpainted one, bearing no resemblance to a royal equippage. Emma quickly examined the casks. They were marked "Stores for Nelson," as were all the crates and boxes now being brought from the palace. Thus labeled, they were safe still, even from the thieves and beggars of the city. In actual fact they contained royal possessions and treasures brought under cover of darkness, and by devious routes, to the Embassy. Tomorrow they would be taken by Nelson's seamen to the *Vanguard*.

"Exciting, isn't it!" Emma cried. "Just like something in a novel."

"People get their throats slit in that sort of novel," Mrs. Cadogan said dryly. "Lord save us, I never dreamed when I left my native village that I'd end up like this."

"You wait here for the last coach," Emma said. "I want to see if there's any definite news from the king."

She went quickly to Sir William's study and, to her intense delight, found Nelson there, wrapped in a cloak and carrying his cocked hat. Sir William himself greeted her querulously.

"Three o'clock, Emma. These late nights are killing me!"

"Is there any news yet?" she asked Nelson.

Nelson scowled. "Within the space of five minutes the king agreed to evacuate, decided against it, agreed again, and decided against it once again."

"And the queen?"

"She seems incapable of any decision, except that the royal treasure must be sent to the *Vanguard*."

"A sufficient decision in itself," Emma smiled. "A little hint that you'll sail without the royal family should be all that's needed now."

Nelson nodded. "The hint has been given." He turned to Sir William, started to speak, then laughed softly. Sir William had fallen asleep in his chair. "Poor old man, he is utterly worn out."

"And so are you, Nelson," Emma said.

Sir William woke with a start. "Nelson, my dear fellow, Emma, my love—if I could be excused? I need sleep. I need it badly."

Pleased at the chance to be alone with Nelson, Emma urged her husband to go to bed at once; and, still apologizing, he tottered from the room, exclaiming that it would break his heart to leave the personal treasures still at the Palazzo Sessa to the French.

"Flight!" Nelson broke out, after a moment's silence. "Evacuation! It goes against the grain, by heaven it does!"

"We are doing the best we can for them," Emma said warmly. She liked the use of "we"; it drew her closer to Nelson, thrust out the world at large. "And the time will come when we shall bring them back again."

"I hope and pray it will," he said fervently.

"It will, Nelson, it will! There is no dishonor in this flight. In the end it will lead to greater honor." She remembered his other favorite word, duty. "We are doing our duty, Nelson, nay, *more* than our duty." She dropped her voice and added, "Do you realize that this is the first time we have been alone since you came back from Leghorn?"

"Yes," he said, his voice barely above a whisper. He cleared his throat and went on loudly. "I have made plans, detailed plans, for the evacuation of the royal family."

"Do you know what I think?" Emma said sadly. "I think you have been trying to avoid me."

He cleared his throat again. "I inspected the secret passage this afternoon. It will serve our purpose well."

"You've been afraid of being alone with me, Nelson."

He turned from her. "When the king finally agrees and the date is settled," he said harshly, "I shall have three barges and a cutter sent to the Molo Figlio after nightfall. I suggest—"

"It has been just as hard for me as for you."

"I suggest," he went on angrily, "the time of half-past seven precisely." He looked at her quickly. "It must have been torment for you, then. Torment!"

"Oh, Nelson, it was, it was!" She took a step toward him. "This struggle against the inevitable is too much for me. Can't you see that? Can't you?"

"But *is* it inevitable?" he pleaded. "Emma, my dear, I value your friendship so much, yours and Sir William's. I want to keep it."

"How differently we look at things," she said sadly.

"Differently?"

"Honor, duty, self-respect . . . Words, just words! Loving you I feel honor for nobody, for nothing, only for you. Loving you I have a duty to nobody but you. I have never loved before, Nelson. Never! I know that now. I shall never love again. If you were to die I would be lost, utterly lost. I might live on, but I would cease to exist!"

She had begun by choosing her words carefully, weighing them, calculating their effect on him; now she knew that she had spoken from the heart. She had meant every word, every single word.

"Love of the spirit," Nelson said urgently, "we have that, Emma, we have that now! Let us be content with it, please let us be content with it. It places us above the world, leaves us untouched by the world."

"And makes us inhuman!" she said passionately.

"We must think of other people, Emma!"

"As if I cared about your wife! And Hamilton, he's an old, old man. He's more like an older brother, or a father."

"For heaven's sake, don't talk like that!" Nelson begged. "You're stronger than I, Emma. Help me by giving me a little of your own strength."

A few more words and he would be lost, his scruples forgotten. Emma saw that clearly. But afterward there would be recriminations, self-reproach. She saw that clearly, too. They were talking too much. That was the trouble. Love as tremendous as theirs should take them up in a wordless wave of emotion. It should just *happen*, and now was not the time.

"Forgive me, Nelson," she said contritely. "I promised to help you and I forgot that promise." Then, to torment him a little, she added, "When we leave Naples it would be better if we traveled in separate ships."

"No!" he said sharply, "I need my friends at my side."

He wanted everything, everything! It was more than flesh and blood could stand. And in the end he would break her heart. She was sure of it, sure of it.

"Do I ask too much of you?" he said miserably.

Before she could answer, one of the Embassy footmen entered the room. He was followed by Queen Maria's confidential secretary who, after bowing hurriedly, spoke to Emma in rapid Italian.

"All arrangements will be made," Emma said quickly. "Tell her majesty that."

"Well?" Nelson demanded, when both men had withdrawn. "Is it the news I was waiting for?"

Emma nodded. "There have been risings in the city. Several people have been killed. There are also reports of a French advance. The royal family will go aboard the Vanguard whenever you say. They feel they will be safe in Sicily, at their second capital, Palermo. Ferdinand awaits your instructions."

The dazzling splendor of the reception given by the Turkish ambassador was almost too much for Emma. Dazed through lack of sleep, she was sitting for a moment in an alcove a little withdrawn from the crowd. Desperately she tried to pull herself together.

Everything was in readiness; and this reception, at which the ambassador had presented Nelson with the Plume of Honor, was fitting nicely into the intricate moves of the general plan. No one would ever suspect that the drama of evacuation would take place on a night like this.

She rose wearily as Nelson and Sir William joined her in the alcove. So short a time, she thought, since Nelson's great naval victory, and now *this*.

"Bless my soul," Sir William moaned, "I feel as if the end of the world had come."

Nelson gave him a brief, sympathetic smile and said curtly to Emma: "The plan of action is fully understood?"

"Yes, Nelson. Everybody knows that another reception has been prepared at the Embassy. I got word just now that sightseers are already gathering there to watch your arrival. Nobody guesses that neither you nor Hamilton nor I will ever go to the Embassy again—until the triumphant return from Palermo, I mean."

"The embassy carriage is waiting outside?"

"Yes, Nelson."

"You understand that it is to be left there, that we three are to go from here by the back entrance, where a plain carriage is waiting?"

"Yes, but we've gone through all this before."

"I want no mistakes, Emma. Tell me what is to happen next."

Like a child repeating a lesson, Emma said: "My mother is already waiting at our private barge. She has taken all our clothes and linen and personal valuables. Sir William will join her at the barge. You and I will go to the palace, enter it secretly, join Maria and Ferdinand and escort them down the secret passage to the Molo Figlio. You will conduct them to the *Vanguard*, then I'll join Mother and Sir William at the embassy barge and we'll go out to the *Vanguard*, too."

"Excellent!" Nelson said. His voice softened for a moment. "How hard you have worked, Emma! What a debt of gratitude the king and queen owe you."

"Nothing compared with the debt of gratitude they owe you, Nelson!" she responded quickly.

He laughed shortly. "In their hearts they probably blame me for encouraging them to attack the French."

"The French would have moved against Naples in any case," Emma said stoutly.

Nelson took out his watch. "Time to make a move. We will leave the reception one by one. No need to speak to the ambassador. He knows all about our plan."

Sir William went first; he was followed a few moments later by Nelson. When Emma joined them at the back entrance Nelson was remarking that the elements were against them. The night was dark and stormy, with a gale blowing up.

Nelson was in full dress uniform; Sir William, in his court dress, even wore new, silver-buckled shoes which, he complained, pinched his feet; Emma had dressed carefully in a green velvet gown with a hampering little train.

In the waiting carriage Emma found a cloak placed there for her by Mrs. Cadogan. Before she wrapped it about her she lifted the skirt of her gown to her knees and tied it there. They drove in silence to the secret entrance of the Palazzo Reale, where they left Sir William to drive on alone to the embassy barge.

In the queen's apartments Nelson and Emma found all in confusion. There seemed to be children and servants everywhere; and Maria, sitting on the edge of a chair, was surrounded by bundles and boxes, while clutched in her hands was her jewel case. Ferdinand himself was strutting nervously about, slapping his hands together and throwing out his chest.

"Actual flight may not be necessary," he said. "Once we are aboard the *Vanguard* I hope to come to terms with my people in Naples and organize resistance against the French."

Nelson struggled to control his anger and contempt when Emma had translated these boastful words. "If the king will be guided by me," he said, "he will go without waste of time to Palermo. Tell him that."

"We will see, we will see," Ferdinand said airily. "Meanwhile let us board the *Vanguard*."

Emma herself led the way into the secret passage, holding in one hand a dark lantern provided earlier by Nelson. From time to time she looked back over her shoulder at Nelson impatiently shepherding the king and queen and the hysterical children, one of whom, the six-year-old Prince Alberto, he held by the hand. Servants brought up the rear, carrying bundles of clothing and blankets and staggering under the weight of casks of gold.

At the Molo Figlio three barges were alongside, guarded by a cutter holding sailors armed with cutlasses. The wind was moaning and a heavy sea was running; the embarkation of the royal family was made with difficulty, amid cries of terror from the younger children. Emma kissed Alberto, told him he would be safe with Admiral Nelson and coaxed from him an unwilling smile. When all were embarked Nelson stepped into the cutter, leaving Emma, a lone figure, her hair streaming in the wind, to wave and call encouragement to the children.

Finally, when the barges and the cutter were lost to sight in the darkness and the black anger of the sea, she made her way along the mole to the carriage that was waiting for her, and presently joined Sir William and Mrs. Cadogan in the embassy barge. Sir William had been seasick already, and Mrs. Cadogan was ministering to him as best she could, talking to him as if he were a child and forcing him to take little sips of brandy. He looked so old and ill and desperate, so little like the active man he had once been, that Emma's heart went out to him.

"Look on the bright side," she said kindly. "We'll all have a nice long rest when we get to Palermo."

"If we ever do get there," he groaned.

The crew cast off, and the nightmare passage to the *Vanguard* began. For a moment fear gripped Emma's heart. She looked in horror at the boiling sea, at the sweating men wrestling with the oars, at the blackness of the night that enveloped them. And then, casting out fear, came an inspiring thought.

"Ma," she cried exultantly, "do you know what we're doing, Nelson an' me?"

"Can't say as I do," Mrs. Cadogan replied.

With shining eyes Emma clasped her hands in front of her and whispered:

"We're making history, *that's* what we're doing!"

Nelson was going with her on what she called "her rounds."

They had just left the king's cabin, where his majesty, groaning loudly, lay prostrate, and were now entering the queen's, where a brisk and businesslike Mrs. Cadogan was in command. Maria was in no better shape than Ferdinand, but she was trying to put a brave face on it. What distressed Emma most was the violent sickness of the little Prince Alberto.

"The storm gets worse," Maria moaned.

"It certainly blows harder than I have ever known it," Nelson said, and added somberly, "Had his majesty not delayed so long in the bay we might have reached Palermo before the worst of it set in."

Emma spoke soothingly to Maria and stroked the little prince's fevered brow. He squirmed in the cot that had been set up for him and stared up at her blankly.

"I don't like the look of him," Mrs. Cadogan whispered. "Just about having convulsions, he is. Better send the surgeon, Emma."

Emma found the surgeon in the wardroom, attending to Acton who, with other members of the government, had been given improvised accommodation there. Then, with Nelson still at her side, she continued her rounds. Such a tossing was the Vanguard getting that at times she found it hard to keep from falling.

"I want you to rest for a few hours," Nelson said. "I insist on it. You've been on your feet ever since we came aboard."

"I can't rest," she told him. "I just can't. The poor queen and all the others—somebody has to look after them. Every single servant seems to be either paralyzed with terror or violently sick."

"What an angel you are!" he said violently.

She smiled happily. Any opportunity of increasing his admiration was welcome, bringing closer as it did his ultimate capitulation. Nevertheless, she judged it wiser at this stage to remain matter-of-fact.

"It is fortunate I have a strong stomach," she said.

Now they went into the narrow, airless cabin occupied by Sir William. He looked at them wildly. He was sitting on the edge of his cot, nursing, of all things, a pair of pistols. His face was green, and when he spoke his voice rose hysterically.

"This storm! This pitching and tossing! This constant gug-gug of water! And what was that crash I heard just now? Tell me, Nelson, what was it?"

"The three topsails, splitting."

"Merciful heavens! Then we shall founder at any moment!"

"Things are not quite so desperate as all that," Nelson said cheerfully.

Sir William brandished his pistols. "Rather than drown, rather than hear myself going gug-gug-gug in the water, I shall shoot myself. 'Pon my soul, yes!"

Emma took the pistols from him. "I'll send Mother to you; she'll cheer you up."

"Give me back my pistols," he moaned.

"Only if the worst happens," she promised.

In the queen's cabin again, Emma found that the surgeon had been unable to do anything for Alberto, whose condition was growing worse every moment. She took the child in her arms, placed him on her knee, and held his trembling body to her breast. He whimpered as she held him, then presently relaxed. Looking up, she saw Nelson standing at the cabin door. He was regarding her with the strangest expression on his face. He came forward, tried to speak, failed, and tried again, his mouth working painfully.

"Why, Nelson, what is it?"

He said brokenly, "Neither of us has children, yet we were *made* for them."

She saw the tears in his eyes before he turned and rushed headlong from the cabin. How providential! she thought. He had seen her in a new attitude, an attitude she had not for one moment thought of assuming. Mother and child! Her child! *His* child! She was sure then that there would be no further arguments. What he called honor and duty would stand no longer between them!

She forgot all this when she felt the child's body stiffen in her arms, relax for one brief moment, then fall into violent convulsions. The surgeon did what little he could and seemed for a time to relieve the convulsions, but they recurred again and again with increasing violence.

When it was all over Nelson came back to the cabin, and Emma rose with the dead child in her arms. She felt as if Alberto were her own child. She had suffered, she was sure, far more than Maria had. She stood there looking at Nelson, the tears streaming down her face.

"Dear God, Nelson," she said, "do you realize that this is Christmas day?"

He came close to her and bent his head to look at the now placid face of Alberto. In a choking voice, audible only to her, he said,

"Pray God, Emma, this will never happen to a child of ours."

17 Emma and Nelson helped a shaky Sir William into the hired carriage, and Mrs. Cadogan wrapped a rug round his knees. Settled thus, he glanced sourly back at the house they had just inspected, the Villa Bastioni.

"Too large, too gloomy," he complained. "And not a single fireplace. Built for the summer only. Not in the least to my liking."

Emma tried to tell him that this villa was the only one remotely suitable in the whole of Palermo.

"We'll brighten it up," she said cheerfully. "We'll hold many a gay reception here, just as we did at the Palazzo Sessa."

"The Palazzo Sessa," he groaned. "I fear I shall never see it again."

"Oh, come, Sir William," Nelson said encouragingly, "life will seem better when you recover your health and strength. And this exile from your beloved Naples is only temporary, I give you my word on that."

Sir William groaned again. "Even if we do return, another sea voyage will finish me."

Emma shrugged in resignation. It had been quite impossible, during the week that had passed since their arrival at Palermo, to shake him out of his mood of depression. For the most part he had remained sullenly in his room at the Colli Palace where the royal family, after a surprisingly enthusiastic welcome by the people of Palermo, had taken up residence. She and Sir William could, of course, remain indefinitely at the palace, but that did not fit in at all with her plans.

"Would it make you any happier, Hamilton," she said, "if Nelson joined us at the Villa Bastioni?"

She stole a quick look at Nelson, but he avoided her eyes. She also glanced at her mother and saw what she expected to see on Mrs. Cadogan's face, a scowl of silent protest.

Sir William brightened visibly.

"Emma, my love, what an excellent suggestion!"

"After all," she went on, addressing herself solely to Nelson, "since Palermo is now to be your base, and your stay here will be indefinite, it would be more sensible, and more comfortable, to live ashore than in the *Vanguard*."

"Much more sensible," Sir William chirped.

"You are far too kind," Nelson said hesitantly.

185

"If it is a matter of pride, my dear fellow, you may share in the housekeeping expenses."

"I should of course insist on that, but—well—"

"Oh, come, Nelson, come!" Sir William cried, almost his old self again, "you and I are the best of friends and we must live together in Palermo. In any case, your presence under my roof would kill the gossip."

"Gossip?" Emma questioned sharply.

"Why, the gossip about you and Nelson, my dear."

Nelson paled, while Emma gave her husband a quick, suspicious look. His expression was gentle and childlike in its innocence, and when he spoke again his voice was kindly.

"Forgive me, Emma, and you, too, Nelson. Neither of you, I know, would be aware of the gossip, yet before we left Naples the whole city was seething with it."

"It was an' all," Mrs. Cadogan interposed.

"Ah, but it takes more than gossip to injure friendship, by heaven it does!" Sir William said.

"Sir William—" Nelson began uneasily.

"Pooh! Why let it worry you, man! People will always gossip. The only thing that matters is that I know there is nothing in it, and I never lose an opportunity, 'pon my soul I don't, of telling people that your friendship, yours and Emma's, is quite, quite platonic."

Emma was looking at him again. His expression was still gentle and childlike; but for a moment, or so she fancied, a flicker of amusement crossed his face. She could have been mistaken—she told herself she *was* mistaken; but she began to ask herself what he knew, what he suspected, and what his game was. She glanced quickly at Nelson. His face was stern and fixed.

"If I were to accept your hospitality," he said stiffly, "it would increase the gossip."

"No, no," Sir William protested. "You have lived with us before. Your refusal to do so now would only increase the talk. It would make people say that we had quarreled, that I had—hum—found you out."

"Hamilton is right," Emma urged.

Nelson hesitated a moment more, looked at her, and was lost.

"I'll gladly join you at the Villa Bastioni," he mumbled, "but I do insist on sharing the expenses." And he added violently, "Let that be understood."

186

Later in the day Emma boarded the *Vanguard* to help gather together the things Nelson would need at the villa. Inside his cabin he was silent and brooding, and she failed to draw from him any response at all when she said she sincerely hoped that he would leave his beloved coffin on the *Vanguard*.

"What's troubling you, Nelson?" she asked quietly.

He refused to answer.

"Don't you really want to come to the villa?" she tried again.

"You know I do!" he said pettishly.

"Then Nelson—"

"I have been placed on my honor," he burst out. "We have both been placed on our honor."

"Yes," she said angrily, "and I'm wondering if that's what Hamilton had in mind."

Nelson looked aghast. "You—you think he suspects?"

"Oh, Nelson," she sighed, "what *is* there for him to suspect? He was right, so very right, when he said that our friendship was quite, quite platonic."

"Platonic in deed, but not in thought!" Nelson said violently. "Oh, Emma, Emma, my dearest, I can still see you with that poor dead child in your arms. I can still feel the anguish that tore at my heart. I am still full of the fear that such a thing might happen to a child of ours." His voice dropped to a whisper, yet the violence was more pronounced than ever. "I have always wanted a child, but never so much as now."

Emma felt anger welling up in her. "Is that your only reason for wanting me? So that you might some day have a child by me?"

Nelson looked bewildered. "But Emma, dearest—"

"Or is it just an excuse you're setting up in your mind? Is it, Nelson, *is* it?"

He looked more bewildered than ever. "You speak so harshly. You seem so set on wounding me. This is—oh, no, this is not the real Emma!"

Her anger melted; tears came to her eyes. She fell unwittingly into an attitude of contrition, dropping gracefully to her knees and holding up her arms in supplication.

"Forgive me, Nelson. To be placed on our honor—the thought of it was more than I could bear."

"And more than I can bear now!"

He turned from her hurriedly and went to the cabin door. He opened it and looked out, then he closed it and locked it from the inside. His face was working painfully.

"I am not yet living under Sir William's roof," he said. He was at her side now as she knelt there still, bending over her, stroking her hair clumsily, and bursting out hysterically, "Was there ever a less romantic sight than a man with only one arm and one eye!"

Afterward he said, "If I was too violent, forgive me."

She said, "I forgive you."

"Dear Emma, you have made me very happy. Believe me, please, this is not just the excitement and ecstasy of a first experience. I feel humble, Emma, humble, and not for one moment do I feel the shame I ought to feel."

But he did, she knew that he did. She placed a finger over his lips.

"We talk too much, Nelson. Talking spoils things. Let's promise ourselves never to do it again."

"I promise," he said.

"And Nelson"—her voice was deep and full and pleading—"no self-reproach, I beg of you."

"No self-reproach," he echoed.

"Just you and me, a little world of our own. A *little* world? No, Nelson, a great, magnificent world. A love that no one has ever known before."

He sprang up. "And tonight, when I go to the Villa Bastioni, and all the time I remain there, I am placed on my honor!"

"And I on mine," Emma said soberly.

But in her heart was joyous laughter and a little voice saying confidently, We'll see about that, Nelson, we'll see about that! Nelson was hers now, really hers. All his victories were her victories, and all his future victories, too. She had achieved her final triumph. Their destinies, his and hers, were fully joined at last.

All the guests except Troubridge, now Commodore Troubridge, had gone; and after the gaiety and laughter of yet another evening of card playing the room, with its empty card tables, seemed unnaturally quiet. Emma, busy counting the money on the table before her, stole a glance at Troubridge. The hardness of his eyes and the stubborn set of his jaw alarmed her. He had been at Palermo a week, having come to report to Nelson on the blockade of Naples, and this was his first appearance at one of her parties. She had sensed at once that he disapproved of the gambling and was surprised that he should have lingered so long. She stole another glance at him. His eyes were fixed now on Nelson, who, slumped forward over the table at her side, was sound asleep.

"Another glass of wine before you go?" Emma asked politely.

"Thank you, no," he grunted.

"Oh, come," she laughed, "Sir William would expect it of you."

Troubridge ignored this, saying stiffly, "I hope Sir William will soon be in better health, Lady Hamilton."

"He seems a little better tonight," she replied, "but these bouts of fever are very weakening. Still, he should be up and about again in another week."

A silence fell.

Troubridge remained there woodenly, standing with his feet planted firmly apart. He seemed unwilling either to stay or to go.

Finally Emma said: "The news you brought of Cardinal Ruffo's progress is most heartening."

Troubridge nodded. "Yes."

From the first Emma had looked upon Fabrizio Ruffo as a romantic, patriotic figure; though Nelson, she knew, secretly disliked him, as, bless his insular heart, he did all "foreigners." As early as January, Cardinal Ruffo had left Palermo for Calabria with a handful of eager supporters and had quickly raised a small army of peasants and brigands. Now that army numbered seventeen thousand and, led by Ruffo, was carrying King Ferdinand's standard slowly and apparently successfully toward Naples.

"With Ruffo advancing by land, and the blockade continuing by sea," Emma said happily, "the French will soon be driven out of Naples. You mark my words, Commodore."

Troubridge grunted, "I hope you are right."

The silence fell again, leaving Emma wondering what next to talk about. Troubridge reminded her, as he always did, of Josiah Nisbet. She saw nothing of the disgruntled stepson now, for Nelson had at last found him a ship and was as glad as she was to be rid of the strain of his presence. Her eyes fell again on the little pile of golden coins on the table.

"Did you enjoy yourself tonight?" she asked. "Did you win?"

"I did not play," Troubridge said sourly. "I have no patience with the gambling that goes on at Palermo, both at the court and—er—"

"Here at the Villa Bastioni?" Emma finished for him.

"If Your Ladyship must know, yes, here at the Villa Bastioni."

"Without a little gaiety we would go quite mad," she told him indignantly. "On the surface the court may seem terribly frivolous; but beneath it all lies hopelessness and heartbreak—or did, until Ruffo raised his army."

But Troubridge was barely listening and had now moved around the table to stand over the still sleeping Nelson.

"My Lord . . ." he said, and shook Nelson gently by the shoulder.

"Really, Troubridge—!" Emma protested.

Nelson straightened up and looked dazedly about him.

Troubridge said determinedly, "Time you went aboard, My Lord."

Emma looked at him sharply. What nonsense was this!

Nelson sleepily took out his watch. "Dear me, the hour *is* late." He rose from the table and stretched his cramped limbs. Only then did he come fully awake. "Aboard, Troubridge? What did you mean by that? You know quite well that my quarters are here at the villa."

"I thought, My Lord," Troubridge said gruffly, "that it might be a healthy change if you returned to the Vanguard for a spell."

"Healthy?" Nelson's voice was sharp.

"No one is more concerned about Nelson's health than Sir William and I," Emma said pleasantly, "but on board or ashore the climate is still the same."

"Your Ladyship will pardon me," Troubridge said, "but I wasn't referring to the climate."

"Whatever you were referring to," Nelson said warningly, "I think you had better take your leave."

Troubridge set his jaw more stubbornly. "Not till I've said my say, I won't. I love you dearly, My Lord; that's why I can't keep quiet any longer."

Emma laughed tinklingly. "Oh, Nelson, poor honest Troubridge doesn't like our midnight card parties."

"That's true enough, My Lord," Troubridge pressed on, "and I know you can't find real pleasure, sitting up all night like this, sacrificing your health and your comfort—yes, and your purse. It's being talked about, too. That and other things." He looked accusingly at Emma. "I don't know what Lady Nelson must think, My Lord. Or your poor father."

"I think you have said enough, man!" Nelson roared.

Troubridge sighed. "I've finished now, My Lord. I'm as jealous of Your Lordship's reputation as any man in the fleet."

Nelson turned his back on him.

Troubridge, all the fight gone out of him, made an ineffectual gesture and went awkwardly from the room.

Emma ran quickly to Nelson's side. "It's my fault, all my fault, Nelson."

"Troubridge was rude, inexcusably rude!"

"Oh, he doesn't like me, I know that, but he spoke from the heart. He loves you like a brother. Promise me you won't turn against him for what he did. He's the best man you have. Promise me, Nelson!"

Nelson turned to her violently. "You have the kindest heart in the world. To plead for him like that! You are *all* heart. Pah! The torment, the utter torment of these months in Palermo."

"Inactivity," Emma said, purposely misunderstanding him, "is a sore trial to a man like you."

He replied as she had expected him to reply. "You know what I mean, Emma. I should never have come to the Villa Bastioni."

"Yes," she sighed, "I know what you mean."

"It was asking too much of a man. It was putting human nature to too great a test."

"Do you think I haven't felt the strain myself?" Emma cried. "I've felt it every minute of every day! That's why I gamble so wildly. Otherwise— Oh, Nelson, I've been half-mad, longing for you, wanting you."

"We promised each other never to talk like this again," he said unhappily.

"And I kept the promise, Nelson! I thought that just to be near you, to see you every day, to hear your voice, to give you comfort when you were ill, make you laugh when you were depressed—I thought all that would be enough. But of course it wasn't. I'm a woman, Nelson. I'm flesh and blood. I can't bear it much longer. I can't, I can't!"

Nelson said roughly, "Nor will you have to. I expect to sail soon for Naples. The blockade needs my supervision."

"That is running away, Nelson."

"I sail tomorrow," he said, and was gone.

Half in anger Emma stared after him. She thought him the strangest man in the world, yet she loved and desired him more than ever. Unwilling to go straight to her own room, she went to Sir William's, ready, almost, to throw herself into his arms and confide in him. But when she found him sleeping peacefully, the fever gone, his face childlike in its peacefulness, she hadn't the heart to wake him.

Still shunning her own room, she went willfully to Nelson's. She told herself that he had only put up a fight, remembered that he was on his honor, because she had made no move herself. She paused outside the door. She could hear him pacing up and down inside.

"Nelson . . ." she said softly.

There was no reply, but his footsteps ceased. She placed her hand on the handle and turned it. The door was locked.

"Nelson!"

He spoke then. "I locked it against myself, not against you, Emma. Please believe me, not against you."

She waited a moment longer, then said quietly, "Good night, Nelson."

She went out of the house and walked in the garden. It was spring in Palermo. The night was calm and still and clear, with not a single cloud in the sky. She looked up at the stars and a little sob caught in her throat. Never in her life had she felt so desolate. She returned slowly to the house and crept up to her room. The candles, lighted hours ago by her maid, were almost guttered.

And there, in the center of the room, stood Nelson.

He said tonelessly, "It was a futile struggle, Emma."

She took him in her arms and held him for a moment as if he were a child.

He said: "How right you were. Honor, duty, self-respect. Words, just words!"

Emma's heart swelled with pride and love and triumph.

Sir William sat back in his seat in the open carriage. There was a happy smile on his face. He beamed benevolently on Nelson and Emma who, with their backs to the horses, sat facing him.

"What do you make of this news?" he asked Nelson. "Does it mean that I shall soon be back in my beloved Naples?"

"On a day such as this," Nelson replied, a trifle sourly, "Palermo is almost as delightful as Naples."

It was a beautiful spring day with a brilliant blue sky and a light balmy wind. The narrow street through which they were clattering on their way to the Colli Palace was crowded with gaily dressed, forever smiling country people carrying baskets of spring flowers. Even as Nelson spoke, he was recognized; the carriage was brought to a halt, and he was cheered enthusiastically while neat little bouquets of freesias and violets were flung into the carriage. Emma, as gaily dressed as any peasant girl, waved and smiled and tucked a bouquet of violets in the sash at her waist.

"But this story of French reverses in Italy," Sir William persisted, once the carriage was moving again, "must mean that our return is close at hand."

"We have heard only rumors so far, not real news," Nelson told him, still speaking sourly.

"Ah, but we are summoned to a council meeting," Sir William reminded him. "There is more than rumor in it. I feel sure of that."

Emma found his eagerness pathetic. The spring sunshine, so warm and cheering, had improved his health; but he was much older in appearance and more childlike than ever in his outlook. Whether or not they returned to Naples, she was afraid he was no longer capable of carrying out the duties of an ambassador.

They were close to the palace now, and the carriage was being delayed once again by cheering country people.

"They worship you, Nelson, they absolutely worship you," Emma said. "The name of Nelson will be remembered here long after those of Ferdinand and Maria Carolina are forgotten."

He acknowledged this with a quick smile of pleasure and for the rest of the journey seemed to be in a brighter frame of mind. She knew what was troubling him. A brig had reached Palermo that morning bringing dispatches and personal letters, and among the letters was one from Lady Nelson in which she had suggested joining him at Palermo. Emma tried to put herself in Lady Nelson's place. Now that Nelson was hers, entirely hers, it was easy to feel sorry for the woman whose husband she had taken. She decided that if she were Lady Nelson and had heard the rumors that Lady Nelson must have heard, she would naturally want to hasten to the Mediterranean. She wondered with the utmost curiosity what Nelson would say in reply.

At the palace they found that the council meeting was only a semi-official gathering composed of themselves, the king and queen, and Sir John Acton.

It was Acton who gave them the latest news. France had declared war on Austria, thus forcing Austria's hand; and now Austrian troops were moving against the French in northern Italy.

"This," he said, "has made the French evacuate Naples. At least, the main French force has been withdrawn. A garrison of five hundred remains in the Castle of St. Elmo."

"Oh splendid, splendid!" Sir William cried, beside himself with excitement.

Emma, glancing at Maria and Ferdinand and Acton, thought it strange that they showed no sign of sharing his excitement. Curious about this, she began to ask questions, trying as best she could to gain a thorough grasp of the situation. She translated the answers for Nelson's benefit; and finally, under his smile of approval, she took control of the meeting.

"As I see it, the situation is this: The French will soon be forced to leave the entire kingdom of Naples. As far as the city itself is concerned, Troubridge's blockade of the bay has encouraged the people on the islands of Capri, Ischia, and Procida to hoist the royal standard again. Then, too, Cardinal Ruffo's forces are in possession of the southern part of the kingdom." She repeated this in English for Nelson and looked at him brightly. "Do I make the position clear, My Lord?"

"Yes indeed," he said enthusiastically.

"Ah, Emma is like a man when it comes to state affairs," Sir William remarked happily.

Emma brushed this aside, saying, "All we need now is the presence of the king in the Bay of Naples on board a British man-of-war."

She repeated this in French, upon which Ferdinand smiled uneasily.

Acton said heavily: "One vital fact has escaped Lady Hamilton's notice."

"And *that*—?" Emma demanded.

"A revolution has taken place in Naples. It was sponsored by the French; and, though the bulk of their forces have now gone, the city is held by the Neapolitan revolutionaries. I consider that it would be madness for the king to appear in the bay at present supported by British naval forces."

He had spoken in French; he repeated his words in English.

"Pah!" Nelson cried, in disgust.

But that was all he said. He was well content, Emma saw, to leave the argument to her. She turned to Maria for support; but Maria, having lost so much of her old fire, remained apathetic.

"I was never afraid of the French as a nation," she mumbled, "only of their revolution, which swept away my poor sister. The French invaded Naples; but, though they have been forced to withdraw, they have left behind them their revolution. Acton is right."

And Acton said: "The king's appearance in the bay with foreign support, and by 'foreign' I mean English, would antagonize the revolutionaries still further. The situation is too uncertain at present for the risk to be taken."

"I take a bolder view," Emma cried. "His presence would put heart into the royalists. There would be a counter revolution."

Maria waved her arms hysterically: "Naples must be cleansed first. I will never cross the water nor permit my husband to cross the water until that has happened."

Emma saw that it was hopeless to argue. Life in Palermo was pleasant enough for the royal family; and the very thought of revolution, in contrast with the safety they now enjoyed, made them quake with fear. She turned to Nelson and told him what had been said.

"A cowardly attitude," was his sole comment.

"Let us wait a few weeks more," Maria pleaded, "then perhaps I shall see my way clear to send my deputy to Naples." She smiled at Emma and repeated, "My deputy."

"You mean Acton?" Emma asked.

Maria smiled broadly and shook her head.

"Ah, Nelson!" Emma cried.

"No, no," Maria laughed, speaking in rapid French, "the good, brave admiral is but an echo these days of the person I have in mind. I would send *you*, my dearest Emma."

Emma flushed with pleasure but stole a quick look at Sir William; he appeared not to have caught Maria's reference to Nelson.

"Your Majesty is joking," she said.

"No, I am most serious, Emma. You will, when the time comes, represent me adequately."

She rose, indicating that the meeting was at an end.

The queen's deputy! Emma thought. It was unbelievable.

Nelson looked up from his writing table. The sheet of paper before him bore nothing but the address and the date.

"Emma," he said, "I need your help."

Emma had been out riding for an hour, leaving him to his letters. She was still wearing the mannish riding costume that he considered so dashing. She liked it herself, especially the tall beaver hat which gave such a jaunty air to the close-fitting, cutaway coat.

She said softly, "If Lady Nelson really wants to come to Palermo, I'll do everything possible to make her comfortable."

"You are kindness itself," he mumbled, "but Fanny's presence here would mean an end of our—" He broke off and cleared his throat. "What am I to tell her?" he asked miserably.

"Tell her the truth, Nelson."

"The—*truth?*"

"Of the position at Palermo. Your movements are uncertain."

"Ah, I knew you could help me!" he said eagerly.

He began to write, slowly and laboriously with his left hand. After a few moments he threw down his pen.

"Emma, where will all this end?"

She laughed gaily. "Why speculate?"

"Fanny suspects," he grumbled. "The time will come when she will *know*. It's going to be awkward, damnably awkward."

Emma said carefully, "If you ever feel it right and proper to go back to her, Nelson, to forget me and go back, I shall understand."

"Emma—"

With a stricken look on her face and a break in her voice she added softly,

"Oh, Nelson, the trouble I've been to you!"

He said harshly, "You have brought me nothing but happiness, Emma, nothing but happiness. Only one thing could ever make me happier than I am right now—the sight of my child in your arms."

"Have you any regrets?" she asked, and added quickly, "I couldn't bear it if you had."

"How could I have regrets, Emma? Except just one. The regret that I can't acknowledge you openly."

"If only that were possible!"

"It may be some day," he said quickly. "Sir William is old and feeble. Each new bout of fever weakens him still more. He— Oh, but this is shameful, shameful! Sir William is my dearest friend!" Nelson was silent for a moment, then broke out again, speaking feverishly. "Fanny is a reasonable woman. Perhaps a little cold and a little un-sympathetic, but surely reasonable." He looked at Emma pitifully. "I hate the word but I must use it. I mean . . . divorce."

Emma went to him quickly. She kissed him tenderly and smoothed back his hair. Even though she had no real understanding of this torment he was forcing upon himself, the sight of his distress tore at her heart.

"Try not to worry," she said. "The time hasn't come yet for that."

He made an angry gesture. "It was a marriage of convenience. Yes, of *convenience*," he stressed, as if striving to convince himself. "Yet I owe

Fanny a duty. I cannot write to her now and tell her I no longer love her. I cannot tell her I never knew what love was until I met you."

Emma kissed him again, no tenderness in the embrace this time. His response was instantaneous; one would never have believed that so frail a body held so much fire and passion.

"To be together like this," she whispered. "Nothing else matters."

"Nothing else," he echoed.

"Then, Nelson, why let your heart be troubled any more? It will all work out for us in the end. Just you wait and see. To the great Nelson all things are possible. Nothing can be denied you, nothing!"

His face cleared; he smiled boyishly.

"Do you know, that's what I often tell myself, only sometimes I forget to remember."

18 "Caracciolo!" Queen Maria's voice rose to a scream. "He shall be hanged! As sure as there is a God in heaven, he shall be hanged! I would play the hangman myself, by the Holy Christ I would!"

King Ferdinand shook his head sadly. "There are traitors on every hand. Even among my closest friends."

Maria broke out again, while Emma and Nelson sat in silence, waiting for the storm to subside. They had been summoned to yet another council meeting, but before anything of importance could be discussed Acton had come in hastily with this news of Prince Caracciolo's treachery.

Nelson caught Emma's eye, smiled briefly, and nodded his head. He had little love, Emma knew, for Caracciolo, one of the few Neapolitans who had dared to criticize his policy; still she had never forgotten the service Caracciolo had done her in the old days in Naples. She always thought of him as a link in the chain of events that had led her on from triumph to triumph.

Caracciolo, who owned large estates in Naples, had begged royal permission to make a secret return, first to work with Cardinal Ruffo, then to save, or attempt to save, his many properties and possessions. And now news had come that he had joined the Neapolitan revolutionaries, had been placed in command of their small fleet, and had fired on royalist ships, including the *Minerva* which he had once commanded.

"He shall be dealt with," Nelson said. "I give their majesties my word on that."

Emma echoed the words for him in French, and at his request asked for precise details of affairs in Naples. Acton spoke up then, first in French, out of courtesy to Maria and Ferdinand, finally in English. Cardinal Ruffo's position was stronger than ever, while the French in northern Italy were being hard pressed by the Austrian forces. In the city of Naples itself, however, the fortress of St. Elmo was still in French hands, while the smaller fortresses of Uovo and Nuovo were held by the Neapolitan revolutionaries.

"But it is only a question of time before Ruffo takes all three," he added confidently.

Nelson gave him a look of disgust. "Obviously Caracciolo thinks otherwise, or he wouldn't have joined the revolutionaries. And just as obviously he was influenced by the inaction and indecision here at Palermo."

Both Maria and Ferdinand received this in silence.

"I, too, have news," Nelson went on, "news which might have encouraged Caracciolo in his act of treachery." He paused, and giving Emma a dry smile, added, "Translate my words as diplomatically as you feel necessary."

"A French fleet has sailed out of Brest. When last sighted it was heading for the Mediterranean. I may be wrong, but I suspect the French of planning an attack on Sicily. I shall, of course, recall Troubridge's squadron from Naples and gather all my ships together south of Sicily at Martimo."

When this had been translated, Maria moaned and Ferdinand said sorrowfully that without Troubridge in the Bay of Naples anything might happen. Emma tried to point out that, at this juncture, the safety of Sicily was more important. Maria quickly agreed—the thought of a French landing at Palermo was more than she could bear—but still she begged that Nelson would leave at least one ship at Naples. Nelson promised this much and named the *Seahorse*, in command of Captain Foote.

"Foote shall work in close cooperation with Cardinal Ruffo," he said, "and keep us informed of all progress made."

Emma remembered then some secret information received by Sir William.

"The cardinal has been ordered not on any account to treat with the rebels," she said. "Or am I wrong?"

"Not on any account," Acton assured her.

"Yet Sir William heard yesterday that to hasten matters he is preparing to offer the French at St. Elmo and the rebels at Uovo and Nuovo certain terms of surrender."

"Unthinkable!" Maria shouted. "One does not treat with traitors. One may as well offer Caracciolo terms. See to it, Acton, that Ruffo is reminded of his orders." Then she indicated that the meeting was at an end.

Emma and Nelson returned to the Villa Bastioni in almost complete silence. Anyone else, Emma reflected, would have accused Nelson of sulkiness; but his unwillingness to make conversation arose, she knew, out of his misery at the thought of leaving her.

199

During dinner his dejection was ever more pronounced. He spoke twice only: the first time to utter his customary grace, "God save the King and bless this food"; the second time, at the end of the meal, to ask Sir William to go to his room with him "for a little private discussion."

The withdrawal of the two men left Emma puzzled and curious. She looked at her mother, who was just as puzzled and curious.

"I wonder what he's up to, Mother."

"Maybe he can't stand it any longer," Mrs. Cadogan ventured, "and wants to tell Sir William the truth."

"How common you make it sound!" Emma said heatedly. "It isn't as if Nelson and I are ordinary people. We—"

"That's what *you* think, girl!" Mrs. Cadogan snorted.

Sir William came ambling back alone from Nelson's room. Emma looked at him anxiously. But there was a happy smile on his face, and beaming on Emma he said that Nelson had added a codicil to his will.

"Our good and faithful friend has insisted on leaving you that beautiful and most valuable diamond-studded box given to him by the mother of the sultan."

"Oh, surely he doesn't think he's going to die!" Emma cried.

"He does, poor fellow, he does. He is quite obsessed by the idea. However, as the good Troubridge once told me, Nelson always expects to die in action, so let us make light of it."

"Light of it!" Emma protested.

"Such a touching gesture," Sir William rambled on. "He showed me the codicil. What a sentimentalist the dear good fellow is, at heart! He leaves you the box as a token of regard, and of respect for your very eminent virtues."

"My—*what?*" Emma gasped, afraid to look at her mother.

"Yes indeed, my love. Your very eminent virtues. 'For she,' the wording runs, 'possesses them all to such a degree that it would be doing her an injustice to mention any particular one.' Touching, most touching, and, indeed, so very true."

Emma looked at him in sharp suspicion.

"So *very* true," he added amiably.

"How nice to be so well thought of," Mrs. Cadogan said tonelessly.

But the expected naval action did not take place.

Nelson's first letter, written in the early hours of the morning before the *Vanguard* actually sailed from Palermo, told Emma that his cabin was a solitary cell. From then on he wrote to her almost every day and dwelt continually on the frustration he felt as he cruised off Martimo, failing still to come to grips with the new French fleet.

He made one curt reference to the retirement of his commanding officer, Lord St. Vincent, whose place had been taken by Lord Keith. Reading between the lines, Emma sensed the bitterness he felt and spoke sharply to Sir William of the ingratitude of the Admiralty.

"Nelson should have been given the Mediterranean command!" she raged. "Nelson and no one else!"

"True, my love, true," Sir William agreed. "I feel as strongly about it as you do; but there has been gossip, you know, dear me yes, and the Admiralty, bless my soul, is just a little bit old-maidish where gossip is concerned."

"Gossip about Nelson and me, you mean?" Emma challenged.

"But of course," Sir William said blandly. "So maliciously untrue, I grant you, but gossip the world over is—gossip. No doubt our elderly Miss Admiralty is quick to say 'No smoke without—hum—fire.' "

He was so pleased with his little joke that he shook with gentle laughter and only grew serious again when he noticed Emma's angry expression.

"I myself will write a stiff letter to the Admiralty," he promised.

A few days later Nelson was at Palermo again, arriving with dramatic suddenness, not in the *Vanguard*, but in the *Foudroyant*, to which he had transferred his flag, and taken Captain Hardy, an officer for whom he had the warmest regard. By this time Emma had unpleasant news for him. Cardinal Ruffo, giving as excuse his fear of the French fleet, had indeed treated with the revolutionaries.

"The wretched man," she told him, "has agreed to an armistice with the rebels on Uovo and Nuovo, and with the French garrison at St. Elmo."

"It was expected," Nelson said scathingly.

An audience with Ferdinand and Maria was immediately requested, and at this meeting it was agreed that Nelson should sail at once for Naples. He pressed their majesties to accompany him; but, while they insisted on remaining at Palermo, Nelson was appointed commander-in-chief by Ferdinand, and Emma, beside herself with delight, became the queen's deputy.

"Why," she told Nelson excitedly, "this makes us king and queen, you and me, in all but name!"

Less than three hours after his arrival in the *Foudroyant* Nelson was on board again. Emma and Sir William were with him—Emma overjoyed at the drama of it all, but Sir William, so rudely torn from the Villa Bastioni, complaining that he was much too old for this sudden upheaval.

"Bless my soul, I scarcely know whether I am on my head or my heels. Will nobody realize that all I want of life is peace and quiet? And the sea!—you know how wretched it makes me."

"We shall have need of you as British ambassador in Naples," Nelson told him gently.

Sir William gave a sharp laugh. "You also have need of a chaperon."

Nelson paled quickly. "That," he said quietly, "was not in my mind."

Sir William made a hasty apology. "Bless my soul, I spoke without thinking; yet I must admit the need to protect, as best I can, the good name of my dearest friend."

"For which I thank you," Nelson said gruffly.

Careful as ever about the use of the left hand, Sir William solemnly shook hands with Nelson; and Emma, looking on, felt first an inclination to laugh hysterically, then compassion for both of them.

Goodness, she thought, real motherly I am at times, and that's a fact.

It was a beautiful tranquil day when the *Foudroyant* slipped quietly into the Bay of Naples. Emma, standing with Nelson on the quarterdeck, remarked that never had she seen Vesuvius look more majestic nor the water so blue, but he was scarcely listening. His face black with anger, he pointed to the white flags flying from the towers of Uovo and Nuovo, and in a shaking voice said, "And there on the *Seahorse*, the flag of truce also!"

He sent a signal at once, commanding Captain Foote to come aboard the *Foudroyant*, and refused to listen when Emma, interceding for the crestfallen captain, pointed out that he had been ordered to work in close cooperation with Cardinal Ruffo.

"Not to the extent of putting his signature to an armistice!" he snapped. "What are the exact terms, Foote?"

"On the surrender of Uovo and Nuovo," Captain Foote faltered, "the rebels will be given safe conduct to France."

"Infamous, infamous!"

"The same terms apply to the French forces in St. Elmo," Foote faltered.

"Pah!" Nelson exploded.

"Have these terms taken effect yet?" Emma asked.

"No, Your Ladyship."

Nelson smiled grimly. "In that case the armistice is forthwith annulled. I refuse to treat with traitors. Annulled, you understand, in the name of his majesty King Ferdinand. The rebels shall surrender to the king's mercy. That and nothing else."

When it was seen that Cardinal Ruffo had no intention of coming aboard of his own free will, but preferred to remain at the royal villa, which he had made his headquarters, Nelson sent for him, spoke contemptuously of his inability to converse in English and finally, tired and exasperated, left Emma to carry on the negotiations.

Ungraciously the cardinal said: "I bow to the wishes of Lord Nelson, not, I hasten to assure you, Lady Hamilton, because he *is* Lord Nelson, but because, foreigner though he is, his majesty the king has seen fit to place him in command."

"Nelson's wishes are my wishes," Emma told him, conscious that the dignity she was assuming was a little pompous, "and my wishes, please remember, are those of your queen."

"He agrees to my orders?" Nelson asked, irritated by the fluent Italian he was unable to understand.

"What else can he do?" Emma said.

"Ask him about Caracciolo."

Ruffo, catching the name, broke into voluble Italian. Translating his words, Emma told Nelson that Prince Caracciolo had fled to the hills at the sight of the *Foudroyant* but was being pursued.

"So you let him slip through your fingers!" Nelson sneered.

"He won't get far," Emma said. "Most of the peasants are faithful to Ferdinand."

Nelson's anger was melting now. He swung around on his heels. "Caracciolo, when caught, shall be made an example of."

Later, with Emma and Sir William to advise him and interpret for him, he conferred with many of the royalists who came eagerly aboard the *Foudroyant*; but it was Emma herself who, forming a new Queen's Party, made the most progress. She remembered Egidio Pallio, the leader of the *lazzaroni*, that irregular band of Neapolitan beggars; and, sending him a secret message, invited him to meet her on the

Foudroyant. He came aboard dramatically when night had fallen.

"If the king were here, as one had hoped and prayed," he announced, "I would have ninety thousand men to place at his majesty's disposal."

"Lord Nelson represents the king; I, the queen," Emma told him warmly. "Place your men at our disposal."

Pallio hesitated for a moment. "At such a time as this one expects the presence of one's king."

"Had his majesty known that such a man as you would be waiting for him," Emma replied diplomatically, "he would have been here. I promise you, Pallio, that the king will return within ten days. All I ask of you meanwhile is to keep the peace in Naples."

"But Uovo and Nuovo, and especially St. Elmo—"

"The rebels on Uovo and Nuovo will soon surrender to the king's mercy; and as for St. Elmo, Lord Nelson will reduce it to a heap of rubble, once we are sure of your own cooperation."

Pallio smiled charmingly. "The Lady Emma is irresistible. It shall be as you wish."

She hastened to tell Nelson of the agreement she had reached with Pallio. He warmly approved of it, called her a clever little stateswoman, and promised to reinforce Pallio's men with a detachment of marines.

"There's only one thing worrying me now," she said, "and that is Ferdinand. I promised to have him here within ten days. Do you think he'll come?"

"Who knows?" Nelson said contemptuously. "If he still hangs back he will deserve to lose Naples forever. I shall send Foote for him in the *Seahorse*."

Hardly had Pallio departed when news came that Prince Caracciolo had been taken by peasants while attempting, in disguise, to reach the country villa of one of his relatives. He was now being returned to Naples. A few days later, after the unconditional surrender of the rebels on Uovo and Nuovo, a group of royalists brought Caracciolo out to the *Foudroyant*.

"It would seem," Nelson remarked dryly, "that Cardinal Ruffo is loath to deal with the man himself. Well, where traitors are concerned no one will ever find *me* squeamish."

The sight of Caracciolo distressed Emma deeply. He had been roughly handled by the royalists. Unshaven, pale and thin, manacled, and stiff from the manhandling he had received, he was scarcely recognizable. He cringed before her and refused to meet her eyes when she spoke to him. Interceding on his behalf, she caused the handcuffs to be removed and sent food and drink to the cabin where he had been placed under guard. Only then did he show a hint of defiance. He refused to eat or drink and uttered one brief sentence, "Dispose of me quickly."

"I do beg you, Nelson," Emma said, "not to act directly in this yourself."

Nelson looked at her in surprise. "I represent King Ferdinand, my dear. This Caracciolo means nothing to me, surely he means less to you."

"He once did me a service," she blurted out.

"Whatever the service, how can we be expected to show leniency to a traitor?"

Emma sighed. "Sternness is necessary, I see that. But will he have a fair trial?"

"He stands guilty before being tried. If the peasants had hanged him without trial, none could have blamed them. A pity they didn't. It would have saved me the trouble."

"Oh, Nelson, how hard you sound!"

Nelson's face darkened. "You were once in love with him?"

"Oh, no!" she cried, horrified that he should grow suspicious.

His voice softened. "I must order a court martial. But I promise to take no part in it myself. There, does that please your gentle woman's heart?"

The court martial took place without delay in the wardroom of the *Foudroyant*. Five officers of the Neapolitan navy, presided over by Nelson's Neapolitan second in command, Count Thurn, heard the evidence. What Nelson had said was true enough; Caracciolo stood guilty without trial. Two hours later the count reported that the prisoner had been found guilty, and that a majority had voted for punishment by death. Nelson ordered the execution to take place at five o'clock that evening, saying: "He fired on the *Minerva*, which was once his own flagship. Let him be hanged from the fore yard-arm of the *Minerva*."

A few minutes before five Emma went quickly to her cabin, but even hiding like this she was unable to blot from her mind's eye a picture of the scene now taking place in the bay. She could see it all so vividly. She might as well have stayed on the quarter-deck and, with the seamen of Nelson's eighteen ships-of-the-line, watched the Neapolitans on the *Minerva* hang their former commander. She listened to the horrible drum roll and shuddered involuntarily when the gunfire, resounding across the bay, announced that the deed was done. Honor, she thought bitterly, had been satisfied. Honor, she raged, honor, honor, honor! In that moment she hated the very sound of the word.

She remained in her cabin until sunset, when Sir William came down and joined her.

"A sad business," he said, shaking his head.

"But you stayed up there and watched it!"

"My dear—"

"And perhaps you enjoyed it. You probably still hated him."

Sir William patted her shoulder absently. "True, I was once insanely jealous of him. But really, my love, I am not *quite* the fool some people think me. It was a trick you played on me, you and Caracciolo. I soon realized that."

"Why, you old fox!"

He coughed. "No, no, I must tell the truth. Queen Maria, unable to keep the joke to herself, told me about the trick after we were married. So you see, I had no reason to hate him."

Then Sir William looked at her quizzically. "I think you must have been just a little in love with him. And I was—yes, I do admit it—not deeply troubled to see the end of him." A thin mean look, reminding Emma of his nephew Greville, touched his mouth for a moment. "And now, by an odd twist of fate, our dear friend Nelson has been the instrument that dispatched him into the unknown."

Emma avoided his eyes. He might not *know* about her and Nelson, but it looked as if he at least suspected.

The heat in the bay during the past week aboard the *Foudroyant* had been nearly insupportable; but this evening, as Emma and Nelson took their ease in Nelson's barge, a light balmy breeze had brought a slight relief, and Emma was glad of the cashmere shawl about her shoulders. They had, of course, begged Sir William to join them on this little excursion, but he had refused and remained on board the *Foudroyant* to discuss affairs of state with King Ferdinand. The king had come back from Palermo on the *Seahorse*. Established now on the *Foudroyant* and holding court there, he had reached the bay in time to witness the fall of St. Elmo, and to be greeted by Pallio's ninety thousand men who had come out in all manner of craft to welcome him home.

"I'm so glad Hamilton didn't come with us tonight," Emma said. "You see, I have news for you."

"I have news for you, too," Nelson said, his face darkening. "I can only hope yours is pleasanter news than mine."

"Oh, mine is pleasant enough, Nelson! It—" She broke off and laughed merrily. "It might even be called the best news in the world."

"The best news in the world," he said harshly, "would be the retirement of Lord Keith. He writes that he is sure the French have no designs on Sicily and he orders me, he actually orders me, to join him with all my forces off Minorca."

"Oh, Nelson, separation again!"

"That, naturally, is Lord Keith's intention. We have had more than one hint lately that he disapproves of you."

"Quietly, Nelson," Emma whispered, "the bargemen might hear."

"You have done so much for England," Nelson said indignantly. "To strike at us like this, to make a personal issue of it, is childish."

"But Lord Keith is still your commanding officer," Emma said quietly. "Orders are orders."

"I have not lost sight of that," he said sourly. "Well, tell me your news."

"How would you like to be a duke?"

"A . . . duke?" Nelson smiled broadly. "What joke is this, Emma?"

"Oh, only an Italian duke, but a duke all the same." She struck a solemn attitude. "It has pleased his majesty, King Ferdinand of the Two Sicilies, to give you the Dukedom of Brontë, in Sicily, as an expression of his gratitude and heartfelt admiration."

Nelson was so overcome with surprise and emotion that he could do no more than stare at her in silence.

"It's the least he could do for you," she went on. "Can you tell me, can *anybody* tell me, that Nelson isn't worthy of the honor? I would have given you more, much more!"

"Knowing you," Nelson said emotionally, "I believe you were responsible, even for Brontë."

Emma smiled modestly. "I prodded Ferdinand a little, that is all."

"You deserve the honor, not I," he went on passionately. "Dear God, if only I could make you Emma, Duchess of Brontë!"

"Emma, Duchess of Brontë . . ." she repeated. "Oh, yes, I'd like that."

"Yet you have given the title to another woman!"

Emma smiled wryly; she had quite forgotten Fanny. Then, watching Nelson carefully, she asked when he expected to sail for Minorca.

For a moment he seemed to be struggling with himself. Finally he said: "I still feel sure that Keith's chief aim is to separate us. Josiah must have written many letters to his mother; and Fanny could, if she wished, make representations to the Admiralty. As a result, I am ordered to leave Naples at a most critical stage. Ferdinand is not yet completely reestablished. Surely it is better to risk Minorca rather than risk Naples."

"Nelson, you mean—?"

"I mean that I shall disobey Keith's instructions and remain here until my task is fully completed." He looked at her for a moment with uncertainty in his face. "I— You agree, Emma?"

She touched his arm quickly. "Of course I do. There's no dishonor in doing what you know is right."

The uncertainty faded from his face.

"Lord Keith shall know my mind at once," he said briskly, and he gave an order to the bargemen, "Back to the *Foudroyant!*" A moment later, when no notice had been taken of this command, he repeated it in a louder voice, upon which one of the men turned and looked at him fearfully.

"Begging your pardon, m'lord," he said, pointing a quivering finger to a spot in the near distance, "but there it is again!"

"There *what* is?" Nelson asked impatiently.

"Gawd 'elp us all, m'lord, it's the phantom of Prince Caracciolo." Nelson rose to his feet. "What nonsense is this!"

"Wait, Nelson," Emma said quietly.

There had been many reports in the past few days about Caracciolo's ghost. British seamen as well as the more superstitious Neapolitans had spoken fearfully of seeing it. Some claimed to have seen it walking on the waters of the bay, moaning, they said, and crying vengeance.

"There's something floating on the surface over there," Nelson said, "but it hasn't the look of a ghost to me."

Emma had seen something, too; and as she watched it drifted closer.

" 'Tis a body, m'lord," one of the men cried. "No mistake o' that."

"But neither walking, moaning, nor crying vengeance," Nelson laughed.

A moment later the floating body was bumping gently but horribly against the side of the barge. The men looked at Nelson, fear and superstition in their eyes. He told Emma curtly to keep her eyes from the sight and spoke sternly to the men.

"This is not the first body you've seen floating in the sea. Most of you have been responsible for not a few Frenchmen in your time. Come now, back to the *Foudroyant*."

When Emma looked again the body had drifted away.

She said in a whisper, "Was it Caracciolo?"

"Yes," he said briefly.

"Oh, how horrible! It makes me feel so wretched. Do tell me it isn't a bad omen for the future!"

"I care nothing for omens, good or bad," he said gruffly. "That was the body of a traitor. Think of it as that and nothing else, but if it pleases you we shall salvage the body and give it a Christian burial."

A sob caught in her throat. "Oh thank you, Nelson, thank you!"

But she could still visualize the floating body, so horribly bloated, so undignified, so unlike the handsome man it had once been; and it was many days before she could rid herself of the superstitious feeling that this was an omen, and a bad one.

19 While Sir William lay in his cot, sleeping through the heat of the afternoon, Emma busied herself writing a letter to Greville. With their former quarters given up to King Ferdinand, Emma and Sir William now occupied the wardroom of the *Foudroyant*, which had been converted for them into both day and night cabin and was used in addition as a study. Though she usually wrote regularly to Greville, giving him her news and still boasting gently of her many achievements, she had neglected him of late. Now she began by telling him that, as Queen Maria Carolina's deputy, she had been much too busy in the last few weeks to attend to personal correspondence; a neat enough way, she thought, of letting Greville know how important she had become. She had written only a few lines when Nelson burst into the wardroom. He had a letter in his hand.

"From Lord Keith," he said, his face strangely impassive.

Emma sprang up from her chair. "His reply to your refusal to go to Minorca?"

Nelson shook his head. A moment later his face broke into the happy, boyish smile that always touched her heart.

He said: "I had meant to tease you, but the news is too exciting to keep to myself, even for a single moment. You are gazing, my dear Emma, on the Mediterranean commander-in-chief."

"Oh, *Nelson!*"

He frowned momentarily. "A temporary command only, I'm afraid. Keith has been called away from the Mediterranean station for a while. He had no option but to choose me. Meanwhile, I am in full charge and am answerable to no man but myself."

"But if this is his reply to your letter—"

Nelson broke in, "Obviously the letters crossed. Mine will eventually reach Lord Keith, but by that time it will be clear that the French have no designs on Minorca. Meanwhile—"

Sir William, grunting like a child, turned in his sleep.

Nelson lowered his voice. "We have little privacy these days, Emma."

"None whatever," Emma said, lowering her voice, too, and looking at the sleeping Sir William.

"Therefore I suggest a little jaunt to Palermo." Nelson cleared his throat. "To bring back the queen and your mother, of course."

"Of course," Emma agreed with mock solemnity.

"The king approves. I spoke to him just now. After all, with Naples liberated, the queen *should* return."

"She should indeed, Nelson."

In a moment both of them were laughing heartily, so heartily that Sir William woke with a start, sat up, and began to laugh too. Finally, controlling his amusement, he asked if he might share the joke.

"We were laughing about Lord Keith," Emma told him, and explained what had happened.

But Nelson had grown sober now and was looking at her sadly. That conscience of his again, she thought, that dreadful conscience . . .

Emma was rereading her latest letter to Greville and frowning as she read. What she had just written, she realized, would certainly give him the impression that life in Palermo these days was a succession of receptions and balls and fetes, and would add weight to the British government's criticism that Nelson was idling away his time at a foreign court.

She tore up the last page, and with a new sheet of paper before her wrote indignantly that the criticism was both false and spiteful. It was true that before leaving the Bay of Naples for Palermo they had celebrated the anniversary of the Battle of the Nile, but could anybody blame them for that? Moreover, it had been a joint celebration, for news had come that Gaeta and Capua, the last remaining points of revolutionary resistance in the kingdom, had fallen. Small wonder there had been a gay dinner on board the *Foudroyant*, a twenty-one-gun salute, fireworks and illuminations, and music till the early hours.

And what, she asked indignantly, if there *had* been a grand fete in Nelson's honor the moment they were in Palermo again? Any gesture by the royal family toward Nelson surely raised British prestige in the area. Nelson had been created Duke of Brontë; it was only fitting that this fact be officially celebrated.

She smiled reflectively and put down her pen. What a celebration *that* had been! The night lighted again and again with magnificent fireworks, before the blowing up of the large model of the French flagship *L'Orient*. And then the grand climax of the evening, the gathering of thousands and thousands of people around the specially constructed Temple of Fame while one of the young princes placed a laurel wreath on the waxwork model of Admiral Lord Nelson. There had even been models of herself and Sir William, placed on either side of that of their beloved hero. A waste of time? What nonsense! "We are at all events appreciated here," she wrote, "if not at home."

And it was unfair to say that Nelson had really been inactive. He had organized the latest move, the attack which Troubridge carried out on Civita Vecchia, an attack which had led to the French being thrown out of Rome itself; and he had sent Duckworth to protect British trade at Oporto and Lisbon. There were people in London, no doubt, who would say that Nelson should have been in all three places himself at the one time; but one was big enough, she hoped, to ignore such carping criticism. Sufficient to say that he was now at Malta, giving all his time and energy and genius to the complete reduction of that island. "Malta has been on his mind for months," she wrote, "but the French hold only Valetta now, and that will soon fall, I feel quite sure."

Even Lord Keith, ill-pleased as he was with Nelson's attitude of independence, must know in his heart that Nelson was doing his duty as no man had ever done it before. But thinking of Keith made her frown. What a pity it was that the man was back in the Mediterranean and Nelson's temporary command had come to an end. She recalled Keith's recent visit to Palermo, during which she had done everything in her power to make him comfortable at the Villa Bastioni. How his attitude of cold appraisal had irritated her; but she had forced him to acknowledge that though Nelson had disobeyed orders the course of events had proved him right. Quite obviously, the French fleet, now bottled up in Brest again, had had no designs on Minorca.

She was sealing the letter when Sir William came stumping into the room. She saw at a glance that he was upset and agitated. Waving a letter in his hand, he fell exhausted into a chair.

"Nelson," he announced, "is furious."

"You have a letter from him!" she cried. "Oh, surely things haven't taken a turn for the worse at Malta!"

"Not in the way you mean," Sir William replied. "The French are more hard pressed than ever at Valetta. No, no, the trouble is the question of the starving Maltese in other parts of the island, and your dear queen's refusal to supply those gallant patriots with grain."

"But there's plenty of grain in the stores in Naples," Emma said indignantly.

"Yes, yes, indeed. *We* know there is, and *Nelson* knows there is. Wait till you read his letter. He curses the day he ever lifted a finger to help the Kingdom of the Two Sicilies. And dear me, to complicate matters for us, there are Maltese delegates in Palermo at this very moment—they arrived this morning—seeking an audience with Maria; but she refuses to receive them."

"Have you seen her yourself?"

Sir William shrugged. "What use would that be?"

Emma smiled. "I am still Maria's deputy. *I* will receive the Maltese delegates. And afterward I'll have a few sharp words with Maria herself." She rose. "Send the delegates to me at once, Hamilton."

He tittered suddenly on a high note.

"What is it, Hamilton? Have I amused you?"

"Dear me, dear me, but the imperiousness of our clever little Emma."

She tried not to be amused, but in the end she was forced to laugh. Sir William rose from his chair but lingered, looking thoughtful yet at the same time rather unhappy. He began to speak, shrugged, then walked slowly to the door.

"There's something else the matter," Emma said. "What is it, Hamilton?"

He turned but avoided her eyes.

"Thirty years of faithful service," he burst out, "and now *this*."

"And now—*what*?" she asked curiously.

"Recalled to London," he stormed. "Replaced by a younger man. I am, it seems, of no further use to my king and country."

Emma watched him as he raged fretfully, a pitiful old man soon exhausted by his anger. And yet, as she watched him, and he still refused to meet her eyes squarely, she had a strong impression that he was more pleased than angry.

"When do we leave for England?" she asked.

"I expect it will be some little time before the official recall comes. There was a private letter from my foster brother. Reading between the lines I could see that her majesty, Queen Charlotte, is at the back of it."

"But why should Queen Charlotte want you recalled?" Emma asked.

Sir William smiled sheepishly. "It has reached her majesty's ears that our dear good Nelson is now completely under the thumb of my wife."

Emma chuckled. "The silly old prude."

"Dear me, dear me, such disrespect!"

"One would think," Emma cried, catching and holding his eyes, "that it were an established fact that Nelson and I are lovers."

"Indeed one would," Sir William said sagely. "Ah me, this great friendship of ours, this great love for Nelson, has been grossly misunderstood." He rose again and shook his head sadly. "Let us hope that the Queen of England will be a little happier when you are in London and Nelson is still in the Mediterranean." At the door he turned for a moment. "My dear, the Maltese delegates shall wait on the queen's deputy at once."

When she was alone she fell to wondering, once again, if he really suspected the truth. Sometimes she was sure that he did, and sometimes again she was equally sure that he didn't.

But to return to England! To be dragged away from her beloved Italy where, in all but name, she was a queen. Worse still, to be separated from Nelson! It was intolerable, intolerable!

A few moments later the Maltese delegates were announced. They bowed low as they entered the room, and as they pleaded with her, she saw that they regarded her as a fairy godmother, capable at the wave of a wand of providing them with all the grain they needed. This was so flattering and gratifying and warming to the heart, that finally, having wept a little over the starving patriots of Malta, she said,

"You shall have the grain. I give you my solemn word."

She went at once to the Colli Palace, found her way barred to Maria's apartments and imperiously forced an entry.

"Your Majesty," she said, slowly and sadly, "it breaks my heart to know that I, your dearest friend, should be stopped at your door. What have I done to displease you? What have I done?"

Maria tossed her head and scowled.

"Your Majesty—"

Maria all but spat. "I fear your great powers of persuasion."

"So you know the purpose of my visit."

"It has been reported, yes, that the Maltese delegates have waited on you."

A quick, angry retort came to Emma's lips but she held it back. Instead, she said cautiously, "There is plenty of grain in Naples."

"That is true," Maria agreed, reluctantly.

"A real surplus, Your Majesty."

"We need a surplus. The French might attack again."

So that was the trouble. Maria was still haunted by her fears of

French aggression. Such being the case, an appeal to her sympathy would fail. Instead, Emma decided to threaten the queen with a still greater danger.

She said softly, "It will not help Nelson in the reduction of Valetta if the patriots in the other parts of the island starve to death. And it will not help to keep Italy, north or south, free of French aggression if Nelson, in exasperation, advises his government to withdraw from the Mediterranean."

Maria sprang up in alarm. "He would never do that!"

Emma seized her hands. "My poor Maria, Nelson is furious, and he is capable of anything."

"Dear heaven, he has already threatened to withdraw!"

Emma did not scruple to lie. "Yes."

"But the honors we have heaped upon him! The ingratitude if he deserts us now!"

"Forgive me," Emma said quietly, "but I feel that it is you who are likely to desert him. Remember his hatred of the French. Remember his single-mindedness in working so tirelessly for their complete defeat. Remember that he has driven them from Naples, from almost the whole of Italy. Grain for the Maltese patriots, Your Majesty, means certain defeat for the French at Malta."

"Pah!" Maria cried. "Very well, you dreadful creature, it shall be as you wish. The wretched Maltese shall have the grain."

Nelson was back again, back with news of the capture of two French warships, the *Généreux* and the *Guillaume Tell*. Nevertheless, he was in one of his blackest moods of despair, and looking dreadfully ill and strained. Poor Nelson, Emma thought, the real trouble was Sir William's recall. A few days ago news had reached Palermo that a successor was on the way out, and this was almost the first thing Sir William had told Nelson when he stepped ashore.

"Yet he knew I wanted to keep it from you till the last moment!" Emma cried indignantly.

"Why did you want to do that, my dear?"

"So that nothing might interfere with your work."

"How sweet and kind and understanding! Do you always know what my duty is before I know it myself? And you were right. It *might* have interfered, though all it did was make me wretched and ill. I can't bear the thought of separation, Emma."

"Oh, Nelson, need we really be separated?"

"No," he said defiantly, "and I am making plans to prevent it. The end of the Malta campaign is within sight. Troubridge can be safely left in charge."

"You mean you would strike your flag and go to England, too?"

Nelson nodded glumly. "When I knew Sir William was to be recalled I wrote to the Admiralty, saying I was weary of ingratitude and criticism. At least, I think I said that." He touched his brow vaguely. "I *know* I said that, far from wasting my time at a foreign court, I came to Palermo for short spells of badly needed rest. The reply was hardly —kind. It said, in effect, that if I was too ill to carry out my duties in the Mediterranean station I was at liberty to return to England."

"Oh, Nelson, how shameful!"

"It is what I want, what *we* want," he said harshly. "So, please, no quibbling. We are going back to England, together."

"But not happily, Nelson, not happily!" She laughed bitterly. "On the one hand we have the Queen of England ordering me back with Sir William, to protect your honor; and on the other we have an ungrateful Admiralty withdrawing you. It's ironic, Nelson, really it is!"

He agreed glumly, then said, "I disobeyed Lord Keith's order. That has been remembered as well."

"You were right to do so. You know you were. And events have proved it."

He smiled somberly. "It will hardly endear me to the Admiralty, to be always right."

Emma looked at him thoughtfully. He was hurt, perhaps, but not so much as all that. No, there was something else troubling him.

"Nelson," she said quietly, "is it your wife? Is it Fanny?"

He nodded. "That and the thought that England will be so different from the Mediterranean. Could we find happiness in England, Emma? You and I? *Could* we?"

"We can be happy anywhere, if we are together. You know that, Nelson."

"How can we be happy in England?" he raged. "Tell me that, Emma! How can we!"

Emma looked to the future, the future in unsympathetic England. It would be winter by the time they arrived, cold and gray and cheerless. Nelson would be obliged to return to his wife. She and Sir William, even if they did have a town house, would spend most of their time—Sir William had already made this clear—in the depths of the country. Tears came to her eyes at the thought of it. Oh, the misery

216

of living in England after the sunshine of Italy and the delightful freedom from convention.

"Brontë," she said suddenly. "Your estates at Brontë!"

Nelson smiled. It was a happy, dreamy smile. His depression had faded rapidly.

"We think alike, as ever!" he cried boyishly. "I have always longed for the life of a country gentleman. If I were not a sailor I would want to be a squire. Well, if I wish, I can become something like that at Brontë."

"Are you inviting us to live with you at Brontë, Hamilton and me?"

"Why not, Emma, why not!"

"Hamilton would never do it."

Nelson started to speak but remained silent, faintly embarrassed now.

Softly Emma said, "A lovely dream, you and me at Brontë; Hamilton and your wife forgotten in England."

Nelson's embarrassment passed. "We could so easily defy convention at Brontë, live openly together there. Oh, Emma, my dear, it would be a most idyllic existence. There's so much I could do at Brontë, for the people there. I would be busy from morning till night."

Emma said quietly, "And your duty to England? Would your honor be satisfied with life at Brontë? Could you live there happily, just because of me, ignoring the war with France? No, no, I know you too well, Nelson. In time, in a very short time, you would be miserable. And you would soon blame me, might even grow to hate me!"

"Duty and honor!" he burst out. "Was it necessary to remind me of those words?"

"They are ever dear to you; they are the real meaning of your whole life."

Nelson sighed deeply. "Yes, the real meaning."

"So Brontë is just a dream . . ."

Nelson scarcely seemed to hear.

"Bonaparte escaped from Egypt," he said, "and is safely back in France. You know that, of course. It was the bitterest day of my life when I learned that he had eluded me off Corsica. Soon, if I judge the man rightly, he will be ruler of France and England's bitterest enemy. While Bonaparte lives there can be no rest or retirement for me, no running away to hide at Brontë." He kissed Emma chastely. "Thank you for reminding me of my duty, and forgive me for depriving you of Brontë."

Emma wondered which attitude to adopt, one of resignation or one of renunciation; but a single glance at Nelson told her that, dreaming now of other things, he would never notice. And dryly she thought, Well, Emma, be honest with yourself. For she could see now that life at Brontë would be intolerable. At Brontë, defying convention, living in isolation, Nelson would be pitied by the world, joked about, then quickly forgotten. A Nelson living in the public view, still seeking out the French and defeating them in one glorious battle after another, would become a greater hero than ever. She was sure of that. She knew his capabilities and his genius; just as she knew that, contriving ever to be at his side, she would live to bask in the glory of his future achievements. She shrugged. She had been honest with herself, had had one more critical look at the real "me." What did it matter if it had brought her close to despising herself? She knew what she wanted and intended to get it.

"Nelson and the future, duty and honor," she said quickly, "that is what life really means to me."

Speaking quickly too, Nelson said: "Some people will say that in turning from Fanny and loving only you, I have forgotten both duty and honor; but how wrong they will be, how very wrong!"

Faintly alarmed by the lack of real conviction in his voice, contemptuous of his uneasy conscience, yet fearing it, too; Emma pressed on with the plans for their joint return to England.

"How soon can you leave the Mediterranean?" she asked.

"When is Sir William to present his letters of recall to King Ferdinand?"

"In perhaps less than a month. His successor should be here by then."

"As soon as possible after that, then, I shall take you and Sir William home in the *Foudroyant*."

Emma remembered Nelson's unsympathetic commander-in-chief.

"Do you expect Lord Keith to permit that?" she asked.

Nelson's face darkened. "He would be exercising a personal grudge if he did otherwise."

Emma stood on the quarter-deck of the *Foudroyant*, her mother on one side of her, Nelson on the other. Mrs. Cadogan, dressed wholly in black, was in the best of spirits; while Nelson, still wearing the full dress uniform he had donned for the departure, had a quiet, happy smile on his face. Emma herself had chosen a new English-style walking costume. She particularly liked the *broderie anglaise* and braid work on the white cambric frock, and she thought the blue velvet spencer most becoming to her figure.

Then, sighing a little, she looked long and earnestly at the now distant shores of Sicily. It almost seemed as if she were losing an old friend, which of course was silly, for there would be one more return to Palermo before they all sailed for England.

She went below presently to see that Sir William was comfortable in the separate cabin Nelson had found for him. He had already put himself to bed.

"This little trip, as you and Nelson call it, is sheer madness," he complained. "The weather is going to be hideous; I can feel it in my bones."

"You could have stayed in Palermo," Emma told him gently.

"I would have been miserable there," he moaned. "Rather a rough sea than a court at which I now have no official status."

He had presented his letters of recall two days ago, upon which Nelson had suggested this little trip to Malta, partly to take Sir William's mind off things and partly because he was still anxious to keep an eye on the blockade of Valetta.

Mrs. Cadogan came bustling into the cabin, suggested brandy for Sir William and began fussing over him, leaving Emma free to escape to Nelson on the quarter-deck. The sky had darkened and a strong wind had sprung up.

"By the look of things we shall have a slow passage to Malta," Nelson remarked when she had joined him.

"Hamilton *will* be pleased," Emma laughed. She glanced at Nelson obliquely. His manner was cheerful and carefree. She risked saying, "Perhaps at Malta we shall hear from Lord Keith."

"Perhaps," he said lightly.

"It would be grand to go all the way to England together in the *Foudroyant*."

"Grand, yes! And so we will, my dear." But he was scowling a little now, beginning to brood, Emma saw, over Lord Keith's lack of response to his request. "Yes," he repeated, "and so we will."

Emma laughed gaily. "Do you realize, Nelson, that I shall have my birthday on board before we reach Malta?"

Nelson laughed, too, his spirits rising happily. "Oh, splendid, splendid! What a gay time we shall have, what a happy celebration. We'll eat, drink and be merry, for tomorrow, after all, we—"

219

She stopped him quickly. "For tomorrow we *live!* The future is ours to do with as we please."

"No," he said soberly, "let us face the truth. The future is ours, yes, but not to do with as we please. The future, whatever it holds, is as fixed as fate."

Emma smiled her agreement, but she laughed to herself. The future, did Nelson but know it, was fixed by Emma Hamilton, the broad lines of the future, at all events. Lord Keith, for instance, might or might not permit the use of the *Foudroyant;* but they would still go to England together, and by some means or other live there together, too. Fate, like life, was what you made it, and she, Emma Hamilton, was making it, for both of them!

Her birthday dinner aboard the *Foudroyant* was the climax of a series of little dinner parties. The meal, a banquet rather than a mere dinner, began at four in the afternoon, an hour later than the routine time on board, and was heralded by a drummer merrily beating out the tune of "The Roast Beef of Old England."

The favored officers were present, as was the ever-popular Mrs. Cadogan herself, songs were sung, speeches in praise of Nelson were made, and hearty toasts were drunk. Sir William, with little head for wine these days, was the first to withdraw. He was put to bed quickly and efficiently by Mrs. Cadogan. Then, one by one, the officers bowed before Emma, kissed her hand, and went off to their own quarters.

Finally only Emma and Nelson remained in the Great Cabin, as the admiral's day cabin was called. It was eight o'clock, long after the usual tea time, and the precise hour at which Nelson normally took a piece of fruitcake with a rummer of punch.

Emma refilled his glass with Madeira, but he set it aside.

"I have had enough, drunk more than usual."

"But a very special celebration, Nelson!" She refilled her own glass. "Just one more toast!" She raised her glass; he raised his impatiently. "To the future, whatever it holds!"

The glasses clinked together and they drank, after which Nelson fell silent and seemed, Emma feared, to be brooding. How foolish of her to have tempted him to drink more than he wanted. On the rare occasions that this had happened before he had become horribly depressed. And, as the silence lengthened now, she wondered how best to restore him to the high spirits he had shown during the party.

"Troubridge!" he burst out suddenly.

She knew Nelson was dwelling again on the contents of the personal letter Troubridge had written to him before they left Palermo, the letter she had hoped he had forgotten.

"He meant well," she said quickly. "He loves you dearly."

"People who in this life are destined to mean well," said Nelson, scowling, "should be strangled at birth."

His words—yes, and the scowl that went with them—amused her; but she decided that it was wiser not to show it. Troubridge, she recalled, had referred to the scandalous talk in England, and had begged Nelson either to leave for home alone or to seek immediate service elsewhere.

"How ironic," Nelson said, staring fixedly at his wineglass, "that the only person in the world who believes in the purity of my regard for you should be your husband."

Emma looked at him uncertainly. Was he making a joke?

"And Sir William," he added pensively, "is fast approaching second childhood."

The seriousness of his voice made it clear that no joke was intended. She thought, as she had thought so many times before, that this man she loved was the strangest man in the whole world. Even she, who knew him so well, came close at times to thinking him a hypocrite. She remained silent, afraid to speak, afraid to risk making matters worse.

"Even Sir William— Pah! Sometimes I feel that even he suspects."

"And would that matter?" she cried. "Oh, Nelson, would it *matter*? He and I are no more than father and daughter—nay, mother and son these days. He clings to me, and to you, too, like a child. And even if he did know the whole truth, he would still believe in the purity of your regard for me, and mine for you."

Nelson's face brightened.

Yes, this was the right line to take, the right attitude to adopt.

"And mine for you," she stressed.

"You really believe," Nelson said eagerly, "that Sir William would see purity in our desire for each other?"

A faint impatience with her lover took possession of her. Soon, whatever he thought, whatever his conscience told him, he would rise hurriedly from the table and lead the way to his night cabin.

"Aren't we faithful to each other, Nelson? Aren't we man and wife?"

"And what would Sir William say," Nelson went on, his face flushed with more than wine, his uninjured eye large and luminous, "if my dearest wish was granted and we had a child?"

221

Emma's heart missed a beat. She asked herself if she should tell him now, or wait until she was absolutely sure. To tell him now and later be proved wrong might disappoint him bitterly, queer man that he was.

"What would he say?" Nelson repeated.

She went around the table to him quickly. "Dear Nelson, why torment yourself like this? Hamilton would regard that child as a pure and living expression of the sacred love that binds us."

Nelson rose abruptly from his chair. Passion and desire were fighting down the mood of depression, yet the depression clung for a moment more.

"It would be my child," he said angrily, "but the law would give it to Sir William!"

"God would know that the child was yours, Nelson."

She had spoken solemnly, all her actress's soul in her eyes. And then she waited, half-expecting from Nelson a shocked protest; but in a moment his face crumpled and a little sob shook him.

"Thank you, Emma," he said humbly, "for reminding me that our marriage was made in heaven."

Nelson, striding about the quarter-deck, was in a towering rage. Emma had never seen him quite like this before. Turning from him, she gave her whole attention to the French shore batteries of Valetta. Another spurt of fire told her that the bombardment of the *Foudroyant* was continuing.

"Emma!" Nelson was at her side again. "I have begged you to go below; now I *order* you!"

"Aye, aye, sir!" she said smartly, but made no move.

"*Emma!*"

She laughed gaily. "But I'm enjoying myself; and besides, we're well beyond range now."

His anger with her melted. "What a spirit you have! You should have begun life as a midshipman, by heaven you should!"

"Under your command, m'lord."

"Under *my* command!"

She glanced at the shore batteries again and smiled. Nelson seemed to take it as a personal insult that the *Foudroyant* had dragged her anchor during the night and ended up, as daylight revealed, within range of the French guns. The officer of the watch blamed the captain and the captain blamed the officer of the watch, while Nelson blamed both of them. Such clumsiness! Such lack of seamanship! And how the French would laugh!

That, of course, was the real trouble—that the French, whom he hated so wholeheartedly, should be given a chance to laugh at him. No wonder he all but danced with rage. Several times during the day, as they sailed in the direction of Marsa Sorocco, he referred to the mishap, saying, "You might have been killed, Emma." But she was not deceived, and though she wanted to tease him about the French she wisely restrained herself.

When they dropped anchor in the bay at Marsa Sorocco, Captain Ball, governor of the British-held part of the island, came aboard with letters from home, and the first one Nelson opened was from Lord Keith. His rage then was worse than it had been that morning.

"Pooh, what does it matter if he *has* forbidden us to use the *Foudroyant?*" Emma said quickly, guessing the contents of the letter.

"Spite, pure spite!" Nelson shouted.

She took the letter from him and read it. A little of Nelson's anger touched her, but underneath she wanted to laugh. Lady Hamilton, wrote Lord Keith, had been in charge of the navy long enough. Of course she wanted to laugh, and triumphantly. But to point out that Lord Keith, without meaning to, was admitting the power she wielded —no, no, that would be most unwise.

So, to pacify Nelson, she said, "As if we care about Keith! We'll go overland, make a royal progress of it, have the time of our lives."

Nelson said dully, "I feel ill."

He was gasping for breath and clutching at his chest. She made him sit down and suggested sending for the ship's surgeon. He shook his head.

"It will pass. I have had these attacks before. My heart has always been weak. I realize that now."

Angry with herself for thinking it, Emma nonetheless suspected that he was just being dramatic. Yet he looked so wretched, so ill, that she soon felt ashamed of herself.

Presently, somewhat recovered, he opened the rest of his letters. One from his wife he thrust hastily aside, unread. Another brought a sudden smile to his face. Fully recovered, he rose and bowed low before her, then kissed her on both cheeks and said:

"My dear sister." He laughed merrily. "My wife before heaven; but my sister, too, it seems."

"Gracious, what's come over you, Nelson!"

223

He gave her the letter to read.

"Oh, *no!*" she cried, beside herself with excitement. "I can't believe it!"

At the instigation of the Czar of Russia, who was Grand Master of the Knights of Malta, the Grand Cross had been bestowed not only on Nelson, but on Emma, too. Dame Chevalière of the Order of St. John of Jerusalem, that was her title now.

"Never conferred on an Englishwoman before," Nelson exulted.

"And think of it, Nelson, the czar has asked the King of England for royal license for me to wear my order in England! Will he grant it, do you think, the King of England?"

"Of course! An obligation he cannot ignore."

Emma clapped her hands like a child. "That will irritate old Queen Charlotte! And Lord Keith, too!"

"Keith! Pah!"

All Nelson's anger was back again. He continued to rage until, gasping for breath and clutching at his chest, he was obliged to take to his bed. This time Emma insisted on the *Foudroyant's* surgeon attending him, but Nelson said pettishly that nothing could be done. He resigned himself, he added, to the dismal fact that the rest of his days would be spent in a naval hospital, the one at Greenwich, no doubt.

He remained ill and dispirited during the whole seventeen days of the Malta visit. True enough, he went ashore to receptions and dinner parties and conferred many times with Ball and Troubridge on the progress of the blockade; but always he returned, again and again, to his bed. "Finished," he groaned, "and at my age!" Finally, in desperation, Emma took the surgeon aside and asked him to tell her frankly, speaking in complete confidence, the truth of Nelson's heart condition.

"I can find no trace of any heart condition," the surgeon said, lowering his voice. "In my opinion, Lord Nelson has a very strong heart."

"But he really is ill. Anybody can see that."

"Fatigue, anxiety, nerve strain, Your Ladyship."

Yes, and anger, too, she thought, the anger of a frustrated child. Unbelievable in so great and brave a man; but there it was, a sort of penalty imposed by his genius.

"To tell Lord Nelson that he has a strong heart," the surgeon mused, "would only aggravate him and make things worse."

"But something must be done," Emma said.

The surgeon smiled. "I leave it to you, Lady Hamilton. A clever

224

woman should have no trouble in finding a way of restoring His Lordship to health again."

Emma considered this for a moment, then laughed merrily.

"I'll fall ill myself and see if that doesn't take his mind off himself."

"Good, good," the surgeon laughed. "You may rely on me to back you up. A little bout of fever, perhaps?"

"That's as good as anything," she agreed.

The night the *Foudroyant* began the return voyage to Palermo Emma went early to bed, complaining of a headache. She sent Mrs. Cadogan to Nelson with her excuses and begged him not to worry. She would, she assured him, be completely herself again tomorrow. The next morning she remained in bed, and the surgeon made a pretense of attending her. Reports were sent to Nelson during the day. He remained in his night cabin, but his many inquiries betrayed his growing anxiety on her behalf. By nightfall the surgeon warned that the roughness of the sea was bad for Lady Hamilton. Nelson immediately ordered the *Foudroyant* to be run off before the wind. The shout "Brace the yards!" reached her in her cabin and made her chuckle. In the middle of the night she awoke from a tranquil sleep to find Nelson bending over her. He made a swift apology.

"I did not want to disturb you," he faltered, "but my anxiety had kept me awake. Ill as I am, I dragged myself to your side. If you were to die I should have nothing to live for, nothing!"

He grasped her hand and, in doing so, half fell over her cot. If anyone had a fever, he had. She thought comically that she had only made things worse. The plan had undoubtedly failed.

"Dear Nelson," she said, making up her mind at last, "this is no ordinary fever—not really a fever at all. I was a little feverish at first, because of the sickness; but, Nelson, it isn't *fever*."

He looked at her quickly. "You have never been seasick since I've known you."

"No," she agreed, laughter in her voice. "A special kind of sickness, it is."

Nelson's face lit up. "Emma!"

She nodded. "Yes, Nelson."

He sprang to his feet and stood there in his dressing gown, his face flushed, his chest thrown out. All sign of strain had gone.

"If I had two hands I'd clap them! I want to shout for joy. Turn cartwheels. Rouse the whole ship. Give the order to splice the mainbrace. Oh, Emma, I want to tell the whole world!"

"Which, of course, you can't."

His face clouded. "Does the surgeon suspect?"

"Of course not, Nelson."

He bent over her and kissed her tenderly. "Thank you, Emma. You have made me the happiest man in the world, and the most grateful." In childlike simplicity he slipped to his knees at her side and bowed his head. "Dear God, I offer thee my humble thanks." He was on his feet again in a moment, striding briskly up and down the small cabin. "We must consider this soberly, Emma, make careful plans. Even though I'm like a dog with two tails, as happy as a lark, as vain as a peacock!"

"What an odd combination," she teased him, "part dog, part lark, part peacock."

He made a dive at her, tore back the bedclothes, and placed his hand on her stomach.

"I can't feel it."

"Of course you can't, not yet."

"When will it be?"

"The end of next January, perhaps early February."

"Splendid!" He was very businesslike now. "That will give me time to go to London and, before resigning, discuss with the Admiralty my ideas for continuing the struggle with France. They may or may not want to follow my advice, but give it to them I certainly shall! You, my dear, will remain at Palermo until I come back, then we will go together to our home at Brontë."

"Brontë? Are you serious, Nelson?"

"I want our child to be born at Brontë. What else can we do now but turn our backs on the world, the ungrateful world?"

This was the last thing she had expected, the last thing she wanted. She was afraid her disappointment might show in her face; but Nelson, gazing at her rapturously, misread her expression.

"You want to remind me again of duty and honor. Remind me, then! I have a duty to my child. Let honor be satisfied with that."

Emma looked at him sadly. "And when he grows up, Nelson, and people tell him that the French who dominate the world would have been beaten but for his father, who withdrew from the struggle—what then?"

"You say *he?*" Nelson cried eagerly. "You feel sure the child will be a boy?"

"All men want sons, of course," she said quietly. "All great men, all ambitious men."

His mood changed at once, his face clouded. "No, I want a daughter. A daughter, you hear, a daughter!"

Emma guessed his meaning and said in a whisper, "A daughter would be better. No son of ours would ever be able to succeed his father, would ever become the second Lord Nelson."

He swept this aside impatiently. "I never hated the French more than I do at this moment. Never! Very well, our plan is this: We make a farewell visit to Palermo, then hasten north to Leghorn and cross Europe by a route yet to be decided; but it will have to be—confound it all!—a route unmenaced by the French. And then—" His imperious manner collapsed. "And then—what? Tell me that, my dear."

It thrilled her that he should need to turn to her like this, but she had to admit to herself that she had no immediate answer to his question. She would have liked to say, I shall have my child in England, and all the world shall know that Nelson is the father; but she felt instinctively that it was too soon yet to utter such a wish.

She said, "What is to be, will be. Just look at things like that, Nelson. And remember, we have more to make us happy now than we ever had before."

"Yes, more than we ever had before!" he echoed fervently.

20 Sir William said: "I had forgotten how cold England can be."

"As if the weather matters when the welcome is as warm as this!" Emma laughed.

Sir William surveyed the cheering crowds again. "True, my love. A magnificent, touching spectacle."

Nelson agreed heartily. "I would never have dared expect such a welcome. *Touching* is the right word, Sir William."

Emma glanced quickly from one to the other. Each had spoken emotionally; each had tears in his eyes. She raised her arms dramatically, including in the gesture not only her husband and lover, but the tumultuous crowds surrounding their carriage.

"What does official criticism matter now!" she cried.

The travelers had reached Yarmouth not an hour ago, having crossed from Cuxhaven by mail packet. The people of Yarmouth were delirious with joy. The greatest naval hero in English history had set foot on his native soil for the first time since the Battle of the Nile and the welcome was breathtaking. As she watched, the people surged forward, the horses were torn from the carriage, and cheering, brawny men took their places. Tears came to her own eyes. How stupid to have gone to Brontë when a welcome like this awaited them in England.

The progress to the inn, the Wrestler's Arms, was slow; and even when they arrived it was impossible for Nelson to retire from the public view. "Nelson!" the crowd kept roaring in unison, "We want Nelson!" With Emma at his side, he went out to the balcony; and both stood there, despite the heavy rain now falling—Nelson in full dress uniform, Emma in a gay muslin dress. And, as they bowed and waved, all the bells of the town rang out and a band played "See the Conquering Hero Comes."

"Do come in, both of you," Sir William called from behind them. "This is November in England, not June in Naples. You will catch your death of cold."

Ever solicitous of her health these days, Nelson forced Emma to obey Sir William's words and insisted that she should warm herself at the cheerful fire. Sir William was already cowering over it, his thin old hands extended to the flame.

"How wise of Lady Nelson not to have braved the weather on a day like this," he murmured.

Emma looked curiously at Nelson. She had wondered about his wife but had refrained from asking questions.

"Though naturally," Sir William added, with a shake of his head, "she is sadly missed this day. I sincerely trust, my dear fellow, that unthinking people will refrain from criticizing her."

"In all fairness to Fanny," Nelson said roughly, "I must tell you that the fault is mine. I wrote to her from Vienna." He glanced momentarily at Emma, then continued to address himself exclusively to Sir William. "At the time I thought we might land at Portsmouth, but warned her there was some doubt about it. So I advised her to remain at Roundwood and await us there."

"*Us?*" Emma asked in surprise.

Nelson cleared his throat. He still addressed himself exclusively to Sir William.

"I asked Fanny to write to you and invite you and Emma to stay with us at Roundwood. I told her she would find you at Nerot's Hotel."

Sir William had written earlier to Nerot's, in King Street, giving an approximate date of arrival and asking for accommodation. He intended to remain there for a time while looking for a suitable house in London, then later a more permanent residence in the country. Greville, Emma recalled, had been asked to help find the London house.

"So very kind of you, Nelson," Sir William was murmuring. "Roundwood, by all accounts, is a delightful place."

Roundwood, near Ipswich, was the small country house which Nelson had bought during his last visit to England but had never lived in. There Lady Nelson had spent most of her time; and there, living with her, was Nelson's old father.

Nelson remarked that he looked forward to seeing the place and added that he had asked his agent to find him a town house as well. Then, excusing himself on the plea that there were letters to be written, he hurried from the room.

"Ah, vanity, vanity!" Sir William chirped.

"I beg your pardon?" Emma asked, her mind on the things Nelson had just said.

"I am referring, my love, to your summer dress. You must put on something warmer, 'pon my soul you must."

"Yes, of course, Hamilton."

"How delightful," he went on, smiling benevolently, "how really delightful, to think that you and the dear Lady Nelson will soon be such great good friends."

"Delightful, yes," Emma replied automatically.

Her mind was now in tumult. Was Nelson insane? A casual meeting with his wife would be difficult enough; the prospect of living under the same roof with her, for however short a period, was unthinkable! Why, in less than three months, the child, hers and Nelson's, would be born. He must be either insane or still in love with Fanny.

When, finally, unable to bear the uncertainty longer, she sought him out in his room, he had written one letter and was busy with a second.

She glanced at his unfinished letter. "You're writing to Fanny."

"Yes, my dear," Nelson said breezily. "I, at all events, must be the first to acquaint her with our arrival. If I get the letter away now it will reach her tomorrow morning at Roundwood and prepare her for our arrival there. If we leave Yarmouth in the morning we shall be at Roundwood in time for dinner on Saturday."

Emma tried to keep all harshness from her voice. "So you're still set on Hamilton and me staying at Roundwood."

"Why, yes," he said mildly.

"But Nelson—why?"

He put down his pen and looked her full in the face.

"I want you under my own roof. I want to repay you both for all the hospitality you lavished on me in Naples and Palermo."

Emma laughed hysterically. Then she said quietly, "I think you must still be in love with Fanny."

"No! No, Emma, I was never in love with her!" He hammered on the table with his clenched fist. "Never! I love you, no other woman. Affection for Fanny, yes. That is surely understandable. And I have a *duty* to her."

"You've got yourself in an awful fix," Emma said, and in spite of herself she laughed.

He was scowling unhappily now. "My duty to Fanny on the one hand, my duty to you on the other."

Emma tossed her head. "I want no man tied to me by a sense of duty! Anyhow, you'll be free of both of us when you go to sea again."

He gave her the most reproachful of looks. "How set you seem on hurting me. And to quarrel like this, on such a happy day!"

"And what," she went on, "about your duty to your child?"

230

He gave a theatrical groan and bowed his head.

Emma looked away from him impatiently. She reflected that although whenever they had spoken of the child he had gone into raptures of delight he had seemed like a man living in a dream world. Such realities as pregnancy, labor and birth never touched him. She looked at him again now. His unhappiness, his utter dejection, filled her with compassion. He was, she thought, a greater baby than any child she could ever bear him. She went to him quickly, smoothed back his hair, kissed his brow. He clung to her then and sobbed.

"Tell me what to do for the best," he said brokenly.

She said: "Dear Nelson, our real problem is the coming birth of our child. Do you realize how long I've been pregnant?" Obviously Nelson didn't, though he was making an effort to remember. "What with one thing and another it was July before we left the Mediterranean, and the journey across Europe took longer than we expected. It's the first week in November now, Nelson."

"Six months or more," he said.

Emma laughed dryly. "Do you want me to have the baby at Roundwood? We could only do that if we told Hamilton first and he agreed to pretend the baby was his."

"My God, how horrible!" Nelson cried.

"Well then, what?"

He smiled engagingly. "My clever little Emma will think of something."

Emma remembered her earlier wish to have the baby with Nelson at her side, proudly acknowledging to all the world that he was the father, but the cold moral atmosphere of England made her aware now that this would be impossible.

Then what to do?

She realized that she had made no plans of any sort. She had allowed things to drift, just as Nelson had. And why? Because the long trip across Europe had indeed been, as she had predicted, a royal progress. They had been cheered and feted everywhere, at Florence, at Vienna, at Prague, at Dresden—at more places than she could rightly remember.

"At all events I have a plan," Nelson said. He was happy and smiling now, completely recovered. "But first I must meet Fanny, meet her and be kind to her, and try to reach an amicable understanding with her."

"You still insist on this visit to Roundwood?"

Nelson smiled slyly. "Dearest Emma, I would be lost without you, utterly miserable. The Admiralty might call on me at any moment. I need you at my side as long as I stay in England."

Emma shrugged helplessly. For perhaps the first time in her life she felt that she was face to face with a situation beyond her immediate control. Incuriously she said, "Tell me about your plan, Nelson."

He slapped her lightly across the shoulders. "You must wait and see, my dear."

Their departure from Yarmouth rivaled in public enthusiasm their arrival the day before. Once again Emma and Nelson waved to the men and women who ran beside the carriage, while the sight of the corps of cavalry, making up an unofficial guard of honor, filled her with additional pride.

In contrast, Nelson's country house, when they reached it, seemed strangely silent and unfriendly. The sky was darker now, the wind moaned and heavy drops of rain were falling. Emma repressed a shudder and tried not to think of Lady Nelson, waiting in the grim dark house.

"The place looks utterly deserted," Nelson complained, as the carriage drew up at the front door.

A single servant appeared out of the shadows. He was a stranger to Nelson, but seeing the uniform and the empty sleeve the man touched his forelock. Nelson questioned him impatiently and learned that his wife had gone to London some days ago, while his father, eager to join her, had left Roundwood yesterday.

"Where is Her Ladyship staying in town?" Nelson demanded angrily.

The servant seemed uncertain of this but said that he had been told to forward all letters to 64 Upper Seymour Street. Nelson looked puzzled.

"That," he decided, "must be the house my agent has taken for me. Apparently Fanny made up her mind to go there and wait." He looked inquiringly at Emma. "This place depresses me. Shall we go on to London by easy stages?"

"Oh, yes, Nelson, please!" She shuddered. "I don't fancy this desolate place any more than you do."

"So much for my wish," he sighed, "to entertain my dearest friends in my own home. Perhaps this new place in Upper Seymour Street . . ."

"We will go first to Nerot's," Sir William decided, and to Emma's relief Nelson left it at that.

After a night on the road they reached a London shaken and battered by its greatest storm in a hundred years. The last hour of their journey was one of pelting rain, vivid lightning, and heavy thunder; and in one of the outer streets of the city a house, struck by lightning, collapsed as they passed it.

When at last the frightened horses were drawn to a halt outside Nerot's, all three travelers staggered thankfully into the hall of the hotel. They were greeted immediately, much to their surprise, by Nelson's father.

"Heaven bless you, Horatio," cried the old man, warmly embracing his son. "Dear me, but one could scarcely say that the elements are pleased to welcome you."

"What brought you here, Father?" Nelson asked. "Here to Nerot's?"

"Fanny, my dear boy, Fanny. She seemed quite sure, goodness knows why, that Nerot's would be the best place to wait for you."

"You mean that Fanny is here, too?"

"Upstairs in her room, resting, bless her heart."

"Her room?" Nelson's voice rose on a high note. "Fanny is actually *staying* here?"

"We both are, Horatio, we both are."

Nelson gave Emma a quick, puzzled look. She shrugged. This must be Lady Nelson's way of saying that she preferred not to receive the Hamiltons in her own home.

Belatedly Nelson introduced Sir William and Emma to his father.

Old Mr. Nelson nodded and bowed and said how delighted he was; and Emma, who had expected and been prepared for a frosty meeting with him, could see that he meant it. She liked him immediately and thought that he looked more like a country squire than a country parson. She told him sweetly that without such a father Nelson could never have been the man he was. The flattery pleased him, and beaming on her amiably he said, "My son's dearest friend, and mine also." Emma all but laughed aloud. If she could conquer the rest of the family —yes, even Nelson's wife!—as easily as this, all would be well.

"Now we must send up for Fanny," Mr. Nelson chuckled. "Oh, how happy the poor girl will be." His eyes twinkled. "But wait, Horatio, wait! Why not run up and surprise her, eh?"

Nelson said quickly, "We'll *all* go up. Come, Sir William, come, Emma."

At the door Nelson hesitated for a moment, then flung it open. It seemed at first that the room, made dark and gloomy by the storm, was empty; but after a moment Emma caught sight of a woman at the window, standing there looking out at the storm-lashed street.

"Fanny . . ." Nelson said.

There was nervousness as well as embarrassment in his voice.

Lady Nelson turned slowly, started to come forward, then, at the sight of the little group behind Nelson, remained motionless. The room was too dark for Emma to see her clearly, but she fancied that Nelson's wife had paled.

Fanny moved at last. "Horatio . . ."

It was Nelson who remained motionless now.

"A stormy homecoming," he faltered.

"Stormy, yes," Lady Nelson replied, her voice a monotone.

"Kiss her, my boy, kiss her!" cried old Mr. Nelson, quite beside himself with excitement.

Nelson moved then, bent forward stiffly and kissed his wife briefly on the cheek. She flinched and half-turned from him; the color came rapidly to her cheeks. Watching, Emma had never felt so sorry for anyone in her life. There was a moment's awkward silence, broken in the end by Lady Nelson herself.

"Introduce me to your friends, Horatio."

Nelson laughed uneasily. "As if introductions were necessary!"

There was another awkward silence, broken this time by Sir William. He ambled forward, took Lady Nelson's hand in his and kissed it with a fine show of elderly gallantry.

"Dear Lady Nelson, how delighted, how very delighted we are to meet you."

She withdrew her hand; her color deepened. Studying her, Emma remembered that she was a few months older than Nelson himself. Nearly forty-three, that would make her, but how much older than that she looked—so staid, so old maidish. Yet in a vapid sort of way she could look pretty, even at forty-three, if she made more of herself, got rid of those drab, old-fashioned clothes.

Sir William broke yet another awkward silence. "Dear Lady Nelson, how proud you must be of this hero we have brought safely home to you."

"Proud, yes," Lady Nelson said flatly, no lift whatever to her voice.

"The savior of England," Sir William ran on, "the bravest man in the world."

Lady Nelson shrugged almost imperceptibly. "I suppose he must have been brave, going into action like that against the French." She seemed to be weighing the question carefully in her mind, an effort that soon tired her. "Yes, I suppose so," she added lamely.

Emma, no longer sorry for her, grew furious. A woman of no imagination, *that* was obvious! The domestic type, more appreciative of a well-run house than the glorious achievements of the heroic Nelson.

"You should have seen the welcome they gave him at Yarmouth," she cried, and went on to describe it at length until she was almost breathless. "It would have done your heart good, Lady Nelson."

Fanny glanced at her coldly. "I expect it was very interesting, Lady Hamilton."

"And the royal progress through Europe," Emma tried again. "The fetes and receptions everywhere! The presentation at the Austrian court, the grand fete given by the Archduke Charles at Prague in honor of Nelson's birthday, the—! Oh, Lady Nelson, if only you—"

But Lady Nelson interrupted icily. "I understand now why the journey took so long."

"To hurry would have been unkind to those who wished to honor me," Nelson said sharply.

"Of course, Horatio."

"What puzzles me, Fanny," Nelson was saying, "is why you should have expected to find me at Nerot's."

Lady Nelson smiled, a smile so brief that it was scarcely noticeable. Her reply came docilely enough.

"You informed me of Sir William Hamilton's intention of staying here with his wife."

Emma tried not to smile. Lady Nelson might just as well have said: *Where Emma Hamilton is, there also will you find Nelson.* She saw that Nelson, sensing this too, had paled slightly.

"But Fanny, this address in Upper Seymour Street—?"

Lady Nelson stole a calm cool glance at Emma. "A forwarding address only, for letters; but your agent has taken a house for us in Dover Street. Are you ready to go there now, Horatio?" Giving Nelson no time to speak she turned to his father. "Do please go down, Father, and have them call us a carriage."

Taken by surprise as she was, Emma felt sure that the silly woman would never get Nelson back by means such as these. She looked at him quizzically. He had hesitated, allowing his father to go happily from the room, but now he recovered himself quickly.

"I had looked forward," he said sharply, "to a little family dinner,

235

here at Nerot's, with Sir William and Lady Hamilton, and that, my dear Fanny, I intend to have. Tomorrow will be time enough for me to inspect the house in Dover Street and decide whether or not I like it."

Fanny said meekly, the meekness obviously covering a smoldering anger, "Whatever you wish, Horatio." Her lips pursed tightly. "As you see, this is a single room. The management will be happy to find us a double one."

Before more could be said there was an imperative rap on the door and a tall young man, dressed like a clerk yet carrying about his person an air of languid elegance, strolled into the room.

"I have the honor to represent the *Courier*," he announced. "If My Lord Nelson would be gracious enough to grant me a few moments of his time I, and our subscribers, would be both honored and grateful."

"Ah!" Nelson cried in delight, "the newspapers!"

Sir William, propped up on the pillows, was busily reading the morning journal which Emma, now eating a late breakfast at his side, had passed to him.

What a fiasco, that family dinner party last night! And how intolerable, those long grim silences imposed upon them by the disapproving Lady Nelson! Emma realized now that she had broken the silence time and time again with bursts of unnatural chatter. And she had boasted too much about the achievements, hers and Nelson's, in the Kingdom of the Two Sicilies. "I wonder you could bear to leave it all," Lady Nelson had remarked, as many as six times, each time a shade more sarcastically. And how Nelson had riled his wife with his constant references to "dear kind Lady Hamilton." Not, of course, that he had intended to annoy her. Still it was clear that he had expected his wife to raise her own voice in praise of "this dear good creature whose ministrations saved my life and restored me to health after the Battle of the Nile."

And Sir William himself, singing Nelson's praises, had annoyed Lady Nelson, too. Perhaps that was why, when Nelson had gaily called for champagne, Emma had drunk far too much. She could still remember the look of disgust on Lady Nelson's prim, pale face. What a relief it had been when the party had finally broken up and each couple had retired to their own rooms. The sight of Nelson and his wife going off together had hurt, but the relief had persisted.

There was a knock at the door, and after Sir William cried, "Come in, come in!" who should appear but Greville.

"Gracious," he said, with a laugh that sounded like a sneer, "what a charming connubial scene!"

"Greville!" Sir William shouted.

"Hamilton!" Greville responded.

He went around to Sir William's side of the bed and bent over to embrace his uncle with rather lukewarm enthusiasm.

"Now come to my side," Emma said, the laughter bubbling up in her. "Your aunt is waiting to kiss you."

Greville's eyes flashed for a moment. He leaned across Sir William and pecked her on the cheek. She knew then, just as she had known at the first sound of his voice, that despite their years of amicable correspondence they were near-enemies when face to face.

"Well, well, well," Sir William was saying, "you have changed but little in the past eight years. Which is more," he added sadly, "than you can say of me."

"Or of my dear aunt, your lady wife," Greville declared, with a thin smile. He was casting his eyes over Emma, whose plump arms and shoulders were clearly revealed by the low-cut nightgown. "Fair, fat, and—forty."

"Nowhere near forty yet," Emma said resentfully, and quickly drew the bedclothes up to her neck. "You are nearly fifty yourself, and look it!"

Annoyed as she was with him, she found herself admitting that he was indeed little changed in eight years. His manner was as precise as ever, and his clothes, from the neat lace ruffle to the black, silver-buckled shoes, immaculate. Age had scarcely touched him. Any change there was showed in his face, which was a little thinner than she remembered, while his nostrils had a more pinched look, as if he was forever bracing himself against a bad smell.

In other words, she thought shrewdly, against life itself, which after all hadn't been too kind to him. He was still a bachelor; his income was a mere pittance and his expectations, unless he outlived her, could not be great.

He was explaining now that he had called at Nerot's yesterday, not an hour before their arrival. He was anxious, he added, his eyes lingering quizzically on Emma, to meet their famous friend. "Such a pity," he drawled, "to find Nelson's splendid arrival marred by those nasty caricatures."

237

"What nasty caricatures?" Emma demanded.

"In the shop windows," he said. "I saw two this morning, one of which was particularly spiteful. And how much larger than life it made you look, Emma."

"Poor Nelson," Sir William groaned. "How deeply this will hurt his sensitive feelings."

"It was your feelings I had in mind, Hamilton," Greville said sternly.

Sir William wagged his head. "I, my dear Greville, am old enough to be tolerant. Nothing touches me now, nothing at all."

Emma saw Greville bite his lip. But almost at once he composed himself and said, "I have excellent news for you, Hamilton."

"Ah, you have found me a suitable house."

"No, but Beckford has offered you the temporary use of his place in Grosvenor Square."

Sir William was delighted. "Oh, splendid! Hotel life irritates me, and after so much wearisome traveling it will be heavenly to live in a civilized house again."

Emma was just as delighted. William Beckford, whom she had met in Naples, was one of Sir William's cousins. He not only traveled in splendor with a large retinue of servants, but lived in the utmost luxury. The Grosvenor Square house, she was sure, would be an absolute delight.

"Do wait below while we dress, Greville," Sir William said, "and then, if you would, good fellow that you are, assist us in our move."

"One other matter first," Greville said. He was looking at Emma, smiling his thin mean smile. "My aunt, I trust, has not forgotten that she possesses a child known to all of us as the little Emma."

Emma very nearly had, but she said hotly, "Of course I haven't!"

"No longer *little*, I grant you," Greville drawled, "and likely to become something of a problem. She is, you know, nearly seventeen. Amazing, you must admit, the way time flies."

"Problem?" Emma took him up. "Has she been misbehaving herself?"

"The way you did at that age?" Greville smiled. "No, I was merely thinking that the sudden appearance of a seventeen-year-old daughter might make her mother feel embarrassingly old."

The girl was still at school in the north, maintained there by Sir William, on whose behalf Greville had always paid the fees and provided other incidental monies. From time to time Emma had written to her aunt, Mrs. Connor, with whom the younger Emma still spent her holidays.

"Well, what are we to do about her?" Greville asked.

"Dear me, dear me, have you any suggestions, Greville?" Sir William wailed.

"She can, if you wish, remain at the school as an assistant teacher."

"Oh, splendid, splendid!" Sir William said.

Greville moved to the door, saying over his shoulder, "Till later, dear Auntie."

The baleful look which accompanied his words made Emma feel wretched. "Oh, Hamilton," she said tearfully, "I don't think I like being back in England again."

"The weather, just the weather," Sir William said placidly.

Lady Nelson sat stiffly on the edge of one of Beckford's elegant brocade-covered chairs. Her face had a pinched look and her plump little hands were blue; but she was much too refined, Emma concluded, to extend her hands to the warm blaze of the fire. Nelson himself was standing with his back to it, a happy, faraway look on his face; while Sir William, worn out after yet another evening's excitement, was dozing in the depths of a silk-covered armchair, his duties as host completely forgotten.

"I must admit," Nelson remarked, "that it flatters me to be received like that whenever I show my face in public."

At his insistence Emma and Sir William had accompanied him and Lady Nelson to Drury Lane Theater where the whole audience, attracted by the full dress uniform with its empty right sleeve, had risen and cheered with gusto.

Nelson and his wife, moving from Nerot's when the Hamiltons had left the hotel for Beckford's house, were now installed in Dover Street and tonight, pressed by Sir William, had "dropped in" at Grosvenor Square for "a bite of supper"—Lady Nelson, of course, unwillingly.

Emma moved her chair back a little from the fire. She felt suddenly stifled, when only a few moments ago she had complained about the cold of the English winter. The Mansion House reception . . . She let her mind dwell happily on thoughts of it. How fortunate, really, that Lady Nelson had chosen to stay at home and sulk. Oh, the splendor of that august gathering! She could see it all still, Nelson of the Nile; Nelson, Duke of Brontë, a resplendent mass of stars and medals and orders; Sir William a gallant figure still, despite his doddering manner; and she herself, Dame Chevalière of the Order of St. John of Jerusalem, standing proudly between them, her order pinned to her breast. Oh, the cheers, the speeches, the joyous shouting—!

Memory clouded. She felt more stifled than ever. Nelson's dapper little figure by the fire danced before her, and Lady Nelson's grim unhappy face hovered as if in a haze. The fire was really much too hot. She half rose, intending to push her chair still farther back and then, toppling forward, knew no more.

It was the sound of Nelson's agitated voice that brought her back to consciousness just as Greville, in her too vivid dream, was reminding her nastily that in spite of public acclaim she had not been received at the English court and never would be. This was true enough. Nelson and Sir William had been obliged to go without her to the king's levee, where his majesty, addressing only a few curt words to Nelson, had quickly turned his royal back on him.

She lay for a moment with her eyes closed. Nelson's voice reached her again. He babbled something about her being dead; and Lady Nelson, speaking harshly, said "Nonsense, Horatio!" She also uttered another sentence, not quite clear to Emma's still befuddled mind, but including such words as "too tightly laced" and "her condition."

This was too much for Emma. She moved her arms slightly—she was covered with a blanket, she noticed—moaned, and slowly opened her eyes.

"Thank heaven!" Nelson cried.

She was lying on her own bed and assumed that servants had carried her up. The only people with her now were Nelson and his wife.

"Apparently I fainted," she murmured. "How silly of me. I shall never get used to this English climate again, never."

"Lie still, I beg of you," Nelson said. "A doctor has been sent for. Sir William is waiting for him downstairs."

"Pooh! As if I need a doctor!" Emma sat up. "See, I'm quite all right again."

Lady Nelson said sourly: "In that case, and the hour being late, we may as well go. Come, Horatio."

"Not till the doctor arrives," Nelson said stoutly.

Fortunately, at that moment, Sir William hurried into the room followed by a doctor. Nelson, after the slightest hesitation, withdrew with his wife, leaving Emma to laugh at Sir William's concern and dismiss the doctor. A narrow escape, she thought. If the doctor had come while she was still unconscious the cat would have been out of the bag with a vengeance. Not that it wasn't a pity, in some ways . . .

When the house had settled down and Sir William had gone to his own room, Emma banked up the bedroom fire and slowly undressed, regretting as she did so the ban placed by her present condition on the employment of a personal maid. Condition? She frowned and tried to remember what Lady Nelson had said. She recalled the other words, *Too tightly laced*. That, of course, was true enough.

Emma slipped into her nightgown, snuffed out the candles and tried to make herself comfortable in bed. For a while she watched the leaping shadows in the firelight of the room. Then she began to feel drowsy. Nothing mattered in this world except your own point of view, getting what you wanted, and, of course, loving somebody. Leave tomorrow's troubles, if troubles they were, until tomorrow. Upon which not very comforting thought, she fell into a dreamless sleep.

It was Sir William's voice that woke her—that and the touch of his cold fingers on her shoulder as he plucked at the bedclothes. He held a candle in the other hand; he was shivering and his teeth were chattering, while his nightcap bobbed ridiculously on his head. The fire had burned to a little heap of glowing embers.

"What is it, Hamilton? Are you ill?"

"No," he said querulously, "but I expect I shall be after this. Nelson is downstairs."

Emma sat up. "Nelson? What time is it?"

"Five o'clock, and a bitterly cold morning. I wonder his knocking didn't rouse you. Go down and minister to the poor fellow, my love. I did what I could, but unless I go back to bed I shall catch my death of cold."

He stumped out of the room, leaving Emma to snatch up a wrap and hurry down to the ornate drawing room. Nelson was huddled over the remains of the fire, absently poking at the dying embers. As she watched from the doorway he snatched up the bellows and tried with his one hand and his knees to blow the fire. Failing, he hurled the bellows aside, then saw her.

"Useless!" he cried. "Useless to myself, to everybody!"

Emma ran to him; quick tears streamed down her cheeks.

"But not to me, Nelson! Never to me. And not to England!"

He flung himself away from her and half-fell into a chair.

"I've walked the streets all night," he said in a low, dazed voice. "Through the Fleet Market again and again, across Blackfriars Bridge.

241

Then, in desperation, I came to the only place in the world I dare call home."

Highly dramatic it was, but pitiful too. And heartrending. He looked so utterly dejected, so shrunken in his oversized cape.

"You quarreled with Fanny."

"Yes. A dreadful, terrible scene."

"You quarreled about me, Nelson."

"And Josiah. She blames *me* for her own worthless son's despicable behavior."

"I expect she blames me for that, too."

"Yes. I never want to see her again. I shall stay with her at Dover Street, a stranger, only until I can make financial arrangements for her."

He roused himself, smiled wanly. "Enough of *my* troubles, we must think now of yours—which, of course, are mine, too."

"Your wife suspects, doesn't she, Nelson?"

He nodded. "She said you were too tightly laced for a woman in your condition." He smiled in sudden boyishness. "I said that was utter nonsense, your husband being so old and frail."

Emma smiled with him, then said, "Did she make any actual accusations about you and me?"

"I think she wanted to, but she was afraid. She must never know the truth, Emma. Promise me that! Help me by keeping it secret. Then she will be powerless to act."

Emma's heart sank. "But don't you want her to act? Don't you want her to sue you for divorce?"

"She would never do that. I referred briefly to divorce; she laughed in my face. But she would make a scandal, ruin my career, do everything possible to hurt the child. I never knew a more spiteful woman, never!" He was looking at Emma uneasily. "In any case, what use would divorce be? You would still be tied to Sir William, and neither of us would willingly hurt Sir William." Nelson was like a bewildered and frightened little boy.

"Try not to worry," she said coaxingly. "Just tell me what you want me to do, though goodness knows how we can keep the actual birth a secret from the world."

Nelson began to look happier, not half so shrunken.

"We can, and we will. Your mother need be your only confidante. She loves us both and she will help us. You will have need of her, in case I am called away."

242

"You . . . expect to be called away?"

He said: "If you can hide your condition till the end—"

"I can do that." And she repeated, "You expect to be called away?"

"I offered myself for immediate service," he said testily. "You know that. Now there is talk of my being given the Baltic command. The call might come any time, the call to duty. I—" He broke off and looked at her pleadingly. "It would break my heart, not to be with you at the time—now here is my plan," he went on quickly. "Foster parents will be found for the child; and later—much later, of course—I shall legally adopt it. It will be necessary to give a false date of birth at a delayed christening to support my story that the child was born abroad before we returned to England, abroad where the parents, friends of mine, died."

Oh, yes, he had a plan, but a crazy one; a broad outline with many details to be filled in, difficulties to be dealt with. He expected her to live a normal life till the very end, then keep the birth a secret. And where did he propose that she should stay during labor? Here at Grosvenor Square?

"You do agree, Emma?" he said anxiously.

"Of course, Nelson."

Emma smiled and was almost happy. Despite the details and difficulties she recognized the drama and mystery, to which the actress in her responded. Nevertheless, she thought, one should strive, if possible, to be practical.

"If we confided in Hamilton," she said quietly, "he would help us by fathering the child. I know he would."

"No," Nelson said violently, "I told you once—!"

She nodded. "I know, Nelson. The child would be yours, yes, but legally his. All this secrecy, it's just a matter of pride, isn't it?"

Nelson smiled shyly. "You don't blame me, do you?"

Emma kissed him impulsively. "It's a clever plan. You'll adopt the child and that way it will be yours legally, too."

He smiled and rose to his feet. He was a very different man now from the one she had seen cowering dejectedly over the dying fire. His back was straight, his shoulders square, and his most charming smile lighted the face she loved.

"Our troubles are at an end!" he cried gaily.

In the weeks that followed the arrival in London, Nelson was with Emma and Sir William constantly, first at the Grosvenor Square house

243

and later at 23 Piccadilly, a smaller place leased by Sir William, the front windows of which offered a pleasant view of the Green Park.

"Here," Sir William declared sorrowfully, "I shall end my days, the greatest event of my life being a cautious little stroll in the park."

He had apparently forgotten all about his earlier resolve to buy a country house and spend most of his time there, and Emma had no wish to remind him of it. He was in poor health again. The cold he had caught after being roused in the middle of the night by Nelson had left him with a cough; and he had been further weakened by a bout of the old trouble, the bilious fever. Emma fussed over him, pampered him, and decided that to keep him an invalid might serve her well during the weeks of waiting for her confinement.

The approach of Christmas brought an invitation from Sir William's cousin, Beckford, to spend the festive season at his country mansion, Fonthill Abbey. The invitation included Lord and Lady Nelson.

"A somewhat ticklish situation," Sir William murmured.

"Fanny would never accept," Nelson said quickly.

"But you yourself, my dear fellow—?"

"How could I bear to miss spending Christmas with you and Emma?" Nelson said warmly. "It might well be the last we shall ever spend together."

"What a thing to say!" Emma protested.

Nelson gave her a gloomy look. "I might die in action long before next Christmas."

"Oh, Nelson," she laughed, "you always expect to die in action."

He refused to laugh with her. "My death in action is as fixed as fate, Emma."

"My dear Nelson," Sir William said, "you have received a new appointment and are keeping it from us."

"No, I know only that promotion has been promised and the call will come soon."

During the short holiday at Fonthill Abbey, where Nelson was as happy and high-spirited as she had ever known him, Emma's mind dwelt often on the promised promotion. With the recent fall of Valetta had come word that Lord Keith intended to retire; and Queen Maria Carolina, a distant figure now in Emma's memory, was pressing the Admiralty for Nelson's return to the Mediterranean. Would he really be given the Mediterranean command? It would be a popular appointment, and both the Admiralty and the Queen of England would take pleasure in placing Nelson as far away from Lady Hamilton as possible. More than once she felt that the future had an ominous look.

244

Nelson was summoned to the Admiralty the day they returned from Fonthill. Shunning Lady Nelson at Dover Street, he came straight to Piccadilly with his news.

"Is it the Mediterranean?" Emma asked.

Nelson frowned slightly. "No, the Channel Fleet. I am to be second-in-command, with the rank of vice-admiral of the Blue."

"It's not enough, not enough by far!" Emma raged. "And why not a full admiral? You do the work of one!"

"Would you rather I went back to the Mediterranean, so much farther from home?"

"I would make any sacrifice for you, hurtful as it might be to me."

"Dear sweet Emma," he said. "Well, perhaps I *had* hoped for the Mediterranean command, and hoped somehow to get you out there, too. A dream, and a foolish one. Impossible, perhaps, to recapture the great joy we knew there once."

Emma tried to be practical. "When do you leave London?"

"Soon," was all he would say, "soon . . ."

He left two weeks later, bound for Southampton and a conference with Sir Hyde Parker before going on to Plymouth dockyard to join his new ship, the *San Josef*. The last thing he did before setting out was pay a call at Piccadilly. With Sir William in bed, suffering from a slight chill, he and Emma were able to snatch a few minutes alone together. They stood side by side at the drawing-room window, gazing at the desolate wintry scene of the park. They spoke in whispers; and Emma, seeing the ill, strained look on Nelson's face, wondered how best to achieve a note of cheerfulness.

"I have seen Fanny for the last time," he said.

"Did she take the parting well?"

"She scarcely cared," he said bitterly. "She has a certain position in society because people, being sorry for her, are kind to her. She has her title. She is Lady Nelson. She has money; I am making her a more than adequate allowance."

"Will she live at Roundwood?"

How silly it was to waste precious moments discussing his wife; but neither of them had the heart, she knew, to speak of the things that really mattered.

"I have arranged to sell Roundwood. She will live at Dover Street, or wherever she pleases."

He added vehemently, "I shall never see her again!"

"And your father, does he know about this final break?"

"I have written to him. He is staying for a time at Bath."

Mrs. Cadogan, newly returned from a visit to her sister in Manchester, came bustling into the room. She was dressed in black, as usual, with a black shawl about her shoulders. Her keys, a smaller bunch than she had carried at the Palazzo Sessa, jangled importantly at her waist.

"It's beginning to snow," she remarked.

They saw that it was; the first light flakes were already giving a fairy-like touch to the bare branches in the park.

Mrs. Cadogan made up the fire, then bustled out again.

"Have you told her?" Nelson asked.

Emma shook her head. "I'll do it later on."

"I am leaving everything to you, it seems."

"My shoulders are broad enough," Emma laughed.

"You're brave," he said fiercely. "Braver than I am. Braver than a man ever could be."

She turned to him and kissed him. He clung to her passionately.

"We should have gone to Brontë, Emma!"

"Come and say that again after your *next* victory!"

He was smiling now and went on eagerly, "A young naval friend of mine, at sea with me, is in love with a Mrs. Thompson. Circumstances prevent him from marrying her, yet she is about to have his child. Mrs. Thompson's friend is, of course, distracted—at his wits' end. So simple, you see, for me to write to you on his behalf and make inquiries about Mrs. Thompson, in whom you are taking a great interest. So simple for you, too, to write to me and tell me about Mrs. Thompson's baby." Nelson looked pathetic in his eagerness. "You do agree, my dear?"

"It's a good idea," she told him cheerfully.

"And what more natural, I being the hero of Mrs. Thompson's friend, than that he should want to call the child after me!"

"If it's a boy, yes."

"And if a girl, the same, with a change of the last letter!"

"Horatio for a boy, Horatia for a girl," Emma agreed.

"Tell me you're happy, Emma," Nelson pleaded. "I can only tear myself away if you do."

"I'm happy, darling," Emma said obediently.

And having said it she thought, in surprise, "I am, at that, I really am."

21 Sir William, wrapped in rugs, his slippered feet on a footstool, sat dolefully by the fire, not even glancing at Greville who was pacing up and down the room, gesticulating indignantly.

"Shameful," he repeated, "shameful!"

He was discussing the government's apparent unwillingness to grant the retired ambassador a pension. Emma, sitting at the other side of the wide fireplace, looked at him in surprise. It was unlike Greville to display so much emotion.

"We shall persist," he went on. "We shall leave no stone unturned. I have already been in communication with his royal highness, the Prince of Wales."

Sir William stirred himself. "A waste of time, my dear Greville. My foster brother the king is the man to move the government, not the spendthrift Prince of Wales."

"I repeat that we shall leave no stone unturned," Greville said.

Tired of the sound of his voice, Emma turned a deaf ear to it and wondered what progress her mother was making. Mrs. Cadogan had gone out again this afternoon in search of a suitable nurse to take charge of the baby when it came. She chuckled to herself, thinking of the sight of her mother's face when the news had been broken to her. Well, she hadn't been shocked, that was one good thing, just "knocked endways over" by surprise. "Good Lord alive, girl, I'd never believe you was that way, an' your time so close!" Nice to know that not even Mrs. Cadogan's sharp watchful eyes had grown suspicious.

"I must confess that a pension would be most welcome these days," Sir William was mumbling, "dear me, yes!"

Emma looked at him in surprise. "Good gracious, you're not hard up, Hamilton?"

Greville shot her a baleful look. "I can well believe that his expenditure these days exceeds his income."

Emma was flabbergasted. "In debt, Hamilton, and you a rich man!"

"Unfortunately the rich are more apt to get into debt than the poor," Sir William pronounced sagely.

"Then the sooner you get a pension the better, that's what *I* say."

"A pension is certainly due to him," Greville said snappishly, "though you must admit, Emma, that it is only made necessary by the burden of an extravagant wife."

"*Me*—extravagant?" Emma gasped. "Hamilton has never complained."

"He has been much too indulgent," Greville said severely. "Really, Hamilton, you have."

Sir William roused himself, laughed foolishly. "Can you blame me, with so beautiful and clever a wife?"

"Beautiful and clever wives," Greville ran on, "have reduced many a man to penury before today. Economy, my dear Emma, is absolutely necessary, otherwise Hamilton will be obliged to draw on his capital."

Emma laughed shortly. She knew now the reason for Greville's vast indignation. With designs on some of that capital himself, he was anxious to see it preserved intact.

"We must tighten the purse strings, 'pon my soul we must," Sir William croaked.

Emma laughed. "I wouldn't know where to begin."

"You employ far too many servants, for one thing," Greville snapped.

Too many servants! She almost laughed aloud again. The servants, presenting as they did one of the problems of the immediate future, had worried her sorely. If she went away to have the baby her absence might attract attention or be remembered afterward, so she and her mother had decided that the best thing she could do was have it here at 23 Piccadilly. But "Risky enough with Sir William in the house," her mother had said, "what about all these servants?" Now Greville had given her an excellent idea.

"Damn you, Greville, how you hate me!" she cried, pointing a finger at him, and then began to work herself up into a most effective fit of temper, finally screaming, "Very well! I'll give them their notice, every single one of them!"

"Emma, Emma, my sweet—" Sir William protested weakly.

"We'll manage, Ma an' me. We'll run the 'ouse between us, you see if we don't!"

"Such delightful language," Greville sneered. "How quickly the artificial culture drops from you."

"You—you—you!—" She was in a real rage now.

"Children, children!" Sir William pleaded. His hands were shaking, he looked a pitiful sight.

248

"There! See what you've done to him!" Emma reproached Greville.

"Done?" Greville shouted.

"Brought on another of Hamilton's attacks. Real sensitive, his poor stomach is. Upset his nerves and it's the bilious fever again."

"Oh, rubbish!" Greville said.

"The dear sweet Emma understands my condition better than you do," Sir William said plaintively.

Emma went to him quickly and helped him out of his chair.

"Come, Hamilton, up to bed with you. Rest and quiet, that's what you need most."

"And peace, too," he moaned, as he allowed her to lead him from the room.

Poor Hamilton, she thought, as she tucked him up in his bed a few minutes later, it was a shame to treat him like this, but necessary to her plans. Only when she had closed his door behind her did she realize how tired she felt herself. Her heart was palpitating and her hands felt clammy.

"Damn you, Emma," she told herself, "you're as strong as a horse, an' don't you forget it!"

She went slowly downstairs, hoping that Greville had taken his leave; but he was still in the drawing room, standing with his back to the fire and a thoughtful expression on his face.

"I keep asking myself," he said softly, "why you feel the need to pamper Hamilton so much. He is old and frail, yes, but not ill. It seems to me that you want to keep him out of the way as much as possible, but—why?"

"You're talking nonsense, Greville."

"I could understand it, of course, if Nelson were still on the scene," he drawled. He looked at her closely. "Are you ill yourself, Emma?"

"Ill—me?" she scoffed.

"I can see sweat on your brow, and you seem to be short of breath."

"It's the fever, that's all. I get little bouts of it myself."

"This is the first I have heard of it, Emma."

"I was never the one to complain."

He laughed unpleasantly. "The noble Emma!" He laughed again. "I do agree that the task of half-carrying Hamilton up the stairs would be no easy one for a woman as fat as you are."

"God 'ow I 'ate you, Greville!"

"Your aitches, Emma, your aitches."

249

She flew at him then, aching to claw at his face. He evaded her neatly, smiled his most supercilious smile and slipped out of the room. Breathless, her limbs shaking, she fell into Sir William's chair by the fire. Tears came to her eyes. She felt lost and lonely, and had an urge to go up to Sir William and confide in him fully.

"Much good that would do," she admonished herself. "An' as for being sorry for yourself, that ain't like you, now is it!" She laughed weakly.

Feeling better, she called the servants together and gave them their notice. There were little cries of dismay; so she spoke laughingly about economy and, knowing that none of them liked Greville, added with a wink, "It's that ridiculous Mr. Greville." She winked again, saying, "No need to go till a week from now, and I'll have you back again in next to no time."

She was in gay, high spirits when Mrs. Cadogan returned, bringing news that she had found a nurse, a Mrs. Gibson of Little Titchfield Street, who was willing to take the baby when it came.

"And find a wet nurse for you, too," Mrs. Cadogan added.

"Oh . . ." Emma said, suddenly depressed.

"Now what's the matter, girl?"

"It's what we wanted, I know, Ma, but now I wish I could keep the baby myself."

"And cause a rare old scandal?" Mrs. Cadogan looked shrewdly at her daughter. "No need to act with me, Emma."

"It's true enough, Ma. It came over me suddenly."

"Lord save us, I do believe you mean it!"

"And why shouldn't I, Ma? It's not like the other time, at Up Park. So why shouldn't I want to keep it and love it?"

Mrs. Cadogan's face softened. "You're a queer one, you are. No mistake of that. An' just about making me cry, you are, damn you, Emma!"

"Not as bad as I'm painted, eh, Ma?"

Mrs. Cadogan sniffed back her tears. "That depends on how you look at things. Vain but not selfish. Extravagant and wasteful, but not mean. Sticking to Lord Nelson because of the reflected glory, but loving him, too, I'll grant you that."

"Been summing me up proper, haven't you, Ma?"

"Believe me, I'm right, Emma."

"Yes, Ma, I expect you are," Emma admitted soberly.

Nelson's first letter had come.

He was at Plymouth now, angered by the fact that the *San Josef* was not yet ready to put to sea. Emma sensed his smoldering rage as she read the three scrawled words, "I hate Plymouth!"

Then skimming through complaints about Lady Nelson, she came to his first reference to the invented Mrs. Thompson. He said how thankful Mrs. Thompson's friend was for Lady Hamilton's kindness and goodness. "Poor man, he is most anxious, and begs that you will, if she is not able, write a line just to comfort him. He is so agitated that he says he cannot write himself, and that I must send for him his kind love and affectionate regards."

How oddly impersonal it seemed, and yet how poignant.

Another letter arrived the next day. In this Nelson again expressed the anxiety of "poor Mrs. Thompson's friend," who desired him to thank Lady Hamilton for her kindness. "He appears so utterly miserable; he says you have always been kind to his dear Mrs. Thompson, and he hopes and prays that you will continue your goodness to her on this trying occasion."

Letter followed letter, each with its oblique reference to Mrs. Thompson and her friend, each giving Emma the impression that Nelson, in spite of his anxiety, was enjoying the little game of make-believe.

Meanwhile, with the departure of the servants, and knowing that her time was close, Emma had persuaded Sir William to spend a few days in bed. He agreed with her that this first winter in England, after so many years in Italy, was a trying one for him. "Yes, yes," he said, "I do see that every care must be taken, and I thank you, my love, from the bottom of my heart." When visitors called they were told by Mrs. Cadogan that the master and his lady were both indisposed. All except Greville expressed the hope that Sir William and Lady Hamilton would soon be well again and went away.

He, accustomed to coming and going as he pleased, refused to be turned away at the door. Emma, resting in her room, sent word by her mother that she wished to be excused. Back came Mrs. Cadogan, scarlet with indignation.

"He won't go away. He's in a towering rage. Real nasty, he looks."

A few minutes later Greville knocked at the door and raged into the room without waiting for an answer. He was taken aback to find Emma really in bed.

"I thought you were shamming illness, Emma!"

"Now you listen to me, Mr. Greville—" Mrs. Cadogan began.

"Better leave us, Mother," Emma said. "You'll only make him worse."

Mrs. Cadogan went reluctantly from the room.

"Fever!" Greville exclaimed. "We shall soon see about that."

He strode to Emma's side and touched her brow.

"I knew it! Warm, but not feverish!"

"It comes and goes," Emma said. "Not a bad bout this time. I'll be right as rain in a day or two."

Greville stood back from the bed and glared down at her.

"I mean to get at the truth, Emma."

She drew the bedclothes up to her chin and half-turned on her side.

"Oh, I know you think I was trying to keep you from seeing Hamilton, and of course I was."

"Yes! In case he died suddenly. You fear he might make a new will and favor me in it more than you. Still, there must be more in these theatricals than that."

"Oh, rubbish, Greville!"

A cunning look crossed his face. "I think I ought to get a doctor for you. A doctor's diagnosis might be very interesting." He moved toward the door. "I shall be back as quickly as possible."

"Greville!"

He turned. His face had never looked meaner. "Well?"

"Ma's as good as any doctor." Emma was struggling for composure, but she knew her words sounded unconvincing.

Greville came and stood at the foot of the bed. "I wonder if she really is? Oh, I admit she knows how to bandage sore fingers and she is handy enough when it comes to cooling a fevered brow—only your brow isn't fevered." He leaned forward viciously. "What does she know, for instance, about the delivery of babies?"

He came round from the foot of the bed and stood over her menacingly. Suddenly his hand shot out, his intention clearly being to tear back the bedclothes.

"Wait!" Emma warned, and held his eyes steadily. "I can only *guess* what you expect to discover, Greville."

"I see we understand each other very well."

She still held him back with her eyes. "Supposing it *is* what you think, what would you do?"

"I would go straight to Hamilton and tell him."

Emma laughed shakily. "You might do yourself more harm than good by that."

A hint of apprehension came to his eyes. "If you have anything more to say I am quite prepared to listen."

"Hamilton wouldn't mind—well, not all *that* much. You know how silly he is about me; he might not even mind at all. And he would help me by taking full responsibility."

Greville laughed blusteringly, but his face had fallen.

"Confound it all, the old idiot is certainly a great fool where you are concerned."

Emma tried to chuckle. "You know what that would mean, don't you, Greville? An heir to the Hamilton estates and yourself right out in the cold."

"Damn you, Emma—!"

"Oh, he'd leave you *something,* a thousand pounds, maybe."

There was rage in his face now, but a helpless rage.

Emma shrugged. "Go to him, if you want to. You might be right about me, or you might be wrong. Either way you'd make a fool of yourself."

"Quite apart from any other consideration," he went on nastily, "I should hate to see Hamilton fathering Nelson's brat. Yet if you wouldn't mind him knowing"—his voice rose questioningly—"why this secrecy? Perhaps Nelson doesn't know either? Or is it that he doesn't want to father it himself?" He laughed for a moment. "All things considered, I can see that he might not; and so off he rushes to sea again to fight the French, gallant little hero that he is!"

Emma, thus taunted, struggled to keep her temper. The struggle tired her, but she even managed to smile pityingly.

"Poor Greville, all this is something out of your own suspicious mind. There's nothing wrong with me but a touch of fever." And then the temper flared up beyond her control. "For God's sake, go, Greville! I hate the sight of you. Go quickly before I tell Hamilton about your vile accusations. He wouldn't love you then, I'm sure!"

Hearing her raised voice, Mrs. Cadogan came running into the room; and seeing Greville standing there, indeterminate now, she seized him roughly by the arm and dragged him away. She returned to find Emma sobbing hysterically into the pillow.

"And I once thought I was in love with him!" she cried.

Mrs. Cadogan bent over her. "There now, don't take on so."

Emma stiffened suddenly. "Ma, it's starting!"

"It's a girl," Mrs. Cadogan said.

"Horatia," Emma murmured lazily.

For a moment she wondered where she was, then remembered that they had decided to use the attic as a precaution against Greville's return, and because of its distance from Sir William's room.

"Well, let's have a look at her," she said, but her eyes were so heavy she couldn't keep them open. "When I've had a little sleep I'll write to Mrs. Thompson's friend." The drowsiness swept over her in delicious waves, yet she felt the need to fight it a few moments longer. "Ma, I didn't make a fuss or cry out, did I?"

"No, Emma, you didn't."

"It hurt, though, it hurt like hell. Lord, don't I sound proud of myself!"

Then, struggling no more, Emma let herself slip gratefully into the deep soft pit of sleep, warm and dark and comforting. She woke refreshed, having slept, Mrs. Cadogan told her, for five solid hours. She woke to a new awareness, staring with bright eyes at the walls of the little attic room, the sloping low ceiling and the little window covered with snow.

She asked for the baby, but it was really Nelson she wanted. She loved him now in a different way. It made her hold her breath in wonderment. Real adoration, that was what it was. And not for the old Nelson, England's hero and hers; but for Nelson the man, Nelson the father of her child.

"What are you smiling at?" Mrs. Cadogan asked her.

"I've never felt like this before. It's a new sort of happiness."

Mrs. Cadogan laughed in her kindliest manner. "Pooh! That's how I felt when I 'ad you."

Nelson's next letter came from Torbay, where he had transferred to the *St. George,* in which he expected to sail for the Baltic. He wrote: "I do believe that poor Mrs. Thompson's friend will go mad with joy. He cries, prays, and performs all tricks, yet dares not show all or any of his feelings. He swears he will drink your health in a bumper this day, and damn me if I don't join him, for none regard you with truer affection than myself. You are a dear good creature and your kindness and attention to poor Mrs. Thompson stamp you higher than ever in my mind. I cannot write. I am too agitated by this young fellow at my elbow. I believe he is foolish. He does nothing but rave about you and her. I own I participate in his joy and cannot write anything . . ."

254

Emma and her mother were safely on the journey to Mrs. Gibson's in Little Titchfield Street. Nobody had seen them leave the Piccadilly house; the snow-covered street had been completely deserted. Sir William, it was true, had given them several moments of anxiety, for he had chosen to get up; and not until he was dozing by the fire had Emma dared to give her mother the word. The driver of the hired carriage, too, had worried her; but she was confident now that with her mother's comfortable figure to shield her he hadn't noticed the baby in her arms.

Mrs. Cadogan said severely, "You shouldn't be out of doors a day like this, much less out of your bed."

"I'm strong as a horse, you know that."

"Yes, an' stubborn as a mule."

There was a sharp argument when they reached Little Titchfield Street.

"I'll take her in to Mrs. Gibson myself," Emma said, when her mother held out her arms for the baby.

"You must be out of your mind," Mrs. Cadogan said.

"I won't make a scene, I promise you, Ma," Emma pleaded.

"Scene or no scene, you'd still give yourself away. One look at you, holding the poor little mite like that, and anybody'd know you was the mother."

"Mrs. Gibson won't know who I am. You told her the child's mother was a Mrs. Thompson, didn't you?"

"Now just you listen to me for a minute," Mrs. Cadogan said gently. "You'll want to come and see your baby later. And knowing Lord Nelson as I do, he'll want to do the same. More than likely you'll come together. Insane it'll be, but you'll do it, mark my words. No hiding who Lord Nelson is, him with one arm and that queer eye. And well enough known it is that the only woman he ever goes about with now is Lady Hamilton. Bad enough that'll be, but if you're Mrs. Thompson one day an' Lady Hamilton the next there'll be the devil to pay."

"I don't care," Emma said fiercely, but she saw the good sense of her mother's words, and with a little sob allowed the child to be taken from her arms. "For Nelson's sake," she said brokenly, "not my own."

They returned in silence to 23 Piccadilly, with Emma sitting stiffly erect the whole time, bracing herself against the back of the seat. Snow was falling again, big soft flakes that clung to their cloaks as they hurried from the carriage to the door. The footprints they had left behind them were half-filled, and alongside them was a new set. A visitor had called in their absence and was still there. "Greville!" Emma exclaimed, for at that moment she saw his face at the drawing-room window.

He came out to the hall to greet them, helped Emma remove her cloak, shook the snow from it and handed it imperiously to Mrs. Cadogan.

"Come to the drawing room;" he said, "Hamilton and I want to talk to you." Emma followed him docilely enough and wondered if he was still set on making a scene about Nelson and the suspected child. She wondered but she scarcely cared. "We were right, Hamilton," he said. "The foolish creature *had* gone for a drive."

"'Pon my soul," Sir William stirred himself sufficiently to admonish, "up from a bed of sickness and out in the snow. Do you want to kill yourself, my love?"

"I felt so much better," Emma excused herself, "and I needed a breath of air."

"Had I come earlier I would gladly have accompanied you," Greville murmured, his eyes full of suspicion, his glance sweeping over her from head to foot. "You have lost weight, Emma."

"The fever always fines me down."

"But not enough. You are still—substantial."

Anger flared up in her. "You said you wanted to talk to me, you and Hamilton. Better get it over with, whatever it is."

Sir William yawned and drew the rugs more closely about him.

"Greville, dear good fellow that he is," he said, "is worried about the caricatures."

Greville squared his shoulders severely. "On my way here, Emma, I stopped at Mrs. Humphrey's print shop in St. James's Street. The crowd about the window was so thick I had to fight my way through it." He appeared to choke. "Gillray has a new cartoon on display."

"Distressing, most distressing," Sir William murmured.

"It is entitled 'Dido in Despair.'" Greville pointed a finger at Emma. "You, of course, are Dido, and larger than life, by heaven! Your arms are thrown out dramatically, there are ridiculous tears on your cheeks. The scene is a bedroom. A fleet of warships can be seen in the distance through the window. An old man in a nightcap is asleep in the bed. Beneath this eloquent drawing is a piece of doggerel verse uttered, presumably, by Dido. Just listen!"

And with a snarl Greville quoted:

Ah where, and oh! Where is my gallant sailor gone?
He's gone to fight the French for George upon the throne,
He's gone to fight the French t' lose t' other arm and eye,
And left me with old Antiquity, to lay me down and cry.

Sir William shook his head sadly. "Old Antiquity—a cruel but correct description of me these days, dear me, yes."

Greville went on grimly. "The crowd shouted with laughter! Something must be done about it, by heaven it must!"

"So it must," Sir William said mildly. "What do you suggest, Greville?"

Emma noticed that Sir William was not as disturbed as Greville would like, was even a trifle bored. She looked at Greville. He was hesitant now and dared not utter what she guessed was on the tip of his tongue, *Turn her out, disown her!*

Mumbling a little, he said: "It is insufferable, Hamilton, your good name being dragged in the dirt like this."

Sir William frowned. "It is Emma's good name, rather than mine. I, bless my soul, am just a figure of fun. And worse, Nelson's good name, too." He straightened up in his chair. "As we love the dear Nelson, something *must* and *shall* be done."

"Hamilton . . ." Emma said helplessly.

He rose with a jerk, grasped his stick and shook it angrily.

"I shall make a public statement," he announced. "One of the newspaper gentlemen will be glad to publish it for me. I shall give the world at large my solemn word that nothing exists between Nelson and my wife but the purest of friendships." He dropped back in his chair, exhausted, and with closed eyes and trembling lips he added, "The *purest* of friendships."

Emma was amazed at the genuineness of his voice and deeply touched by it. She had thought from time to time that he suspected the truth, but it seemed now that he had never suspected. She stared at Greville unsmilingly, her lips framing the words, "Well, you asked for it." With a gesture of rage he turned his back on her, but she was no longer interested. She thought of the baby she had just left at Little Titchfield Street. A *public denial?* She thought of Nelson, lonely and anxious and delirious with joy. Denial? Oh no! her heart cried. A public admission, made fiercely and proudly, that or nothing else.

"We must be ever jealous of the good name of our dearest friend," Sir William said, opening his eyes.

257

"Of course," she said obediently, "of course . . ."

Emma could scarcely believe her eyes. "Nelson!"

He came striding excitedly into the room with Mrs. Cadogan, who had opened the front door to his knock, hovering just as excitedly behind him. To Emma's surprise he was wearing civilian clothes, the coat and breeches a deep red velvet, the stockings a pale pink cotton.

"Leave," he announced. "At least three days of it."

"I can't believe it! How I longed to see you, but how impossible I thought it. Oh, *Nelson!*"

Emma glanced meaningly at her mother and Mrs. Cadogan, with a toss of her head, went reluctantly from the room.

"We can talk freely," Emma told Nelson. "Sir William has gone to the foreign office to discuss the vexing matter of his pension." She looked at him with an ache in her heart. "But only three days, Nelson!"

He told her then that he was to sail soon for the Baltic under the command of Sir Hyde Parker; and, scowling, he reminded her of the changes that had taken place in Europe since they had left the Mediterranean. Bonaparte had forced Austria to sign a treaty with France; King Ferdinand had agreed to close all ports to British shipping; even Portugal, England's ancient ally, was cowering beneath the threats of Spain, while Spain, itself menaced by France, seemed likely again to join forces with England's enemies.

"And all because I permitted Bonaparte to elude me when he returned to France from Egypt!" Nelson raged.

Then, to make matters worse, Bonaparte had cleverly reached an understanding with the Czar of Russia, under whose pressure Denmark, Sweden, and Prussia had agreed to maintain an armed neutrality.

"Which means that the Baltic will be closed to us, so—to the Baltic I must go. But retirement, honorable retirement, that is my one real aim now."

He threw himself into a chair.

"You're tired, Nelson."

"Yes, but in high spirits. I traveled all night, only stopping to change horses, and just now at Lothian's to reserve a room."

"As if you couldn't stay here!"

"And set tongues wagging afresh?" But he smiled boyishly. "I'll live here, only sleep at Lothian's."

Smiling, Emma said: "This is the first time I've seen you in anything but naval uniform."

He laughed delightedly. "Disguise. I put a shade over my eye and wasn't recognized at Lothian's. Do I disappoint you in the dress of an ordinary gentleman?"

She was saved from answering by Mrs. Cadogan, who came in with a tray of refreshments. For a few minutes Nelson ate ravenously and drank the steaming chocolate in great excited gulps.

Presently he looked up. "How cruel and heartless you must think me. How soon can I see Mrs. Thompson's baby?" But he gave Emma no time to answer. "Is she beautiful, the baby? She must be, with her mother the most beautiful woman in the world."

They went that afternoon to Little Titchfield to see the child, and to Emma's amazement Nelson insisted on taking Sir William with them. He told her eagerly that it was part of a plan he had conceived. It was a way of preparing Sir William for the day when he adopted the child, and to make the old man see how natural it was that Emma herself should take an interest in her. "An ordeal for you, I know, holding back your true feelings, but necessary, Emma, necessary."

"An unhappy story," Nelson told Sir William, before they reached Mrs. Gibson's house. "I have a special interest in this young fellow, an admirable officer. He begged me to see this child and later, on his behalf, make provision for it. Marriage is out of the question with both their families against it. The poor mother, my heart bleeds for her."

"Both are fortunate to have the interest and help of Nelson," Sir William pronounced.

Mrs. Gibson, hurriedly warned by Mrs. Cadogan to expect three important visitors, was in something of a flutter when Emma, Sir William and Nelson trooped into her little house. She was quiet, reserved, and homely, and her home was delightfully spick and span. Emma liked her on sight and felt happier on Horatia's account. They grouped themselves about the cot, Emma and Nelson afraid almost to speak, Sir William vaguely interested. The child was awake, and when Nelson silently touched her tiny hand the fingers closed eagerly about his thumb.

"May I—" Emma steadied herself; this was Mrs. Thompson's child, not hers. "May I take her in my arms, Mrs. Gibson?"

Mrs. Gibson lifted Horatia from the cot and placed her in Emma's arms. Emma held her close, rocked her gently, and made little croon-

259

ing noises over her. How hard to believe that it was only three weeks since she had given birth to this child in the attic at 23 Piccadilly.

Sir William grew quite sentimental. "A most touching sight. I love to see you like that, Emma. It makes you look—dear me, yes—*complete*."

"I adore her already," Emma said. "How I wish she were mine."

"What have they called her?" Sir William asked.

Nelson nodded and smiled. "The young fellow had the happy thought of Horatia. And he even begged me to be the godfather."

"And who is to be godmother?" Sir William asked.

Emma could have hugged him for uttering this cue.

"Why not me?" she asked, trying to keep her voice steady. "That is, if your friend hasn't someone else in mind, Nelson."

"You, Emma?" Sir William pondered.

"You wouldn't mind, would you, Hamilton?"

"Dear me, no, Emma. An excellent suggestion." He laughed playfully. "The responsibility might be good for you. Bless my soul, I wouldn't mind being godfather myself."

"My friend," Nelson told Emma emotionally, "would be more honored than he could ever say." He was trembling now, unguarded. "Such a lovely child. Would to heaven I had two arms and could hold her safely myself."

As unhurriedly as possible Emma placed the baby back in her cot. Nelson was finding the ordeal too much, and unless she got him away soon he would betray himself completely. She bent and kissed her daughter's brow.

"I'll come again soon," she told Mrs. Gibson.

"Dear Nelson," Sir William murmured, "how much you have wanted a child yourself."

"To be a godfather is better than nothing," Nelson said thickly. "Later, if possible, I shall adopt Horatia."

That night, with Sir William gone early to bed, Nelson excitedly discussed the christening of his daughter. He wanted it immediately and he nominated no less a church than St. George's in Hanover Square. Completely carried away, he strode about the room, gesticulating with his one arm, an almost frightening sight with his blind eye fixed and staring, the other inflamed and watering.

"Publicity is the last thing you want," Emma reminded him.

"A private christening, then!" he cried. "That is always permissible."

"Wouldn't the parents have to be there?"

"The parents are abroad. You hear, Emma, abroad. Their names only, that is all we need."

"Mrs. Thompson and friend . . ."

"Oh, there are difficulties, I admit it," he said, pouting like a child.

"And the parents of a three-week-old baby abroad, even the mother?"

"She is in London, then, but too ill to leave her bed!"

"And the place of birth?"

"She—she was born at sea. Yes, at sea!"

"Oh, Nelson," Emma said warmly, "what does it matter?"

"What does it matter!" he echoed, vastly shocked.

"She's ours and we love her. That's all I know and care. I"—Emma's voice broke—"I can't stand up in a church, not just yet I can't, and act as godmother to my own child!"

Nelson came to her quickly, anxious and concerned.

"Forgive me, Emma," he said quietly. Then he stood away from her and went on briskly, "You are right, as you always are. Even with a private christening the truth might leak out. It will be safer later, a delayed christening, as I planned before. And another thing"—he was flushed and excited again—"once we are married, how could we acknowledge her as ours if we had forsworn ourselves at a deceitful christening?"

No more was said during the remaining two days of Nelson's leave. They were quiet days, spent together at Piccadilly. He did not want attention, and miraculously enough his presence in London went unnoticed by the general public.

During the last afternoon they went again to see the baby. At Nelson's insistence, Emma took a small pair of scissors with her and, when Mrs. Gibson's back was turned, clipped a lock of Horatia's silken baby hair. He would carry it in a locket, he said, and never part with it as long as he lived. In the carriage afterward, his own large German traveling carriage which was to carry him through the night to the coast, he was silent and brooding, and spoke only once.

"I was never afraid of death before. But I have so much to lose, now."

Later, after a hasty supper, and in the presence of Sir William, his farewell was brief.

"I am too full for words," he told them both, and to Emma, as she went out to the carriage with him, he whispered, "Everything I feel I will put in a letter, everything!"

The letter when it came was free of subterfuge. Addressed directly to Emma, it contained not one reference either to Mrs. Thompson or to Mrs. Thompson's friend.

> *My dear Wife, for such you are in my eyes and in the face of heaven, I can give full scope now to my feelings.*
>
> *You know, my dearest Emma, that there is nothing in this world I would not do for us to live together, and to have our dear child with us.*
>
> *I love you alone. I never did love anyone else. I never did have a dear pledge of love till you gave me one. You, my beloved Emma, and my country, are the two dearest objects of my fond heart. All I have ever wanted in this world, ever asked, ever sought, is one true heart. That I found in Italy, in my own dear Emma's beloved breast.*
>
> *Kiss and bless our dear Horatia.*

Delirious with joy, Emma read this letter again and again. One phrase, bringing tears to her eyes, stood out above the rest. *One true heart . . .* Yes, and that heart hers!

22 Out of the increasing jumble of Nelson's letters Emma was able to follow his movements. He had first left Portsmouth for Yarmouth in the *St. George* to join his chief, Sir Hyde Parker. Soon he was sailing from Yarmouth for the Cattegat through fog and bitter winter storms, and then he was writing sorrowfully of the frustration he felt when told by Sir Hyde that diplomacy was to be tried first. How he hated the diplomats, the "pen-and-ink fellows" sent to negotiate at Copenhagen!

A later letter revealed his delight in the knowledge that diplomacy had failed. The Russians, he said, were afraid of the French, and the Danes were afraid of the Russians; a peaceful understanding with the Danes was therefore out of the question. In obvious delight, as well as in a fever of impatience, he wrote that he was to be placed in the front of the coming battle. Of one thing he was absolutely sure, the *St. George* would add an additional ray of glory to England's fame and to the fame of Nelson, *if* he survived.

"Keep me alive in your remembrance. My last thoughts will be of you. I judge your heart by my own. May the great God of Heaven bless and protect you, now and forever more!"

And he added: "Tomorrow will be a proud day for England and for Nelson."

Affected now by his expectation of death in action, Emma waited in a fever of anxiety for his next letter. And when, after an alarming delay, it came, the brief momentous news reduced her to a flood of tears of joyous relief.

> I have had the happiness of witnessing, under all its circumstances, the most hard-fought battle and the most complete victory ever obtained by the navy of my country.

Gradually, from personal letters and official reports, Emma and Sir William were able to piece together the full story of Nelson's latest triumph, the Battle of Copenhagen, as everybody was beginning to call it. He had indeed been "placed in front," and of the twelve ships under his command two had grounded and one had failed to clear the shoals of the channel.

"Nine ships only," Emma cried, "against the eighteen Danish! Pooh, with Nelson in command *six* would have been enough!"

She tried to picture him, blinded by the smoke of battle, walking the starboard side of his quarter-deck and exclaiming, as the *St. George* engaged the Danish flagship, "Warm work, by heaven!" Yes, and adding in almost the same breath, "But not for a fortune would I be elsewhere!" Those were his very words; Emma had them before her in his letters, yet how hard it was to believe that her frail little Nelson, maimed and blinded, could strut that quarter-deck, fearless in the intensity of his enjoyment.

More thrilling still was the risk he had taken in the Nelson touch of disobedience. She tried to reconstruct the scene. There stood Nelson on the quarter-deck of the *St. George*, his signal lieutenant at his side anxiously reporting Sir Hyde Parker's signal to withdraw. As clearly as if she had been there herself she could hear Nelson's impatient, contemptuous "Damnme if I do!" as well as his "Keep the signal for close action flying, man!" and his quick impish smile as he added, "With only one eye I have a right to be blind sometimes."

"It has made a hero of him all over again," Sir William commented gleefully. Then he added soberly, "Though, had the battle gone against him, it might have meant a court martial."

But the battle had not gone against him, chiefly because, as Emma learned later, he had offered the Danes a truce at the right moment. The truce had been accepted, and Nelson had been able to remove his ships from an admittedly dangerous position.

"The luck of the devil," Greville remarked, annoying Emma deeply.

While she waited for her hero to come home, fretting that negotiations in Copenhagen should delay him so long, she busied herself with the task of redecorating the Piccadilly house, which Sir William admitted was dull, uninspiring, and scarcely comfortable enough for a permanent residence. Greville, of course, protested loudly.

"How set you are on reducing Hamilton to penury!"

"Oh, come," Sir William said mildly, "things are hardly as bad as that, Greville. What does it matter if, at my time of life, I spend a little of my capital?"

Greville looked stern. "Capital, once touched, has a way of disappearing over night. You have placed me in full control of your affairs"—this was a surprise to Emma—"and I warn you solemnly that to redecorate the house at this time is—"

"Uneconomic?" Emma put in sweetly.

"Yes, *uneconomic!*" Greville thundered.

Emma turned to Sir William with a frown. "Is Greville really in control?"

Sir William nodded. "I myself have no head for business these days." His voice became a low complaining murmur. "Peace and quiet, that is all I want. And since Greville assures me that we cannot afford a house in the country, 'pon my soul, I am determined to have peace and quiet here in Piccadilly."

"That's why I want to make you as comfortable as I can," Emma said.

"If it were your own money you were spending," Greville smiled, "no one would have the slightest objection." His smile broadened. "You have a fortune in jewelry. Why not sell some of it?"

"I'll do it gladly!" she was taunted to retort.

"Splendid!" Greville declared. "And while on the subject of raising money without touching capital—dear me, I should have thought of this earlier!—there are far too many pictures in the house, pictures, my dear aunt, of you."

"Sell them," she stormed, "sell them all!"

Sir William said hesitantly, "Beckford *did* tell me that many of them, the Romneys especially, are worth three or four times the amount I paid for them."

"Our dear Emma," Greville jeered, "is worth more on canvas than she is in the flesh. The best pictures were painted in those faraway days when she was young, beautiful, and—slim."

"Quite so, quite so," Sir William said absently. "Ah well, let us be practical. Make a selection, Greville, and have them put up to auction."

What a change from the old days, Emma thought sadly, when Sir William, at the height of his infatuation, had treasured her on canvas almost as much as in the flesh. However, after she had sold much of her jewelry, he sent only three "Emmas" to Christie's auction rooms. One of them was Romney's "St. Cecilia," always so much admired by Nelson; and Nelson, hearing of this "dastardly" move, instructed his agent to bid for it. He wrote later that it had cost him three hundred pounds and stoutly affirmed that he would have been glad to pay for it with three hundred drops of blood.

"I shall have it with me at sea," he added, "enshrine it in my cabin, and change the title to 'St. Emma.' "

The weeks were slipping by and still Nelson had not returned. His one aim was to crush the coalition which the Danes had been forced to join. And during the illness of Sir Hyde Parker, Nelson had become commander-in-chief in the Baltic. A grateful government had pushed him up still higher on the peerage ladder; he was now a viscount. Why not Earl Nelson of the Nile? Emma demanded indignantly.

The weeks soon became months, with Nelson as busy as ever at Copenhagen. There were banquets and levees, discussions and arguments, and then, at long last, an armistice which, he told her hopefully, would soon be a permanent peace.

While Emma waited, pleased with Nelson's success yet impatient at his continued absence, she completed the redecoration and refurnishing of 23 Piccadilly. For a time this was exciting—she was especially pleased with the Italian-style music room—but her interest soon flagged. She went frequently to Little Titchfield Street, longing each time to bring her baby back with her; and once she went to visit George Romney in the country. She found him an old man, vague, irritable, scarcely pleased to see her; and she returned in sorrow to London where two letters from Nelson awaited her.

The first dealt with his earlier wish to buy a country house. "I would like a good lodging in an airy situation where you and my other dearest friend, Sir William, may loll at peace and ease."

The second was a love letter.

> My dearest Beloved, to say that I think of you by day, by night, all day and all night, but faintly expresses my feelings of love and desire. Oh, how I have loved you, from the first moment of our happy, dear, enchanted blessed meeting! There is no desire of wealth, no ambition, that could keep me from all my soul holds dear. Ever, forever, I am yours, only yours, my wife in the eyes of God.

She laughed and cried over this. What did it matter that at their first meeting he had never once looked at her as a woman! Surely he was entitled to at least a little poetic license.

And now he was home again, after an absence of three full months. He lodged first at Lothian's, but soon, to Greville's disgust, Nelson was in permanent residence at 23 Piccadilly. Emma found him thinner, his face more deeply lined, his hair slightly gray, but his vitality higher than ever. With the approval of the Admiralty he had resigned his command. He knew that Bonaparte would give him little time in England, but such was his excitement he refused even to think of that.

His first thought was of the baby, and he would talk of little else until he and Emma had visited Little Titchfield Street. There, castigating Mrs. Gibson, he grew indignant on the subject of wet nurses. Two of them, one lazy, the other dirty, had been dismissed and a third temporarily engaged; but Mrs. Gibson was all for weaning the child.

"I forbid it!" he cried. "A hasty weaning will make the poor child lose weight and color and ruin her future beauty. I forbid it, you hear!"

His next thought, such was his high-spirited mood, was a fishing holiday; and Sir William, a keen angler in his youth, vowed that nothing would be pleasanter. The summer weather, after the rigors of winter, had improved Sir William's health and spirits.

They went, the three of them, to Staines, where they put up at the Bush Inn. The old-world garden of the inn, bright with roses, led down to the Thames, and there, on the bank of the river, they fished during the long twilight of the summer nights. Greville joined them for an afternoon, a Greville polite to Nelson's face but ready to sneer behind his back.

After Greville, and spoiling the idyll completely, came Nelson's brother William and his small, chattering, well-meaning wife. Emma had met the Reverend William Nelson before, briefly, had even written to him during Nelson's absence; but she had disliked him on sight. He was polite to her, as Greville had been polite to Nelson; still all the time there was disapproval in his suspicious, inquisitive eyes, disapproval and a flickering, guarded *something* which, rightly or wrongly, she took for a physical interest. She thought shrewdly that to the Reverend William she represented sin, and sin attracted him.

In London again there were constant visits to Mrs. Gibson's; gay little dinner parties; and a number of day excursions to such places as Turnham Green to inspect country houses, none of which, however, was quite what Nelson was seeking. Over all this happiness, ignore it though they did, hung the threat of French activities. Bonaparte, free now of war on the Continent, was planning an invasion of England.

And so, three weeks after Nelson's arrival home, he was summoned to the Admiralty, and from a conference held there returned to 23 Piccadilly with a long face.

Emma's heart sank. "Is it separation again, Nelson?"

267

He nodded. "I have been appointed commander-in-chief of a special fleet for the protection of the southeast coast. Bonaparte is gathering together a large army which, heaven curse him, he has called the Army of England. There's talk of it in the papers today and panic in London and a slump in stocks and shares. They tell me at the Admiralty that they need the name of Nelson to put heart into the people of England."

"Which is true enough!" Emma cried.

Three days later, in the early hours of the morning, he left London for Sheerness. "Find that dream house in the country for me," were his last words to Emma. The assignment did little to cheer her, but she set to work with a will. Early in August, while Nelson was planning an attack on a French flotilla at Boulogne, she was forced to report that she had found nothing better than a house they had seen at Turnham Green. He left the decision to her and then, later in the month, after his attack had unfortunately failed, she joyfully reported the discovery of Merton Place in Surrey.

"It has everything you want, Nelson. The house is pleasant and gracious. There's a farm attached and a stream running through the land, a tiny Nile for us to go boating on. And it's within an hour's easy drive from Piccadilly."

Nelson's immediate reply was, "Buy it!"

Negotiations for the purchase dragged on until the middle of September, when Merton Place became Nelson's property with occupation guaranteed by October tenth. Writing that he could not expect to get leave until the twenty-second, he gave her a free hand with the renovations and in the choice of furnishings. He begged her to have everything in readiness for him; and, hinting that his leave of absence would be a long one, he spoke of the secret negotiations which were taking place between the English and French governments. Peace, for which they had both longed, was now within sight.

Nelson arrived before breakfast on the morning of the twenty-third. Roused from her bed by the sound of his post chaise, she had a little pang of doubt. In the gray light of this late October morning the two-storied, hundred-year-old house looked grim and forbidding, and the drive desolate with its carpet of fallen leaves, while the rooms he insisted on viewing at once, their grates black with the burned-out fires, were cold and cheerless.

"Well?" she asked tentatively.

"Merton Place, you call it," Nelson said, his voice shaky with emotion, his face creased in smiles; "I have a better name for it—Paradise!"

They settled in quickly, once they recovered from the excitement of Nelson's first night in his own home. What a night it was, with the whole village illuminated and Nelson mingling happily with "his people," as he began at once to call the villagers. He took particular delight in drinking ale with the tradesmen, with Gadd the baker, Greenfield the butcher, Woodman the chandler; and simply and sincerely he replied to their stumbling, unrehearsed speeches of welcome. This was the real England, he said emotionally, these were the people he had fought for and made safe from Bonaparte's aggression. He was home at last, home in a sense he had never believed possible.

Toward the end of the first week Nelson said:

"This is Naples and Palermo, the Palazzo Sessa and the Villa Bastioni all over again, only better, much better! Not yet a week, and it seems as if we have been here all our lives."

Sir William agreed. "Nevertheless, my dear fellow, Emma and I must think soon of returning to London. Dear friend that you are, to impose on your generosity too long would be—bless my soul—ungracious."

"Leave Merton?" Nelson exclaimed. "Unthinkable! How could I live here alone? I would be better at sea again than that."

"My dear Nelson," Sir William said gently, "I was thinking of Lady Nelson's attitude."

"Fanny?" Nelson's voice rose sharply.

"An unhappy situation, I do admit," Sir William went on somewhat hesitantly, "and forgive me for referring to it, but now that the war is over— It occurred to me, Nelson, that Lady Nelson might wish to forget past differences and—hum—join you here."

"Fanny would never join me here," Nelson asserted.

"Perhaps not while *we* are here—" Sir William began.

"That is beside the point. We have had certain correspondence, Fanny and I, and have failed to reach an understanding. I prefer now to leave the past *in* the past."

Emma knew that Fanny had written to him; he had shown her the letters. She remembered some of the sentences. "I cannot be silent in the general joy throughout the kingdom . . . my thankfulness that it hath pleased God to spare your life . . . let me entreat you to believe no wife ever felt greater affection for a husband than I do . . . to the best of my knowledge I have invariably done everything you desire . . . if I have omitted anything I am sorry for it." Nelson had set this particular letter aside unanswered; let Fanny read again his earlier letter, he had told Emma, the letter that had bluntly stated his own attitude: "Living I have done all in my power for you, and after my death you will find I have done the same. My only wish is to be left to myself." Poor Fanny, Emma thought now, infinitely sorry for the woman; if Nelson were to write to her like that she would die.

She said: "I don't believe Hamilton really wants to leave Merton."

Sir William looked apologetic. "How well you know me! I love the place as if it were my own. I would like nothing better than to end my days here."

They argued then, he and Nelson, about the financial aspect. Sir William wanted to buy a half share in Merton Place. Nelson, fiercely proud to be the sole owner, refused to consider it for a single moment, but he finally agreed to share all housekeeping expenses.

"And the Piccadilly house," Sir William declared, "I shall retain for our joint or separate use whenever we wish to stay in town."

"While the excellent Mrs. Cadogan," Nelson concluded, "shall run them both for us."

By Christmas they were well established with the house completely furnished to their liking. "Overfurnished," said Greville, when he made a brief uninvited visit on the plea that he must discuss business affairs with his uncle. Merton Place, he murmured, was like both an art gallery and a museum; an art gallery dedicated jointly to Lady Hamilton and Lord Nelson, a museum dedicated to the naval hero alone.

"Paintings of every size and shape, every attitude, on every wall, in every room, even on the *staircase*. And in the rooms the Nelson coat-of-arms, the Nelson plate, the Nelson china, even the flagstaff of *L'Orient*. Surely, my dear aunt, a little—just a *little* in bad taste?"

"It's a valuable collection," Emma said complacently. "You're just envious."

"Heaven forbid!"

With the utmost politeness, Nelson invited Greville to stay for the Christmas festivities; and Greville, with like politeness, refused. Emma was vastly relieved; they were like a couple of dogs, walking around each other, sizing up one another before flying at each other's throats.

Even more unpleasant to Emma than Greville's visit was an unexpected letter from Lady Nelson. Fanny addressed Nelson as "My dearest husband," and wrote, "It is some time since I have written to you. The silence you have imposed is more than my affection for you will allow. I now have to offer for your accommodation a comfortable warm house. Do, my dear husband, let us live together again. I can never be happy until such an event takes place. I have but one wish in the world, to please you. Let everything be buried in oblivion."

"I feel so sorry for her," Emma cried impulsively. "I know how I would feel if you'd set me aside. I would write just like that, truly I would."

"In stilted language, without any expression of tenderness? I doubt it, Emma!"

With an impatient gesture he started to tear up the letter; then, changing his mind, he found pen and ink and scribbled on the back of the letter, "Opened in mistake by Lord Nelson but not read."

"It shall be sent back to her." His face clouded. "We would be doing ourselves a great wrong if I went back to her, just as now"—his voice broke—"we do our daughter a great wrong by keeping her separated from us."

Emma's heart began to beat excitedly. "We had planned to have her with us, hadn't we! What a completely happy place Merton would be then, Nelson! Horatia here, acknowledged only as our godchild, but to us, our very own!"

Nelson shook his head sadly. "We want everything, everything!" He avoided her eyes. "Horatia is not yet a year old, still too young to care whom she is with. Leaving her with Mrs. Gibson, who is good and kind and gentle, we deny only ourselves. And Fanny would make trouble if she knew we had a child here."

"It might make her consider divorce!"

"No, Emma, she would hate you more than ever, grow more vindictive. I know her, I know her. I am determined to persuade her to divorce me when—well—" He broke off. "We must keep Horatia a precious secret till then."

When . . . Till then . . . He meant, of course, the death of Sir William.

"There is also my father," Nelson added.

"Your father?" This was an argument he had never brought up before.

"If he knew about Horatia it would break his heart. I wouldn't be able to face him. We must have patience, Emma, patience . . ."

But Emma, on the spur of the moment, sent a hurried note to Mrs. Gibson, instructing her to hire a post chaise for Christmas Day. She told her that to drive by way of Clapham Common would be the quickest and easiest route; and she added, almost as an afterthought,

271

"Bring little Miss Thompson with you; we will all be happy to see you." Just for once, she told herself, just for the first Christmas Day.

Afterward, when the little family party was over, when Sir William and Mrs. Cadogan had gone to bed and Mrs. Gibson had driven away again with Horatia, Nelson declared with tears in his eyes that he had never in his life spent so happy a Christmas.

"I was tempted to keep her with us always, so very tempted."

"Then, Nelson—"

"Soon, perhaps, soon," he promised. "Trust to my judgment, Emma. Be patient, and wait."

23 With the cold winds of March had come official news of peace with France. This peace, the Treaty of Amiens, was not to Nelson's liking.

"It gives the wretched Bonaparte, who, I see, now calls himself consul, a breathing space. Consul! He has his eyes on the *throne* of France. This peace, this patched-up peace which makes me want to hide my head in shame, will never last. We must make every moment at Merton a happy one, Emma, remember that!"

But with the spring came word that his father, now permanently residing at Bath, was ill. Though no actual estrangement had taken place, father and son had seen less and less of each other, Nelson resenting the old man's constant attempts to reunite him with Fanny. And while he admitted now that he ought to go at once to Bath, he delayed, being afraid that his father, perhaps believing himself about to die, might exhort a death-bed promise of reconciliation. While he delayed, waiting for more news, old Mr. Nelson passed away; and Nelson, making himself ill with self-reproach, left the funeral arrangements to his brother William. Then he took to his bed and, pleading a recurrence of the earlier heart attacks, remained at Merton until after the services.

"I am finished, completely finished," he told Emma despairingly. "How fortunate we have peace, uncertain as it is. I would be useless to my country now."

Gradually she restored him to the lightheartedness that usually marked his life at Merton, first with a party, small and restrained, for their neighbors, then with larger, gayer diversions. Soon Sir William was grumbling that the house was always crammed with guests and peace and quiet had deserted Merton Place.

"I would be better off at Piccadilly. The town, I do declare, is quieter than the country."

Spring lengthened into summer, summer into autumn, an autumn bringing news of George Romney's death, and soon it was Christmas again. While the first Christmas at Merton had been a quiet one, Emma this year filled the place with guests, brought in the neighbors, and did all she could to make the festive season the gayest she had ever spent. Nelson enjoyed himself immensely; but Sir William, worn out with all the excitement, did nothing but complain. When Emma gave a similar party to welcome in the new year, he muttered that this was the end, ordered the post chaise which he used for day trips to London, and departed in a temper. On the third day of his absence Nelson grew restive.

"Gossip is sure to arise out of this, Emma. It may even get about town that you and Sir William are estranged."

"I do see," she teased him, "that we need a husband to chaperon us."

But Nelson was not amused, so she wrote at once to Sir William, asked him to come back without delay and promised that in future life would be more restful at Merton Place. He replied that Piccadilly was restful enough; he preferred to remain there for the present, cataloguing his books and attending an occasional art auction.

"This is ridiculous!" Nelson said angrily.

Emma smiled placatingly. "Very well, I'll slip up to town and bring the truant back."

At 23 Piccadilly she found Sir William in the small library, deep in consultation with Greville. They sat at either end of a small mahogany table, account books and papers spread out between them. Sir William greeted her with a shamefaced smile, Greville with a look of triumph. She had suspected all along that Greville was at the back of his uncle's determination to remain away from Merton.

"You came at a most opportune moment," he told her. "We were discussing you, Hamilton and I—at least, we were discussing and deploring your extravagance."

She threw her cloak on a chair, dragged another up to the table, and glanced with a smile at the account books.

"This reminds me of the old Edgware Row days," she said merrily.

Sir William wagged a finger at her. "We have a letter here from the bank. The good Mr. Coutts has been obliged to notify me that the balance of your account is exactly twelve shillings."

"Shameful!" Greville declared.

"But gracious," Emma exclaimed, "didn't you say the government was granting you that pension at last?"

"It has been granted, yes, but not yet paid," Greville told her. "In any case, economy is still very necessary." He turned the pages of one of the account books. "Look at this, Emma, just look at this! In one week, *one* week, mark you! your expenses at Merton Place amounted to sixty-six pounds, seventeen shillings, and one penny." He turned another page. "And here, another week—just *one week only*, the staggering, incredible, shameful sum of one hundred and eleven pounds, thirteen shillings, and four pence."

"Nelson pays half," Emma said flatly.

"Even so it is out of all proportion."

"Retrenchment, my dear Emma, retrenchment," Sir William murmured.

"Take your expenditure on wine alone," Greville went on— "gracious heaven, you must have a cellar at Merton worth every penny of three thousand pounds. A fortune, in wine!"

Emma shrugged. "Hamilton likes his wine even more than Nelson does. A gentleman must keep a proper cellar." But when she saw that no good would come of starting an argument she added, "Go and get ready, Hamilton, and leave Greville to me."

"Ready?" Sir William echoed.

"Hamilton, my dear fellow," Greville said softly, "remember your resolution."

Sir William squared his shoulders. "I have arrived at an age, Emma, when some repose is necessary, and for the comfort of both of us we must endeavor to make the best of it."

He coughed. He was delivering what sounded like a rehearsed speech. Emma expected him to break down at any moment and be prompted by Greville, the writer of the lines.

"I by no means wish to live in solitary retreat, but to sit down almost nightly at Merton with fourteen or more at table is irksome to me and—"

"To say nothing of the expense of jointly entertaining so many people," Greville simply had to interpose.

"—and more than I can sustain," Sir William went on, frowning at the interruption. "I feel now that my wife's attention is entirely taken up with Lord Nelson and the running of his house."

"As it is, as it is!" Greville put in.

"I well know the purity of Lord Nelson's affection for my wife—"

"Ahem!" Greville coughed.

"—for my wife and— Really, my dear Greville, I do wish you would refrain from these irritating interruptions. Where *was* I, now? Ah yes, for my wife, and I know how uncomfortable it would make the good Nelson if a separation should become an accomplished fact. I—"

"Separation?" It was Emma's turn to interrupt. "Between you and me, you mean?"

"Quite, quite," Greville purred.

"However, for Nelson's sake as much as my own," Sir William hurried on, frowning at Greville, "I am determined to do all in my power to prevent such an extremity."

"My dear Hamilton—" Greville's face had fallen.

"Oh, be quiet and let him finish!" Emma cried, delighted to see that Sir William had deviated from Greville's obvious instructions.

Sir William bowed over the table. "Thank you, my love. As you know, I cannot expect to live many more years, perhaps not many more months, which makes me determined to be my own master and pass my time according to my own inclinations. There are moments, I admit, when the thought of a—hum—well-concerted separation"—he glanced briefly at Greville—"has recommended itself to me, but as I say—" His voice quavered, and he looked utterly bewildered. "As I say—" he broke off again. "Bless my soul, I have quite lost the thread of my—of my—"

He fell back into his chair and with his elbows on the table buried his head in his hands. So old and frail he looked, scraggy at the neck, gray cheeks spotted with angry red, that Emma burst into tears as she jumped up and ran to his side. He raised his head after a moment and looked at her.

"Tears, Emma? And for me?"

"Pah!" said Greville, under his breath.

"Merton is quiet now," Emma said. "A real country farm. We get up early, we go to bed early. You should see me playing the milkmaid, Mother feeding the hens, Nelson trying to guess the weight of the pigs. And the air, it's so crisp these mornings, with frost on the ground. Better, oh, so much better, than the London air. Why not come back, Hamilton, and let me nurse you for a while?"

Sir William clung to her for a moment. "What a good sweet creature you are. Still, this is no time for trifling and such nonsense." His voice was stronger again. "I propose to live my own life, and if I come with you it will be because I *want* to come with you. That is understood, Emma?"

"Goodness, yes!"

"Well, well," he sighed, "let us bear and forbear. What say you, Greville, my dear fellow?"

But Greville, for once, was speechless.

After a week in bed at Merton Sir William, surprising everybody, appeared suddenly at the dinner table and asked petulantly why everybody and everything was so quiet, so quiet to the point of deadliness.

"I never felt better in my life," he declared, though he staggered a little as he said it, "and hanker for a little gaiety."

Nelson laid aside his newspaper. "The patched-up peace has all but run its course. Oh, yes, I know the papers are full of rumors, but beneath the rumors is a hint of truth. If gaiety is your wish, Sir William, by all means let us have it while we may."

The next morning Nelson received a summons from the Admiralty, and Sir William, his manner strained and feverish, insisted on accompanying him to town. He wanted to look in at Christie's and pick up some books at 23 Piccadilly. In the late evening Nelson returned to Merton alone. Sir William had decided that it was time to complete the cataloguing of his books, and he wanted to attend a meeting of the Literary Society. A week, perhaps two, and he would be ready for Merton again, dull as it was.

"And your own news?" Emma asked Nelson.

"Whether it is to be peace or war again, nobody knows, but I am to hold myself in readiness. If it is war I shall be commander-in-chief in the Mediterranean."

"I knew it was all a dream, this paradise at Merton," Emma said sadly.

"But a paradise to return to! Remember that, Emma. Hold on to it. Keep it in mind always. A paradise to return to!"

Sir William spent two weeks in London, returned for a week at Merton, then went off again, restless, his mind unnaturally alert, the skin of his face so pallid and tightly drawn that he looked already dead.

Three days later the message came, sent hastily by Greville and received by Nelson, who broke the news gently to Emma.

"Sir William, my dear, a sudden collapse. And now, unconscious."

Sir William moved slightly, opened his eyes, and stared vacantly round the bedroom. He closed them with a little groan, only to open them again immediately. They held a frightened look.

"Dear heaven, where am I?"

Emma, speaking softly, told him that he was in his own comfortable bed at 23 Piccadilly. He looked round the paneled room again; the fear passed from his eyes. His claw-like hand reached out and grasped Emma's with a fierceness that made her shrink back.

"Nelson is here? And the good Mrs. Cadogan?"

"Yes, Hamilton, and half mad with anxiety."

His grasp relaxed. "And Greville?"

"He calls every day. Do you—want to see him? He can be sent for immediately."

"No, no, Greville is sure to come, whether we send for him or not." A faint twinkle lit his eyes. "Anxious, like the rest of you." He was silent for a moment. "This, of course, is the end."

"No, Hamilton, don't say that!"

"Sweet Emma, in spite of everything, you still do care. How silly of me, old and useless that I was, a father to you more than anything else, ever to have been jealous of Nelson."

"Goodness," she tried to laugh, "you were never that!"

"And not the jealousy of a father, bless my soul, no."

"Hamilton, you'll tire yourself. Try to rest."

But Sir William went on speaking as if he had failed to hear her. "Even when I could be nothing else but a father the jealousy persisted. A strange, strange emotion, loving and admiring Nelson as I did, as I still do. Many times it made me peevish, spiteful." He laughed softly. "You remember my recall from the Kingdom of the Two Sicilies. I pretended disappointment but it pleased me. I can tell you now, two years earlier I secretly asked to be recalled. Jealousy of Nelson again? No, not entirely. I wanted to protect his name. In the end, when he decided to come, too, I left you both to fate."

"So you knew about Nelson and me, you knew all the time."

"I beg your pardon, my dear? Speak up, I beseech you."

His eyes were blank again. And before she could say any more he ran off at a tangent.

"The eruption of '79, it was. How foolish people thought me, climbing up the stream of lava just after the outer crust had cooled. But how I enjoyed it, dear me, yes!"

"Hamilton—"

He rocked his head on the pillow. "Please send for my solicitors. My will . . . I must do something. I— What *was* it I wanted to do?" He smiled happily. "Of course! A bequest. Some small thing for my friend Nelson."

Obediently she sent for the solicitors. Their arrival coincided with Greville's. At the sight of them, his suspicious eyes asked the unspoken question: *What have you persuaded Hamilton to do?* Poor Greville, Emma thought, when all Sir William wanted was to make a bequest to Nelson.

After the solicitors had gone the old man fell into a peaceful sleep. Waking in the late evening he said, "Bless my soul, I never felt better. I can hear Vesuvius rumbling and shall go up as far as the observatory tomorrow." The doctors, in constant attendance now, shook their heads and feared he might not last the night. Emma and Nelson took turns sitting by the bed, while Mrs. Cadogan, already in tears, remained downstairs with Greville.

Shortly before dawn Sir William woke again. Emma, alone with him, watched as he tried to speak. The end, she felt, had come; but to her amazement he rallied.

"As we were saying," he said, as if continuing the conversation broken by his request for the solicitors, "I was not always the blind old fool you thought me."

"I was never sure, Hamilton, never really sure."

He chuckled. His voice was low and clear when he added, "It amused me to keep you like that, never really sure. But forgive me. I intend no reproach now, I wish you no harm. And I have of course made adequate provision for you. Snatch at your happiness and, if you can, keep it. But Emma, my dear—"

"Yes, Hamilton?"

"Take good care of the child, the little Horatia."

"You knew even that!"

"I only suspected, now I do indeed know."

He fell silent. She thought he had fallen asleep again, or into the coma expected by the doctors. But when the door opened and Greville tiptoed in, saying "Emma, I could bear it no longer—" Sir William said softly, "Ah, Greville, my dear fellow. So very welcome. We were talking, Emma and I. You would have been interested." Emma's heart missed a beat; the tired old eyes settled on her for a moment. "Emma is afraid of what I might say."

"No, Hamilton, not me!"

"Tell me, my dear, did you ever regret leaving Greville and coming to me?"

"Really, Hamilton," Greville protested, "such an embarrassing subject."

"And in bad taste too, I'll be bound!" Sir William mocked. "Well, Emma, did you—ever?"

All the past came back to her then in that moment. Edgware Row; the gratitude she had felt toward Greville and called love; his sending her to Italy, tired of her yet falsely swearing to follow her later; Sir

William's goodness, kindness, and generosity. She thought of it all till her heart swelled in her breast and tears rolled down her cheeks.

"Oh, Hamilton, never, never! Everything I am and everything I have I owe to you."

"Thank you, dear Emma," Sir William said, with a deep sigh. "You make me very happy."

He closed his eyes. He was so dreadfully still now, the faintest smile about his lips. She sent Greville for the doctors. The expected coma had come. A few hours later, at a little after ten in the morning, they pronounced him dead.

Emma sat in her upstairs room at 23 Piccadilly, waiting for Greville to call her, as he had promised to do, when the solicitor arrived to read Sir William's will. Though a month had passed since his death, and two weeks since the funeral, she still felt dazed. She had lost more than a husband who in his later years had resembled an elderly parent; she had lost the best friend a woman could ever have. She realized that now, fully. And be honest, Emma, she told herself, you can't forgive yourself for the way you tried to deceive him.

Nelson too was full of self-reproach. She wondered if he had arrived for the reading of the will. She knew he had been summoned to the Admiralty this morning and might well be delayed there. Since it was necessary for him to be much in London these anxious days, he had taken rooms at 19 Piccadilly, a few doors away, rooms above a saddler's shop. He had warned her, too, that for the sake of propriety, and out of respect for Sir William, it would be wiser for them not to stay together at Merton either. And Emma herself, knowing that this Piccadilly house was too large for her, and possibly too expensive, had already found a smaller one in Clarges Street, to which she planned to move later on.

At the sound of footsteps on the stairs she rose quickly and inadvertently caught a glimpse of herself in the mirror. Thinking sadly that the deep mourning was not becoming she half-regretted having cut short her hair in the prevailing fashion of the day. It made her head look too small, her body too large. Hideous, that's what it was, hideous; then she grew angry with herself for showing vanity at a time like this.

Greville knocked and entered. His face was solemn and he walked on tiptoe. That he was grief-stricken was obvious; that he was concerned about the contents of the will was equally obvious.

"Has the solicitor arrived?" she asked.

"Yes. Nelson, too. Are you ready to come down?"

"Yes, Greville."

"I—" He hesitated, cleared his throat.

"Poor Greville," Emma said quietly. "If Hamilton has made greater provision for me than for you, you won't find me ungenerous."

Greville said solemnly, "Hamilton, I feel sure, has done the right thing."

Nelson met them in the hall, at the drawing-room door; and, as he led Emma in to a chair held for her by the bowing solicitor, he whispered that it was neither peace nor war yet.

"But I am advised to hold myself in readiness and remain in London; and I am now in command of the Mediterranean fleet."

Emma felt as if she were choking. Hamilton dead, Nelson soon to be taken from her. A vision of the loneliness of the future swamped her. She sat down. Her mother was also in the room, wearing deep mourning too, and weeping quietly. The solicitor, bowing to Emma again, made a tiresome, sincere little speech about the sad loss they had all sustained. A horrible silence fell. Nelson broke it by asking Greville, unnecessarily, if he objected to his presence.

Greville's eyes gleamed for a moment. "No, My Lord, it is only natural, surely."

Nelson colored. "I—"

"Natural since you were always such a good friend of Hamilton, and being mentioned, I presume, in the will, as Mrs. Cadogan is."

"Quite, quite," the solicitor said, busying himself with his papers.

Emma closed her eyes. What did it matter who was mentioned in the will? Or whether or not she had benefited to a greater extent than Greville? She had lost Hamilton, was soon to lose Nelson. Life had become dull, unhappier than she had ever known it, the future unthinkable. She was vaguely aware that the solicitor had started to read the will. Greville was named the principal executor. That, of course, was something she should have been prepared for, since he had acted as Sir William's man of business. She began to listen with more attention. Sir William's debts and legacies were to be paid out of his personal estate; if that proved insufficient, out of his real estate. There was a legacy of three hundred pounds for Lady Hamilton.

She said faintly, "I beg your pardon?"

"Three hundred pounds," the solicitor repeated, "to be paid immediately. And for Mrs. Cadogan, also to be paid immediately, one hundred pounds."

Greville cleared his throat. He was trying not to smile but he leaned forward eagerly.

"Pray proceed."

"The residue," the solicitor continued, summarizing the will rather than reading it, "is bequeathed to the Honorable Charles Francis Greville."

"Ah . . ." Greville breathed.

Nelson made an indignant gesture.

"In addition," the solicitor went on quickly, "the Honorable Charles Francis Greville is directed to pay Lady Hamilton the sum of eight hundred pounds yearly; and Lady Hamilton in her turn is directed to pay her mother, Mrs. Cadogan, the sum of one hundred pounds yearly during her lifetime."

"Dear Hamilton," Greville murmured, "was always most fond of the good Mrs. Cadogan."

Emma, dazed no longer, thought indignantly, Only eight hundred a year! And a hundred of that for Ma. So this was what Hamilton had called adequate provision!

"And now," the solicitor was saying, "we come to the codicil."

Emma pricked up her ears. Codicils, she knew, often changed the whole aspect of a will. But this one only made a small provision for her debts and stressed Sir William's desire that the annuity should be paid in advance. Her indignation softened; Hamilton had been at least a little thoughtful.

"Finally," the solicitor concluded, "there is a bequest to Lord Nelson, a miniature of Lady Hamilton, in enamel. The bequest is made with the following words: 'A very small token of the regard I have for his lordship, the most virtuous, loyal, and truly brave character I have ever met. God bless him and shame fall on those who do not say Amen.'" The solicitor coughed, looked down his nose and said, "Amen."

"Touching, most touching," Greville said softly. "Er—Amen, by all means."

The color quickly flooded Emma's face, partly in shame, partly in anger. The sarcasm, the hateful, spiteful sarcasm!

Presently, when the solicitor, Mrs. Cadogan, and Nelson had gone, Greville announced that he proposed to take up residence at Piccadilly while straightening out his uncle's affairs.

"Whether I want you here or not?" Emma challenged.

"I understood that you had taken a house in Clarges Street."

"Are you ordering me to go there at once?"

"You may please yourself, but I should think that Lord Nelson would object to our sharing the same house. In any case, it would be ridiculous to keep it on. The tenancy will be relinquished at the end of the month. I give you till then to remove your personal belongings."

"*And* the furniture," Emma snapped. "It was bought with the money I raised by selling some of my jewelry."

"So it was. What a pity!"

She wasted no time in following Nelson to his rooms at 19 Piccadilly. She saw at once that he was still upset by the wording of Sir William's bequest.

"Oh, Nelson," she said, trying desperately to make her voice sound convincing, "I'm sure Hamilton meant it sincerely. He was a simple soul at heart, we both know that. And he loved you like a brother."

Nelson looked happier. "You really believe that, Emma?"

"With all my heart and soul."

"You take a load off my mind. Very well, let us give him the benefit of the doubt."

Then she told Nelson about Greville's attitude, adding, "We'll go to Lothian's or Nerot's, Mother and me. Today, I mean. And stay there till we can get the new house ready."

"I have a better idea," Nelson said. "I must remain in town myself, so that leaves Merton vacant. Go back there, Emma, where you belong. Merton is yours. I have already made a new will, leaving it to you. Go back, please—keep it open and lived in, your home and mine, till I return."

"You haven't gone yet, Nelson."

He turned away, as he did whenever he had something unpleasant to say to her. "I omitted to tell you earlier that I am expected to leave London in ten days' time."

"So it's war after all!"

"Apparently."

"How long a separation this time, Nelson!"

"God knows." He turned back to her. "I know my duty, but I take it hard this time, harder than ever before." He grew excited then. "This time I do not go to sea expecting to die in action. I go expecting to come back and make you my legal wife."

283

"There's still Fanny."

"Hard and uncompromising, I know, but one person might persuade her to set me free. My brother William. She writes to him often, seeks his advice, regards him as a spiritual director."

"William . . ." Emma mused. "You know he disapproves of me."

"Then make a friend of him. Make him our ally."

She thought of the Reverend William Nelson's sour face, his sanctimonious airs.

"It won't be easy."

"What? Not to the cleverest woman in the world?"

"Oh, I'll try, of course I'll try."

Nelson paced the room for a moment. "There is something else. Horatia's christening. We have delayed too long already."

The child was christened three days before Nelson left to take up his new command. It was a quiet, almost doleful ceremony, with Emma steeling herself to brave the ordeal she had shrunk from earlier. What if there were tears in her eyes, and in Nelson's, too? Certainly one was entitled to feel and show emotion at the christening of one's own godchild.

Horatia Nelson Thompson, that was the full name Nelson had finally decided upon. And the parents? They, poor things, had died abroad, where the child had been given into the care of Lord Nelson and Lady Hamilton. And the date of birth? Nelson quoted October 29th, making Horatia three months older than she really was and "proving" that she had been born before Emma and he had returned from Italy.

Afterward, when Mrs. Gibson had carried the child back to Little Titchfield Street, Emma said:

"When can I take her to Merton?"

"Not yet, Emma. Bear with me a while longer. Have patience. If my brother William saw the child at Merton—and you will be inviting him and his wife there—he might grow suspicious." He smiled in sudden happiness. "Horatia Nelson Thompson . . . Very soon, I hope, the 'Thompson' can be dropped, making her Horatia Nelson."

For the remainder of Nelson's time in London Emma busied herself between 23 Piccadilly, the little house in Clarges Street, and Nelson's rooms above the saddler's shop. She slept at Merton, leaving early for the drive to town and returning late at night. At 23 Piccadilly she superintended the removal of her possessions; at Clarges Street (she

284

had decided now that she needed a town house as well as Merton)
she arranged newly purchased furniture, and at Nelson's rooms she
helped to pack his heavy luggage. She was deliberately keeping herself
busy so that she wouldn't have time to fret.

When she reached Merton on the night before Nelson left for sea
duty her mother and all the servants had gone to bed. The house
seemed unusually quiet. She turned away from the dark stairway and
went into the drawing room, where she settled in a chair by the fire.
Real sleep was out of the question. She decided to sit up and wait
for Nelson; he was attending to last-minute naval business in London
and expected to reach Merton at dawn, en route for Portsmouth.

"I want no sad good-bys," he had admonished roughly. "I shall call
in passing, like a casual visitor."

She shivered and made up the fire. Late spring it was, but the nights
were still cold. Presently, in spite of herself, she fell into a doze. She
dreamed of Greville, who stood over her with a whip, while behind
him Sir William leered, wagged a finger, and said, "Nelson, my
virtuous friend."

The sound of carriage wheels woke her. The candles had burned out
and it was still dark; but here was Nelson, at least an hour before the
expected time. Emma rushed to open the door for him. He refused to
come in.

"There's a clear sky. I want to see the sun rise."

Then, struggling out of his cloak, he insisted that Emma put it about
her shoulders. Together they walked down to the little stream, their
"Nile." They stood on the little Italian bridge and watched the gray
eastern sky turn slowly crimson.

"I can bear no more," Nelson cried suddenly, and without a backward glance ran heavily toward his waiting carriage.

Emma remained on the bridge till the sun was above the elms,
then walked slowly back to the house. The grounds of Merton Place
had never looked lovelier. The laburnum and lilac were in full bloom,
and the tulips in their neat beds stood erect like rows of soldiers. But
Emma was aware of one thing only; Nelson's cloak was still about
her shoulders.

A symbol, she thought, and laughed hysterically. It might be months,
years even, but Nelson would have to come back in the end, if only
to claim his cloak.

24 "I must admit," said the Reverend William Nelson, "that it comes as a surprise, not to say a slight shock, to find Your Ladyship in complete control here at Merton Place."

Emma struggled to keep her temper. "It was your brother's wish, Mr. Nelson." She smiled sadly. "And to those of the many friends who love him, his wish is law."

The Reverend William sniffed irritatingly.

How pompous he was, like Greville but lacking Greville's refinement. Again she struggled to keep her temper. Mindful of Nelson's wish—he had reminded her again of it in his last letter—she had written to the Reverend William, inviting him and his twittering wife to spend a few days at Merton. And now he had come, *alone*, not to stay, but merely to pay his respects in passing.

"You have, I trust, had news of Horatio."

"There have been several letters."

The first, she remembered, had arrived by special courier only a few hours after Nelson's hurried departure. En route to Portsmouth, he had paused for a moment at Kingston-on-Thames to scribble some lines ending, "Be assured I have been, and am, and always will be, your most faithful and loving husband." The second letter, in the same vein, had come from Portsmouth and had referred in fond language to Horatia, while the third had been written aboard his new flagship, the *Victory*.

"Has he sailed yet?" William asked.

Emma nodded absently as her mind dwelt on the phrasing of that third letter. "Being afloat makes me feel we do not tread the same element . . . when you look upon our dear child, call to your remembrance all you think I would say myself were I present . . . my heart is full to bursting . . . may Almighty God bless and protect you . . ." Memory of it brought tears to her eyes.

"My dear Lady Hamilton . . . !" William Nelson exclaimed in alarm.

"Forgive me," Emma said, studying him cautiously, hoping that her distress would soften him. "Recently bereaved as I am, your brother's absence is an added blow."

He said unctuously: "Those who can find comfort in prayer are indeed fortunate."

Was he advising her to pray, or suggesting that she was beyond the pale? Should she seek his spiritual help? She turned from the idea in disgust, but said pleasantly, "My dear Doctor, how right you are."

He almost smiled at this unexpected form of address, and Emma recalled how he delighted in signing himself the Reverend William Nelson, Doctor of Divinity.

"It was Nelson's wish," she went on, "that you and I should be friends. He spoke of it often, and he still speaks of it in his letters. And it is my wish, I do assure you, that I might find comfort and inspiration in such a friendship."

She saw that the words "comfort" and especially "inspiration" pleased him. He strutted a little, even arched his back, and once again he looked at her with an interest that was surely and nauseatingly physical. He even rubbed his plump, thick-fingered hands together slowly and thoughtfully, a gesture as revolting as the way he had of licking his lips.

"It is ever my aim to comfort those in need of comfort," he said pontifically. "And if my words have ever inspired in the needy a little hope, a little faith, I offer up my humble thanks to my Maker."

For one horrible moment Emma suspected that he was about to kiss her on the brow and pronounce a benediction; but, to her intense relief, he merely inclined his head, asked her to keep him informed of his brother's movements, and took his leave. She went with him to the door and watched his post chaise roll down the drive.

Perhaps a little progress had been made when none at all had been anticipated. She walked for a while in the rose garden, absently admiring the first of the early roses. She would persevere with William Nelson, and try desperately to win him completely to her side. Impulsively she plucked a rose, deep red and in full bloom, and placed it in her hair.

"For you, dear Nelson," she said, in a whisper.

Emma tried to rouse herself. The pressure on her shoulders was so insistent. Hazily she realized that somebody was shaking her. "Oh, leave me alone," she muttered; but the shaking continued, and none too gently.

"If I had the strength I'd thrash you right soundly, grown woman though you are!"

It was her mother's voice. She opened her eyes, struggled to raise herself from the table, and stared about her. The candles had burned out long ago; the only light in the room came from the dying fire. She remembered everything then and burst into a fit of uncontrollable sobbing.

"Lord save us," Mrs. Cadogan cried, "not only drunk but crying drunk!"

"I was that lonely," Emma sobbed. "Yes, an' real desperate."

She straightened up angrily. "I'm not drunk now, I'm stone cold sober."

"An' fair ashamed of yourself, I hope!"

"It's never happened before, Ma. And it won't happen again, I promise you."

"I should think not! What would Lord Nelson say?"

"You won't write and tell him!"

"Give me credit for a bit of sense, girl!"

Emma pushed back her chair and stumbled across to the fire. Eight months, and still no sign of Nelson coming home. That had been the trouble. That and Horatia. Nelson away, Horatia still with Mrs. Gibson. First she'd felt lonely, unbearably lonely; then she'd started feeling sorry for herself. She looked back at the table in disgust, at the empty bottle, the spilled wine, the broken glass.

Her other daughter had been part of the trouble, too. If I can't have Horatia, I'll have little Emma, she'd thought. *Little* Emma! The child was quite grown up now, tall, slim, very self-assured and just a little disdainful. After a lengthy argument Mrs. Cadogan had agreed to fetch her; and the girl, wondering what it was all about, had come reluctantly. Miss Emma Connor, assistant schoolteacher, was not impressed with Merton, not impressed with the mother she had grown up to regard as a cousin. Emma had been almost glad to see her go, though her going had left an ache in the heart. What if estrangement made this same thing happen to Horatia?

Miserably she recalled other events of the past eight months. Nelson had urged her to be gay; so she had given dinner parties and musical evenings, filled Merton with people, entertained again and again (Nelson was allowing her a hundred pounds a month for housekeeping). But in her heart there had been no gaiety, only frustration and loneliness. Life had been as futile for her at Merton as it had been for Nelson at sea, patrolling the Mediterranean; blockading Toulon; trying but failing, again and again, to tempt the French fleet out to action.

There had been quarrels, too, with Greville who, meaner than ever these days, had actually deducted tax from the income due to her. And as for William Nelson—she was on good terms with his wife, on good terms, too, with the Nelson sisters, Mrs. Matcham and Mrs. Bolton—he had remained aloof, refused all her invitations.

"Ma," she said suddenly, "I want Horatia. It's more than I can bear, not having her with me."

"Bring her to Merton," Mrs. Cadogan said flatly.

"Nelson wouldn't approve."

"Write to him, then. Tell him how you feel, Emma, and he'll change his mind."

She wrote at once, sent the letter in care of the Admiralty, and hoped that it would reach him quickly. Nelson's reply came six weeks later, written off Algiers where he had refused to go ashore. "I have vowed never to leave these decks till my account with the French is settled." The letter had a feverish tone, like most of his letters now.

He was sick with despair. All day and all night he thought only of Emma, Horatia, and that which kept him from them, the elusive French fleet. He was so ill he doubted if he could continue much longer, yet continue he must. He had a distressing cough, frequent headaches, a mysterious lump in his side, alarming heart attacks. He only hoped that, in spite of the cough, his lungs were still sound, but he doubted it, strained as they were with cursing the French. Her question, her all-important question, he left unanswered.

She wrote again, suggesting she join him in the Mediterranean. She would at least see something of him then. She could live at Naples, as in the old days, and he could visit her there. "Only it would be better now with Horatia at my side." But she had overlooked his vow, "never to leave these decks," and in his reply he pointed out that it would be impossible to have her and the child on board ship. "Not that I do not want you both, you especially. My longing for you, you may readily imagine. Thoughts of you set me on fire!" Enclosed with this letter was the answer she had longed for, his decision about Horatia and Merton. It was couched, this separate communication, in the most guarded language, a letter she could, if necessary, show to anyone.

> *Dear Lady Hamilton,*
>
> *I am now going to state a thing to you and to request your kind assistance. Before we left Italy I told you of the extraordinary circumstances of a child being left to*

my care and protection. On your arrival in England I presented you the child, the dear Horatia. You became to my comfort attached to her, as did the good Sir William. She has reached that age when it is necessary to remove her from the care of a mere nurse. My earnest wish is that you take her to Merton.

Nelson and Brontë

And so, with joy in her heart and greater love than ever for Nelson, Emma made all arrangements for the three-year-old Horatia to move to Merton. This done, she wrote briefly and happily to Nelson: "Your daughter has come home."

"I came," said the Reverend William Nelson, "to see the child."

Emma, caught unaware, tried desperately to compose herself. So the story of Horatia's arrival at Merton, surprising all her friends as well as Nelson's, had reached the reverend gentleman at last.

"I considered it my duty," he added.

Emma looked at him curiously. "Your duty to . . . whom?" she faltered.

"To my brother, who else?" He spoke stiffly, and with little jerky movements was rubbing his hands together. "When Horatio spoke of this child in his last letter I was naturally surprised. Surprised, I must admit, that a man placed as he is should for one moment think of adopting a child."

So Nelson had written to William about Horatia! He might have warned her!

"Nelson has the kindest heart in the world," she said warmly. "Ask anything of him and he will gladly help you, at whatever cost to himself."

The Reverend William looked at her plaintively. "So I thought, until recently."

"Why, Doctor, what do you mean?"

"So small a thing, really, yet Horatio hesitates to ask a favor on behalf of his own brother. And so, even though he is himself a national figure, a member of the House of Lords, I remain, and am likely to remain, a country clergyman. I want nothing more for my own sake, but one must think of the dignity of the Nelson family as a whole."

"Of course," Emma murmured.

"Now this child . . ." he said.

She answered his questions calmly. Perhaps because of his preoccupation with Nelson's refusal to help him he felt, or appeared to feel, no suspicion; and he agreed that it was quite natural for Nelson to turn to her for help in the matter. As they talked Emma grew a little preoccupied herself. At the back of her mind, struggling to present itself fully, was the germ of an idea.

"I take it, Lady Hamilton, that you never met the mother."

"Unfortunately, no."

"Horatio says she died abroad."

"Yes, poor soul."

"The child was then brought to England by a nurse."

"Yes."

"And the father—Horatio made no direct reference to him, but I assumed that he was dead also."

"Yes." Her mind was wandering in her struggle to catch and hold the elusive idea.

"You never met him either?"

"No, Doctor, though I know very little of the circumstances. One moment, please, while I find Nelson's letter for you."

William read the letter slowly and deliberately.

"He should have spoken to me before he left England. To wait until now seems silly. Unless he thought I might try to persuade him against such an altruistic course."

"That's more than likely."

Smiling a little, almost gracious now, William said: "You seem to be as great a victim of his altruism as I am, Lady Hamilton. A greater, since the care of this orphan had devolved upon you alone."

"Oh, it isn't a burden, I do assure you, Doctor."

He looked at her in silence for a moment; he was rubbing his hands together slowly and thoughtfully now. This hand rubbing fascinated her. So clearly did it express his state of mind that she almost felt he *thought* with his hands.

"Let me be frank with you, Lady Hamilton. The influence you exert over Horatio is the one thing I have held against you."

"You think it . . . evil, Doctor?" The idea had come to the surface now, fully developed, but how to put it into practice! "Please don't say you think it evil, please!"

The hand rubbing ceased, although the hands remained clasped in front of him.

"Perhaps not *evil*, but not entirely *good*, either."

"And yet," pleaded Emma, big-eyed with sadness at the thought, "and yet my aim has always been to help your brother, and through him the England we love so well. Naturally"—she allowed a resigned indignation to show now—"there are those who resent my success in Naples when, before the Battle of the Nile, I was able to give substantial help."

"True, true," William acknowledged, "though some people are stubborn enough to argue that you—"

"And believe me," she broke in, inspired now by his use of the word "stubborn," "Nelson is not the man to be moved by a bad influence. In my late husband's words, Nelson is the most virtuous, loyal, and truly brave character I have ever met. God bless him"—her voice quivered of its own accord—"and shame on those who do not say Amen!"

"Amen!" the Reverend William ejaculated.

"Unfortunately he is also a stubborn man."

"He is, he is indeed!"

"Take his attitude toward you. Not, of course, that he doesn't *want* to help you. No, he has simply made up his mind that to use influence on your behalf would not be *right*." She sighed. "Yet we must respect him for this, even if we don't agree with him."

Her subtle use of the "we" brought them conspiratorially together. The hand rubbing, starting again, had a childlike eagerness about it now.

"You don't agree yourself, Lady Hamilton?"

"No," she said vehemently. "I think it's a shame that the brother of so great a man should remain in the obscurity of a country living."

"So kind of you, so very kind."

"Still, we must be patient, Doctor. I'll give Nelson my own views on the subject and perhaps, in the end, the influence I exert, and which you disapprove of, will break down that stubbornness of his."

"You actually offer me your help? How wonderful! If *I* can ever help *you*, Lady Hamilton, only ask me, only ask me!"

She smiled at him candidly. "All I ask of you, Doctor, is friendship and understanding."

"You have that now, my dear Lady Hamilton."

"Mind you," she warned, "it might take time, and no definite arrangement can be made till Nelson comes home."

William's face fell, but a moment later he was all brightness and optimism again.

"God grant him a great victory and a quick return."

"Amen to that."

So entranced was he now by his dream of future importance that he asked no further questions about Horatia and quite forgot that he had wanted to see her.

"God bless you, Lady Hamilton," he said, and took his leave quite happily.

That night Emma wrote to Nelson. "Your brother wants to be a bishop, and why not, my dear good Nelson? As a bishop, with all the authority of the church behind him, his influence over Lady Nelson will be greater than ever."

Emma woke, panting.

It was the nightmare again. This was the third time in as many weeks; and, as before, it left her weak and trembling, the lingering depression of the dream heavy upon her. She could still see Sir William's face, as diabolic in the world of nightmare as it had been gentle and kindly in life. And his voice, harsh and unreal, still rang in her ears, telling her, with bursts of horrible laughter, that Nelson's next battle would be his last: "Only wait and see, he will die in action as he always fears."

She flung herself out of bed and went to the window. The morning sun had touched the garden with a soft yellow haze. It was spring again, two years almost to the day since Nelson had left Merton to rejoin the fleet. The sight of the laburnum, cascade upon cascade of delicate yellow; the lilacs, varying from pale mauve to deep purple; and in the distance the spreading carpet of bluebells, cheered her. Memory of the nightmare faded.

She dressed, choosing a gay pink summer gown, and went to Horatia's room. The child greeted her with a whoop of joy and insisted on wearing a pink gown, too. How beautiful she was! Four years old now, bright, talkative, the best of company. And clever, too; already, under Emma's tuition, she could speak a little French and quite a lot of Italian. Everyone adored her. Even William Nelson declared her the finest child he had ever seen, while the Nelson sisters doted on her, Mrs. Matcham especially, who loved to hear the child call her "Matchie."

Emma smiled as she thought of Nelson's brother. William was her dear friend now, her ardent admirer, for Nelson, taking the hint, had written that they must certainly make him a bishop. All stiffness, all disapproval, had vanished; they were "Emma" and "William" to each other, and fond he was, in his wife's absence, of caressing Emma's hand. But he and his wife, as well as all the other Nelson relatives, were much at Merton, especially when such anniversaries as the Battle of the Nile, Nelson's birthday and Emma's own were celebrated. It almost seemed that William Nelson approved of everything Emma did, meanwhile possessing his soul in patience until the hero, the influential member of the family, returned.

A letter came that morning from Nelson, and with it a parcel for Horatia, a Spanish picture book in which the child became instantly immersed. The letter told Emma that Nelson had sailed, "in something of a temper but all eagerness," for the West Indies in pursuit of the still elusive French fleet. Memory of the nightmare came back then. For two frustrating years he had sought out the French. If only the frustration could continue until peace was declared at last!

Nelson's letter was followed quickly by another, stiff and formal in language, making it clear to any who might question his wishes that Lady Hamilton was, had been, and must remain the guardian of his adopted daughter, Horatia Nelson Thompson. His intention was all too evident; he anticipated a naval engagement; he expected, as ever, to die in action; he wanted to make sure that Horatia should remain with her acknowledged godmother.

And then, for more weeks than Emma could remember, weeks of agony and anxiety and nightmare after nightmare, there was silence.

"No news is good news," Mrs. Cadogan told her.

"That's the stupidest saying I ever heard," Emma raged. "No news can be bad news, too."

She was ashamed of herself, but how could she be hopeful, how could she look on the bright side when her heart and mind and soul, her whole life, depended on the safety of one man, and that man Nelson. How *could* she!

"Have it your own way," Mrs. Cadogan said huffily. "But let me warn you, Emma, don't go turning to the bottle again."

Emma was shocked and indignant. "It was only that once, Mother. It hasn't happened since and it won't. You know it won't. Not unless you go on reminding me."

But it did. It was like a fever attacking her, beyond her control, irresistible, an offer of escape from anxiety when other ways were closed to her, escape and forgetfulness. This time she was wise before the event and locked herself in her room. Afterward she was sorry and ashamed and angry. It was her mother's fault. She should never have reminded her, tempted her . . .

Another week passed. Letters by the score came to Merton Place—letters from friends; from Greville, who scolded her about a request for money in advance; from unknown people begging money, asking favors. It was these latter, addressed in strange handwriting, that she feared to open. If Nelson were dead the news would come to her from a stranger.

And finally, when she could bear it no longer, two letters reached her in quick succession. No news of the French, no mention of any engagement, only the brief announcement that Nelson was home again. That and the heart-warming, heartfelt sentiment of the one clear sentence:

"God send us a happy meeting."

Oh, and what a happy meeting it was! Happy in spite of the bitterness of his mood, happy because of her resolve to live for the moment, the moment and no more.

Nelson's letters had preceded him from Spithead, where the *Victory* had anchored. He reached Merton the next afternoon, a changed, tense Nelson, unable at first to relax.

"I return a disappointed man. I bring home no honor for my country. Faithful servant that I am, I return empty-handed."

"You bring yourself, Nelson. Nothing else matters."

"I broke my vow," he said somberly. "I went ashore at Antigua." His face was more deeply lined, the skin sallow, his hair lank and gray. "I have suffered the torments of hell. Two years and three months of it."

"And now there's Merton, Nelson. Our own private paradise."

"For how long, Emma? One day? Two? A week? Perhaps not even a week. How can I rest with my task unfinished? Pah! With my task not even begun!"

Gradually he relaxed.

"So hard, Emma, to believe that I really have come home. How I thought of you, longed for you, alone in that cabin on the *Victory*. I pictured you at Merton, I pictured you as I had known you at every meeting in the past, every moment spent together. I dreamed of you in waking dreams until you seemed to be there with me, there but beyond reach. Elusive, untouchable."

"Not elusive now, Nelson; not untouchable now."

Live for the moment, that was the thing!

The first dinner was a delight beyond all expectation. With pride and complete satisfaction Emma glanced around the table at the snow-white linen, the china and plate decorated with the Nelson coat-of-arms, the sparkling crystal, the gleaming candelabra . . . Oh, the happiness, the incredible happiness of having Nelson there again at the head of his own table, of seeing him with Horatia prattling excitedly at his side, sitting on his knee, listening to the ticking of his great watch, showing off a little at the piano. "A family group," he said, emotionally, "the happiest in the world."

After the first day there were hordes of visitors, entertained graciously but soon sent away again. Merton, now, was a refuge to be jealously guarded; time enough later to open wide the doors. Among the visitors came the Reverend William Nelson, glad to see his brother for his own sake but anxious for his help, too.

"My brother, the bishop of—well, of *where*?" Nelson teased.

Invitations poured in from all over London. Nelson had brought no new honor to his country, no new victory; but his country was ready to lionize him, now more than ever before, it seemed. Nevertheless he preferred to stay quietly at Merton. Society, fashionable society, could wait. Then, too, his visits to town, for official conferences at the Admiralty and Downing Street, were made hurriedly and kept as brief as possible.

A week passed, though Nelson had not expected even that much time at Merton. Miraculously it was soon two weeks, with a promise of more stretching out into the future. Then, halfway through the third week, swift as summer lightning, came the urgent summons to the Admiralty. This was the end of the idyll. Emma sensed it on his return to dine with her. There was a quietness about him, a sense of waiting and at the same time withholding. All her doubts and fears were back again, yet another week dragged by before the final blow fell.

"News of the French fleet," he said curtly. "The chase is on again."

"When?"

"A carriage will call for me."

"Tonight?"

"Tonight."

The room, for all its leaping firelight and yellow candle flame, seemed chilly. They talked quietly, about ordinary everyday matters; it might have been for minutes or hours, she was never able afterward to remember, and then came the sound of the carriage in the drive.

"Nelson!"

"Let it wait!"

They went together to Horatia's bedroom. The house was silent, too silent. Mrs. Cadogan had gone; the servants had gone, too. They knew, and in their kindness had stolen away. Emma and Nelson gazed down on the child, warm, rosy-cheeked, one plump hand on the coverlet.

"You love her," he said.

It was a statement of fact, not a question.

"With all my heart, Nelson, but you—you I *idolize*."

He fell on his knees at the side of the cot. Emma, standing dry-eyed above him, placed a hand on his shoulder.

In a strong voice Nelson began to pray.

"May the great God I adore enable me to fulfill the expectations of my country. May He bring me back to Merton and my loved ones. May He guard and protect my daughter Horatia, now and in the years to come, and give her peace and happiness. His will be done."

Greater fear than ever gripped Emma now. Nelson was going away for the last time. She would never see him again.

He rose, squared his shoulders, and flung back his head.

"How strange," he said, smiling, "but this time I do *not* expect to die in action."

"Oh, Nelson," Emma sobbed.

He kissed her tenderly. "Yet you feel differently."

She clung to him fiercely. "I can't help myself, Nelson. It's— Oh, Nelson, without you life would have no meaning. I might turn to drink, get into debt, grow mean and spiteful. I know I'd do all the wrong things. But out of *desperation*, Nelson. Desperation and longing to be with you again."

"Dearest Emma," he said, "such nonsense you talk! Yet what if all that really happened? Those who know and love you would never blame you. They would remember you as you really are. The good and lovely Emma. The warmhearted, generous, loyal friend. And Nelson's inspiration! Nelson's very self—for without you, Emma, Nelson *has* no other self."

He turned hurriedly to the door, but was back at her side the next moment.

"What a coward I am! One word from you, one word only, and duty and honor will go for nothing."

"I have that power?" she said brokenly.

"Heaven forgive me, you have."

In a whisper she said, "Oh, Nelson, what can I say!"

"You can say 'go,' or you can say 'stay.' "

Still in a whisper she said, "Your country, and Emma, and your own true self expect that Nelson will do his duty."

She watched him go softly to the door. When he turned she feasted her eyes on him. The pain in her throat was choking her.

"Till our next and happiest meeting," he said, and was gone.

25 She was paying only scant attention to the Reverend William Nelson as he paced the floor, cleared his throat, spoke a few pompous words, then paced the floor again. His voice sounded indistinct and faraway in her ears; his figure, in its clerical black, looked blurred. It was the same with all who surrounded her at Merton these days. Even Horatia seemed unreal. It's the waiting, she told herself, the dreadful waiting. She found she was saying this aloud.

"It's the waiting, the dreadful waiting, William."

"Yes, yes, we all feel it, Emma. A month now, is it not?"

"More than a month. Only one letter, then silence. No more letters, no news. No news of any sort. If only I knew where he is, what he's doing now . . ."

"Gentlemen," Nelson said, addressing his assembled captains, "we are some twenty miles west of Cadiz. The French fleet, supported by units of the Spanish fleet, is sheltering in Cadiz harbor. Therefore, we wait impatiently, day by day, hour by hour, minute by minute, for the enemy to put to sea."

The Reverend William cleared his throat.

"We were discussing—I beg your pardon, my dear Emma—we were discussing my brother's wife."

"Fanny? Were we?" Emma made an effort to recall the conversation. "Of course. You had seen her recently."

"Yes, and found her singularly vindictive."

Emma tried to concentrate. "You actually broached the subject of divorce?"

"Not in so many words." He was rubbing his hands together smoothly, with long easy strokes. "No, no, one must move cautiously, even circumspectly. I very much fear that it will be difficult to bring her round to our—hum—way of thinking."

"Still, when you're a bishop, with the full authority of the church behind you—" Emma broke off, wanting idiotically to giggle at the picture her mind conjured up of William dressed as a bishop, gaiters and all. She controlled herself. "What I mean, William, you being a Nelson too, all we ask of you in dealing with Lady Nelson is a little of the Nelson touch."

"By the Nelson touch, gentlemen, I mean the bringing of the enemy fleet to battle on the most advantageous terms to Nelson himself, and by that I mean the laying of our ships close on board the enemy as expeditiously as possible, and continuing there, without separating, until the business is decided."

Captain Hardy led the round of applause.

"My object," Nelson continued, "has always been to break the enemy line and overwhelm one end of it. The whole aim of the British fleet must be to overpower the enemy from two or three ships ahead of my flagship, to overpower him from the rear of his fleet. This, let us say, will leave twenty enemy sail untouched. But it will take some time for twenty sail to perform a maneuver designed to bring a compact force close enough to engage us or to aid their own stricken ships. Something must undoubtedly be left to chance, but if, for instance, signals from the Victory are unreadable, no captain can go wrong if he places his ship alongside that of an enemy ship."

"And keeps it there!" Hardy roared.

"And keeps it there! Go back to your ships, gentlemen, and wait with patience for the day of battle. God grant us victory and a lasting peace!"

"Ah yes, when I am a bishop," William murmured. "But if Horatio—" He stopped and cleared his throat. "That is, Horatio has done nothing whatever, yet, nothing whatever."

He had almost said, "But if Horatio dies in battle." He had, she knew he had!

"To let you into a little secret," she lied, "he has done more than you think. Had he not left so suddenly he would have told you."

William's face brightened. "This is heartening news."

"He spoke to the prime minister the day he left. Busy as he was, William, he still had time to think of you."

"You overwhelm me!" William cried. "And the prime minister said . . . ?"

She was tired of the lie she was telling, tired of William's presence and wished he would go.

"Yes, my dear Emma . . . ?"

"The matter will be discussed fully when Nelson returns. Meanwhile, the prime minister will speak to the Archbishop of Canterbury. I feel sure you need have no fear now, William, that—that—"

She stopped, her head cocked on one side in an attitude of listening.

"Is something the matter, my dear?" William asked solicitously.

"I—it was the strangest thing. I thought I heard someone speak my name. No, not just someone, but Nelson. I heard it distinctly. 'Emma Hamilton,' he said . . ."

"It's a codicil to my will, Hardy," Nelson said. "I'm trying to knock it into shape, and later I want you to witness my signature. Listen to what I've written. You see, I want you to know that I am in sound mind while writing it."

"I can vouch for that sure enough, My Lord," Hardy laughed.

"Listen, then . . . 'Whereas the eminent services of Emma Hamilton, widow of the Right Honorable Sir William Hamilton . . .'

"I was never so afraid in my life, William," Emma cried. "I heard it, I distinctly heard it! Oh William, could it possibly mean that—that—?"

Shaken, the Reverend William said heavily, "This is too fanciful, Emma. Superstition, sheer superstition. In any case, would Horatio, if —well—in great anguish of mind, call out to you like that? Surely he would call 'Emma,' not 'Emma Hamilton.'"

Emma laughed happily. "Of course! How stupid of me!"

"A very pretty child," Greville remarked, and gave Emma a sly look. "I believe Lord Nelson has been heard to declare that she resembles her mother."

"I never met her mother," Emma said woodenly.

"No?" Greville inclined his head. "Personally, I think she looks more like her father."

"Oh, damn you, Greville. Leave me alone!"

Greville laughed. "What I meant was, girls usually show a greater resemblance to their fathers— Is anything the matter, Emma?"

"I was listening for Nelson's voice," she said softly. "I heard it yesterday, or perhaps the day before. I can't remember which. He spoke my name. Just once. Funny, though, that he should say 'Emma Hamilton.' But I did hear it, I swear I did, Greville."

Greville backed away from her. "You must be feverish, Emma."

"I've listened ever since, so very hard," she said earnestly, "but I haven't heard a thing, not a thing."

Nelson went quickly to the quarter-deck, Captain Hardy close on his heels.

"Well?" he demanded of the signal lieutenant.

"Frigates signal combined enemy fleets coming out of port, My Lord."

Nelson very nearly danced for joy.

"Thank heaven for that! We will engage them off—yes, off Cape Trafalgar. What's the weather, Hardy?"

"Well, it couldn't be better just now, My Lord, but the wind seems inclined to shift to the west. Heavy showers, that would mean, and a possible gale."

"You're an excellent sailor, Hardy, but a damned poor weather prophet—I hope!"

Greville was still standing at a cautious distance from Emma, staring at her. He said: "You may not be feverish, but you must be out of sorts. Perhaps you need a change of air. Why not a few days at Brighton? Very bracing there at this time of the year."

Emma laughed scornfully. "That's not like you, feeling concern on my behalf."

A puzzled look crossed Greville's face, then he laughed negligently.

"I might not always have been kind to you, but I often feel a certain responsibility."

"Is that why you like to keep me short of money?"

The angry color touched his cheeks immediately. "You have sufficient for your needs. Do you expect me to give you money of my own, in addition to Hamilton's annuity?"

"The money you call your own was Hamilton's first—!"

She broke off abruptly. The last thing she wanted to do was quarrel with anybody. She rose and moved aimlessly about the room. She wished Greville would go. Why, for that matter, had he come in the first place? She frowned in an effort to remember. Of course! He had been making representations to the government again, trying to persuade those in authority that a portion of Sir William's pension should be paid to her during her lifetime. He had come to tell her that he had failed. His concern made her suspicious, and she said,

302

"I can't understand why you bothered about the pension at all."

Greville smiled his familiar thin, mean smile. "No?"

Emma laughed then. "You know I'm in debt and always will be. You're afraid my creditors might be able to claim on Hamilton's estate. Better government money than yours, eh?"

"Precisely!"

He went at last, leaving Emma to wander aimlessly around the room again. She stopped to look out of the window. There in the garden was Horatia, helping Mrs. Cadogan to pick flowers, and chattering, Emma could see, like a magpie. She turned from the window. Horatia's toys were scattered about the floor. She began to gather them together, the sailor doll dressed in admiral's uniform, the small, perfect model of Nelson's German traveling carriage, a battered picture book, and finally a seashell. She fell on her knees and held the shell to her ear, as Nelson had taught Horatia to do, listening like a child herself for the sound of the sea. Listening, she thought, for Nelson's voice, but hearing nothing.

"I want to send a general signal to the fleet," Nelson told the signal lieutenant, *"so make haste, Mr. Pasco."*

"Very good, My Lord."

"Send this one first. On second thought I'll send two. Here we go: 'Nelson confides that every man will do his duty.' No, wait! Change 'Nelson' to 'England.' I am apt, as usual, to take too much on my own shoulders."

Pasco hesitated. "My Lord—"

"Well, what's the trouble?"

"There's no signal flag for the word 'confides,' My Lord. It will take seven hoists to spell it out. If I may suggest it, My Lord, 'expects' would be quicker."

"Then let the message read, 'England expects that every man will do his duty.'"

Pasco sent the signal; and, as ship after ship received it, tumultuous cheering rose and echoed across the sea.

"Now," cried Nelson, "send my second signal. Number 16 it is, Pasco, and the one I love best."

A few moments later, as the signal for close action flew challengingly from the top-gallant masthead of the Victory, *Nelson smiled his satisfaction.*

"For England, Emma, and Horatia," he said softly.

Emma was still on her knees when Mrs. Cadogan and Horatia came in from the garden, each carrying an armful of autumn flowers.

"Gracious heaven," cried Mrs. Cadogan, "what are you doing there on the floor?"

"Just listening to the sea," Emma said and, still clutching the shell, rose to her feet.

"You don't look well, an' that's a fact," Mrs. Cadogan commented.

"We'll go up to town tomorrow," Emma decided, "and stay at Clarges Street for a few days. We might get news quicker there."

"You're shivering," Mrs. Cadogan said. "You've taken a chill, more than likely. Them flimsy gowns you wear! Asking for trouble, that's what I say."

Emma felt a childish inclination to burst into tears. She hurried from the room to the privacy of her bedroom. Presently, sitting at the writing desk Nelson had ordered specially made for her, she tried to write to him. "Dear husband of my heart . . ." she began, but could get no further. She opened the desk drawer and found his last letter, which she had read a dozen times already. In it he had described his departure from Spithead and spoken of the plan of action he was busily designing—"So simple that it must surely succeed, my Nelson touch!"

She noticed that she had carried the seashell upstairs with her and dropped it on the desk. She picked it up again and held it against her ear, pressing it harder and harder but hearing nothing. Oh, Nelson, her heart cried, why can't I hear your voice!

Nelson was on his knees on the quarter-deck, trying vainly to raise himself with his left hand. As Hardy came running up, he swayed and fell on his side. Hardy bent anxiously over him, and a smile twisted by pain broke over Nelson's face.

"They've done for me at last, Hardy."

"For God's sake, My Lord—!"

"Cover me up, get me below, hide me from view," Nelson panted. "Nobody must know, nothing must hold up the action. Victory first, Hardy, remember that!"

Deafened by the din of battle, choked by the stench of it, they got him below and laid him among the dead and dying in the bloody shambles of the cockpit. With the surgeon on one side, the chaplain on the

other, he tried to sit up. Hardy would have supported him from be-
hind, but Nelson sent him back to the quarter-deck.

"News of victory, bring me that, Hardy, nothing else."

Later, gasping for breath, choked by the blood which gushed contin-
ually in his chest, he asked for details of his injury. The surgeon told
him that the ball had penetrated deep through his chest, had probably
injured his spine.

"A mortal wound," Nelson whispered. "It broke my back. I felt it."

He closed his eyes and clenched his teeth against the pain. When he
spoke again, hours later it seemed to those at his side, it was to ask
for Hardy. Captain Hardy was sent for and came immediately.

"How goes the battle, Hardy?"

"Very well, My Lord," Hardy replied, his voice broken with grief.
"We have a dozen enemy ships, perhaps more. The day, My Lord, is
yours."

"Nay, Hardy, England's. Come closer, Hardy." Hardy knelt and
placed his ear close to Nelson's lips. "Remember, I leave Lady Ham-
ilton and my adopted daughter as a legacy to my country. Now Hardy,
kiss me."

Hardy, tears coursing down his face, kissed Nelson on the brow.

Near complete exhaustion, but fighting still, Nelson whispered,
"Thank God I have done my duty," and finally, convulsively, "Lady
Hamilton and my daughter . . . never forget Horatia."

Petulantly Emma threw the seashell across the room. It struck the
wall, bounced back, rolled on the carpet, and lay still. Taking up the
pen again, she made a great effort at concentration. Little phrases
formed in her mind. "Oh, Nelson, how many more letters must I write
before you return? . . . Need I tell you again that you are all in this
world to your devoted, adoring Emma? . . . God grant you a great
victory and send you swiftly home to Merton, Emma and Horatia . . ."
These thoughts formed in her mind, but the pen lay unmoving between her fingers.

They told her she had been ill for weeks, at times barely conscious.
Weeks? It might well have been months. She had lost all sense of
time. But . . . barely conscious? It was true enough, yet out of the
black despair of the past weeks, the unendurable anguish, more than
one clear memory remained.

She turned in her bed and lay flat on her back, staring up at the ceiling, trying with the solemn concentration of a child to put her memories in strict chronological order.

There was that first letter from Nelson's chaplain, Dr. Alexander Scott, the letter addressed to Mrs. Cadogan. "Hasten the very moment you receive this to dear Lady Hamilton and prepare her for the greatest of misfortunes." Yes, she could remember that most clearly.

And then there was Captain Thomas Hardy, calling to see her here at Merton. Captain Hardy, with his clumsy, sincere attempts at sympathy, breaking down and weeping while she herself remained dry-eyed. Captain Hardy bringing her the miniature of herself that Nelson had worn around his neck. And giving her his unfinished letter, reading, "As my last writing before the battle is for you, so I hope in God I shall live to finish this afterward . . ."

After that there had been more letters from Dr. Scott, anxious in his inquiries, but determined to stay near the remains of Nelson till the end. He was at Greenwich now, waiting with the body, for the state funeral, the day of national mourning.

There had been a visit from Greville, too—Greville precise in his sympathy; Greville trying to be kind to her, offering help, saying, "Call on me at any time." So rash of him, she thought, without humor.

And Nelson's sisters, Mrs. Matcham and Mrs. Bolton, both weeping bitterly, both anxious on Horatia's behalf, Mrs. Matcham saying with the utmost sincerity, "My home is hers, if ever she needs one."

Not only the sisters, but the brother, the Reverend William. She remembered him with equal clarity. A little withdrawn from her now, he seemed to be. Grieving, devout, pompous, speaking in measured tones of God's will. Poor William, there was no Nelson now to make him a bishop. Bishop? Why should he fret about that since, as Nelson's next-of-kin, he had automatically become Lord Nelson? He had all the importance he craved now, surely—the title, the seat in the House of Lords.

"How clever of me," Emma whispered, "to remember all this so clearly."

To remember, when forgetfulness was all she wanted.

With a bitter cry, a cry torn from a tight and painful throat, she turned her face to the wall.

"I want to die. Why can't I die too!"

Her mother, being practical, had said: "Face facts, stir yourself, make an effort, if only for Horatia's sake."

Well, she was doing that now, wasn't she? She looked around the dinner table, at William Nelson, at his wife, at the Matchams and the Boltons, at her mother, ready at all times to give her an encouraging smile. Perhaps, after all, she had misjudged William Nelson, had been wrong to think him withdrawn and unsympathetic, for here he was, spending a few days in London with his wife and gladly accepting hospitality at Clarges Street. And yet, deep down, she felt that she was foolish to trust him. She had been suspicious right from the first even when, as Nelson's executor, he had assured her calmly that the codicil witnessed by Captain Hardy had been forwarded to the government.

The codicil . . . *Whereas the eminent services of Emma Hamilton, widow of the Right Honorable Sir William Hamilton* . . . How careful Nelson had been to list these services, the matter of the King of Spain's letter to King Ferdinand and the provisioning of the fleet before the Battle of the Nile. *Could I have rewarded these services I would not now call on my country . . . I leave Emma Lady Hamilton a legacy to my king and country that they will give her an ample provision to maintain her rank in life. I also leave to the beneficence of my country my adopted daughter, Horatia Nelson Thompson* . . . Well, his king and country had never yet acknowledged Lady Hamilton's services and were hardly likely to do so now. But if something was done for Horatia nothing else would matter. How generous would the beneficence of his country prove to be?

"I understand," William Nelson said, leaning forward to address her, "that you intend to sell Merton Place."

"Yes. Merton is hateful to me now, full of loneliness."

"And no doubt you need the money."

"Yes."

"A wise decision, then."

She wondered if he resented Nelson's bequest, which included Merton Place, a cash sum of two thousand pounds, and an annuity of five hundred pounds, drawn on the Brontë estate. Perhaps he did, and resented also the trust fund set up by Nelson for Horatia. She remembered his odd little laugh when he had informed her that his majesty the king, in recognition of the services of the late Admiral Lord Nelson, had decided to raise the new Lord Nelson still higher, in fact, to make him an earl. "I admit a certain pride in the fact that I, a humble country clergyman, should suddenly become an earl; but on what, I ask you, am I to support my earldom?" Yes, she decided, he probably did resent Nelson's bequests to her.

"I trust you will obtain a good price for Merton Place," he remarked.

Growing weary of this conversation, she said casually that Nelson had spent a lot of money on Merton, adding, "It should be nearly twice as valuable now."

"Say rather," he chided her, his voice playful but his eyes unsmiling, "that *you*, my dear Emma, did the spending for him."

Emma shrugged and made no reply.

"And having obtained a good price," William wound up, "I would advise you to secure your capital in some safe investment."

A little silence fell, leaving Emma conscious of an uneasiness at the table, a sense of apprehensive waiting. None of the others had spoken much; they had the look, all of them, of puppets waiting to be controlled by the illustrious new head of the family, Earl Nelson.

William broke the silence by dwelling, as he loved to do, on the somber magnificence of his late brother's state funeral: the thirty-one admirals, the hundred captains, the countless sailors and soldiers, the procession so long that the vanguard had reached the cathedral before the rear guard had even left the Admiralty; the final lowering of the coffin—yes, the coffin Nelson had kept behind his chair in his cabin—into the tomb at St. Paul's.

Emma, listening in horrified fascination, reflected bitterly that no provision had been made for her to follow Nelson's remains to the last resting place; reflected bitterly, too, that pride had kept her from mingling with the crowds, a silent, unrecognized mourner.

William went on talking, yet as he talked Emma gained the impression that his mind was not on his words. Now and again he glanced at the door, lost the thread of what he was saying. And he still seemed distracted when the party withdrew to the drawing room. Once, when a servant entered the room he leaped to his feet.

"Is something the matter, William?"

"No, no." He sat down again. "Nothing."

"Are you expecting a visitor?"

"Dear me, no," he laughed, but there was a cunning look in his eyes. "At least, not a *visitor* . . . say rather a—er—messenger. I may as well tell you that affairs relative to the Nelson peerage are being debated in Parliament today. The matter of a grant, among other things."

Emma was puzzled. "But I thought that had been settled long ago.

Fanny Nelson was granted an income of two thousand pounds a year soon after the funeral."

"True, true," was all William would say.

Actually it was Greville, not William's messenger, who brought the news. He apologized for interrupting what seemed to be an amicable little family discussion.

"However, Earl Nelson"—he inclined his head ironically in William's direction—"will be just as interested in what I have to say as you yourself, Emma."

"What are you talking about?" William said sharply.

"I came straight from the House. Permit me to offer Your Lordship my heartfelt congratulations."

"Tell me the result of the debate," William said briskly.

"My dear Earl, you have been voted a pension of five thousand pounds a year, and the sum of ten thousand with which to purchase a suitable estate."

"Ah!" William rubbed his hands together energetically.

Emma was flabbergasted. "But—*why?*"

"Why else," Greville said tartly, "but in honor of the late Lord Nelson's glorious achievements?"

It was then that Emma lost her temper. "I never in my life heard of anything more stupid, no, nor more disgraceful! Why, the humblest sailor on the *Victory* did more for his country than William Nelson ever did!"

William paled, said tensely, "I might have expected *that* from a person of your antecedents, Lady Hamilton."

Emma was quickly sorry for her outburst and said so, almost humbly. But William turned away from her, mortally offended. Well, she thought, that was the end of any help she might expect from him. Actually the fault was not his; it was the government's. In his lifetime Nelson himself had never been more than a viscount, never even more than a vice-admiral. But now his brother—a *brother*, not even a child —was an earl with a pension of five thousand pounds a year. The stupidity, the sentimentality of it!

William, having fumbled in an inner pocket, was facing her again. He tossed a pocket book toward her; it fell at her feet.

"Useless to you, but you may as well have it."

Greville picked it up for her. Taking it she saw in amazement that it was the pocket book in which Nelson had written the codicil. She turned the leaves quickly. It was there still; the page it had been written on had not been torn out. A moment later the full significance of what William had done struck her.

"You held it back! You never did forward it to the proper quarter! You lied when you told me you had sent it to the government. You held it back until your own greed was fully satisfied. Oh, shameful, shameful!"

William colored. His wife set up an instant twittering, the Boltons and the Matchams looked acutely embarrassed.

"The codicil has been seen by the highest legal authorities in the land," William said. He turned to the others. "Lady Hamilton is somewhat distraught. I wish to talk with her alone. Would you . . . mind?"

Led by Greville the others trooped from the room. With frigid politeness William asked Emma to sit down and punctiliously held a chair for her. Almost without feeling now, she sat and watched him as he stood above her. He seemed to have increased in stature. The earl, puffing himself up, feeling his importance! After a moment he laughed, as if at an amusing thought.

"After all, it is not as if my brother left you anything, or the child Horatia anything, in his hastily drawn-up codicil. On the contrary, it was his country he had in mind. He made a bequest to his country. He left you and the child to England, and England, I fear, has no use for you."

Emma shrugged. Let him say anything he liked, this onetime man of God. She didn't care.

"It is to be admitted, however, that my brother intended England should do something for you both. The codicil, therefore, falls into two parts, leading you, in the first part, to expect some reward for services allegedly rendered by you some years ago at Naples. We can dismiss that briefly: had the government recognized those services as other than the sentimental ravings of a man in love, the reward would have been given at the time . . ."

How William talked, how he loved to listen to his own voice!

"In the second part the codicil leads you to expect from the government monetary support for my late brother's adopted daughter. Yet it must be pointed out that 'adopted daughter' is only a figure of speech. There was never a legal adoption. A claim, therefore, would be laughed out of court."

Roused a little, Emma said, "Before he died Nelson spoke to Hardy of his *daughter*, not his *adopted daughter*."

"A slip of the tongue. Quite understandable when one considers the state poor Horatio was in."

Emma said, "Nelson was her father."

"Oh, come," William protested. "The parents died abroad. The child bears the name of Thompson."

"Horatia Nelson Thompson."

"The surname is Thompson."

"He was her father," Emma said stubbornly.

"And . . . who was her mother?"

Emma saw that William regretted having asked this question. He was looking at her now as if afraid of her answer, afraid of the truth. Well, she was afraid of the truth, too. Would it help Horatia to say, "I'm her mother"? No, it would only make things worse for the child.

Finally she said quietly, "I never knew her mother."

"Nor her father either." William was looking vastly relieved. "Nelson was her godfather, that and no more. He provided for her when he set aside that trust fund."

"Yes, William. Two or three pounds a week."

"You, as godmother, may do more yourself. And you are at liberty to submit the codicil to the government. I, for my part, have done all I intend to do. If the child is too great a responsibility for you, you can place her in an orphanage." He went to the door. "Good-by, Lady Hamilton. My wife and I will leave this house immediately."

Greville said: "You must admit you have only yourself to blame." But Emma was barely listening. How long, she wondered, was it since Nelson's death? How long for that matter since, giving up the Clarges Street house, she had moved to this smaller one in Bond Street? In her state of utter depression she neither knew nor cared.

"Myself to blame for what?" she asked.

"I was speaking of your extravagance. At Nelson's death your debts were unbelievable. Had he lived you would have beggared him."

"I don't know why you bother yourself about me, Greville."

"You asked for my help and advice."

His tone was unexpectedly kindly, if unavoidably scathing. Warming to his subject, he gave her a detailed account of her financial position. She had sold Merton Place for a goodly figure; but when Nelson died he still owed money on it, and the alterations she had undertaken while he was at sea were still unpaid for. In addition there had been an "incredible, fantastic, staggering sum" owing to the tradespeople.

"As a result, my dear Emma, you have practically no capital left."

Emma, not really caring, frowned. "But Nelson did leave me a clear two thousand pounds."

"Gone," Greville moaned, "all of it gone."

"Well, never mind."

"To sum up, Emma, you have eight hundred pounds a year from Hamilton's estate and the income from the trust fund set up by Nelson. The money from the Brontë estates is too irregular to be counted on, so we will forget it. Nevertheless, you have an income large enough for you, your mother, and Horatia to live on in moderate comfort."

"I'm a poor manager," Emma said flatly. "I don't think it will be enough."

"You were a good enough manager in the old Edgware Row days, but of course you had me to watch and guide you then."

The old Edgware Row days . . . Another age, another life.

Surprising her, Greville said, "On the whole those were happy days."

She looked at him incuriously. "Were they?"

Smiling just a little foolishly, he went on, "I like form and order in life. In life as well as in art. Your life would describe a full circle, perhaps become a complete whole, if you went back to Edgware Row."

Emma stared at him blankly. "I don't know what you mean."

Impatient now, he said, "I like the district. I love Paddington Green. In fact, I am buying another house there, a larger one."

The continued blankness of her look irritated him. He came to her quickly and shook her by the shoulder.

"What's the matter with you, Emma? The life seems to have gone out of you. Surely you are not still pining for Nelson!"

Even this last jibe failed to touch her.

"A hero? Pooh, that was simply his good fortune. The surgeons performed an autopsy on the body before the funeral. And what do you think they found? In spite of his complaints about heart attacks and all manner of mysterious pains, he would have lived to a ripe old age but for that fatal musket shot. All the vital organs, every single one of them, perfect! He might have been a man of twenty, they said, not forty-eight. Call him a hero if you must; *I* call him a weakling."

Calmly she said, "He faced the bloodiest of battles. He never murmured when they hacked his arm off." She was growing tired of her visitor. "Why don't you go, Greville?"

He flushed. "Is that all you can say to my offer?"

"What offer?"

312

"I thought I had made it clear that I was once again offering you my protection."

Emma considered this as if it were a weighty problem, but she was still devoid of feeling.

"You'd take all my money, of course; dole it out to me, bit by bit."

"Only in order to keep you from destitution."

"Would you marry me, Greville?"

He looked flustered. "One can scarcely marry one's uncle's widow. Still one doesn't like to see one's own creation going to seed. A personal insult, that is."

"Well, fancy that!"

"I created you, Emma. I gave you education, turned you into something closely resembling a lady. I made it possible for you to mix in real society, become the confidante of royalty. So in a way, if it hadn't been for me, Nelson never would have won the Battle of the Nile!"

"You must be mad, Greville."

"Mad to offer you certain security? You and the child, and your mother, too, while she lives?"

"Please go, I'm tired."

She was surprised to see a look of utter dejection on his face. He struggled with himself for a moment, then spoke again.

"You force me to humiliate myself before you. There was never anybody else. Never a woman before you, never one since. I was jealous of Hamilton when I saw you together after you came back from Italy to marry him, and later I was jealous of Nelson, too. *Now* will you consider my offer?"

"No, Greville. All the same, I'm sorry if you're lonely."

"But, Emma, what will you do?"

Emma made no answer, yet when he had gone his final question still rang in her ears. *But, Emma, what will you do?*

She went to the sideboard, took up a bottle of wine and a glass. In something like disgust she put them down again.

But, Emma, what will you do?

All the wrong things, of course. She had told Nelson that at their last parting at Merton. She had told him also that without him she would be dead, too. When your heart was dead within your body, you were truly dead. Back from the past she thought she heard Nelson's voice saying: *Without you, Emma, Nelson has no other self.*

313

"Oh, Nelson," she cried, "I have no other self either. It went when you went."

She picked up the bottle and glass again, and this time she filled the glass. Carrying it with her, she stumbled to the writing desk and began to search with growing desperation for a letter. One thing was worrying her. "Horatia," she kept mumbling, "Horatia . . ." She found the letter at last and spread it open on the desk. She had received it yesterday from Nelson's sister, Mrs. Matcham. It was about Horatia, so kind and genuine a letter. Nelson's sisters, it seemed, had each received a government grant of ten thousand pounds, and because of that Mrs. Matcham was eager to offer Horatia a home. Dear, kind Mrs. Matcham. Whatever happened now, Horatia's future was assured.

The sound of footsteps made her look up from the letter. Her mother and Horatia were returning from a walk. Their talk and laughter, reaching Emma through the wall, made pleasant hearing. An old woman and a child, both at an age to have much in common.

A letter had fallen on the floor. Emma stooped and picked it up. It was Nelson's unfinished letter, written before Trafalgar. "As my last writing before the battle is for you . . ."

All feeling came back then. Her throat tightened, her heart swelled in her breast. She fumbled for a pen, tried twice to dip it in the ink, and sobbed quietly as she wrote on the back of the letter:

"Oh, miserable, wretched Emma, oh glorious, happy Nelson."

"Miserable, wretched?" She heard the voice quite clearly then, Nelson's voice. Softly but distinctly Nelson repeated the last words he had spoken at Merton:

"Till our next and happiest meeting."